THE CONTRACT

A Paul Stanton Thriller

Chris Darnell

CONTENTS

Title Page   i
Contents   ii
Copyright   iv
Dedication   v

THE KILLER   1

PART I – ONE OF OUR MEN IS MISSING   11
Chapter One   12
Chapter Two   20
Chapter Three   30
Chapter Four   44

PART II – PRETORIA   55
Chapter Five   56
Chapter Six   63
Chapter Seven   70
Chapter Eight   80

PART III – DIRTY BUSINESS   91
Chapter Nine   92
Chapter Ten   104
Chapter Eleven   117
Chapter Twelve   127

PART IV – BAD PEOPLE, FRIENDS AND LOVERS   136
Chapter Thirteen   137
Chapter Fourteen   152
Chapter Fifteen   167
Chapter Sixteen   175

PART V – DEAD BODIES   189
Chapter Seventeen   190
Chapter Eighteen   201
Chapter Nineteen   209
Chapter Twenty   217

PART VI – THE LONG ROAD TO BEIRA   225
Chapter Twenty-One   226
Chapter Twenty-Two   239
Chapter Twenty-Three   249
Chapter Twenty-Four   262

PART VII – CLOSING THE LOOPS   272
Chapter Twenty-Five   273
Chapter Twenty-Six   283
Chapter Twenty-Seven   294
Chapter Twenty-Eight   306

REQUIEM FOR THE GOOD GUYS   319

Historical Note   327
About The Author   334

COPYRIGHT

DEDICATION

This novel is for my wonderful children, Bryony and Marcus. My wish is for you to have a life as full of excitement, challenge and reward as mine has been.

THE KILLER

MANNIE COETZEE WAS a killer. He was also filthy, ugly, evil and prejudiced.

Right now Coetzee was in Mozambique, in a concealed clearing in the water-starved reed beds of the Save River, leaning against the cab of a *bakkie*, an open-backed 4x4 utility truck, which belonged to the white man Coetzee had just killed and whose body was in the back of the truck. The killing had gone to plan, but despite this, things were just not right and his twisted mind was in a state of uncertainty. The situation was *kak*, man, no two-ways about it.

It was nothing to do with the place: it was shit and still a long way from where he needed to be, but he was pretty sure he was secure here for a while and could get the next part of the business done. It wasn't the two renegade Renamo soldiers either: they were going to leave him after they'd all completed the journey south and finished the business. No, it wasn't the place or the black men that had started to fuel Mannie Coetzee's darkening mood.

It was the white man's fucking diamonds.

He'd killed the man four hours ago at a place one hundred and fifty kilometres to the north, in Zimbabwe, and he'd done it with the help of the two Renamo. The man in Pretoria, who had the links to the Renamo rebel warlords in Beira, had planned it all and arranged for the men to be at the agreed meeting place. And he'd been right, because without them and their knowledge Coetzee couldn't have got

1

this far. But true as it may have been, this realisation did not make Coetzee's situation any better.

He'd made the journey from Pretoria and been picked up by two ex-Rhodesian Army mercenaries in a beaten out Land Rover at Bietbridge, the border-crossing into Zimbabwe, and five hours later dropped off on the gravel road that ran north from Melsetter up to Cashel, in Chimanimani, an area parallel to the Mozambique border. It was close to the RV where he was meeting the Renamo and where he would kill the white man. The Zim mercs hadn't given him a weapon or any rations, nor did they wish him good luck, the fucking bastards! But the weapon didn't matter, since Coetzee had his holstered Makarov pistol snug under his left armpit, and he had a bushpack with brandy and biltong in it. So he'd walked the short distance to the rendezvous and waited in the shelter of the bush for the Renamo to get there. Which they had.

The plan was simple. He'd got the Renamo to drag a large branch of deadwood across the narrow road and they'd waited in ambush. The direction of travel didn't matter, although he'd been told it would likely be north towards Cashel. The man would be on his own and Coetzee had his description and that of the bakkie. Two other vehicles had come and both times he'd let the driver and passenger clear the road and then drive off. Twice more the Renamo had dragged the obstacle back across the road.

Then, two hours later, the man had arrived and Coetzee had identified him by his long, greying hair. Fucking hippy. As soon as the vehicle came to a halt, Coetzee had calmly stepped into the road and shot the man twice in the head through the open driver's window. Thirty seconds, start to finish. The man had an FN 7.62mm self-loading rifle by his side - no one travelled without a weapon - but he hadn't even moved for it.

Coetzee had taken the weapon out, shown it to the Renamo, and then thrown it as far as he could into the bush. He didn't need it and nor did they. There was an old tarpaulin in the back of the truck and the Renamo had wrapped up the man's body, loaded it into the back and climbed in. Coetzee had headed directly across the border into Mozambique and then south, using old game tracks known to the Renamo.

The plan had worked perfectly, but then the diamonds had fucked everything up! Whilst the Renamo were dealing with the body, Coetzee had found the stones hidden in a box of vegetables on the passenger side floor. He'd dug underneath the carrots and potatoes to feel the edges of the package, pressed at the hardness of the contents inside the oilskin wrapping and lifted it out, then hurriedly put it back, covering it up again. His instructions had been explicit: *You bring the consignment back. It is a small package of blood diamonds. No one else knows about it or sees it. The Renamo are foot soldiers, paid by their Beira warlord. They leave you when you've finished with them. Give them nothing!* Fine. But his instructions had been wrong: the package was too big, and it weighed at least two kilograms. Even Coetzee knew that was a fuck-load of diamonds!

So, four hours after killing the white man, with the discovery of the diamonds gnawing at his mind, Coetzee called a halt in the reed beds on the approaches to the Save River. It was the end of September, the rains hadn't come yet and the ground was cracked and hard. It was a perfect place for the work in hand and close to some passable fords across the big river. This close to the border neither the Zimbabwean nor Frelimo Governments had the strength to deploy any kind of force in the area.

Coetzee came to a decision: the situation was shit, but hey man, that was the story of his life, so let's finish the job. At least the fucking Renamo had no idea about the diamonds. He levered himself upright from where he was leaning against the cab of the bakkie, turned towards the back of the truck, to the two men sitting there, and let his mood flow into his words, 'Get the white bastard out of the bakkie and chop him up. Cut through all the joints and break the ribs and backbone into bits. Cut off his head. Be quick, leave no spoor and do not fuck it up.' The two men looked at him with blankness in their eyes. Coetzee spoke a mix of Afrikaans and Tsonga and he knew they understood him because he'd been with them for over six hours. But it was as if they hadn't, because the men didn't move and their look was stony.

Coetzee felt his anger rise. It may have been 1989, and the bastard politicians in Pretoria might have been talking to the black leaders, but for him apartheid was not dead yet, far from it. These men were kaffirs and there was an order to things that wasn't about to change in his world. He felt the reassuring hardness of the holstered Makarov pistol under his left armpit, and he mentally rehearsed the few actions required to bring the weapon into his hand. The safety was on but there was a round chambered. It was dead simple and he'd done it many times before. He could waste these two kaffirs before they could blink, and maybe that's exactly what he should do?

But then it was as if the Renamo read his mood, and his anger was deflected, 'Ja, baas,' came the reply and Coetzee checked his thoughts and looked at the speaker. Not so stupid after all. It was the older of the men, the one called Alves.

'Good.' But as he watched them, they made him realise afresh just how much he needed to get on and get away from them. 'No mistakes, Alves, you hear. You are practised. Yes?' Coetzee laughed at his own poor joke. Of course they were practised. Renamo had been butchering their Frelimo enemy and Mozambican civilians for ten years. The two men opened up the truck's tailgate and said nothing. Coetzee frowned at the silence. 'What's the fucking matter with you, Alves? Cat got your black tongue, hey, kaffir?'

Alves stopped what he was doing and looked around at Coetzee. His smoky, red-veined eyes shone out in the muted dark, but his look said nothing. 'Nothing the matter, baas, we will do as you say. It is work for us, and we are practised.' Alves motioned to the other Renamo and they started to lift the tarpaulin-covered body out of the bakkie.

Coetzee felt the disdain in Alves' voice like a force. He moved closer to the men at the back of the vehicle and spoke again, 'Do what I say and do it good.' His anger was rising and he suddenly felt the need to say more to these Renamo, to tell them what he was, 'In the Border War, in the west in Angola, I killed plenty. And then in the Recces, I

4

killed even more. And now, I am free-lance. Ja, now I am a free-lance killer. What a joke, hey. You know about the Recces, Alves?'

'I have heard, baas, but only heard.'

'They were the best, man, I tell you. We were the best. We went deep inside Angola on our raids and did mayhem with those fucking installations the Cubans and Russians were funding. And we killed plenty of the SWAPO bastards from Namibia as well.' Coetzee paused and allowed himself a few moments of nostalgia. Then he started again. 'So, Alves, you are both Renamo still, or have you also become *free-lance*?'

'We were Renamo, baas. But now we work for Señor Ramon Lima in Beira and he has told us we must do this job with you and then return.' Alves' tone was empty of feeling.

Whatever he had thought to provoke, Coetzee gave it up. He looked around him and said, 'OK, enough of this dreaming, hey. Get to work.'

'Ja, baas.' The Renamo took the rolled tarpaulin out of the back of the Toyota, threw it on the ground and unfolded it to expose the man's fully clothed body.

Coetzee said, 'Four hours only it took us to drive here, and look already at how the bastard's started to stiffen. But it will be no problem for your blades, hey?' Alves and his comrade each carried a tapanga, fifty centimetres of blued and balanced steel sharpened to cut through bone and muscle like butter. No problem. 'Alves,' Coetzee continued, 'strip off all his clothing and collect it. When we have butchered this man, we will burn his clothes and the tarp. There will be no traces. But we will do that further south. Give me his wallet and papers.'

Coetzee held out his hand as Alves rifled into the side pockets of the dead man's bush jacket, found the bulky wallet and gave it to him. There was still some light, so Coetzee opened it up and took out some business cards, reading the words. He stiffened, and immediately stuffed the cards back inside and pocketed the wallet in his bush vest. He suddenly felt a tremor of fear and involuntarily he said, 'Hurry! Fucking hurry!'

Alves was standing watching him and must have sensed it, 'What have you found, baas, who is this person? And what is in this man's bakkie that you seek?'

'No one, this man is just a fucking dead white man, and there is nothing but vegetables in that dead man's bakkie.' Fuck, fuck, fuck! He needed to divert them, get them focused back on the job, 'This is a great spot, Alves. Ja, man you have brought us to a good place. So much for local knowledge, hey?' He tried to sound unworried, but he didn't.

The atmosphere was now tense and only reluctantly, it seemed, did Alves respond, 'Ja, baas, no one will see or hear us.' Alves walked over to his comrade and the two of them started their grisly work.

Coetzee knew he'd betrayed something to the Renamo, and it had instantly made his situation far, far worse. The mutual distrust and incipient hatred between him and the Renamo was deep-rooted. Here, they had been brought together by their respective contacts in Pretoria and Beira to do a job, and only this kept their relationship in a state of fragile balance. Coetzee had inadvertently tilted that balance. And if they suspected the existence of the diamonds...

He moved away towards the front of the bakkie. He felt the stab of uncertainty shiver through his body again. First the diamonds and now the man himself. He leant back, resting on the bullbar and struggled to rationalise his thoughts. This was definitely bad, man, very bad. His hands were shaking as he pushed his filthy slouch hat off his brow and went in search of a smoke, patting the pockets of his bush vest and quickly finding his crumpled packet of shag-cheroots and his treasured Zippo, with the Recce Battalion badge on it. He didn't smoke many of them but he needed one now. He lit up, sucked the acrid smoke deep into his lungs and held it inside the barrel of his chest. Christ, but that was *good* shit! He exhaled slowly and tried to relax.

The Renamo rebels had finished their bloody work as Coetzee walked back to the rear of the bakkie. He spoke, forcing normalcy back into his tone, 'What we do with this bastard's bits is we find the edge of the swamps and feed those filthy crocs the large limbs and the head, and the smaller bones and pieces we put into the homes of the driver ants. They will eat it all and the bones will stay buried. Leave anything else for the wild dogs and hyenas, and those fucking vultures.'

* * *

COETZEE DROVE TOWARDS the Save River and crossed it easily, and the butchered remains of the white man he'd killed were duly fed to the beasts of the river's swamps and the savannah bush. Now he was headed for the Limpopo and South Africa.

The going was better and he was able to pick a route through the rocks and scrub with relative ease. His mind was clear now, like the stunningly bright night that gave him most of the light he needed to drive by. He had the bakkie's sidelights on but the world around was deserted. He used the stars to navigate, but he had a pocket compass as well, and checked it occasionally. Coetzee visualised the border area between Mozambique and South Africa in his mind's eye. There was a particular place where he was going to cross back into his land, *ons land*, South Africa.

But before he got there he had more killing to do.

Coetzee checked the odometer. He had done a hundred kilometres. It was time to finish things. He was fifty kilometres from the Limpopo River. He pulled up by a large koppie and switched off the vehicle's engine and lights, pocketed the keys and felt for the hard lump of the white man's wallet in another pocket. The large package of diamonds was still in the vegetable box on the passenger side floor. He got out of the cab and motioned to the two Renamo in the back, 'Here's where we burn the tarp and the clothing. Alves make a fire in the lee of the koppie. Keep it sheltered. Here,' Coetzee threw his worn Zippo to Alves who caught it deftly, 'use this.'

'Ja, baas.'

Coetzee watched as the other Renamo offloaded the bloodied tarpaulin and the bundled collection of the white man's clothing as Alves gathered some dry kindling with which to start the fire. The two men squatted on their heels as they made the blaze. The wood was soon roaring, contained within a rocky scrape, and the tarpaulin was already smouldering. Now was the time. Alves heard Coetzee's footfall because he looked around towards him. The other fed the fire. Coetzee never hesitated. He shot Alves between his startled eyes and then moved the pistol the few degrees and shot the other Renamo in the side of the head as the man half-turned in the instant recognition of the sound. The heavy Makarov 9mm bullets blew both heads apart. Over a thousand feet per second muzzle velocity did terrible things to human bone and tissue at point-blank range.

Coetzee was pleased. 'You had it coming, you kaffir bastards. And don't pretend you black fuckers wouldn't have chopped me into lion meat once you'd got your filthy hands on the diamonds.'

He dragged the bodies away from the fire and left them. He stuffed the clothing into the flames and watched it burn for a further five minutes. The pistol shots had cracked loudly into the night air, but anyone hearing them would imagine them to be caused by one of any number of things. This was a warzone and he wasn't worried about the sound of two pistol shots. He was worried about other things.

Coetzee sat in the driver's seat of the Toyota and thought again about his instructions from the man in Pretoria. The white man was nobody, a courier. The package was small, some blood diamonds. The Renamo were his foot soldiers and guides and knew nothing. He hauled the box up onto the seat beside him, fished out his torch from his bush vest and tipped the vegetables on to the passenger side floor. He stared at the oilskin package for a few seconds and then lifted it out. It was about twenty-five centimetres long and fifteen centimetres deep. The thickness was not consistent but was at least four centimetres, and he could feel the roughness of the stones and the density of their packing through the coarse material. Yes, it weighed at least two kilograms. The package scared him because, if he was any kind of judge, he was holding a very large sum of money, *not a small package of blood diamonds!* He placed the diamonds inside his bushpack, closed the flap and threw the vegetable box back into the floorwell.

Coetzee turned his mind to the white man, which was another fucking matter entirely! His hand went to the lump of the man's wallet in his vest pocket and he pulled it out. He found the business identity card and his heart lurched in anticipation.

Victor Stanhope Fitzsimons
Regional Director Manica/Sofala Provinces
MozLon Corporation
Country Office, Beira. Head Office, London

Coetzee's mind buckled and he felt the sweat break out under his armpits. *This man was not a nobody!* How in God's name could he have been a diamond courier? Coetzee pocketed the wallet and looked all around him into the dark. Suddenly he was scared, and it was an unusual feeling for him. The fire was almost burnt out. He started up the Toyota and switched on the sidelights. He saw the two corpses. As soon as he left the area he knew the hyena would have a field day. What would anyone find? Two dead Renamo renegades, shot with a Russian handgun commonly used by Frelimo, and left beside their campfire to be eaten by the wild animals. He had no worries on that score. His worries were about bigger things.

His man in Pretoria had been given inside information about the shipment and the routes. Coetzee never asked how the man got his information or from whom. He was Intelligence Service and his was a black world of whispers and informers and double deals. Coetzee knew he'd been brought in to do the dirty work and the arrangement was fine by him. Thievery and murder were his trades. *But not ever had it been on the cards that the courier would be a director of some fuck-off big company with a head office in London. Nor was it ever mentioned that the diamonds would be two kgs in weight.*

He knew he'd been right to kill the blacks, because if word ever got back to Beira about the package, then the hounds of hell would really be let loose.

Coetzee drove slowly southwards, picking up the track he wanted. He was going to cross back into South Africa at Crook's

Corner, where the borders of Zimbabwe, Mozambique and South Africa met and formed the historical no-man's land where thieves and renegades were untouchable by the law agencies of any of those countries. He would ditch the bakkie just a couple of klicks out and cross over on foot. At this time of year the Limpopo was a dry riverbed. He would avoid the pools of water and the crocs and walk across. As for the bakkie? Well it was too far south to be traced back to Zim, so let Frelimo have it, or anyone else for that matter. He didn't give a flying fuck.

He drove on and the silence of the night closed in around him and the magnificence of the moon and stars illuminated his way. Mannie Coetzee, the killer, frowned as he made his way south. He felt a worm of dread start to move through his mind. It wasn't the diamonds, it wasn't the white man's identity, nor was it the blacks. It was something small and very recent, and it concerned what he had or had not done, but he couldn't nail it down.

PART I
ONE OF OUR MEN IS MISSING

CHAPTER ONE

THE WALK FROM Pimlico to Duke of York's Barracks in Sloane Square had invigorated Paul Stanton. It was Wednesday morning, the 11th of October, and the day was chill but bright and warming up, and there were plenty of people thronging the pavements as they made their way to work. It had been an Indian summer and the day was going to be fine again. The girls were wrapped up but they were London girls, the most striking in the world, and they were beautiful and vibrant. They made him think of *his girl* and when he might next see her.

He climbed the stairs to the office corridor in Headquarters Director Special Forces and was walking past the doorway into the Briefing Room when the voice rang out and stopped him in his tracks.

'Well will you look at the state o' that! Christ all bleedin' mighty, boss. Look at ya, all decked out like a city slicker. What 'appened!'

It was broad cockney, irreverent, friendly in tone and underlaid with inverted respect. Paul knew exactly who spoke the words but couldn't fathom why the man should be here. He had a stupid thought and it was a moment of madness. He decided to try and ham it up, but even as he decided this he knew he'd come off worse. His opponent was an expert and he wasn't. What the hell, it might be a bit of fun. He smiled and turned back into the doorway of the room.

'Corporal Evans! Don't you boss me, you horrible, pug-ugly, fake Welsh-Cockney, it's Lieutenant Colonel Stanton to you now.'

Paul stopped as the laughter burst out unrestrained from the two men who stood directly in front of him like a pair of lop-sided East London Bobbsey Twins. Lop-sided because one was tall and lean and the other was smaller but built solidly. Paul knew them both. They were dressed almost identically in worn Levi's, black-laced boots and leather jackets, holding a plastic cup of coffee in one hand and wearing a broad grin that split their gnarled faces. Shit! Here it comes. Paul smiled back in anticipation of the onslaught, and he wasn't disappointed.

'Come on, boss, you can't 'ardly talk, what with that big bent bloody nose of yours an' all those 'orrible scars. And don't come the raw prawn. We all know you're only an actin' 'alf colonel, and they've gotta be ten-a-penny nowadays, ain't they? And besides, it's Staff Sergeant Evans now, and I may 'ave been born in Welsh Wales, but I've never set foot in the bleedin' miserable, always rainin' country, not since. Well, not if you don't include 'Ereford, that is.'

'You daft, thick bastard, Taff.' The man next to Evans said this and belted him not too gently on the shoulders, laughing again as he did so. Paul noticed a third man who'd been at the far end of the room, moving towards them.

Evans continued unchecked. 'But good on yer, boss, on the promotion, that is. The boys were all really pleased to 'ear about it. Well deserved, they said, but me, I don't know about that!' And now all four men roared with laugher and Evans stepped towards him hand outstretched, and Paul felt the warmth and humour bubbling inside his chest and stepped further into the room. God it felt good to hear the banter again.

Paul held out his hand and immediately realised it was his second misjudgement in the space of seconds. Taff Evans, dark-haired, stubbled and hard as old iron, was a pocket battleship of trouble and violent danger when roused, with a handshake that could crush yours to mashed bone and flesh. Paul's eyes betrayed him. 'I saw that, boss! No worries, I've mellowed, ain't I. No more of that arm wrestlin' rubbish. Got betta things to waste my energy on. Squashy and cuddly as a teddy bear, I am now. You tell the Colonel it's true, Lefty.'

'You're talking shite as usual, Taff, but I reckon the Colonel can take care of himself anyway.' The man next to Evans was standing his ground but his face wore a broad and genuine smile. He brought back gold-and-black memories to Paul, as did Taff Evans.

Evans' handshake was firm and friendly and his face open and honest, as it always had been. In a flash Paul was transported back to *this* place, Duke of York's Barracks, but three years ago, and to Evans giving him his weapon and gear for the covert operation in West Belfast, the black operation sanctioned by HMG and run by Brigadier Charles Grace. And then he had met Evans again, when the Corporal had been with Grace, in a safe house outside Belfast, just before Paul had gone south into Eire; and one killing had led to another...until Berlin. His heart raced and he felt a jab of pain in his chest and rubbed it involuntarily.

Paul realised the two men were looking at him with a touch of concern in their eyes and a small frown on their faces. He needed to say something, 'Well done on the promotion, Taff. I'm really pleased for you. And unlike me, it's well deserved.' It broke the freeze and everyone laughed again and there was movement.

'Bollocks, Colonel! Don't be a soft wanker, beggin' yer pardon, that is. You know it comes up with the rations. But thanks anyway, boss, it means a lot.' Then Evans tugged on his arm to get him moving and Paul felt normality start to return as he looked at the others and stepped further into the room.

'How are you, Lefty? It's good to see you after so long.' He shook the taller man's hand and his mind flooded with memories. It had been seven years. He knew the man had been passed fit long ago and returned to duty with the Regiment, but he hadn't seen Lefty Shoesmith since just after the Falklands, when he'd gone to visit him in Headley Court.

'I'm fair fine, boss, many thanks, and it's excellent to see you, too. Congrats on the promotion.'

Paul was just about to extend the discussion when he was conscious of the third man standing next to him, and he was at least an inch taller and felt imposing. He turned to introduce himself but was beaten to it.

'Hello, Colonel Paul, I've heard a lot about you.' They shook hands. Paul was intrigued. He thought he knew the man's face but he'd been out of the Regiment for so long that he just couldn't place him. Shoesmith and Evans moved a few paces away. 'I'm Ted Bakerswell, which as you can imagine causes great mirth amongst the drunken and licentious soldiery. I'm currently OC A Squadron.'

Paul liked the man's manner and style. He was clean-shaven and looked fit and hard. Bakerswell might have a name the boys could play word games with but he looked as if he could hold his own. His clothes were a give-away, though. His tan cords were faded and worn and matched his scuffed suede desert boots. Underneath the open, ragged Barbour jacket Paul saw a heavy jumper and the frayed collar of a striped shirt. Very SAS officer in mufti and on reconnaissance in London, and in complete contrast to Evans and Shoesmith who looked like London thugs, with their close-cropped hair and swarthy faces, which wasn't far from the truth, he thought.

'Good to meet you, Ted. I'm Paul Stanton.'

'I know, Colonel. And you were in A Squadron in the Falklands. The action in West Falkland is one of the legends we cherish and hope to be able to emulate. And it's where you and Lefty fought together, I guess?'

It was said without a trace of self-consciousness and Paul was surprised by how he felt as a result. He felt good. He seldom if ever spoke of it. He hadn't realised others in the Regiment did. 'Yes, it was,' he said. Paul's mind was instantly transported back to that bible-black, wind-torn, bitter night on West Falkland in June 1982, when Argentinean forces ambushed his patrol. The intelligence had been completely to cock and somehow their move into the final lie up position was compromised.

'The mission was bollocksed from the start and the boss didn't know it, none of us did. Wasn't that right, Colonel?'

'It was, Lefty. But only after it all finished did we find out the radio transmissions had been monitored by Argentinean SigInt. We underrated their listening capabilities badly.'

'And as a result we got fucked.' Paul still couldn't believe it was being talked about like this. They were all looking at him now. Shoesmith continued. 'Micky Rollins and Pete Hardcastle copped it and I got my leg shot-to-buggery and was completely useless. And then the boss here, Captain Paul, broke the rest of the boys out of the killing zone and counter-ambushed the bastards. Killed a fair few of the Argies and baled us all out. Got smashed up by a grenade in the process but got us all out of it, including Micky and Pete. It was bloody brilliant, Colonel, and I probably never told you so before, not even when you visited all those times in Headley Court, but it was.' Paul's mind was there, as Shoesmith spoke. He'd been hit by grenade fragments, in his side, but they had torn flesh and muscle only, nothing that hadn't been repaired and stitched up. And nothing to compare with what had happened to him in Berlin.

'Got the MC for it,' Shoesmith concluded matter-of-factly.

'As I said, Colonel, the type of action we need to remember.' Bakerswell's words brought Paul back to 1989. He smiled at them. In a way it had been good to talk about things.

'Thanks, Ted, it's nice to know. But what are you guys here for?'

'A Squadron's just taken over the counter terrorism role. We're here to get briefed up. Lefty's a Sergeant now, one of the troop sergeants, and Taff's the Squadron Quartermaster Sergeant. So we're the recce party, loitering with intent here in the Briefing Room, waiting for the programme to start.' Bakerswell turned and waved his arm around the large room. 'Pretty impressive set-up you have.'

It was, and to be expected for the SAS at its headquarters in Duke of York's Barracks, London. A built-in projection screen took up the front wall. A raised briefing platform had a matched lectern at both sides, the SAS shield mounted on each. The dais worked the controls for the audio-visual and black out blinds. But for now the room was still and light, the Chelsea autumn morning colours flooding in through the big windows. The seating was comfortable. At the back end of the room a large clock hung over a row of tables, on which sat big, bulky black weapons bags. It seemed the men were here to collect some serious gear as well as be briefed.

Evans spoke, noticing where Paul was looking. "Ad to pick up a bit of specialist ordnance and other stuff from the stores down below, you remember the place, don't you, boss.' It was a statement. Of course Paul knew it. Taff Evans used to be in charge of the armoury. It was where he had given Paul his untraceable handgun. 'Cor blimey, Colonel, I still can't believe them days. It was absolutely fuckin' freezin' that winter, and you was not to be seen by anyone. An' I 'ad my orders from the Brigadier...'

Paul cut him off. It was rude, but he didn't want to and couldn't go into it all again, in front of those who hadn't been involved. He was still under the strict terms of the Official Secrets Act. The mission had been deniable, a black operation, a personal charge from the Prime Minister, and not to be discussed.

'Ted,' he said, looking at the clock on the far wall.

Bakerswell anticipated him. 'Yes, Colonel, we must let you get to work. From the rumours we picked up in the Regiment, what you were involved in back in eighty-six sounds like it must have been hairy.'

'An' the Colonel got plugged again,' put in Evans helpfully, 'in the chest. Fuckin' nearly copped it, so I 'eard.'

Paul grimaced and then smiled. It was useless trying to evade it with the likes of Taff Evans around. 'Yes, I did, Taff, but as you can see I'm still here and for now please shut that gob of yours and let me talk to your OC about the briefing.'

'Yes, I saw from the programme we're due to get some sort of specialist info on the political side from you, but a little later on,' Bakerswell, again. Paul sensed the man's intuition at work. They could be good friends, he thought, if the circumstances allowed it.

'You're right, and you will.' Paul looked around the briefing room and the others followed his eyes. On the three walls, wherever there was space, huge aerial photographs and large-scale maps of buildings, installations, barracks and street areas had been fixed. Paul had studied them all when he first arrived here. They were the Met Police Anti Terrorist Squad's current list of high priority terrorist targets. There was a gallery of mug shots, too, the most wanted terrorists, mainly IRA, but not exclusively. Paul knew most of the faces.

He went on. 'It's not just the direct threat of the Provisional IRA that seems to be fussing the Met, and you know all about what the bastards did to the Marines in Deal last month, it's the possibility the Provisionals will take advantage of the Government's civil vulnerabilities to attack non-military targets again. The PM's got her hands full at the moment firefighting factions and splits within Cabinet and contending with rising popular unrest about Europe and the bloody Community Charge. So that's where I'll be adding some flavour to everything else you'll get given.'

'Interesting,' said Bakerswell.

'It is. But frankly it's politics that's Mrs Thatcher's biggest threat at present, not the IRA. She's most likely to get tripped up by her own team and the perceived loss of popular confidence and votes. What the Provos do will always be a major concern, will always challenge her plan to bring Dublin into affairs, but no one knows more about it or how to handle it than she does. Especially after a major incident such as Enniskillen.' Paul looked at Evans as he said this. He could have added *and H23*.

'You're right there, boss,' Evans replied, knowingly.

'Anyway,' said Paul, 'that's all for the briefing later.' He felt momentarily tired. Psychosomatic, he told himself. It's all the talk of the past. He needed a coffee. He looked at the clock again. 'It's only eight-thirty and I don't think you guys are due to start getting briefed until nine-thirty, so shall we grab a cup of proper coffee? I haven't had my morning fix yet.'

'Good idea,' they all said, and started to move.

Paul heard the footsteps in the corridor. The Director's personal staff officer stood in the doorway. He saw something in the man's expression.   The others turned to him as the words were spoken.

'There you are, Colonel Paul, the Director's looking for you. He's had a call from a General Grace, who wants you over at the Old Admiralty Building, apparently, and you're to be there at ten-thirty hours. In fact the General has asked you to call him and you're to do it from the Director's office.'

Paul acknowledged with a nod of his head and mixed thoughts ran through his mind. Déjà vu. So much for his new posting here. The staff officer disappeared back down the corridor.

Evans spoke it for him. 'So the old Brigadier's a General now, is 'e, Colonel? Well that's not surprising, really, seeing as what 'e did for Maggie. So I guess we won't be gettin' that briefin' from you after all.' And he chuckled to relieve the tension that seemed to have crept into the room. 'But we've still time for that coffee. C'mon, sir, and the rest of you all, boss, Lefty. I know a place, as they say. I'll lock the room. The gear'll be secure 'ere 'til we get back. C'mon, the Colonel's paying. He's loaded now, and besides, if General Grace's got anythin' to do with it, boss, you most likely won't be needin' any dosh.' And Paul had a thought that Evans might just be right.

Bakerswell threw in a comment as they started to move. 'That's Military Intelligence, isn't it?   The Old Admiralty Building. Probably world affairs?'

Paul looked at the others as they trooped out of the room. They were all pilgrims. They were part of a close band of people forged by the common purposes of duty, adventure and comradeship. James Elroy Flecker had created Ishak and Hassan and set them amongst the pilgrims who left the corruption and sleeze of Baghdad to take the Golden Journey to Samarkand. As a pilgrim it meant you never really knew what might happen to you. But, as Paul reflected, he wouldn't want it any other way. He smiled to himself. It was definitely time for a coffee. He patted Taff Evans on the back as they moved and looked at Shoesmith.

'It's been *really* good to see you both again.'

CHAPTER TWO

MAJOR GENERAL CHARLES Grace had summoned Paul to the Old Admiralty Building. He said he wanted to discuss *a world issue close to HMG's heart*. Grace had told him to come into Admiralty House from Horse Guards: *I'll be in the FCO, Room fifty-six on the second floor*, were his exact instructions.

On the short tube journey from Sloane Square to St James's Park and then during the walk across Horse Guards Parade, Paul had begun to rehearse what he knew of events unfolding with alacrity in the Eastern Bloc. This, it seemed to him, must surely be top of the pops of world issues facing the departments of Defence and Foreign Affairs, both of which Grace seemed to work for in some ill-defined way.

He had been wrong, and typical of the man, Grace got right down to the business in hand and pointed out the error of his thinking. 'Tell me what you know about the civil war in Mozambique, Paul, and the regional politics. Tell me what you know about what is happening now, at this time, and what is likely to happen in the near future.'

Mozambique? Not even in the pop charts of Government business, surely? So as Paul opened his mouth his thoughts leaked out. 'Mozambique, General, what about Mozambique?' It was the wrong response and he should have known what the General's retort would be - caustically personal, as a minimum - but in fact he'd been thinking of something else completely. His mind had suddenly leapt back ten months to those five days in Kathmandu last December, and to Nikki Walker-Haig's meetings in London in July with MozLon, and all the talk about what Danny Dalloway's Gurkha Connections Limited was planning to do: *In Mozambique!* And of course since then, GCL had started to deploy its manpower. There couldn't be any connection to what Grace wanted to discuss, surely not?

'Paul, I know many would probably rate Mozambique as a very low geopolitical priority right now, but I had hoped your lateral approach to life might have extended to your grasp of world affairs and enabled you to think out of the box. As we both know, geopolitical events are of relative importance depending on how multi-dimensional their component parts are, and how those parts can and do have so-called *Grand* effect. Agreed?' Grace moved from where he was standing behind the large table at one end of the room.

'Yes, General.' That was a fairly minor rebuke, Paul thought. But what in hell was Grace talking about? And as he thought these simple questions, Paul had a soft lurching feeling in his chest. Nothing that Grace had ever said to him in the past had been in isolation; everything Charles Grace talked about had connectivity to Paul's life, in some way. This was ominous. The man's words cut back into his deepening thoughts.

'So there is every possibility Mozambique could be more important than might appear so from media coverage?'

'Yes, General.' Paul still had no idea what Charles Grace was getting at, but he was racking his brain to remember what he'd learned whilst in Kathmandu and what little information he'd gathered in the intervening ten months, particularly during his discussions with Nikki, *his girl*.

'For goodness sake, Paul, sit down. Engage that modest intellect of yours, open your mind to new possibilities and pour yourself a cup of coffee. And me, too, please, and just look at the view from up here.'

Paul Stanton should have been used to Grace's quixotic mind changes, but he had got out of the habit it seemed. Paul decided he needed to relax his mind and deal with what was coming as he usually did: expect the unexpected, adjust your thinking accordingly and don't let anyone see a chink of uncertainty. So he sat down in one of the group of fragile looking armchairs arranged around an informal table on which was set a large tray containing everything needed for coffee for two.

The chairs were period, late Georgian, and in keeping with the architecture and décor of this large, high ceilinged room in Admiralty House. The assemblage had been deliberately positioned to look out of the wide, low sash window framed by the drawn and gathered velvet curtains. Huge oil paintings of England's naval history seemed to watch Paul from all walls where they hung on heavy chains, their large gilt frames holding the dark canvasses from which blazed the gunfire of Aboukir Bay, Copenhagen and Trafalgar. Paul wondered why on earth Grace had commandeered one of the building's Historical Rooms as a meeting place. Why not his office? He leaned towards the table to start pouring the coffee and looked out of the window.

Grace spoke gently. 'Doesn't it make your heart glad to be an Englishman?'

'It does, sir.' The General's words checked Paul's thoughts and he was reminded that Charles Grace did have a soul.

The room was on the second floor of the grand old building. The sun was almost overhead and bathed the whole of Horse Guards in its warm, mid-October glow. To the right, the trees of St James's Park still held their leaves and the scarlet oaks and plane trees were an absolute picture of rich golds, ambers and russets. The late tourists to London milled and ambled across the parade ground as they sought out the Park and the attractions of the Mall and Buckingham Palace. Many of them, Paul registered, moved through towards Whitehall. Would they turn up towards Trafalgar Square, to stand for a few moments under Nelson's stony stare, he wondered, as he was right now sitting under the oily gaze of the Little Admiral's famous sea battles? Or would they walk down towards Parliament Square? Both, probably, Paul reflected. Grace was right. It *was* a very English scene. It was *London*, and it did make Paul feel a tinge of pride for the city where he worked and had his home.

'No two-ways about it, Paul, and to corrupt the title of one of Christopher Hill's seminal works, God *was* an Englishman and a day like today proves it.' And Grace laughed deeply and spontaneously at his irreverent wit. 'Know who Hill is, Paul?'

'Yes, General, I do. An historian. And he was referring to Oliver Cromwell, as you know. And I doubt the Irish would agree with you. About God being an Englishman, that is, and I doubt Hill himself would agree since he espouses a Marxist dialectic in his historical theses, as a committed, albeit seemingly confused Communist, would.'

'Smart arse!' Grace smiled broadly and moved over and joined Paul, carefully sitting down in another of the antique chairs. Grace was a tall and large framed man, quietly powerful. Paul thought that had he felt like it, Grace could just flex his arms and the chair would burst apart. It would be Charles Atlas's Dynamic Tension at work, surely? 'And let's not talk about the Irish. After all we left that behind us three years ago.' Grace's words momentarily took Paul's mind away from Mozambique. Paul often thought about the dark and mad period that Grace was referring to, and the earlier chance meeting with Taff Evans had brought it all back to him. Paul shuddered involuntarily. Grace noticed it. 'My apologies, Paul, it was tasteless and insensitive of me to remind you of the personal cost of those days.'

'Not at all, General, but you caught me on the hop when you asked me about Mozambique, because I was in fact thinking about the Wall, in terms of geopolitics, as you put it.'

'Quite right and you should be, too, Paul.' Grace gazed out onto Horse Guards and his voice took on a serious and far-seeing tone. 'I suspect your regular contacts in GSG 9 are keeping you abreast of the whirlwind blowing through East Germany and Berlin of course. It's stunning how rapidly the so-called Peaceful Revolution has generated tempo there. I can tell you from the gossip I pick up in the corridors of the Foreign Office that speculation about Erich Honecker's continued position is rife. He'll go, so the mandarins are saying. Our Foreign Secretary, Mr Major, is reported to be quite concerned, although why, I can't imagine. The man clearly lacks a sense of destiny and imagination. Honecker *has* to go. After all, it's only just over two years ago that President Reagan challenged Mr Gorbachev to tear down the wall, and lo and behold, now Gorby is struggling to hold the Eastern Bloc together and Honecker's grip on things is shot.' Grace drank from his cup and looked at Paul, and Paul saw the General's mind at work. It was beginning to be like old times. Sooner or later, Paul knew, Grace would get around to the real reason for calling him over. 'Look at Hungary. Four months ago it was as tightly bound into the Eastern Bloc as ever.'

Time seemed to stop as Paul's thoughts took another jolt at Grace's mention of Hungary. What in hell was going on? His mind, once again, was suddenly elsewhere. There was just too much déjà vu, too much personal history about this conversation, and Paul momentarily tried to tie it all together and relate it to why he was here.

First there was The Wall. Paul and Charles Grace had history with West Berlin and the Wall, down in the derelict zone of Wedding. Paul remembered the frenzy of the shoot-out in the old cinema building, and the cacophony of the massive sky-breaking storm that literally swamped the black deeds of the afternoon, when he and his friends had killed three evil men. But in the gunfight Paul had been shot and nearly died. He had the damage to his right lung and the surrounding muscle groups to remind him, along with the deep scarring on his body where the brilliant West Berlin surgeon had drained the blood from his lung, cut him open, extracted the bullet and repaired all the internal damage. The man had saved his life. Grace, in a way, had saved his life, because of the contingencies he had made.

And of course Christina had saved his life because she and the others had been there and had driven him through the raging storm to safety. And in the months afterwards she had done much to repair him. She had given him love but he had been unable to return it in the way she wanted. There was something dark and black in his soul that troubled her. He had killed three men in cold blood and accepted it without question. Of course he did. He was a soldier, a serving member of the SAS, someone who executed terrorists and those who helped them. He was a tool in the deniable black world of British politics. He was unaccountable as long as he was uncatchable, and he was good at it. So he and Christina had parted as the fragile love between them died.

Then there had been Kathmandu and the Hungarians. That was his tenuous link to Mozambique; because Paul had only gone there to help his old Gurkha friend, Danny Dalloway, establish his Gurkha security business. But in doing so Paul and some of his ex-Gurkhas from the Kathmandu Rifles had killed the Hungarian criminals who had badly hurt and tortured Dalloway and threatened his business enterprise. And there in Kathmandu, and then months later, only this summer in fact, Paul had met and fallen in love with his girl, Nikki Walker-Haig, who worked for Gurkha Connections Limited, GCL. But she was back in Kathmandu and Dalloway was starting his contract with MozLon in Mozambique. That Charles Grace didn't know any of this, Paul was as certain as he could be, but it was typically eerie of his history with Grace that he should be summoned to talk about Mozambique!

Time started again and Grace brought Paul's thoughts back to London, to the sun and light. He must have sensed Paul's concentration waver. 'Did I say something odd, Paul?'

'No, sir, no, I just had a thought about Hungary, that's all.'

'Yes, Hungary, bless her. Then it opens its blasted border with Austria and within the space of six weeks over thirteen thousand East Germans have fled into Austria! Stunning is what I call it. The Wall will fall, Paul, mark my words, and soon. Then Mr Major will really have something to occupy his dull mind. Apart from cricket, that is. Although, if I know the PM, she'll have him out of the Foreign Office before that happens.'

'Do you think so, sir? The man's only been Foreign Secretary since July and I thought he was being groomed for the heights.'

'Well he might be, you're right. Who knows, he could even end up as PM. That's a thought now.' Grace finished his coffee. 'Come on, Paul, let's get out of this grand but depressing room and sample the fresh air of the lovely mid-day. We'll walk over to the Park and I'll buy you an ice cream. We'll shake the Berlin blues out of your head and talk about Mozambique. I really do need to talk to you about Mozambique. It's going to be, more than likely, your next mission.'

* * *

PAUL KNEW ONLY too well how skilled Grace was in manoeuvring the military machine in order to serve the wider and sometimes less obvious needs of HMG, but his words had really surprised him: *your next mission*. Paul didn't see how this could be so, but equally he had been sufficiently surprised by Grace's influence in the past to realise it was eminently possible.

Paul had been in his new appointment only three months. Surely he couldn't be sprung from it quite so soon? The Director Special Forces had pulled him in to the lieutenant colonel's post in the Headquarters in DOY's Barracks to head up a new branch. It had been this or the possibility, much later, of a directing staff post at the Staff College in Camberley. No contest; and Paul had been secretly pleased to have been given his acting rank so soon after the promotion list was published. He was young for the rank, thirty six, he was well aware of it, and others would be envious, but it was a break of luck, it was extra pay and it meant he could continue to live in his home, his flat in Pimlico. And now Charles Grace was telling him it was all going to change. How exactly was the great man going to do this? And why did he suddenly feel both ill at ease and charged with anticipation? Was it the prospect of challenge and danger, the foods that fed fundamental elements of his being?

The two men sat on a bench close to the cafeteria by the edge of the big lake in the heart of St James's Park. Paul felt the warm flow of air and registered the splash of water and the background noise of tourists all around him. They They sat, relaxed for the time being, suit jackets unbuttoned, munching away. Grace had gone one better than an ice cream and bought them both sandwiches. The feeling of balance couldn't last, not when Grace had summoned him. Not when Grace had talked about Mozambique rather than Eastern Europe. Paul sensed it coming but he had no idea what form it would take.

'Read this, Paul.' Grace pulled a piece of folded, stiffish A4 paper out of his inside jacket pocket and handed it to Paul almost diffidently. 'Read it carefully and then we'll have a discussion about what it all might mean. It's highly sensitive, Paul. You're the fifth person to read it. It only arrived at Number Ten yesterday, so the first and second people to read it were the PM's Private Secretary and then herself. Mrs Thatcher gave it to The Chief of Staff of Number Ten and he called me over. He's a man of sense in my view. He bypassed the Foreign Secretary, which given the circumstances and what is likely to happen, was probably a judgement call bordering on genius. So you're the fifth. Read it. Don't get your sandwich all over it, please. It has to go back to Number Ten and it's the original.'

Paul took the letter gingerly and unfolded it carefully. His hands were clean. The feeling of balance was totally gone. His blood fizzed and he had a keen sense of anticipation. This was the PM and only her most closely trusted advisors again, just as it had been in Ireland and Berlin.

He read the letter.

Private Office
Sir Reginald Hanlon, KCMG
Chairman and Chief Executive, MozLon Corporation
46-48 Lombard Street, London EC3

Personal for The Prime Minister
The Right Honourable Mrs Margaret Thatcher, MP
10 Downing Street
London SW1

10th October 1989

Dear Prime Minister

It is with a proper sense of caution that I write this letter. I do most sincerely recognise that in doing so I am drawing greatly on your favours, yet given the nature of the issue at hand and its possible impact upon the delicate state of the Mozambique Peace Process, I have no other course than to pen this letter. With all that is implied for British commercial interests and relations with the neighbouring countries, I know Her Majesty's Government will have a vested interest in the ramifications of this matter.

To be brief, Head Office MozLon has recently been informed that the Regional Director for the Central Provinces in Mozambique had gone missing. After exhaustive enquiries, we are now certain that this man has disappeared permanently and is most probably dead. Although we have no precise knowledge of the circumstances in which this event occurred, internal investigations have uncovered what I can only describe as 'uncertainties' concerning the man's activities in recent months.

These activities may or may not have led to his disappearance, but if they are substantiated, then their significance has the potential to impact upon a number of Her Majesty's Government's initiatives in southern Africa. Indeed, Prime Minister, the circumstances impact directly on my own continued involvement in attempting to facilitate the peace negotiations between the Frelimo Government and Renamo, and I am, as you know, due to be in Pretoria at the end of this month and in Nairobi in early December, engaged on precisely this business.

I am reluctant to put much more in writing, Prime Minister. I would, therefore, be most grateful if you felt able to assist me in uncovering the true scope of what has happened in Mozambique.

I remain, respectfully,

Reggie Hanlon

Sir Reginald Hanlon, KCMG

MozLon! Paul could hardly believe it! He kept his expression neutral, finished reading and looked up. Grace held out his hand and Paul handed the letter back.

'Clever man is our Sir Reggie Hanlon, oh yes he is, but he's taking a fairly sizeable risk in writing such a letter.'

'Why's that, General?'

'Because despite the fact that he and Mrs Thatcher have a certain amount of history, in the sense that Reggie's sizeable commercial ventures in Southern Africa have enjoyed Government support at times, the nature of relations in Mozambique and with its neighbours has changed in recent years. Reggie's a monolithic, pioneering business force, a latter-day Rhodes some might say. MozLon's his modern day British South Africa Company, and he's brought wealth generation and a certain political influence into the UK as a result; hence the knighthood and the ability to write personally to the PM. But Mrs Thatcher's moved our position in Mozambique in the last five years, she's had to, and it's left Sir Reggie slightly in the cold, with a waning political mandate and substantial commercial investments that are now seriously threatened by the evolving politics of the Region. So, in a nutshell, the PM doesn't need Reggie as much as he now obviously needs her. Still, Mrs Thatcher's loyal to those who work for her, as you and I know. So that's why I have the letter and why you've been the fifth person to read it.'

Grace got up from the bench and stretched. The sun had gone behind the clouds and Paul looked around him. It seemed as if the clouding of the sun had forced the tourists and the office workers inside. He checked his watch as he stood up. It was gone one o'clock. Lunchtime was over for most civil servants. He wondered what was coming next and waited for Grace to get to it in his own time, calmly contemplating that it was unlikely he would be going home to his flat in Pimlico at the end of each day for very much longer.

'It's a pretty enigmatic letter, General, a lot of innuendo and a barely veiled hint of forthcoming danger if HMG doesn't rush to his aid or help him in some way. Does anyone else say such things to Mrs Thatcher?'

'Hah!' and Grace laughed out loud, fluttering the pigeons pecking close by. 'You're right, Paul. So come on, let's walk awhile and I'll explain what's going on and try to fill in the gaps in Sir Reggie's missive. Then, we'll have to get things moving fairly swiftly.'

CHAPTER THREE

CHARLES GRACE OCCASIONALLY glanced at the tall, rangy man beside him as the two of them walked through St James's Park. He hadn't seen Paul Stanton for the best part of two years. Stanton's face was lean, the main features as prominent as he remembered them: the badly broken nose, chips of scar tissue around his jaw line, the piercing, weather-blue eyes and the close-cropped fair hair. He looked fit and powerful despite the disguise of the polished black half-brogues, the tailored double-breasted dark suit and the faceless patterned tie. All of which were de rigueur for service personnel working in London. The war in Northern Ireland still raged as intensely as ever and those in the military were targets wherever they were. Grace himself was dressed in similar mode.

He laughed quietly, and caused the man next to him to turn with a quizzical look. Grace didn't speak. Faceless? No, not ever could that soubriquet be applied to Paul Stanton. But he was relieved Stanton was fully fit again. Grace could never forget how seriously wounded Stanton had been in West Berlin. It had taken a long time for the man to be well enough to be moved, clandestinely, from the private clinic back to UK. As the months - and years - had inexorably rolled on, Charles Grace had been keeping a quiet check on Paul Stanton's physical fitness and his recovery to full health. He owed it to the man. It was an essential duty of care and the least he could do having sent Stanton into harm's way.

Until this last June, when Grace had been delighted, but not surprised, to see Stanton's name on the promotion list to lieutenant colonel, Stanton had been running a major's desk in the Ministry of Defence's Main Building in Whitehall and living in his bachelor flat in Pimlico. Stanton had done a good job servicing the equipment and requirements needs of Her Majesty's Special Forces; and he'd got himself fit again. When he'd known this meeting was inevitable, Charles Grace had checked Stanton's medical status with Army Personnel, just to get the official verdict, and now he could see the evidence in the man himself. Which is good, he thought, because he's going to need to be strong.

Charles Grace had only known Stanton since the middle of 1985 but there were unlikely bonds that linked the two of them, and despite the passage of time since 1986 and the lack of direct military contact, he still felt comfortable with the man. He was Stanton's mentor in a way. He had been a brigade commander in Northern Ireland when Stanton's unit had come to South Armagh in 1985. The battalion had been under Grace's direct command and Paul Stanton, as a company commander, had been responsible for the unpleasant and dangerous operational area of Crossmaglen, down on the Irish Border in Bandit Country.

Grace recalled the scuttlebutt about this supposedly talented officer at the time. Stanton was SAS, had won a Military Cross in the Falklands, and there was a current of envy as well as respect in the talk about him. Grace remembered it all as if it was yesterday. How could he forget? He'd instantly liked the man. Stanton's experience had struck chords of empathy with his own earlier service. Grace had a deep background in security and intelligence work. He had strong liaisons with the Police and Security Services and thankfully, as it happened, with Number 10. Stanton was a good officer, a very good officer. The man was tough on his men but fair, and they had clearly loved him for that. His operations had been active and imaginative. But it had all gone wrong, and he, Charles Grace, had missed the signs until it was almost too late.

Someone within the Royal Ulster Constabulary had betrayed Stanton's operations and the Provisional IRA launched a direct, heavily armed attack on one of his vehicle checkpoints. It was a classic of the Provisional IRA at the time, a so-called flying column attack on the little-known, nothing place the Army had dubbed Hotel 23, H23. The casualties had been significant and it was on the face of it a military and political disaster at a highly sensitive time in the PM's dialogue with Dublin and her Peace Process initiative. Mrs Thatcher had been seriously unamused.

Grace shuddered silently at the memory. Actually she had been incandescent with rage. It had been touch-and-go whether or not he could right the wrongs of the situation. In the event, with the help of a few friends in the security and intelligence business and some minor miracles, he had gained sanction from the PM to send Stanton undercover to hunt down and kill those responsible. It had been a cold and bloody business, and Charles Grace couldn't really begin to imagine what it had cost Stanton in personal morality, let alone what he knew it had cost him in physical pain. He was aware there was a dark side to Paul Stanton – the man killed without remorse - but then again, Grace reflected, Stanton had been trained by the best black operations unit in the world, so what should anyone expect?

And then there had been Christina Dahler, the MI5 Researcher who Grace had introduced into the mission. Had he done the right thing? He had believed so at the time, and she had been crucial to the outcomes. But now, walking through the early autumn balm of St James's Park, Charles Grace wasn't so sure. He couldn't have failed to notice Stanton's reaction when they discussed the Berlin Wall earlier. The covert mission had taken them all from Ireland to West Berlin, and Stanton and Christina had fallen for each other along the way. In the darkest depths of the ruined city, Stanton had confirmed the corruption and racketeering in one of the Army units and dealt with it in a proficient and final manner. The work necessary had been brutal and illegal, unsanctioned officially. The girl had witnessed unimaginable acts and had been in great personal peril. In the aftermath of it all, Grace believed, it was probably too much for the relationship to last. But what did he know? Anyway, he consoled himself, it's likely to have been for the best given what I think lies ahead for Lieutenant Colonel Paul Stanton.

'The letter, General, you were going to expand on Sir Reggie's situation?'

Stanton's words brought Charles Grace back to the present. 'Yes. I was. And am. But let me first congratulate you on your promotion, Paul. Well done. Much deserved. And well done to your Director in Duke of York's for getting you into a post where you can wear the rank. It makes such a lot of difference to your influence, and the pay helps, I can assure you.' Grace checked his step and looked about. There were still a few tourists. He needed the conversation to be secure. 'Let's walk up towards Buckingham Palace at a non-military pace and see where we end up, eh.'

'OK, sir, that's fine by me. As long as you're not planning to take us inside when we get there.'

'Stupid officer! Although I expect you know the inside pretty well don't you? All the gongs you've got. Anyway, the letter, yes, where to begin? I'll start and see how we go. Tick me off if I ramble incomprehensibly; but remember, since I read the blasted letter only yesterday, I've had to do some serious homework with the briefers in the Foreign Office just to understand what in hell's name is going on in the region. Not easy for a man of my advancing years and deteriorating mental faculties.'

'Yes, sir.' Paul had no sympathy for Charles Grace. The man had a mind that worked on the principles of Occam's Razor.

'Since the early seventies MozLon has been doing two things, and this is the Janet and John version remember. First, expanding British commercial interest into Africa, principally southern Africa, and secondly, meddling in the politics of the respective countries over there, and back here in the UK.' Grace couldn't help but chuckle at the scale of understatement in what he had just said. The fact was, Hanlon had been at times and still was, an ocean-going pain-in-the-arse.

'I vaguely remember some scandal involving a distant member of the Royal Family, who was a MozLon director, and something to do with MozLon supposedly sanction-busting in Rhodesia,' Stanton said. 'And wasn't the Royal the man who recommended Hanlon for the top job?'

'Yes, you're right. The man in question's business career was ended because of it. In fact that was the time when Sir Reggie was in the process of being taken to the High Court by a number of his directors who wanted him ousted for unethical management, or something similar. The action failed. The shareholders backed Reggie. He was good for shareholder wealth. But the PM, the famously indecisive Ted Heath, criticised MozLon in the Commons and called it, if I can quote correctly, "an unpleasant and unacceptable face of capitalism". But let's not forget, despite being a copper-bottomed nuisance, Reggie was taking MozLon to places where British Industry needed to go and taking factions of the political fraternity with him. The seventies were stagnant and depressed times and Reggie was going to stir it all up. And he did. It took him a while, but he did.'

'How exactly?'

'MozLon's an established Company, but it wasn't always so profitable. Hanlon's an immigrant to this country, did his service in the last war, worked in the City and then went to Africa and made a small personal fortune through a variety of businesses. MozLon recruited him into the top post in the sixties. The Board liked his style and approach to wealth generation, and he used the Company's base of gold rights in Ghana, platinum rights in South Africa and the oil pipeline from Beira in Mozambique to Zimbabwe, to make it what it is today. Even though he's fallen out with the Board and almost everyone else since those heady days.' Grace paused, but he didn't notice the thoughtful look on Stanton's face, otherwise he might have broken stride and asked him what was on his mind. He knew that what he was saying was beginning to sound like a lecture, but he wanted to tell Stanton about how he had interpreted Hanlon's letter to the PM, and it was vital for tomorrow's meeting that Stanton had a good understanding of the background. 'Sir Reginald Hanlon owns about fifteen percent of MozLon and the share price is strong. Last year the Company posted sales of over three billion pounds. Reggie's worth somewhere in the region of one hundred and fifty million pounds.'

'Christ!'

'Yes, indeed, which is why he can still write directly to the PM and be taken seriously. He's survived all the in-fighting and the furore surrounding his highly public attempted acquisitions. He's diversified the Company so that it now operates in the automotive distribution field, the oil and gas infrastructure field and the top market hotel and resort business. But, and here's where I'm gradually bringing this school-masterish diatribe back to the letter, MozLon's roots are in Africa. Sir Reggie's an Africa-hand and always will be. And in this case, at this time, we're talking about Mozambique.'

'But how can the disappearance of a senior manager in-country have political effect?'

'That's a very good question, Paul. How indeed? I'll try to answer it in a minute, but a little more background first, since you'll need it for the meeting we have tomorrow.'

'Meeting? With whom, General?' Grace looked at Stanton as he spoke and smiled to himself. At least Stanton hadn't bothered to raise irrelevant questions about how, and why and what for. No, he thought, the man's a pragmatist. No wasting of time on trying to duck the issue. He could sense the two of them were already moving from where they had been in their lives only just a few hours ago. The feeling of the unknown was starting to exercise its familiar grip on him. He wondered if Stanton felt the same. He was sure of it, if the past was anything to go by.

'We're meeting MozLon's Head of Security at Lombard Street tomorrow at ten hundred hours.'

'I beg your pardon, General!' exclaimed Stanton.

Grace looked quizzically at the younger man who had broken stride and seemed genuinely surprised. 'Yes, Paul. Are you OK? Do you know the man?'

'No, sir, no of course not.' But he knew *of* him.

'Well I do, as it happens. His name is Frederick Etherington.' I know him all right, thought Grace, and I'm not very happy it's him.

'You recall I spent time in the past working with the Met Police's Anti Terrorist Branch?' he went on. 'Well I bumped into Chief Superintendant Fred Etherington during those days. He was with the Fraud Squad. Not what I would call an all-round pleasant man, unfortunately, but he's Sir Reggie's Head of Security and has been for five years. So we're meeting him tomorrow and we're obviously going to have to get on with him.'

'That'll be no problem, sir. I'm legendary for my charm and tact, as you know.'

Grace laughed. Stanton seemed to have regained his composure and the two men had resumed their stroll. 'OK. Well back to Africa then,' said Grace.

Stanton mumbled, 'Sounds like the title of a film. And I've never been there, so there's no *back* for me, just a first time.'

'Let me try to draw you a verbal picture,' Grace continued, ignoring Stanton's comment. 'It's an old-fashioned wheel hub with several spokes radiating out from it. The hub is Mozambique. Inside the hub there are a number of bearings and they're a mixture of commercial and political in nature and they're rubbing up against each other and causing friction. The spokes link the hub to the UK, other non-African countries, and count Portugal and the US as prominent in those, and then to South Africa, Zimbabwe, Zambia, Tanzania and Malawi. The bearings are MozLon Corporation, the Frelimo government and the opposition Renamo, and there may be more, like breakaway elements in both Pretoria and Harare. But the point is that if the wheel stops turning then there's the strong possibility some of the spokes will break and the resulting imbalance will cause unacceptable strain on others. So HMG has a part to play in keeping the wheel turning, and thus far it still is, slowly, and regional affairs are in balance, just, and the Mozambique peace process moves on. Getting the picture?'

'I am. Clearly, thank you.'

'Good. And by the way, Paul, I'm not going to try and draw any conclusions from all this, because to be honest, I can't. It's too unclear to me at the moment. I suspect tomorrow's meeting will clarify things a little more.'

'I understand, sir. Go ahead.'

'And that's enough of the wheel metaphor.' Grace noted they were almost at Buckingham Gate. 'There's a pub in Petty France, Paul, the Bunch of Grapes, or something, let's head for it and we can sit down in a dark, dingy, boozer and have a glass of lemonade or preferably something a touch more manly. Where was I? Oh yes. I'm assuming you've heard of Frelimo and Renamo. It's been a bloody twelve-year civil war and Frelimo's been in power all the time. For the past year, though, a recognisable peace process has been underway. Frelimo has always been Marxist-Leninist and enjoyed certain and obvious global support for being so, but it's actually changing right now, and is offering the Mozambicans a liberal, multi-party government. Since nineteen eighty its principal support has come from Zimbabwe, where Mugabe has needed routes to the sea, and Zambia, for the same reasons. Tanzania was where Frelimo was founded and remains a staunch ally. All three countries have at varying times in the past offered safe havens for refugees, deployed forces in support of Frelimo, secured borders, etc, in return for trade and safe routes to the sea. And Sir Reginald Hanlon has long and strong personal relations with Mugabe, Kaunda and Nyerere. He's quite a man.' Grace paused and looked at Paul. 'We're here, come on, let's go in and sit down and get a drink. I don't know about you but I could murder a pint.'

* * *

THE BUNCH OF Grapes pub was quiet and the two men were indeed sitting in a dark and dingy corner that was permeated with that pervasive pub-only odour of stale smoke, beer, liquor and humanity. It was perfect for anonymity and the business in hand, even though it was early afternoon.

Paul's mind was reeling with the connections being fired into his thoughts by Grace's words. Last year he'd been working in a steady and interesting staff job in Whitehall, getting his medical status and personal fitness back, dealing with his beloved and well-known Special Forces, when out of the blue an old and good friend from the Kathmandu Rifles, Major, retired, Danny Dalloway, had called him from Kathmandu and asked for help. Help of a kind that only someone like Paul Stanton could provide: physical help, danger help. So Paul had gone. He'd taken ten days pre-Christmas leave and gone. And that was where he'd first heard of Mozambique, MozLon, Sir Reggie Hanlon and Fred Etherington. That was where he and the Gurkhas had killed the Hungarians. They'd had to. There had been no choice. What they'd done in those five dark December days last year had been necessary for Dalloway's safety and for his fledgling company, Gurkha Connections Limited, *to win a contract in Mozambique*.

And that was where he'd met Nikki Walker-Haig, GCL's business manager, who'd then come over to London this summer and stayed with him, because she had *contract meetings with MozLon's Fred Etherington*. He and Nikki had fallen in love. So now, Paul thought, my business and personal lives are inexorably interconnected. Christ! No, I can't escape this; destiny is at work in a very powerful way. He forced his thoughts back to the present. Grace had been articulate and careful in his explanations of what was a complex situation, but Paul still had little clear understanding of how it all linked back to the damned letter of Hanlon's that he'd read. Grace's picture was fine, but what did it all have to do with him? And did it have anything to do with what he now knew Dalloway's GCL was doing? He drank gratefully from his pint glass and waited.

The big man settled comfortably on the stained and well-used wall seat and looked at him with those serious eyes Paul had once known so well. His face looked concerned. Paul thought he looked older. But then he must look older, too. And like him, Grace had been promoted, and was now a Major General, so he'd also come out of the Ireland-Berlin affair with credit. And the man was still wheeling and dealing behind the scenes in military politics, with the remit to pull people like Paul Stanton in any way he chose. Amazing.

Grace resumed the narrative. 'Renamo was created in nineteen sixty-seven by Rhodesia's Central Intelligence Organisation to monitor and disrupt terrorist activities and movement from Mozambique into Rhodesia. Obviously the Lancaster House Agreement, the creation of Zimbabwe and Mugabe's election, changed all that. South Africa became the tacit sponsor of Renamo's efforts as it switched its aims to a war to topple Frelimo, and that's what it's been doing ever since, until now, that is. Right from those early days Hanlon, and therefore MozLon, has been involved in some way or another with Renamo.' Grace took a long drink and sighed gently. 'Most welcome, this, eh Paul?' Grace went back to his narrative. 'Sir Reggie's links to high government in Pretoria are well known. Five years ago things shifted and Reggie's activities did, too. South Africa and Mozambique signed a non-aggression pact, the Nkomati Agreement. And that's when Reggie really started to wheel and deal and that's when Mrs Thatcher's relationship with him started to coalesce. But I bet the Iron Lady's regretting it all now.'

'Why's that?'

'Sir Reggie started doing two things and it all caused serious heartburn in the Foreign Office. First, because of his commercial interests in Mozambique he started pumping millions of dollars into the coffers of Renamo, to leave his business operations alone, and they repaid him by laying waste to both the land and the civilian population and effectively alienating themselves from regional sympathy.' Which is why, Paul thought, he wants to engage private military companies such as GCL. 'And Hanlon's still doing it,' Grace continued, 'albeit on a reduced scale. In nineteen eighty-six even Hastings Banda in Malawi was forced to reject Renamo, and he's been a supporter of theirs from the start. Renamo took things too far, in many people's view, including HMG.'

'How so, sir?'

'In nineteen eighty-seven they massacred thousands of civilians in the Gaza Province, in southern Mozambique. Elements of the South African Defence Force were implicated and you can be sure Pretoria was definitely involved. But the second thing Hanlon did was to interject directly into the political process. And I mean *directly*. And this was when he and HMG started to drift apart.'

'How was that possible, General?'

'Sir Reginald Hanlon knows no bounds. He's driven, it seems, by the demands of his ego and brooks no obstacles. After Nkomati in nineteen eighty-four he used his wealth and the services of his private jet to coerce and shuttle various regional leaders into meetings in neutral territory in order to energise a peace process for Mozambique. He's committed to bringing Renamo and Frelimo together, to establishing Renamo as a legitimate political force in Mozambique. You've got to admire the man in a twisted way. He chose Kenya and President Moi, or more correctly Moi's mediator, Bethuel Kiplagat, as the fulcrum for his efforts. Just this August, when the talks in Nairobi between Renamo and Frelimo failed to make headway, Reggie took a hand. Last month he went directly to Lisbon and got Portuguese agreement for his active part in the peace process. He's due to take Kiplagat to Pretoria at the end of this month. That's what he was referring to in his letter.' Grace took another drink and frowned.

Now he's getting to the heart of things, Paul thought. 'I see that, now. But I still fail to grasp why the disappearance of a MozLon man can bring this level of interest from Number Ten Downing Street.'

'Maybe he's flying a kite. Maybe he's attempting a mind-job on the woman with the toughest mind in world politics. Pity him! A man's gone missing, an important man, supposedly, but that act alone doesn't generate pressure sufficient to get HMG to act. This is not Don Pacifico for God's sake. Mrs Thatcher may want a Foreign Secretary with the balls of Palmerston but this is not the Greek War of Independence and Maggie's hardly going to deploy the Spearhead Battalion to civil-war Africa for Hanlon, now is she?'

'Unlikely,' offered Paul.

'Absolutely. So, buried in the MozLon investigation of what's happened are goings-on, which Reggie believes might be embarrassing or meaningful to the PM or might be significant to the peace process. That's my guess. He'd better be right.'

'So how has HMG played in all the regional events you've described?'

'Back in 'seventy-nine when Mrs Thatcher had just won the Election, the outcome of the Lancaster House talks presented her with a real situation. She had been in office for just seven months and her Africa policy was nascent, at best. There is evidence to suggest that she favoured putting her support behind Bishop Muzorewa to form a government in Zimbabwe. Sir Reggie, through his personal relations with Kenneth Kaunda, who was Head of the Commonwealth Conference then, acted behind the scenes to change her mind and plump for Mugabe, and so far it's worked. So in a sense Mrs Thatcher owes Reggie a favour and at least an ear.'

'I see, but that's not all is it? There are conflicts, aren't there, General?'

'There are. As I said, Reggie's pumped millions into the coffers of Renamo and into the fabric of Mozambique and a great deal of the wealth created has come back into UK investments. But HMG cannot be seen to support Renamo since it stands for instability in the Mozambique-Zimbabwe-Zambia-Tanzania balance. So Mrs Thatcher supports Frelimo: she supports the peace process of course as well, but she is still cognisant of MozLon's business activities in Mozambique and how they might or might not involve Renamo. And of course, in the not-too-distant past, HMG was more open towards Renamo.'

'Hah. So what you said earlier is probably right then. Sir Reggie needs help, all is not right in the state of Mozambique, he knows things, or thinks he knows things important to the PM, and is calling in a favour from the British Government.'

'Simply put, Paul, and probably not too far from the truth of it. But I'm damned if I can guess what it is he thinks will move the PM. However, with her usual perspicacity the Prime Minister has sensed something and so I am charged by her Chief of Staff to *follow it up and report back, urgently, General Grace*, which were his exact words.' Grace suddenly sat upright, finished his drink and stood. The big man paused, looked at Paul and then sat down again.

Paul sensed something unsaid. 'What is it, sir? What else is there?'

'The Charles Grace insight, Paul, totally unofficial you understand. The letter's a bomb in my view, about to go off, but I'm damned if I have a clue why. You know the Inspector Clouseau films. Well it's one of the black, fizzing bombs in Blake Edwards's comic images. Just like the hapless Clouseau we've got to get to it and pull out the fuse before the bloody thing explodes, but I haven't a clue where to start looking.'

Paul watched Grace closely. 'But there's more, isn't there?'

'Yes. These are difficult days for the PM. Mrs Thatcher's third term is not the smooth ride she wants it to be. The Government's domestic policies are a cause of serious concern to the Cabinet. The Community Charge is another fizzing bomb, if you like. Yes, as you said earlier, the Foreign Office is focused on Eastern Europe, but, and this is the bit that affects us now, the Africa-watchers are warning of seismic events in southern Africa, too. The election last month of F W de Klerk to the Presidency in South Africa and his apparent new tolerance of the African National Congress could lead to the release of Nelson Mandela very soon. And then what might happen? The eyes of the world will be watching such events very closely and Mrs Thatcher will not want to be caught out or wrong-footed in any way by sub-level activities such as those Sir Reggie Hanlon might be up to. As for Zimbabwe...well cracks are beginning to emerge, so the gurus say, and the Government may well be forced into a new or changed position vis-à-vis Mr Robert Mugabe. And as we've just discussed, both countries are contiguous to Mozambique and this situation of Sir Reggie's does and must, my instincts tell me, have certain repercussions for HMG in the affairs of the Region.'

'Not straightforward, then?'

'No, and not likely to be when characters like Hanlon are involved.' Grace stood up. 'Come on, Colonel, my head is spinning with all this conjecture. I need to get back to Admiralty House and you need to clear your lines with the Director Special Forces. He knows what's going on, so he'll be expecting to talk to you. It's Thursday tomorrow and most of the day will be taken up with the meeting with Etherington. You need to be at the MozLon Head Office by zero nine thirty hours and bring your wits with you. Remember where they are?'

A trick question, wondered Paul? 'Yes, General, from the letterhead.'

'Excellent. Lombard Street of course, in the City. So I'll see you there.'

'You will, General.' He wondered what Charles Grace would have thought about the fact that he knew exactly where the MozLon Offices were, because of Nikki Walker-Haig's meeting with the very same Fred Etherington.

'Good. It will leave Friday clear for the various briefings and research you're going to need to do. You can rearrange things accordingly, can't you?'

Of course he could. When had his life been anything but unpredictable and short notice? At least Nikki wasn't in London with him. 'Of course, General.'

Grace looked at him with just the tiniest trace of sympathy in his eyes. 'Thank you for your input today, Paul. We have interesting times ahead of us, I believe.'

We do, thought Paul Stanton. We do.

CHAPTER FOUR

'THERE YOU ARE, sir.' With a beaming smile the British Airways hostess placed the glass of whisky on his seat table and set down a small bowl of nuts next to it. 'Would you care for some water with that?'

'Thank you, but no,' he replied. The woman left him. He eased his body back into the comfort of the airline seat and tried to relax. He cast a glance around the dimly lit cabin. It was the middle of the night and most of his fellow long-haul travellers were sleeping, or attempting to. They'd eaten their dinner three hours ago. There was another six to go. A good spell of time to sleep; but he couldn't. At least HMG was flying him business class to Johannesburg so he'd use the time and the relative luxury to think about what it all meant and what he was going to do. When the plane landed Paul would be met and transported to Pretoria by someone from the British Defence Attaché's staff. Then it would all start, in a rush, and he needed to have his mind clear with at least an outline plan before that time, so he sipped his whisky, munched cashew nuts and thought about what had happened at the MozLon meeting.

Paul had not taken to Frederick Etherington, Sir Reggie Hanlon's Head of Security. He was short, punchy in manner and had a weak handshake. Paul hadn't initially trusted him despite the fact that he was an old drinking buddy of Danny Dalloway from their Hong Kong days and despite the fact, as Grace had told him, he and Grace had a relationship that stemmed back to Etherington's days in the Met's Fraud Squad. But during the meeting he'd parked his prejudices, listened and learned. There was a collision of destinies at work here: Etherington had favoured Dalloway's company with the Mozambique contract and the man was a personal friend of his boss. And he had to work with Etherington, after all.

The meeting took place in the MozLon Board Room. Initial introductions were made, Etherington called for coffee and then the three men were alone.

Grace spoke. 'Lieutenant Colonel Stanton, Paul, is going to be my man on the ground, Fred,' which caused Paul to raise a glance at the man who seemed so able to change the balance of his life without so much as asking him, let alone warning him. Grace ignored the look, and as if to mollify him said to Etherington, 'Don't worry, Fred, this man I trust, and so might you,' which made Paul smile inwardly. Good on you, Charles. Etherington quizzed Paul through a steady stare and then clearly thought better about it all and cut to the chase.

'You've obviously seen and read Sir Reggie's letter to the PM, Charles,' Etherington stated the obvious, 'and you, too, Colonel.' Grace held his counsel. 'I don't want to overplay the metaphor but it's a ticking bomb,' and Grace flashed a telling look at Paul before Etherington continued, 'and it hints at much but deliberately says nothing specific.'

'What are the specifics, as you put it, Fred? A bomb? That sounds highly dangerous.'

'Hmm. It is. Listen to this, and let me show you,' and Etherington moved to a large wall map. 'This is MozLon in southern Africa.' It was exactly as Grace had explained to Paul the day before: Reggie Hanlon's commercial empire was spread like a measles rash across the map. All the old-new colonial country names had been infected with his business presence. 'Our main headquarters is here, in Maputo, in the south, but we have a subsidiary HQ in Beira. Both are international ports and both are redolent of the grand old Portuguese colonial style, although now battered and wrecked to varying degrees by the shock and impact of prolonged civil war.' Paul listened closely.

'We've put a sound structure in place. Telex and international 'phone links back here to London and again between London and all the other country capitals. We've linked all the country managers.' It was Grace's hub, with the spokes, just as he'd described. 'In country we have as good a comms set up as the indigenous infrastructure will support. So in Mozambique we have a web of interconnected regional offices all linked back to Maputo, and we have an established contact, reporting and call system. Which is why we know one of the Regional Directors is missing.'

'Who is he,' asked Grace, 'and why would he go missing? Why *is* he missing, more to the point? And how long has it been? Sir Reggie's letter was dated the tenth of October, three days ago.'

'Whoa, Charles, one step at a time, please. If this situation is as portentous as I believe, I need to make everything clear to you both,' and here he cast a glance at Paul, who, sitting at the conference table, returned his look but said nothing. He turned his head again to the huge map and carried on memorising its story. The geography was going to be important. It always was. 'His name is Victor Fitzsimons and he's the Regional Director for the provinces closest to the Zimbabwe and Tanzanian borders,' continued Etherington, 'the central areas adjacent to the Beira-Zimbabwe oil pipeline.'

'So the Manica and Sofala provinces,' said Grace looking closely at the map. 'Is that correct?'

'Yes,' replied Etherington, 'and vitally important provinces they are, too, for a number of reasons.'

Which is why the man's disappearance is also vitally important, thought Paul. The areas, vast tracts of territory, judging by the map, were split almost equally by a railway-road-oil pipeline from Beira in the east and on the ocean, to Mutare on the border between Zimbabwe and Mozambique. He calculated the distance from the scale line at the bottom of the map to be around three hundred kilometres. Deceptively important land, obviously, but why?

Etherington continued. 'It's a bugger's muddle,' he said, 'and like everything Sir Reggie does, the business and the politics are damn nearly impossible to separate.' He turned to Paul. 'Everything I tell you is strictly confidential. Do you understand?' Unnecessary caution, Paul thought, so he half-nodded and looked at Etherington with interest. This man had to trust him. 'You must be about the same age, I'm guessing,' he continued. 'Do you know an ex-Gurkha officer, Kathmandu Rifles, by the name of Dalloway, Danny Dalloway?'

'I do,' Paul replied. He knew where this was going. Grace looked slightly quizzically at him.

'Well I knew him in Hong Kong. He's a wild man but a very competent operator and his Gurkhas always worshipped him.' And still do, thought Paul. 'He's formed a security and protection company called Gurkha Connections Limited, GCL,' continued Etherington, 'based out of Nepal using recently retired Gurkhas. It's all above board and sanctioned by the Government there, the Panchayat, and by the Brigade of Gurkhas. Anyway, MozLon's given him a sizeable contract in Mozambique, which he's in the process of implementing on the ground. I was personally responsible for persuading Sir Reggie and the rest of the regional decision makers that Dalloway should get the deal.' And *I* know who helped persuade *you*, thought Paul. Nikki Walker-Haig!

'OK, Fred,' said Grace thoughtfully, 'but how is this of geo-political import and how is it linked to Sir Reggie's concern about your missing man?'

'I'll get to it, I think, if my deductions are correct. The GCL contract is to provide area and onsite security for our collective farms and to be capable of mobile response security for attacks on the pipeline.'

'Collective farming?' Grace questioned. 'Sounds very Marxist-Leninist.'

Etherington smiled wryly. 'You don't know how close to the truth that comment is.' Grace cocked his head and raised his eyebrows. 'It is, or it's planned to be, large scale agricultural production of tomatoes, to start with, then sugar, cotton and tea. But here's the thing: the areas concerned fall within Fitzsimons' provincial responsibilities.' Etherington's look became quizzical. 'The deployment of Gurkhas is going well. It's very early days but the first farms are up and just about running in Nhamatanda and Manica. Fitzsimons had reported back to us on both the projects.' He paused. 'And now we've lost contact with him. Literally.'

Paul was studying the map intently. 'So both farms very close to the road, rail and oil line, and the second one you mentioned very close to the Zimbabwe border at Mutare.'

'Exactly. We deliberately planned to support GCL's logistics from the Beira end and from the Zimbabwe end, where MozLon has some presence and good relations with the relevant government ministries.'

Grace said, 'Apologies for being so direct, Fred, all very interesting as this is, what exactly is it that Sir Reggie and you want help for? I'm not seeing the connections between GCL's security activities and your problem. Sir Reggie says explicitly in his letter that Mr Fitzsimons' disappearance has impact on regional activities, activities of concern to HMG. So far, though, you haven't really given us anything tangible to substantiate this concern. All this talk about security contracts is interesting but is it relevant?'

'Actually it might be; but you're right,' said Etherington and sat down. For the first time he looked stressed and uncertain. 'Let me speculate for a minute,' he confided. 'If, and I mean, if, our man has disappeared in circumstances that might in any way be proved as nefarious, illegal, unsanctioned, then it is potentially a big drama for MozLon and HMG will urgently want us to deal with it, which is why Sir Reggie wrote the letter.'

'What could those circumstances realistically be?' asked Grace.

'I believe, and I've managed to convince Sir Reggie, that Fitzsimons' has been, was, helping to move hard assets from Zimbabwe through to Beira, and from there, presumably to offshore locations.' Etherington looked at the two of them. 'And what's worse, if this is the case, then he's probably been doing it with the help of criminal accomplices in South Africa and possibly Zimbabwe, and Renamo renegade factions in Beira. I can't prove it, yet, but that's what I suspect.'

'Christ,' said Grace, which was most unusual for him.

Paul interjected quickly, 'And do you believe GCL has any involvement in this?'

'No, no, definitely not,' said Etherington hastily. Thank God, thought Paul. 'Whatever Fitzsimons may have done or did, it was way before Major Dalloway's company hit the ground there. I mention it because, with such a reliable presence on the ground in Fitzsimons' areas, we at least have some support in country. Should we need it,' he finished lamely.

Grace ignored the exchange. 'So,' he said deliberately, 'there's Sir Reggie, dedicated to supporting HMG's policy of help to Mugabe's Zimbabwe, which is alarmingly starting to fray at the edges, unfortunately,' he paused as he marshalled his thoughts. 'He's also overtly assisting Frelimo to make peace with Renamo and ploughing millions into the country in an endeavour to create growth and stability through these farming and other development contracts, as well as make MozLon's additional fortune, of course.'

'And Mrs Thatcher's policy is support of Frelimo,' said Etherington, 'as well as limited tactical support for the release of Nelson Mandela and the legitimising of the ANC in South Africa.' He took a drink from his coffee cup and screwed up his face at the obviously cold liquid. Almost fatalistically he continued, 'Which is made even trickier because Pretoria is only just beginning to drop its overt support for Renamo, in order to move with the rest of the region to secure a lasting peace.'

'Certainly,' replied Grace. 'And Sir Reggie's latest round of regional politicking takes place in Pretoria at the end of this month, and if MozLon has been seen in anyway to be involved in actions that might offend us, the UK, South Africa, Zimbabwe or Mozambique, then his credibility will be shattered.'

'As will his business interests in the region,' added Etherington.

As will Danny Dalloway's GCL enterprise, thought Paul. Yes, an unexploded bomb. He asked the key question. 'What makes you believe Mr Fitzsimons was trafficking, and clearly for some time before his disappearance?'

'First off, because I am personally friends with Ken Rose, the head of the Central Intelligence Organisation, the CIO, in Harare, and he has some tangible evidence in his keep.'

'Which is?' asked Grace.

'A patrol of the Zimbabwe Police Anti-Terrorist Unit made a targeted cross-border foray near Malvernia, about fifty kilometres north of the Limpopo River and found a recent campsite. The patrol was technically illegal but was part of Rose's covert intelligence gathering plan.'

'Which is why what it found is not in the public domain,' stated Paul. The other two men looked at him. 'I would have picked it up in the intelligence digests where I work,' he said. In Headquarters Special Forces, he didn't add. 'What did they find?'

'The remains of a big fire with partially burned clothes and a tarpaulin,' responded Etherington. 'The scraps of tarpaulin had what looked like blood on it. But more significantly they found some of the bones, including their skulls, of two men, big men. As the patrol and what it found were eyes-only for Rose, the patrol commander brought the clothing and skulls back with him. Both had been shot in the head. There were two shell cases, nine millimetre, probably from a Russian pistol.'

'But,' Paul said, 'I'm guessing neither skull belonged to Mr Fitzsimons. Is that correct?'

'Yes. Both were Africans.'

'When did this happen?' Paul knew the answer already.

'On the fifth of October, three days after we received the news of Fitzsimons' disappearance.'

'And the clothes?'

'What was left were charred scraps. They could have been European.'

'Two Africans,' said Grace, 'who could have been Renamo but could have been anyone else, for that matter, most likely murdered, and the burnt scraps of possible European clothing which might or might not have belonged to the disappeared Victor Fitzsimons. And this is why Sir Reggie would like HMG's help in finding out what really happened?'

'Yes, Charles, but here's the second reason.' Grace's look asked the question of Etherington. 'Ken Rose and I have been communicating regularly for years. He's the one who alerted me some months back to the increasing uncertainties amongst the whites in Zimbabwe and the fact that some of them might be trying to put their wealth offshore. When Fitzsimons went missing I told him, just in case he'd heard anything. That's when he gave me the information from the PATU patrol in strictest confidence. I shared it with Sir Reggie. Rose is absolutely sure that the Zim businessmen and farmers will only have trusted their activity to someone above board, someone out of view from the prying eyes of Mugabe's intelligence thugs, someone who can move freely and securely between the Zimbabwe border at Mutare and Beira.'

'Someone such as a MozLon Regional Director for those very areas,' said Paul. 'Mr Fitzsimons.'

'Anyone else know all this?' asked Grace.

'No, apart from you two, now. But there are more reasons to support my beliefs. Ken Rose is one part of my covert network. We also have limited ears and eyes in Beira that keeps us informed of events in Frelimo and Renamo. Beira had no specific knowledge of the trafficking, but told me that Renamo renegades are being used for criminal activities possibly in Zimbabwe. Rose confirmed this when I asked him.'

'Wonderful,' said Grace.

Etherington ignored the resigned sarcasm. 'Finally, I have a well-placed contact inside the South African National Intelligence Service.'

'What did he have to contribute?' asked Grace.

'That it was more than likely ex-South African Defence Force soldiers were now being used as mercenaries to act inside Zimbabwe and Mozambique.' Etherington paused.

'And one or some of all these groups were involved in Mr Fitzsimons' disappearance?' asked Paul.

'Yes, I do think so. The PATU patrol found something else. They found a Zippo lighter with a military badge on it. The Reconnaissance Battalion.'

'Part of South Africa's Special Forces,' said Paul, who knew these things. 'But,' he continued, 'the Recces haven't really been active since the end of the Border War, earlier this year, have they?'

'Which is why a number of them have probably gone rogue, according to my source in Pretoria, to bolster their earnings and to work off their ongoing hatred of the blacks in this dawning era of tolerance towards the ANC.'

And so the meeting had concluded.

After they'd left the MozLon building Grace had been silent for most of the journey back to Whitehall. Then he'd said: 'I'll clear it with Number Ten tomorrow so as to ensure all the diplomatic help you'll need, but I'd like you to get there and sort out this mess, Paul. It reeks of complication but what the Government stands to lose by way of association with such a situation cannot be tolerated.'

'Yes, General,' he'd replied.

'Ultimately Sir Reggie and Etherington have to make the changes in their organisation and satisfy Mrs Thatcher that the problems have been fixed before the politics of it all becomes uncontainable. But I don't trust them to be able to do it. It's my blasted hub and its spokes again. We've got renegades in Mozambique, Zimbabwe and South Africa all trying to take the wealth from the white Zimbabwe nationals, and all of them very comfortable with killing with impunity anyone who gets in the way. And we have corruption inside MozLon, in country. How far does that extend, I wonder?'

'On the plus side, sir, we have Major Dalloway's Gurkhas in country, and I will know a number of them, I'm sure.'

'You will? Of course you will, from your secondment to the Kathmandu Rifles. Well that's good. And you're the man to give me eyes on, a clear and sensible assessment, and to take action if needed.' Grace broke off, thinking furiously. Paul said nothing. Grace spoke again, 'As I said, I'll fix everything in two days. Book your air ticket.

Your initial point of contact will be the Defence Attaché in Pretoria. He's a brigadier, a good man. His name is Colin Bullock, a Green Jacket, so understands soldiering. You'll need to work with him and other UK assets in the region. We also have a British Military Advisory and Training Team in Zimbabwe. I'll send the details of it all over to Duke of York's later today. I'll also ensure the secure comms links are in place so you and I can stay in touch.' Grace looked at Paul and his expression was tired. 'Apologies for buggering up your life once again, Paul, but if my experience is anything to go by, there's more to this situation than any of us think.' The General's face lightened, 'You never know, it might be exciting. And as you are friends with this ex-Gurkha chap, Dalloway, it will be a help, I'm sure.'

'It might, sir.' And Paul returned Grace's look of unsure optimism with one of his own.

* * *

THAT HAD BEEN two days ago and so his world had changed. He had a mission of National importance wrapped inside the uncertain reality of complex regional politics and business issues in countries he had no experience of, with repercussions that his intellect could only guess at. The moving pieces and how they acted in the game Etherington had described, and which he and Grace had subsequently discussed in the manic series of briefings at the Foreign Office and in the Ministry of Defence, made his mind reel.

Paul eased his shoulders back into his seat and drank his whisky. He pushed the thoughts of MozLon to one side and let his mind turn to Nikki Walker-Haig and where their relationship stood. It was inevitable. He thought about her most of the time now when he wasn't manically busy. They'd agreed work had to come first since many others depended on them being committed and focused. They had the future ahead of them, so no need to rush; at least that's what they thought.

Since July they had only seen each other once, for a glorious ten days, when she had coerced Danny Dalloway to give her home leave so she could look for a flat to buy in London, as a base, which she'd achieved with Paul's help. Dalloway hadn't asked her how she'd suddenly acquired the money and Nikki didn't offer an explanation. It was none of his business. Only she and Paul - and Nikki's sister and Paul's close friend, Barry Radford, from his SAS days - knew the money had been a late-legacy gift from a Great Train Robber! It had been Paul and Barry's one and only foray into what they called justifiable crime; and contrary to popular advice, it had paid!

But that *had* been back in the summer.   Over the months they'd spoken occasionally, when Paul could get a 'phone line through to Kathmandu, and the two of them exchanged air letters roughly every ten days. But he hadn't had a letter for a while and the last call they'd shared had been her calling him, which was unusual, and that had been over a week ago. Yesterday Paul had managed to get through to Gurkha Connections Limited in Kathmandu to speak to Nikki. She wasn't there, the office said. She'd left Nepal two weeks ago and was most certainly in Zimbabwe, where they had a permanent base close to Mutare, which was safe, and they were sure that's where Major Danny Dalloway would have wanted her to be. *Two weeks ago!* Which would explain the fragmentation of their communications, Paul had realised.

He looked at his watch in the dim glow of the cabin. He had less than six hours before his odyssey would start when the plane landed in Johannesburg. So he finished his whisky and closed his eyes. He'd leave the immediate future of the next hours to the gods. He'd find his girl soon. That was for certain.

PART II
PRETORIA

CHAPTER FIVE

THE PLACE REMINDED Major Richard de Castenet of the squalid down and out bars in Berlin where he'd met that mad bastard Corporal Shaggy Drinkwater three years ago, when his world had catastrophically imploded. Those Berlin days when Drinkwater had blackmailed him over a security lapse in Northern Ireland and Brigadier, now General, Charles Grace had effectively handed him over as a sacrificial lamb in the British Army's worst security scandal in memory. He'd lost seniority and been parked, seemingly until the end of his career, on the Army's postings and promotion blacklist. But at least Drinkwater had died.

He'd been down on his luck ever since. Until six months ago. Although his latest posting as the officer responsible for training liaison in the UK's Defence Staff in the British Embassy in Pretoria had seemed yet another career backwater, the place and the post had changed his fortunes...or so he hoped. However, here he was now dealing with another Drinkwater-esque mad bastard, some renegade mercenary called Coetzee, and what was worse, the evil little man smelt like a shithole, quite literally. But at least de Castenet was more sure of the outcome of this meeting.

He looked across the shabby table at Coetzee and he hated what he saw. The man was fat, stocky fat, with dangerous, close-together pig-like eyes, that leered out at him from under the brim of the filthy, sweat-stained slouch hat he never took off. It made de

Castenet feel extremely uncomfortable. What made him feel even more uncomfortable was the fact that Coetzee worked for him; well, strictly speaking he worked for Schuman, de Castenet's business partner, but de Castenet had somehow been given the role of Coetzee's handler and he hated it. But it hadn't actually been very hands-on and it wouldn't be for much longer. This meeting would be the last between the two of them.

Coetzee was volatile, repulsive and dangerous. He wore a loose canvas jacket over his bush vest, presumably to hide the holstered weapon de Castenet knew the man kept under his left armpit. A Makarov, always loaded with a round chambered, but with the safety on, of course, man, Coetzee had boasted when they'd met the first time. Richard de Castenet wouldn't have put it past the lunatic bastard to use it here and now in this low life shebeen on the eastern outskirts of Pretoria. He looked around him. Would anyone notice if he did? Not at all, in de Castenet's view. The drink-sodden clientele comprised a cast of broken down labourers and other layabouts, and the barman was a scar-faced Afrikaner who exuded all the dying prejudices of white South Africans steeped and reared in apartheid. So in all probability he wouldn't give a damn if violence broke out. de Castenet loved the country, especially given the freedoms he had to travel, but he had no time for the racist politics and social practices.

'So then, Major,' Coetzee spoke in that awful accent of the native Afrikaans speaker wrestling, unfamiliarly it seemed, to enunciate the English language, 'what's next, hey?'

What's next? Richard de Castenet didn't have a clue, although he did know what was planned for Coetzee. The man had been their collector for Schuman-de Castenet Enterprises' only job, and *had been* was the operative phrase, since Coetzee was about to be sacked. 'There's nothing on the cards at the moment, Mr Coetzee,' he replied.

'What exactly is that supposed to mean, man?' de Castenet repressed the desire to tell the man to fuck off. The creature was too volatile.

'The consignment you brought back from Mozambique has caused us problems.' The truth was it had brought his and Schuman's dirty business to a grinding halt just as it had got started. They had planned this job meticulously and it had taken time and all Schuman's extensive network of crooked contacts to execute. Coetzee had come back to Pretoria ten days ago and de Castenet had met him as planned to take possession of the consignment. But something had been wrong. Coetzee had kept something back, they were sure of it. What was planned later tonight would prove Coetzee's duplicity or not. Right now the man had to be placated.

Coetzee said, 'I've still to be paid. You and your colleague in the National Intelligence Service still owe me, fucking right you do.'

'We know that. Your money will be paid to you.'

'I killed people for you and your partner. You know that, also, right?' de Castenet *did* know that, but he didn't know exactly who or when and how this mad bastard mercenary had committed the various murders and he certainly didn't want to, either. Schuman kept these details to himself. 'Their bodies are animal food. Gone.' Coetzee chuckled evilly and drank his beer. de Castenet shuddered involuntarily. 'Not squeamish, Major, are you?' Coetzee said dismissively. 'You fucking Poms never had the stomach for what's needed in this sort of business.' Which was a stupid and insulting comment but de Castenet ignored it.

'The package you brought back was unexpectedly large,' he said evenly. 'Sourcing buyers for such a quantity of stones is not easy. You can understand that, surely?'

'OK, Mr fancy accent British Army officer, I'll wait, but not for too long, hey. Buy me one more Castle lager, man. You owe me that, for sure.'

de Castenet pulled some money out of his trouser pocket and counted out a large number of Rand banknotes. 'Have a few more beers on me, Mr Coetzee. There's enough for some Klipdrift chasers and some late evening entertainment, too.' He needed this man to be drunk, seriously drunk and distracted. 'I'll arrange the next meeting in a week. Stay strong. Goodbye for now.'

'*Totsiens*, Major.'

Major Richard de Castenet left the shebeen bar. He breathed in the October Sunday evening air and put on his lightweight jacket. The sun was dipping and it was still a touch chilly. He needed to get out of this fringe township locality and back into the Arcadia area, to the relative serenity of the British Embassy cantonment and his bachelor lodgings. He needed to be as far away from Mannie Coetzee as possible.

As he walked he thought about the next stages of his business with Major Wentzel Schuman, Head of Border Operations in South Africa's NIS. He'd met Schuman at one of the endless rounds of diplomatic cocktail parties and they'd talked and then started to socialise and play golf. Observing the proprieties and cognisant of the fact that either or both of them might be talking in the wrong code and so might be misunderstanding the verbal signals, they had discovered and agreed mutual interests of a criminal bent, in order to redress the perceived unfairness in their lives.

Three months ago they'd started to plan their future fortunes - or at least the means they believed would deliver them. Schuman had inside security knowledge and direct contacts with counterparts in Harare and Beira. These were people who knew people who would carry out contract work of any description. Schuman also knew the operatives in South Africa who would do the same type of fieldwork. Men like Coetzee; men who would kill for a price. Schuman had the network that could span the three countries and cross their borders, and de Castenet had the blue chip credentials of a British Army diplomat who could travel with immunity back to London. It seemed like perfect foundations for executing dirty business. And the beauty and simplicity was that their business could be disguised inside the chaos of racial politics, social unrest and civil war, all of which existed to some extent either openly or nascently in the three countries concerned.

Southern Africa was on the verge of seismic change, Schuman said with hatred and passion. The demise of Afrikaner South Africa was imminent and those kaffir bastards in the African National Congress would take power. The newly elected F W de Klerk *would* release Nelson Mandela, it was written in the stars. And when that happened he, for one, wanted to be out of this place, man. The NIS bosses and some of the middle ranks would be replaced with black men, his post for sure. Fuck that for a future life. So he had a plan, and because de Castenet could travel freely with diplomatic immunity between Zimbabwe, South Africa and UK he was the perfect man to join with in partnership to make the plan work. Was he interested? It was highly illegal, though, and fraught with danger. *Was he interested?* Too bloody right he was! Being an object of pity in the British Army's list of passed-over majors was not an ongoing career choice for him. So he'd accepted the risks and gone to work with Schuman.

And now, because of the consignment Coetzee had brought back, the two of them were on the road to becoming very rich, staggeringly rich. He pitied Coetzee, but the man had played his part. No, actually, he didn't pity the man at all. He stank and the bastard had almost certainly tried to steal from him and Schuman. He deserved all he got.

Confident that Coetzee would be taken care of, de Castenet thought about his next problem, one far closer to home than Mannie Coetzee. It was a problem that had its genesis in those bad, ill-fortunate days of Northern Ireland and Berlin: *Lieutenant Colonel Paul Stanton, MC.* The bastard man was arriving in country tomorrow morning and his first port of call was the Military Staff of the Defence Attaché in the Embassy. Stanton was his nemesis and just to rub salt into his not-healed wounds, was now a blasted lieutenant colonel! de Castenet had no idea why this man was arriving, none whatsoever, but the coincidence of it all made his skin crawl and all of a sudden he was not so confident about his new found future.

And to make matters even worse he'd been ordered by his Brigadier to task a driver and car tomorrow morning and go to the airport to meet this important visitor from London.

* * *

LATER, MUCH LATER on that fateful Sunday night, Mannie Coetzee staggered out of the shebeen bar and stumbled drunk towards a brothel he knew. He was not a totally happy man and sensed inside his stewed mind that he was being played along by the smooth-talking Pommie bastard whose name he didn't even know; but at least he had the money for a good time with some coloured girl who would ease his worries, if only for a short while.

Coetzee never saw the man nor heard his death approaching. He was mumbling and stumbling. The narrow streets were black-dark and deserted. Who in their right mind would be on the streets of east Pretoria at that time of night? His assassin was, paradoxically, a white man, an old colleague.   There was no loyalty it seemed between comrades when it came to money and survival.   The bullet was silenced and nine millimetres in diameter. The force of the bullet, which entered Coetzee's head at an angle of forty-five degrees from the base of his neck, blew his pickled brains out through the top of his slouch hat.   He felt nothing.   His   troubled   world   passed instantaneously into oblivion.

The killer wasn't worried about the body. He'd been told to leave it.   The scavengers would find it and then the police.   So he stopped only long enough to pick up the brass cartridge case and pick through Coetzee's pockets in his bush vest and overjacket. He found the remainder of the banknotes, which he'd been told he could keep, and the Makarov pistol, which he could also keep.

Much more importantly he found the cowhide pouch of diamonds secured by leather strings around the hairy belly of the man. These he would hand over to Major Schuman tomorrow. It would be him lying in a pool of his own blood next in some shithole alleyway if he didn't. The Major from the National Intelligence Service who had somehow tracked him down and blackmailed him into becoming one of his fixers was a dangerous bastard to tangle with. The man knew too many secrets and you should never try to double-cross him. That's what Schuman had said to him. But that was fine, because he had heeded the Major's words and was smarter than that fat fucker,

Coetzee. Besides, do this right, Schuman had told him, and there would be more opportunities.

The assassin-mercenary slipped away from Coetzee's body and walked swiftly southwards.

CHAPTER SIX

MONDAY MORNING THE sixteenth of October and it took over an hour, with the commuter traffic, to drive from Johannesburg airport into Pretoria. Paul didn't talk much to his host; it was too difficult and too false to do so. He'd recognised the two British Army personnel by their tropical uniforms in the airport's arrivals area. One of them was a lance corporal, obviously the driver, the other was a major in the regimental livery of the Loamshire Regiment, which Paul knew well, and he also knew the man wearing it. *Richard de Castenet.* How it could be, Paul had no idea; although de Castenet had obviously been told who was arriving because he'd shown no surprise, simply exhibiting a moderately polite diffidence. The two men exchanged muted and awkward pleasantries and kept their counsel until whenever.

Paul remembered de Castenet clearly from the days in Northern Ireland. Although the man had been in West Berlin Paul hadn't seen him, nor had he seen him since, but he knew what had happened to him. The Army's grapevine was second-to-none. The man was a typical career Infantry officer, fit and smart and seemingly competent and good at his job. Now, however, he looked out of condition; his medium height and the cut of his tropical uniform couldn't hide the extra weight de Castenet now carried. There was tiredness around his eyes, a touch of seediness about his features and his mousy-coloured hair was receding and thinning. The man had evidently lost a good measure of his self-esteem and professional pride, but Paul felt no pity for him. Not surprising, really, if you thought about it, which Paul didn't.

He sat back in the elevated seat in the rear of the Toyota Land Cruiser and absorbed the surroundings. From what he could see from the huge expanse of sun-filled blue spring sky, it was going to be a hot, clear day. The countryside was low rolling scrubland and looked parched. Rains hadn't come yet to the Highveld, but they were expected anytime soon. As they hit Pretoria, Paul felt the sense of history, both old and new, that the buildings and the layout of the city imparted. The skyline of the Central Business District dominated as the driver took the vehicle into the heart of this iconic city, Jacaranda City. They passed the solid, classic Afrikaner Palace of Justice and Church Square with the imposing statue of Paul Kruger, and finally into the wide leafy thoroughfare of Park Street, the heart of the suburb of Arcadia.

This was the diplomatic quarter, de Castenet told Paul in a dismissive manner, the British Embassy was here, of course. So also, Paul noticed, were the Art Museum, some parts of the University and the Union Buildings. But fascinating and interesting as it all was, the history of the place could wait; he had more urgent issues to address.

'Whom am I meeting first?' Paul asked, as the driver took the Land Cruiser through the manned security gates, showing his pass to the uniformed Ministry of Defence policeman, and driving into the large, garden fringed compound in front of the doors to the British Embassy.

'The DA,' replied de Castenet, 'Brigadier Bullock. Do you know him?'

'No, I don't.' But he'd heard of him, as a close friend of Charles Grace.

'Grab your bag and I'll take you up to his office. I'm sure he'll fill you in on whatever your mission is.' Paul ignored the deliberate tone of false self-deprecation.

The Embassy was large, airy and flooded with sunlight. Paul immediately felt comfortable. The building had character. He could imagine what it might have seen through the years in its tall-windowed or balconied walkways that gave access to large, ceiling-fanned offices and gracious meeting rooms. History-changing debates and decisions, that was for sure. As he followed de Castenet up well used stone stairways to the higher levels of privacy and quiet, he glanced through the open balconies down on to the gardens that surrounded the buildings in green and emerging colours. Despite the lack of rains, the gardens looked luxuriant and vibrant.

He examined his feelings: he was tired but not jet-lagged since there was only one hour's time difference between here and London; but on top of everything else he now had the issue of de Castenet's presence which would have to be dealt with in some way and fairly soon. He imagined his office at HQ DSF and quickly put it out of his mind. When might he see it again? His thoughts turned to Charles Grace and what he could be up to. He'd certainly be waiting for Paul's first report back, that was a given. Time to focus, Stanton, he chided himself.

de Castenet knocked on a large, heavy door and opened it, ushering Paul inside. 'Thank you, Richard,' a voice said, and de Castenet left Paul to the Defence Attaché, Brigadier Colin Bullock of the Royal Green Jackets.

Paul's first impression was of a sprightly, lithe, good-looking man, probably in his early fifties. Bullock said nothing, but came to him from behind a large mahogany desk with a hand extended in friendship and a genuine smile on a thin, weather-beaten face that sat neatly below a cropped head of grizzled greying hair. He looked like a soldier's officer, which was good. Bullock wore a green coloured tropical uniform, probably made from some sort of Dacron, Paul guessed, which was marked out by the distinctive black buttons of his Rifle regiment, the red collar tabs of his general staff position, the black crown and three stars of his rank on its epaulettes, and the broad, rifle green stable belt. He had polished black brogues on his feet. He was shorter than Paul, but it was clear to see there was steel toughness in the sinews and flesh of this man. He would make a good ally and Paul intended to ensure this was the case. He placed his battered, trusty travel bag on the floor inside the door. The two men shook hands and Paul sat in one of the chairs to which Bullock gestured.

He glanced at the walls and registered the panoply of prints and framed memorabilia that told the stories of the office itself and the man who was now its occupant. Paul was suddenly aware of how out-of-place he felt in his travel-worn polo shirt, Levis, desert boots and linen jacket. He scratched his face and felt the bristle of his day-old beard.

'We have a berth organised for you, Paul, and I expect you'd welcome getting to it sooner rather than later in order to spruce up a bit,' said Bullock, who had taken a chair next to Paul's and was pouring coffee out of a thermos into two large mugs, 'but we need to talk first, I'm afraid. After we've done so and you've met the key people you need to, my driver will take you to a rather pleasant little hotel just outside the Embassy grounds. You might even ask him to familiarize you a little with your surroundings. He's at your disposal. Milk and sugar?'

'Yes, Brigadier, thank you.'

'The flight's not too bad, is it? Not in the welcome comfort of business class, anyway,' continued Bullock. He was clearly getting the niceties out of the way early. Then he said: 'I expect seeing Richard de Castenet was the last thing you would have expected at the airport. Am I right? I know a little of the history involving the two of you, but only because I was in Army Manning and Records before this post and the files came across my desk in nineteen eight-six. I thought it best to get your first meeting out of the way from the outset. There will be a need for you to work with him. He's responsible for our training liaison here, across the border in Zimbabwe and even with the Mozambique Armed Forces. I'm sure the opportunity will arise for him to brief you on what he does.' Bullock sipped his coffee and gave Paul an enquiring look with his sharp dark eyes. 'What say you?'

Paul dropped his eyes to his coffee and drank gratefully. So de Castenet had a responsibility that touched all the military pressure points in the region and could travel. Most interesting, he thought. He looked at Bullock and said: 'Frankly, Brigadier, I thought God was having a laugh!' Bullock's face split into a broad smile and he leaned back in his chair. Suddenly the thought flashed through Paul's mind: had Charles Grace known? Surely not? Grace had the same low regard for de Castenet as he did. The fact was that this man, his predecessor in command of the Army's base in Crossmaglen in 1985, had been complicit in a security breach so catastrophic that it had led to the death of Stanton's soldiers. And in Berlin he'd been blackmailed by one of his own corporals, the feral, congenitally evil, Drinkwater, the man Paul had killed there.

'Of all the serving people who might have met me,' continued Paul, 'I'm not sure I could have guessed at the odds of it being Major Richard de Castenet. If I was a superstitious man, I'd think the portents of such coincidence to be alarming.' Bullock's face turned serious and he raised his eyebrows. 'Only *because* of our history,' emphasised Paul. And now de Castenet was somehow going to be a part of this latest mess in southern Africa. No, without a doubt, God was having a massive laugh.

'I understand,' said Bullock. 'But, now, getting down to business. Charles Grace has briefed me in so far as he wants me to know the ins-and-outs of your task here. And I'm fine with that, Paul, in case you might think I'm peeved or feel left out of the higher demands of HMG's secret world.' Paul looked intently at Bullock and the man was being serious. He clearly wasn't someone who felt precious about his rank and position and needed to know everything going on, which made Paul's life much more straightforward. The Brigadier continued: 'I'm to be of maximum *practical* assistance to you, which I'm delighted to be, and includes everything from human to logistic and communications support,' Bullock said. 'I'm to introduce you to the Embassy's First Secretary, John Sawyer, who is the MI6 Head of Station, and he will put you in contact with his counterparts here in the National Intelligence Service, and in Harare. I'll do the same for you with regard to the Army side, particularly in Zimbabwe, where, as you know, we have the BMATT and we provide support to the Zimbabwean Battle School at a place called Nyanga.'

'That sounds fine, Brigadier.'

'I'm to be your last resort for help.' Bullock looked at him earnestly. 'You're a senior officer, deeply experienced in special operations, highly capable in your professional skills, but you might, just might, need to call for help; and I'm the man to call. General Charles wanted you to know that. He has also given me a direct, secure channel of access to him, we're old friends, and I'm pretty well regarded in this neck of the woods, even if I say so myself. So between myself, John Sawyer and Charles, we ought to be able to handle whatever might come up.'

'Thank you, Brigadier, very much.' Bullock's words had prompted a chill in Paul's being. He was conscious of the lack of drama in Bullock. The man was experienced and hands-on. But *whatever might come up*? Paul doubted it. In his experience no matter what you planned for, the unexpected always caught you out. But that was what he was good at: dealing with the unexpected. Meanwhile, having the Brigadier's assurances was as good as he could hope for at this stage.

'Come on, we'll get you started.' Brigadier Colin Bullock took Paul into the SIS quarters, which were in a secluded area in the back of the Embassy but reasonably close to the small suite of offices that housed the Defence Staff. They didn't talk as they walked through the cool corridors nor did they see anyone else. 'This is it,' said Bullock as they approached a closed door with a keypad on the wall beside it. Bullock had the code and let them in to an outer reception area where a female secretary at a desk was expecting them. Paul took it all in. The reception room was small and friendly but it was clearly an outer room only, because behind the desk there was strongroom-type door that obviously gave access to the secure MI6 communications and office areas. 'Good morning, Giselle,' Bullock introduced them, 'this is Colonel Paul Stanton, just arrived from London. John is expecting him, I believe.'

'He is, Brigadier. I'll call him now.'

Bullock turned to Paul, 'I'll say goodbye for now, Paul. Remember my driver is yours for this afternoon and in the morning should you need him. I don't know of course, but it may be that your talk with John will necessitate something.' Bullock paused. 'Rest assured, no one really knows why you're here, other than John Sawyer and myself. As far as I've had to, I've dressed your visit up as a liaison and fact-finding trip, which will do for the ears of those who think they want to know. Like our mutual friend, for example.' Bullock chuckled, smiled at Giselle and said, 'Touch base with me before you leave the Embassy, if you would, Paul.'

'Thanks, Brigadier, I will.'

CHAPTER SEVEN

THE STRONGROOM DOOR opened and the man called John Sawyer came out. 'Thanks, Charles,' he said as Bullock left. 'Good to meet you, Paul,' and he ushered Paul inside the secure area and proffered his hand in welcome. 'You've met Giselle, obviously. Giselle, please look after Colonel Stanton's bag, will you?'

Sawyer was bright-eyed, sharp and friendly and dressed in a well-cut, lightweight dark grey suit. He led Paul to a seat in front of an operations display setup that reminded him only too starkly of a Northern Ireland Army base and shut the outer door behind them. They were on their own. Paul could see at least three other doors that must lead to briefing rooms and offices. One door was made of steel. The Communications Room? 'More coffee?' asked Sawyer.

Paul checked his watch. It was still only ten-thirty hours but felt like it was mid-afternoon. He'd need some food soon since the effects of the British Airways breakfast had long passed. 'Thanks, John, yes please. Don't suppose MI6 runs to a biscuit of any description, does it?'

'We can do better.' Sawyer pressed an intercom link. 'Giselle, Colonel Stanton needs mid-morning sustenance as well as great coffee. So, two strong brews and some fresh bread rolls, please, from the restaurant, with special honey.' He turned to Paul, 'That's what you need to feed your brain. Let's start,' he continued, 'so you can then get yourself kitted-out and orientated before the day's worktime is over.

It'll be pitch black here by six-thirty when the sun dips, and then everyone battens down the hatches and stays home.' He paused and changed conversational tack, 'I've been briefed by Charles Grace and by Number Ten. The Deputy Director of MI6 in London is also in the loop and he's told me to get on with it. The whole matter is on a close-hold need-to-know basis and you're the spearpoint, the man carrying the responsibility on the ground. But from what I've heard about you that'll be no problem.' There was a knock at the door and Sawyer leapt up to take a tray of goodies from the secretary Giselle. He placed it on the desktop in front of them. 'Dig in, Paul. Get some energy inside you. Where was I?'

'Telling me who knew about what it was I was about to do,' Paul chewed into a delicious, warm bread roll, cleared his mouthful and continued, 'which is good, because even I don't know what it is exactly I'll be doing.'

'Put some of the honey on the next one,' said Sawyer. It comes from the bees that feed on the fynbos, the local shrubs and bushes only found in the Western Cape, so it's travelled a long way. I love it and it's delicious.' They both drank some coffee and Paul relaxed - a touch. He would listen closely to this man, because he knew he was going to be *very* important to his mission.

'Go on, John.'

'Yes.' Sawyer looked at Paul and there was a slight frown of what could be described as sympathy on his youthful face. 'You're about to step into something that none of the people I've mentioned to you know the scale or depth of. Nor do I, although I expect, given my naturally suspicious nature, it is likely to be more of a mess than we might think. How does that make you feel?'

'Perfectly normal, thanks. You're right about this honey, it's delicious.'

Sawyer laughed. 'Well I won't waste any more portions of my sympathy ration on you then, Colonel Stanton! I can see you have exactly the sense of humour and philosophical approach to life, with which to find your way through the complex maze that is this part of the African continent.'

'Do I?'

'Yes, I think you do.'

'How so, the complex maze?' Paul was focused.

'Because this dark country is, in our considered and much debated view within Her Majesty's Foreign Office, about to emerge into the global spotlight and it will either be with massive violence and bloodshed or with truth and reconciliation. It will either earn the continued disapprobation of the so-called civilised world or its ringing applauses for creating a miracle. Sounds apocalyptic doesn't it?'

'Just a touch,' Paul replied as he ate and drank his coffee, but he knew exactly what Sawyer was talking about: F W de Klerk and Nelson Mandela.

'We're on the frontline of a global political struggle here. Most of the planet is clamouring for more sanctions against South Africa and its immoral apartheid government and we, HMG, with Ronald Reagan's US Administration, it must be added, argue that radical economic sanctions will make what is an already difficult situation one that is impossible and ineffectual.'

'Impossible?'

'Yes; because plenty of states, including many in Africa, would bust any sanctions.' Sawyer shifted his position. 'But this isn't the real point, Paul. Since eighty-seven I've been part of an SIS team here that has had one specific political mandate: to help facilitate HMG's foreign policy initiative to empower the ANC, whilst preserving the existing and emerging social and political balance of the country. Our Government has poured millions into black township development projects to end apartheid. We've created township diplomacy as a new diplomatic art form. Our diplomats, accompanied by my section, have penetrated deep into areas in this country where previously no sunburnt pink-skinned people, other than toughened South African policeman, had ever been. We've delivered micro-projects aimed at empowering local communities.'

'Such as?' asked Paul.

'Such as new water pipes, handicraft groups, village halls, church roofs; all aimed at community organisations that support the ANC.'

'Whilst somehow not alienating the Afrikaner classes?' quizzed Paul.

'Yes; and mighty difficult it's been. But F W de Klerk is the man to do it and sees and shares our intent whilst pursuing a much wider agenda. Despite pressure from his hardliner Afrikaner colleagues he won't relent. For the first time in two generations South Africa has a visionary as its leader; and he'll release Mandela soon, mark my words he will. You'd be surprised how much ground-level information I pick up hosting and joining smart Pretoria and Johannesburg dinner parties, which I'm then able to turn into intelligence to aid the strategies of Mrs Thatcher's cabinet. In truth, Paul, it's where I've been able to pick up the underworld gossip and wider impact feelings of this momentous change process. Which brings us in a roundabout way back to you.'

'In what way?'

'Massive change is also imminent in both Zimbabwe and Mozambique, so the same is happening, but not in the same way if that makes any kind of sense.'

'It might,' replied Paul, 'but go on.'

'Just north of here, across the border in Zimbabwe, Mugabe's actions will, in the not too distant future, start to isolate his country from many others,' Sawyer paused. 'And I'm afraid to say there is a greater degree of certainty for the bloodshed outcome.' Paul said nothing. 'You're going to experience some of this at first hand, Paul. You'll go there and feel and see and taste it for yourself. It'll touch you in some way, I'm sure, if you're the man I believe you to be.' Sawyer sighed. Paul felt one of those inner feelings that he'd always trusted. This man was intelligent, articulate and very experienced in this beautiful but dangerous part of the world and he was giving Paul some invaluable insights. He looked at the large-scale operational map displayed to his front. It was a picture of his immediate future, though he didn't yet know how. It would govern where he went and whom he encountered. He suddenly felt lonely and isolated. *Where was Nikki?* Sawyer must have sensed the sudden change in his karma, and said, 'Are you all right, Paul?'

'I am, thanks, John, but I must admit I'm striving for some clarity with regard to my actual mission.'

'I'm not surprised. I can give you the benefit of my knowledge and insights. I can tell you what I think, but only you can be the master of determining and defining your mission. No doubt you have restraints imposed by London, and no doubt events on the ground will impact on how you go about executing it.'

Paul looked at his watch and then immediately apologised. 'I'm sorry. That was rude of me.' It was eleven-thirty.

'No, I quite understand,' said Sawyer smiling. 'We'll stop inside the hour anyway, because I've agreed with Colin Bullock that I'll hand you over to his driver who will take you to get some lunch and then help sort out your gear and take you to your lodgings.'

'Thanks. So please tell me more about Zimbabwe and then, of course, the Mozambique angle.'

Sawyer took up his thesis: 'Mugabe's unravelling the past history of that great country and disavowing the Lancaster House Agreement with his deliberate policies of alienating the white communities. Christ,' Sawyer exclaimed, 'it makes me weep sometimes. As I said, I've been here three years, and in that time Zimbabwe, Rhodesia as it was, God's Country, is fast losing its beautiful, bountiful countenance. Mugabe, God rot him, is launching a long-term plan to rape and pillage the land. He's going to fuck the place over. Excuse my French, but mark my words. And the white businessmen and farmers who have made Zimbabwe Africa's bread basket for over thirty years are wise to his and his goons' intentions. Which is why, if it's true, they may be planning to ship out their hard wealth and bank it offshore; which, believe me, they'd have to do covertly or it would all be impounded and they may well be imprisoned. Which is why you're here.' Sawyer smiled gently and enigmatically. 'Well part of the reason you're here, if what Charles Grace told me is correct.'

'It is,' replied Paul, but said no more. He'd always worked on the principle of letting the other man or men tell you everything, then decide to talk or act or both. So he waited for Sawyer to continue and absorbed all the intelligence and insights he could get from this influential man.

'And the other part of why you're here is of course the power politics of our eastern contiguous African neighbour, Mozambique. And specifically, the marauding business and political antics of Sir Reggie Hanlon! That's the hornets' nest of this situation, Paul, isn't it?'

'Is it? Have you met Hanlon?'

'Yes. Impressive. Charismatic, self-opinionated and an ocean-going nuisance. And I'm to be his inside man when he visits Pretoria at the end of this month and then at the Mozambique Peace Talks in Nairobi in December, which I'm not thrilled about. He'll try to bully information out of us and give us very little of his. What a pleasure that will be!' Sawyer expostulated. 'Even though I admire his efforts in the Region I can't say I really *like* the man.' Sawyer's expression of his feelings was heartfelt and, Paul suspected, unusual. Despite having just met him, the Head of MI6 in South Africa seemed to be one of the most balanced and sensible men Paul had encountered.

'And how does the Mozambique part fit into all this?' Paul asked. He suddenly experienced a wash of tiredness and needed to move his body. He wanted John Sawyer to end his briefing so he could get moving and get into action; whatever that might be.

'The hornets' nest,' said Sawyer, and sat back, sighed and then fixed Paul with a look of earnestness. 'I've seen Hanlon's letter,' which made Paul think that even since his journey started, so within two days, Grace must have realised he couldn't be the sole owner of such information. 'And having read the copy Charles Grace sent me I've been digging around, discretely.'

'What have you found?'

'A time bomb, is what I believe I've found. Which as I understand it, is how Hanlon and his man Etherington view it.' Paul kept his counsel; the ticking bomb analogy *again*. Sawyer said, 'So, Paul, let me see if I can tie all this gobbledy-gook I've been talking about together, neatly.' The man lent back in his chair, steepled the fingers of his hands, looked at Paul and said, 'And I need to tell you that I'm privy to all the information the heads of intelligence in Harare and Pretoria have pulled together. We had a secret crisis conference call last night. I believe you were told some of what had been discovered by Ken Rose, my opposite number in Harare, by Frederick Etherington before you left London?'

'I was.'

Sawyer continued, 'We have imminent seismic political change here in South Africa that Mrs Thatcher's supporting. Such change finds favour in Harare because Mugabe supports any initiatives that empower the ANC; and of course Mrs Thatcher is *still*, in the eyes of the world, backing Mugabe's regime even though she and her closest advisors know the bastard is beginning a deliberate policy of raiding the whites and breaking the structure of the country. With me, Paul?'

'Right there with you, John.'

'Thought you would be. *So*, anything that destabilises this little duet would be a problem for HMG.'

'Like, for example,' Paul offered, 'the white Zimbabweans moving their wealth, and therefore some of the assets of the country, out of Zimbabwe, and doing so with the help of South Africa, whether sanctioned by Pretoria or not?' Sawyer raised his eyebrows. 'And even if Mrs Thatcher in London denied any knowledge and F W de Klerk did the same, it would cut no ice with Mugabe. Am I close?'

'Spot on,' said Sawyer. 'But, to this duet, add Mozambique and Sir Reggie Hanlon and things really get tricky. Over the years Hanlon's spent a fortune trying to broker peace in the civil war in Mozambique. Overtly investing in and supporting the Frelimo government in Maputo and toadying with the Portuguese colonial ex-masters in Lisbon and the regional heads of state here in southern Africa. But at the same time he's been, and still is, offloading huge sums of money to Renamo in country to buy them off and stop them attacking and destroying the commercial infrastructure he's putting in place for Frelimo, which would destabilise the Mozambique peace process. What a man! What a situation.'

'Which is one of the reasons why he's just let a fairly big contract to a Gurkha security company to provide security and train local militia to protect his farms and other installations, I take it.' Paul felt compelled to say this: to see what Sawyer did or did not know.

'Yes. But such business actions are not likely to be a major play in Reggie's political master plan. However,' and here Sawyer emphasised his words, 'I'm not sure I'd want to be on the ground with them, because despite Renamo's tacit agreements with MozLon to keep their hands off Reggie's properties in country, they don't always do so. There are a number of incidents where such security forces have been caught in the crossfire of this ongoing dirty war.' None of which information made Paul feel any better about where Nikki Walker-Haig might be and how she might get caught up in this increasingly uncertain situation. But he'd focus on this later.

'How does Mozambique fit into the scenario of the ticking bomb, then?' Paul asked.

'Simply and confusingly,' was Sawyer's enigmatic reply. 'And it centres on MozLon and how a UK-registered company might be seen. Which is why, in my opinion, Hanlon wrote his letter to Mrs Thatcher.'

'Simply?'

'Because if a MozLon senior manager *has* been complicit in illegal, cross-border, activities then those actions prejudice Sir Reggie's business interests in Mozambique and his political integrity in the Region.'

'And this would reflect very badly on HMG in London.'

'Exactly.'

'You said *has* been involved? You think Fitzsimons might not have been acting for illegal personal gain?'

'I'm not sure, Paul. What does *illegal* mean in this case? The Zimbabwean whites are a strong, tightly bound, hardheaded community and commercially quite savvy. I think they might have decided on a course of action that would preserve their future livelihoods, but which of course would be seen as illegal to Mugabe, and I think they'd be very sure about whom they dealt with.'

'Which is the confusing side of things, I guess,' said Paul.

'Exactly,' said Sawyer, with firmness. 'If, for example, Fitzsimons was one of their chosen conduits to move wealth out of country and was acting with help from South Africa as well as Zimbabwe, which he might have been, given the forensic evidence recovered by the Police Anti Terrorist Unit patrol and given to Ken Rose in Harare, then the potential damage to South African-Zimbabwe relations is huge, exactly at the time when Pretoria wants support from Harare.'

'Clearly,' said Paul, 'because Fitzsimons was acting without sanction from either government. But neither knows about it, yet, officially, do they?'

'No, thank Christ!' responded Sawyer, and continued. 'And *if* Fitzsimons, with his help in Zimbabwe and maybe here in SA, has *also* been dealing with renegade Renamo warlords in Beira, which the recovery of the shreds of evidence might indicate, then this would de-rail Hanlon's political credibility with Frelimo and in the Region as a whole and scupper his ongoing business in Mozambique.' Sawyer leant forward in his chair and fixed Paul with a penetrating look. 'Not only would it scupper Hanlon, but because Hanlon operates with the given blessing of our Government in London, it would make Mrs Thatcher's ongoing relations with all governments in the Region very hard to sustain. Hanlon's tied our PM into his dirty business, and if one of his men has gone rogue and it gets out then Mrs T stands to lose a political foundation stone of her overall Foreign Policy. It would be a total clusterfuck, if you'll pardon my German.'

'And,' offered Paul, 'whoever has been entrusting Fitzsimons with their hard assets will be expecting him to have delivered. And if he hasn't then they'll start raising hell, which will quickly become apparent to Harare, Pretoria, Maputo and London. And then what you've just described starts: Mrs Thatcher's southern African policy meltdown. Wow,' Paul frowned, 'that is a ticking bomb.'

'Time's against us, Paul.'

'Hmm, it sure is,' Paul was thinking furiously. 'But what if Fitzsimons was acting out of altruism, helping out because he *could* travel between Zimbabwe and Mozambique?'

78

'He might have been. It's a possibility. But no one other than the Zim whites, you and I would ever see it that way.'

'Yes, you're right. So how do you see my part in all this?'

'Honestly? I see you finding out exactly what has been and is going on. I see you meeting my opposite number here in Pretoria, in the National Intelligence Service, and I'll fix this for tomorrow morning, and it will be a meeting just between the two of you. We've discussed what he'll talk to you about. He's agreed to this. His name is Stephen Langlands and he's solid. I see you then going into Zimbabwe to meet Ken Rose in Harare. I see you going into Mozambique, if necessary, no almost certainly, and I can arrange all the diplomatic clearances for this and anything else, and I'll tell Rose to expect you. We'll get everything sorted out within twenty-four hours.' Sawyer was on a roll. He continued: 'And I see you needing help; and you're the best person to decide what help that might be.'

Paul was sure of it. He would need Special help; and he knew those he wanted to provide it. So he'd fix it.

CHAPTER EIGHT

SAWYER TOOK PAUL into the Communications Room and introduced him to the duty operator. It was coming up to twelve-fifteen local time, perfect for a call to London. Pretoria was a relatively large SIS station and the Communications Room had everything. Paul was familiar with the set up. He asked the operator to prepare to send a Secret fax to Charles Grace in the Ministry of Defence using the CRYPTEX system. He took a message pad, sat at a table and quickly wrote a succinct summary of his mission so far and an outline of what he intended to do next. He did not mention his own concerns or the potential complication of de Castenet.

'Please send this now,' he said to the operator. Paul turned to Sawyer, 'I'd like to keep a totally separate log of all the transmissions relating to my mission here. Is that OK?'

'That's exactly how I imagined you'd want to operate.'

'And for our eyes only, with the exception of the duty operator?'

'Yes. I'll be the immediate contact here in Pretoria,' added Sawyer. 'Got that?' Sawyer turned to the operator, who nodded his understanding. 'I'll make sure all the duty operators are briefed,' he said to Paul.

'Thanks. I just have one other thing to do, which is put a call into Headquarters DSF. I need to touch base with my Director and I need his help. I'm guessing your BRAHMS system has a direct line into Duke of York's.'

'It does. Here, I'll set you up.' Sawyer took Paul over to the secure telephone system, which was housed in a special soundproof cubbyhole. 'If you have no joy, then you can always send him a message using the CRYPTEX.'

Sawyer left Paul to it.

Paul made his call and felt a sense of relief that his recent boss, the Director Special Forces, didn't waste time asking questions, but agreed to put the contingencies in place Paul had asked for and provide the help which Paul had asked Charles Grace to sanction. His Director ended the call by saying: 'Expect the two men to be in Nyanga within seventy-two hours. They'll wait for you to make contact there.' Paul finished the call. The white noise of the scrambled 'phone line ceased and he appreciated the moments of silence.

Nyanga. From the briefing information he'd had before leaving UK and what Bullock had said to him earlier, Paul knew what was in Nyanga and could therefore guess why his Director had chosen that place for him to meet up with two of his SAS colleagues. He could guess how his men would get to him, and they'd bring the gear and weapons he'd asked for. So he had to be there and inside three days.

Paul had a feeling the fates were converging in and around Nyanga. Brigadier Bullock had told him that Richard de Castenet had a training liaison responsibility for Zimbabwe, and so had, in all probability, frequently visited Nyanga. Geographically, Nyanga was close to Mutare, the border crossing adjacent to Manica Province, which had been Fitzsimons' area of responsibility in Mozambique. Fred Etherington had said that Danny Dalloway's security work was well underway at the first two projects, one of which was at a MozLon farm near Manica.

No, the geographical coincidences were too much to be ignored. But the clincher for Paul was what he'd been told by Dalloway's man in Kathmandu when he'd asked for Nikki Walker-Haig's whereabouts: *She was most probably in Zimbabwe, saheb, where they had a permanent base close to Mutare, which was safe.* But *was* she

81

in that place and was she safe? He'd get there - he had to anyway - and he'd damn well make sure she was. Somehow

'Are you all right, Paul?' Sawyer asked when Paul rejoined him.

'Yes, thank you, I am, but I need to be able to contact you or your comms room wherever I am.' Paul's mind was working through all the uncertainties he believed might arise. 'And I think your domain here needs to be my main reporting point.' He paused. Sawyer watched him. 'The DA has offered himself in this role but I think he stands to be compromised by his staff more easily than you do. What do you think?'

'I agree. It won't be wittingly, but his team can talk and information might leak. Probably would.'

'Exactly. And besides, I don't need the additional load of carrying military comms equipment. So how can I do this?'

'You can have one of our Inmarsat portable satphones, plus the recharging gubbins, it's a touch bulky but it works, and you'll be able to call through to this Station wherever you are. We'll give you landline numbers as well. We'll act as the necessary conduit to Colin Bullock. I'll brief him personally whenever I hear from you.'

'Thank you.'

'I'll fix your meeting in NIS for eight hundred hours tomorrow. Go straight to Director Langlands' outer office. He'll be expecting you.'

'I will. Many thanks.'

'Oh, and Giselle will organise all the travel clearances you'll need. They'll be with the DA by mid-morning tomorrow. I can't see you starting for Zimbabwe before then?'

'I'm sure you're right.'

And with that Paul Stanton collected his travel bag and went to find Bullock's driver so he could get some lunch and set himself up. He needed to update the DA and there was more practical admin he had to sort out. He'd brought with him all the field gear he needed for the moment and he'd get the rest in Nyanga, but he needed maps for a start. He'd decided he'd find his lodgings as early as he could and get a good night's sleep so as to be sharp for his meeting early tomorrow with Sawyer's opposite number in the NIS, the National Intelligence Service, the dark heart of South Africa's Government.

He wondered how Colin Bullock would react to his need to travel into Zimbabwe urgently? He would have to tell him that Sawyer was fixing a meeting for him in Harare, with the Head of Zimbabwe's Central Intelligence Organisation, and that he'd contacted London and was going to Nyanga, supposedly fact-finding, but with the need to get there rather quickly. Paul felt sure the DA wouldn't be surprised. He'd also tell Bullock about his arrangement with Sawyer concerning communications. It was reliable and secure and therefore made sense.

Paul would need a guide for his journey and he knew instinctively who might be suggested: Major Richard de Castenet. It had to be. What a joke! Paul decided he'd tell Bullock outright that he wanted de Castenet to accompany him. After all, liaison with the Battle School at Nyanga was part of the man's job, and as he'd thought about everything he'd heard and had suggested to him so far during this day in Pretoria, Paul had a hardening feeling that de Castenet was somehow a player in this dirty business.

What was it Sun Tzu had allegedly said: keep your friends close and your enemies closer? Richard de Castenet certainly wasn't a friend and he was probably an enemy; the fates would decide one way or another but he wanted him within seeing distance that was for sure.

* * *

'HAVE YOU HEARD anything yet?' de Castenet asked.

'The Police found Coetzee's body earlier today,' said Schuman. 'His ID was on him. The scavengers had left it. They didn't find anything else,' he said knowingly. 'As soon as the Police checked the records and saw he was ex-military they contacted the NIS.' The man took a drink of his Castle Lager. 'They don't want to investigate any of that kind of shit. They won't dirty their hands with something that might run across our Government departments.'

'Will the NIS take the investigation further?' asked de Castenet with a trace of nervousness in his question.

'No, man, there's no chance. It's with me.' Wentzel Schuman lit a cigarette and inhaled deeply. 'I'll bury it. The Chief won't even hear about it.'

His head was caught in the lights that illuminated the deck bar area. Schuman's skin was burned mahogany brown and his thick dark hair was cut very short so that it lay like tufted grass across the plain of his head. His countenance was not unpleasant or unfriendly, but de Castenet knew the man to be ruthless and tough as the hardwood planks of the deck area on which they and other small groups of people now sat. He reckoned the man was several years older than him, somewhere in his mid-forties, with the experience and attitudes that fitted a well-placed career official in an all-powerful Afrikaner regime. Except, of course, that like him, Schuman was disaffected. Which was why they were meeting here, at Eastwoods.

It was a good place to meet, Eastwoods Bar in Park Street, Arcadia. It was close to the Union Buildings where Schuman's office in the department of the NIS was located, and being in Arcadia was close to the British Embassy and de Castenet's centre of gravity. His small self-contained flat was not too far away. You didn't want to have to travel long distances in this city, especially after dark, and he had no car that he could use for social and personal reasons; so short walks were the ideal and Eastwoods was just a short walk.

But the meeting wasn't a social one; no, more like a crisis meeting and called by de Castenet. He asked, 'So you have the rest of the diamonds, I assume?'

'I do, bru, they're safe,' the square-faced man replied. 'I was right. That sleeze-bag Coetzee had siphoned off what he thought he could get away with. But Christ man, he must have been shitting himself during the past days.' He must have been, de Castenet mused. 'But he's in the mortuary now,' Schuman continued, 'so our worries on that front are over.'

Coetzee had come back from his job visibly jittery, that's how he'd seemed to de Castenet at the first meeting, and his instincts had been alerted. When Coetzee had handed over the diamonds de Castenet had understood the reason for the man's jumpiness. The coarse oilskin package of diamonds had obviously been tampered with. The man had been clumsy. So de Castenet and Schuman had discussed the import of this and decided the man needed to be eliminated, which he had been - last night. But now, where did that leave de Castenet and Schuman? They had discussed options this evening but had they reached any conclusions? Not really.

The package had contained just over two kilograms of mixed diamonds, some cut and brilliant and some not, but good, nonetheless; they'd been the possessions of white Zimbabweans, their hard assets, after all. And this was the unforeseen problem that had brought their illegal operation to a standstill. Neither he nor Schuman had agreed what to do next because even using their rough calculations, the stones had a laundered value in the UK of over two million pounds sterling!

'Are you sure our worries are over?' de Castenet asked. 'Are you really sure so?'

'What do you mean, bru? If you're worried about the stones, man, then don't. I keep them with me all the time, and I mean *all* the time.' Schuman looked down at the battered canvas satchel on the floor by his chair. The chair leg was inside the shoulder strap. 'I've put the stones that Coetzee stole in with the rest. They're all there, bru.'

'Well, that's good, but we're at a standstill, and who in Christ's name knows how we break out of it.' de Castenet gave vent to his deepening worries. The arrival of Paul Stanton that morning and his complete lack of knowledge as to why the man - *that man* - had suddenly arrived in Pretoria, added to the Coetzee murder and the quantity of diamonds he and Schuman had in their possession, had unnerved him. 'You're going to have to hold on to them. It's impossible for me to take that quantity and value of stones back to London,' he continued, 'fucking impossible. I have no idea which fence or organisation in London or Europe would take such a stash. And besides, I'm not due a home visit for some time yet.' Schuman smoked and looked at him intently. 'When I met with that evil shit of an animal yesterday he taunted me with the people he'd had to kill in order to bring the diamonds to us. Do we even know who he's killed? Do we have any worries on that score?'

'No, man, we don't.'

'Well I don't doubt your confidence, Wentzel, but how do we know this? I mean the shipment out of Zim was two weeks ago. Obviously I'm not privy to the detail of how the Beira end works, except for the existence of your man, Ramon Lima, nor do I know how you organise the network inside Zimbabwe, but we've got a collective of influential whites in Zim who will be waiting for confirmation that their offshore wealth has actually *arrived* offshore,' and de Castenet deliberately emphasised the word, 'and I'm assuming we've got fellow fucking criminals in Harare, maybe elsewhere in Zim, like Mutare, but definitely in Beira, all of whom will be waiting for confirmation of their share of the steal.' de Castenet stopped and took a drink. Having articulated his concerns so forcefully he was even more perturbed. Another thing occurred to him. 'And who exactly was the courier of the diamonds? Who was this man that Coetzee obviously murdered and, as he so graphically told me, left for wild animal food somewhere in the wasteland of Mozambique?'

'You don't need to know that either, man.'

'Well, think about it, Wentzel, presumably he's already been missed by someone or some organisation that in all probability is looking for him and raising questions.'

'Well it won't be the whites in Zim that's for sure. Any hint of what they're up to and that crazy bastard Mugabe and his secret police goons will be all over them.'

de Castenet let his thoughts shift. They could spend all night talking around this conundrum without reaching any hard conclusions. He wanted to talk about the other problem. Stanton. 'This British Army officer arrived from London this morning.'

'So what, man?'

'So nothing, maybe, except...' de Castenet hesitated and Schuman sensed it.

'Except what, boet?'

'I collected him from Jo'burg Airport this morning. I know him from the past. I didn't know he was coming out here and I still don't know the reason why. And he's dangerous.'

'Dangerous for us, man?' Schuman got right to the point. 'How could he be? No one outside our Beira and Harare contacts know what shit we're dealing with or how we're doing it. That's for sure, hey?'

'Yes, that's what you've always told me, but are you sure?'

'Of course I'm sure, man. No problem. So what's got to you?'

'Just a feeling. Do you ever get one of those, Wentzel? It's as if something from your past is suddenly back in your life and you have this lurking sense that because the probability of it all happening is so remote that somehow this person or that event is going to put a curse on what you're doing.'

'Fuck me, man, no, that's black magic nonsense.'

'Well this man is British Special Forces, SAS, and a proven killer. He has reason to hate me and I'm not comfortable with the coincidence that he of all people has suddenly arrived here and none of us in the military staff know why.'

'Now what is it exactly you're telling me, Richard? Speak, man, this sounds serious.'

'His name's Lieutenant Colonel Paul Stanton and as I said, he's SAS, served time with the Gurkhas and was in the Falklands War. He's a fucking war hero back in UK, Wentzel, highly decorated and I know he operated under cover in Northern Ireland.'

'So he's a Brit hero. So what? He's on a fact finding mission for your bloody Government or something similar, he must be?'

'He could be. But what makes me slightly uncertain is that he went straight into the DA's office and after a session with him I was told he spent a long time with our Head of Station for the Secret Service.'

'No, man,' said Schuman, and his voice sounded thoughtful, 'that's worrying, so I think you're right. If he did that then there must be something your spies back in London are interested in, and it must be something that needs a military man to do it.'

'Or he's working on a black operation for our Ministry of Defence and needed briefing in by the Head of Station.'

Schuman lit a cigarette and took a drink of his lager. 'So why does he hate you, bru?'

de Castenet studied his gin and tonic and took a drink. He lent back in his chair and looked up at the night sky that was smouldering and rippling with stars. It was a wonderful sight and one of the many things he loved about this country. He answered Schuman's question, 'I'm not actually sure that he hates me, but back in nineteen eighty-six this man, Stanton, was instrumental in ruining my life.'

And Major Richard de Castenet proceeded to tell Major Wentzel Schuman about his apocalyptic meltdown in West Berlin in 1986, that traced its roots back to Bandit Country, South Armagh, Northern Ireland in 1985, and had as its causal centre the destructive force that had been Major Paul Stanton, SAS.

'Shit, man. This guy sounds like very bad news.'

'That is an understatement.'

'And you know, boet, I now know that I've heard of this man, but not directly.'

'How so?' de Castenet was interested.

'Simple, brother, my family is still in Berlin. In the East. I'm second generation Afrikaner. My family's from Germany, from Berlin, obviously, and I always get the updates from the home country from my parents. They stay in touch. There's some big shit brewing there, I tell you. The world will change soon.'

'Stanton?' de Castanet reminded him.

'That man was not named specifically. It was about an old-time faithful of Ulrike Meinhof, called Otto Krenselauer, the one-time Baader-Meinhof quartermaster and fixer, the hero of the so-called German Autumn, and how he was arrested and his racketeering business smashed apart.' Schuman smoked his cigarette and drank again. 'Krenselauer's men were killed. Down by the Wall, in the West. No one knew who did it. Although some British soldier was found there. A low-life. Anyway,' he went on, 'it certainly made the news and caused a hell of a disturbance. It damaged my family's business, too, boet. They did work across the Wall for Krenselauer.'

'That was Stanton,' de Castenet said in a resigned tone. And the low-life British soldier was one of his corporals, the demented, evil, blackmailing, treacherous fucker called Shaggy Drinkwater. 'And now the bastard is here.'

'That's fucking shit, man. It really is. But he doesn't know, you said?'

de Castenet fought to think clearly and objectively. He needed to bury the past if at all possible. And it could be. What he was embarked on now with Schuman was surely the new beginning he'd dreamed of; and Paul fucking Stanton wasn't about to ruin his life for a second time. 'He can't do,' he said. 'I have no real idea why he's here, but I can't believe it's anything to do with our activities.' He looked up at the stars again and sampled the cool of the October evening. The High Veldt of South Africa. It was magical. He took a drink and looked intensely at Schuman. The Afrikaner was outwardly calm, smoking gently and drinking his lager. He took strength from this: the man was tough, seasoned and experienced, he was a safe pair of hands. 'I've been detailed to escort him up into Zim tomorrow, leaving in the early afternoon. He's visiting the Battle School at Nyanga. So I really think Stanton's out here on a liaison trip. Fact-finding.'

Schuman cocked an eyebrow at this piece of information. 'I think you're right, bru, and I tell you why. The Director has called me for a quick office brief tomorrow morning. Rumour from his secretary is that some Brit bigwig is visiting and that I'm going to be his nursemaid on a trip up country. How fucking lucky would that be, hey! We'll be travelling together.' Then Schuman became serious, 'Let's hope his visit is what we think it is, let's really hope so, because if its not then we might have to kill the bastard. It might turn out to be our only option. Now are you up for that, my brave English man?' de Castenet did not answer. 'Killing one of your own so that we survive and become very rich?' de Castenet stayed silent. His mind was too far away from that possibility just yet. Schuman said, 'I'll bring the diamonds with us. We might be able to do something with them in Zim.'

* * *

SOME MINUTES LATER, having finished their drinks and discussion, the two accomplices left Eastwoods Bar and went their separate ways. They had made their plan. Tomorrow would bring new perspectives. They'd be on the road and the Brit SAS man Stanton would be with them. Neither de Castenet nor Schuman were totally at ease with their thoughts but nor were they unduly worried. There was no solid base for them to be, surely?

But they were wrong. On three counts.

They knew that Stanton was to have a meeting in the NIS tomorrow morning with Director Stephen Langlands and that Schuman, Head of Border Operations, would most likely be tasked as a sensible travelling companion and guide for his trip into Zimbabwe. But they did not know that Langlands would tell Stanton about certain private concerns.

Nor did they know that Stanton had a meeting planned with the Head of Zimbabwe's Central Intelligence Agency in Harare, Ken Rose. Rose, who had alerted Sir Reggie Hanlon and Fred Etherington to the scraps of evidence found by the Police Anti Terrorist Unit during the cross-border patrol into southern Mozambique; the scraps of evidence that had indirectly launched Stanton on this odyssey. Rose, who had well-founded suspicions about the dirty business he believed was being conducted in and outside his country.

And then of course de Castenet and Schuman had completely underestimated Paul Stanton.

He wasn't that easy to kill.

PART III
DIRTY BUSINESS

CHAPTER NINE

THEY WERE SOUTH of the pipeline road, at least a hundred kilometres west of the MozLon farm at Nhamatanda, and travelling in two vehicles, when out of the blue, bullets whipped and cracked all around, like a spattering string of Chinese firecrackers exploding on the ground, kicking up pockets of dirt and trackside shrub.

Immediately Major Danny Dalloway floored the accelerator of his Toyota Land Cruiser, scanning the ground for a quick exit from the ungraded dirt track on which his vehicle and the Land Rover behind him were travelling. *Gunfire dead ahead, no, slightly left, small arms, sounds like AK-47, sporadic, not effective - yet. OK*, he thought as he jerked the steering wheel to the left and the vehicle roared forward, bumping and bucking into the bush scrub, *let's get in amongst these fuckers!*

He shouted to the man in the back of the Toyota, 'Pinto! You've got a fix on the enemy's firing position, yes?' He risked a quick look behind him where the young Mozambican militiaman was nodding his head uncertainly and struggling to manhandle his FN MAG light machinegun into the open window on the right side. 'Fuck!' Dalloway expostulated and fought to control the Toyota. 'Where's the Rover?' Pinto didn't answer. Dalloway could no longer hear the crack of the gunfire over the screaming engine and the tortured noises from the suspension as he zigzagged and fought to control the lurching vehicle, but then he registered that at least two bullets slammed into the rear of the cab somewhere. If they were AKs then the bullets were 7.62mm short rounds. They packed a punch but they'd done no real damage because the vehicle was still moving. 'The enemy's somewhere to your half-right, there's a clump of big trees about four hundred metres away, up on that little koppie.' Dalloway had seen the midday sun glint off something in amongst the trees on the small hill feature ahead: rifle barrels, bandoliers of brass-cased bullets, something. They were lazy soldiers; their camouflage and concealment had been shite. He shouted into the back of the vehicle, 'Get some fucking covering fire down on that area now or we're going to be buggered by these Renamo scum bastards!' Pinto didn't speak great English but he would have got the message. 'Stop pissing yourself, man, and get that machinegun into action!' Which seemed to do the trick because there was a sudden roar of ear-splitting medium machinegun fire and tracer rounds started arcing to the front right of the Toyota and tearing up the bush and scrub roughly in the area that Dalloway had indicated. The inside of the Land Cruiser was instantly transformed into a cockpit of fighting mayhem: burning hot empty brass cases pinged and bounced off the metal interior and singed the tatty upholstery and the cabin was suffused with cordite fumes. The noise was cacophonous and the cabin temperature ratcheted up a few degrees. 'Good man, Pinto!' roared back Dalloway who was now partially deaf in his right ear, 'That's the ticket!' Blind in his left eye, momentarily half-deaf in his right ear, breaking out into a sweat, what a state, he thought, and laughed out loud.

'Sir!' shouted the man in the passenger seat, who was another member of Dalloway's militia force, a bright young Mozambican who'd been trained as a radio operator.

'What's up, Nesto? Can't you see we're busy? Have you sent a contact report back to base yet? Don't tell me, comms are buggered. Well if they are, get that gun of yours out of the sunroof and put some fucking bullets down on the target. Just make a bleeding noise, eh?' Ernesto, Nesto, spoke reasonably good English; but he wasn't really a fighting warrior.

'Yes, sir, I mean, no, sir...'

'What the fuck do you mean, Nesto? Pinto, keep firing! Keep a check on your ammo usage. Shit! Where's that other gunfire coming from?' An arc of heavy tracer rounds was zeroing onto the enemy position from the right of the Toyota, slashing into trees and cutting up the bush in a violent storm of spraying ground and vegetation. The noise was fearsome. Dust and debris was flying up into the air. Dalloway swerved the Toyota away from it.

'That's what I was saying, sir,' said Nesto. 'The Land Rover is coming from the right of us.' Dalloway glanced at the man. He liked Nesto; he was bright and hard working. The man's eyes were wild and the expression he wore was sheer terror.

'Fucking brilliant! Well done, Nesto. Good old Gopal. Right, men, we're going in for the kill. I just hope Gopal knows when to stop firing or we'll be chopped to mincemeat by our friendlies.' The Land Rover had a Russian 12.7mm DShK heavy machinegun fitted on its roll bars. It was a fearsome weapon.

'Gopal can, sir, I'm sure,' said Nesto with something less than certainty.

'What the hell are you talking about, Nesto. Oh yes, 'course he does. He's a Gurkha for Christ's sake. Best trained and best fighting men on the planet. And he's seen it all. No offence to your fighting spirit, men, of course.' Dalloway was smiling through his teeth now, his blood was up and he had found a rough patch of animal tracks; elephant probably, he thought irrelevantly. But the tracks led up to the koppie, where the beasts must have sheltered and fed on the leaves and thorns of the trees - and from where the enemy had ambushed him. *The enemy: break away rebel groups of Renamo, the witless bastards.*

Suddenly the Toyota was climbing the small height and was in amongst the trees and scrub, and Dalloway braked and spun the wheel right and left to manoeuvre over the area. The firing had stopped - *all the firing had stopped*. 'Where are they, boys, what can you see? Anything?' Dalloway was frantically scouring the ground all around him. The trees were broken down over the whole area. He stopped the vehicle and listened and watched. The engine steamed. The silence was enormous after the cacophony of the short engagement. There was no movement he could see…but there was a track, heading off to the left, southwards, from the koppie back towards to the Zim border area. That made sense. He suddenly realised he was hot, burning, sweating hot. Well, it was thirty degrees in the open and they had just been involved in a fucking great firefight! What could you expect?

'Saheb!' Dalloway lurched himself to his right where the Land Rover had miraculously appeared alongside. Gopal Gurung, standing up behind the DShK, was shouting and gesticulating. His driver, a skilful Mozambican militiaman whom Dalloway had nicknamed Eusebio because of his addiction to football, had the engine gunning ready to set off. Dalloway tried to shake the ringing noise out of his ears. Gopal spoke in Nepali, 'Saheb, the enemy have gone south. They are on foot. We can get them easy. Do we kill them?'

'Yes. Go to the right of this track. I will go to the left. Take it gently, brother, they will be cunning and try to hide from us.'

The two vehicles set off, cautiously, lurching downwards initially and then crawling through the open patches of the scrub bush. Dalloway wanted these men dead. How many were there? He didn't know, but probably four or five, judging by the amount of incoming gunfire. There was no benefit in bringing in dead rebel bodies. These groups obeyed local warlords, men who had broken away from the mainstream Renamo leadership that after a decade of bloody civil war was trying to politicise itself and gain a share of the future government that at present was held by the Lisbon-backed Frelimo fat cats. No one would be interested in a handful of dead nobodies. There was no reward, no gain. The only potential gain was that when they failed to return or their bodies were found, it would be a deterrent to others who believed they could wage war on the agricultural farms and villages that were trying to bring some prosperity to Mozambique. The MozLon agricultural collectives that it was Danny Dalloway's contract to protect.

They had travelled less than a kilometre and Gopal saw them first. He was standing up and his eyesight was hawk-like. 'In front, saheb,' he shouted.

Dalloway saw them. The rebels were a straggly group of four men. One was limping badly, being dragged along by a comrade. As they drew closer, Dalloway could see that they were all dressed the same: worn bush fatigues, combat boots and belts of bullet pouches strung over their body webbing. They had AK-47s and they were going to make a fight of it; but the ground wasn't on their side, there was no cover, and they didn't have the firepower or the willpower. They were dead rebels. They stood and fired first, always a difficult firing position, especially with the adrenaline flowing, fatigue and the shock of a post-contact situation. Their marksmanship was as effective as it had been earlier. The rounds whipped around the two vehicles, hitting neither of them.

Dalloway leaned out of his driver's window and shouted across to the Land Rover. 'Eusebio, keep in line with me. We're going in closer. Gopal, a few selective bursts from the DShK as we advance, then when I stop, debus and we'll go in on foot. The two of us.'

'Hunchha, saheb,' and with that the two vehicles drove closer to the enemy and the Gurkha let rip with the heavy machinegun and tore the enemy to pieces.

Dalloway stopped the Toyota a hundred metres short of where the rebels had gone to ground and was out of his vehicle as the firing finished. 'Stay firm, boys,' he said to the two men in his vehicle. 'Do we have any comms yet?' He didn't wait for the answer. He knew what it was and it didn't matter. They were too far from home base to have reliable VHF communications and besides, unless he and Gopal had got this horribly wrong, they didn't need back up - even if there had been any to hand. He deliberately left his AKM in the cab of the Toyota and unholstered the Browning 9mm that he habitually carried as his sidearm. Gopal was abreast of him, ten paces away, AKM in one hand and his kukri drawn in the other, the classic image of the fighting Gurkha closing with the enemy in order to kill him at close quarters.

Which was what happened.

Dalloway found two of the rebels first. They were a crumpled smashed heap of clothing and flesh. Several of the heavy 12.7mm rounds had hit both and killed them instantly. Neither man was young. They had died for their cause. Had it been worth it? Now the bodies would be food for the wild game. The families of the men would probably say they wished their men to be in their village, behaving sagely, with grace, and drinking home-brewed heavy beer as each watched and felt old age come crawling up to him. Dalloway moved on, the ground was broken and studded with scrub bushes. A flicker of movement to his right made him turn. Gopal's kukri caught the sun and the blade flashed as he brought it downwards in a cruel, killing stroke. So one of the bastards had been alive. Now where was the last one? Gopal found him. Dead, killed instantly by the lethal machinegun fire.

Dalloway and Gopal dragged the bodies into a loose heap and searched their possessions for any intelligence. And there was some: several folded sheets of paper on which were scrawlings and markings that looked ominously like a map. 'We'll take their AKs and the ammo, Gopal.'

'Je, saheb, no point in leaving them for other rebels.'

The two men walked back to their vehicles and climbed in. As they did, Dalloway said, 'Back to that little koppie, Gopal. Then we'll get a brew on and see what state we're in and what we have here. When we get up there, Nesto, get that shagging radio ready. We'll rig an antenna up in the trees. I need to try and speak to base.'

In the event, Dalloway could not get communications back to his base; and as he studied the crude markings on the papers he had found and considered the geography of it all, he realised the radio call was insufficient. He needed to get back in person.

So the five men checked over the vehicles, which were largely fine, and brewed a hasty mug of tea, laced with sugar, and a nip of Gurkha rum. They all needed energy and a fast release from the adrenaline stress of the firefight.

Dalloway had wanted to carry out a fairly deep reconnaissance of the road and track routes adjacent to the pipeline road that was the sole viable travel route between Beira and Mutare, between the two MozLon farms at Nhamatanda and Manica. He wanted to assess how difficult or easy it would be to travel and he and Gopal had agreed they also needed to identify if there was any obvious threat in the areas around them. Well they'd found that out all right, in dramatic style, which was all well and good; but they were at least a hundred kilometres from their base in Nhamatanda and they needed to get back onto the road and head southeast for home. There was a job to do.

* * *

'THEY WERE MOST likely Renamo rebels,' Danny Dalloway said to the assembled group in the canteen of the MozLon farm complex at Nhamatanda. He'd taken time to collect his thoughts and he gathered them together just after the evening meal had been cleared away. He'd fixed the large map of the area on the wall behind where he now stood. They sat on chairs, huddled around in a close semi-circle, their eyes intently focused on him. It felt just like being back in the Army again: an important orders group or operational briefing. 'But it is important to understand that they were break-aways, guerrillas, and there were only four of them. They were bad men. Destructive men. They did not believe in the peace process that is trying so hard to bring a good life for everyone here in Mozambique.'

He spoke in slow and simple English and he knew they would understand him. He'd got to know them all well over the past two months in country. Danny Dalloway hardly ever politicised when he talked to people but on this occasion the inference was necessary. His audience right now might include some individuals, or their family members, who had their ethnic origins in the same people of southern Mozambique as the Renamo. It was unlikely given the demographics, but it was possible. The bigger problem though was to debunk the Renamo mysticism and *any hint of a possible larger scale Renamo link*.

'Can you tell us if this affect our lives, sir,' said the MozLon project manager here at Nhamatanda. He was tall and thin with the lovely features and skin colouring that resulted from the historical blending of the original Portuguese colonisers and the indigenous Mozambicans. His name was Mia Couto and he was good: his under-managers responded well to him and he was energetic and dedicated. His family was also lovely. It was a great question.

'I do not believe what happened will place any of us in peril, Mia,' Dalloway responded. He didn't know this for sure but he needed to say it. These were mainly civilians, practical men, educated and unused to direct contact with warfare. He had to protect them both physically and psychologically. He went on, 'We were attacked by them here,' and Dalloway pointed to the spot on the map where the contact, six hours ago, had occurred, 'and as you can see, we were south of the pipeline road and it is over one hundred kilometres from Nhamatanda. Also they were on foot and when we pursued them they were going south towards the Chicamba Dam and the Vumba Forest area, the Zimbabwe border.' A long way from Nhamatanda, Dalloway thought, *but not from Manica.* 'They were on their own. They had no communications and no back up.' He finished by saying, 'And we killed all of them.'

Dalloway looked back at his audience to try and judge the impact of what he had said. All of them were studying him keenly. What did they see? A big man, six feet two inches tall, fair-haired and with a horribly scarred face and only one eye! But a soldier, dressed like a soldier, fit and hard again from over two months in this harsh, testing environment of Mozambique, and the man who was ultimately their security provider. There was a rustle of movement amongst the audience and silent exchanges of sideways glances. Couto's sub-managers were all present: the chief engineer, the chief of production, the factory manager, the logistics and equipment manager and the field farm managers, of which there were four because the real estate being farmed was huge and the product range diverse, from tomatoes to cotton to coffee. They were all, like Mia Couto, of mixed race origin. They would be nervous but hopefully reassured by what he had told them. Their focus was business, MozLon and their own productivity, and they had come to trust Dalloway's military security regime. He hoped to God their trust was well placed.

Also present were Dalloway's Gurkha Connections Limited employees: his ten Gurkhas brought from Nepal, their leader being Gopal Gurung, and his six locally recruited Mozambican militia leaders with their section commanders. These twenty-four men had been MozLon workers and had shown the desire and the competence to be fighters and defenders. They included Ernesto and Pinto and Eusebio, the football maniac. Dalloway had organised the militia into six platoons and the platoon commanders and their three subordinates were present. So, the command structure of the Nhamatanda Militia Force, his force, was present; and although they were all of Ndau origin from Sofala, elements of the Ndau had historically supported Renamo, hence the *possible Renamo link*. Would they all be reassured? The Gurkhas would be of course, because they feared absolutely nothing and Dalloway was their Saheb. But the local militia...probably, but he'd need to up their training and taskings and keep them busy and confident in themselves, and he'd need to watch them for any signs of subversion.

Danny Dalloway thought about this and about the papers he had recovered from the dead Renamo terrorist and which he'd shared with Gopal but which he was *not* going to share with his leadership team right now. Christ, he had so much to do.

He needed to finish up this briefing as quickly as possible.

* * *

LATER, DALLOWAY AND Gopal sat drinking rum and smoking in the small mess they had established at the back of their accommodation hut. There was much on their minds. The two men had examined and discussed a range of issues. Dalloway had been unable to get through on the landline or the HF radio to the GCL sister farm complex at Manica, two hundred tortuous kilometres west of Nhamatanda on the pipeline road, the second MozLon agricultural endeavour entrusted to GCL's security. Manica: commanded by Omparsad Pun, Dalloway's second-in-command. Manica: only thirty-five kilometres from Mutare and the Zimbabwe border. Manica: adjacent to the Chicamba Dam area.

'What do you make of it, Gopal?'

Like Omparsad Pun, whom they'd been discussing, Gopal Gurung was a veteran Gurkha soldier, or ex-Gurkha soldier to be accurate, the second in order of seniority and level of responsibility of Dalloway's principal lieutenants. As with all Gurkhas, he was of only medium height but tough as teak and fearless. He'd killed the enemy in combat in the jungles of Borneo whilst in the British Army and he'd killed the enemy in the bush of Mozambique this afternoon. His weathered Mongolian-Indian features showed his visible concern. He said, 'I think there is trouble on the way for Omparsad and his project, saheb. We must help him prepare.'

'I agree. I also read the danger signs in these pictures and words,' and Dalloway indicated the sheaf of tatty pages on the table between them. 'And even if it turns out to be nothing,' he continued, 'then Om must know. We will try again in the morning with the landline and if it comes to it, then I will go by road to Manica.'

'Hunchha, saheb, I agree.' Gopal rose to his feet and stood up straight. 'I will check the sentries and the radio room, saheb. Good night.'

'Goodnight, brother, and thank you. Good work today.'

Dalloway poured himself another glass of rum and lit a cigarette. He was tired and his eye ached and hurt. He fingered the olive green eyepatch he had worn all the time, since the brutal attack in Kathmandu last December had left him sightless in his left eye and savagely scarred from his forehead down through to the line of his cheekbone. There was also scarring around the eye socket. The Hungarian criminals who attacked him had smashed the bone of the socket's structure. The fact was, although he looked like a pirate, the left side of his face was a mess. Thank God it wasn't his master eye, he thought, or he'd be a useless ex-soldier who couldn't shoot! Thank God he'd been able to see the fucking enemy today!

He smoked and thought of Paul Stanton, as he often did when his injury intruded into his thoughts and his memory danced back to those dark December days last year in Kathmandu. Stanton and Dalloway's Gurkhas - Omparsad and Gopal were there - had killed all four of the Hungarians and burned their remains in cremation ceremonies at the Pashupatinath Temple. He smiled to himself at the ironic justice Stanton had delivered for him and wondered idly where Paul Stanton was now. Then he thought of Nikki Walker-Haig, his business manager and Stanton's love interest.

Nikki Walker-Haig was the one who had really secured this deal with MozLon through her business skill and talented, persuasive persistence. She had gone over to London in July to meet with the MozLon decision makers and it was as much due to her achievements, as his and his Gurkhas', that GCL had now been on contract in Mozambique for just over two months. But whilst in London she had happened to fall in love with Paul Stanton. Christ, what an outcome! As a result and ever since, Dalloway had felt the unwanted burden of responsibility for her welfare. And what made this responsibility even more difficult was that Nikki was wilful and Dalloway knew he couldn't really control her. The blasted woman had refused to stay in Kathmandu, where he'd told her to remain, and had come over to Zimbabwe. Two weeks ago. She'd eventually made the Mutare Country Club her base, since GCL had established a small but comfortable command and control hub in some rooms there, but in truth he didn't know if she was still there. He hadn't been able to talk to her for over ten days.

'Fuck, fuck, fuck,' said Dalloway to no one. His mind was racing and his heart lurched with rapid beats of panic. From the Mutare Country Club GCL was able to have links back to Kathmandu as well as monitor the activities in Manica where Omparsad Pun was in control of the MozLon farm collective. So whilst hoping that Nikki Walker-Haig was in Mutare, orchestrating things, he wouldn't have put it past the woman to try and get to Manica, just to see what was going on. But then he realised that if she had, Omparsad would have got the message to him. No, he reassured himself, she was in Mutare, which was good, because if anything happened to her, Paul Stanton would...well, it didn't bear thinking about. He had a serious duty of care towards her.

There were too many loose pieces in his command, and control and it was totally unprofessional. Another burning question forced itself into his manic thought processes: where, for Christ's sake, was Victor Fitzsimons? When was the man coming through to Nhamatanda again? It was the 17th of October today and the MozLon Director for Manica and Sofala provinces, and his principal conduit to MozLon headquarters in Beira, hadn't contacted him for two weeks. *Two fucking weeks!* Dalloway had no idea why the man had gone off the grid but it was unusual and he had reported the fact back to Beira. From the beginning of the GCL contract, Fitzsimons had come through Nhamatanda on his weekly run from Mutare to Beira, but not for the past fortnight. Maybe he'd seen Nikki Walker-Haig in Mutare?

Danny Dalloway stubbed out his cigarette, drank his rum and decided to take himself off to his bed. On second thoughts, he paused, and picked up his tumbler and the bottle of rum and went outside to sit on the *stoep*, to reflect on life and look at the night sky.

No point in going to bed. He wouldn't sleep much this particular night. Tomorrow was going to be another busy day. And even if he couldn't satisfy his doubts about where Nikki was, he had to get up to Manica and brief Omparsad on the threat from Renamo rebels that he believed lay to the south.

In the forests close to the Chicamba Real Dam.

CHAPTER TEN

THE HERCULES C-130K aircraft left the Royal Air Force base at Brize Norton with its crew of five just after midday on Tuesday the 17th of October; it had only a Land Rover and two passengers on board. It was going to be at least a nine-hour flight to Nairobi so the two men, having secured and lashed the vehicle firmly in the cavernous rear deck area, and having stashed all their considerable gear inside it, put on cold weather clothing and crawled inside the olive green sleeping bag laid out in each of their hammocks. They'd rigged the hammocks low enough to swing with any slight movement of the aircraft and to enable them to reach down to the metal deck for the thermos mugs of sugared coffee and the chocolate biscuits they had brought as in-flight refreshments. Nine hours was a long time in the back of a Herc, a fucking uncomfortable plane at the best of times, but both men were seasoned veterans and knew how to make the passage of time pass as pleasantly as was possible. Warmth, body fuel and sleep.

The C-130K was operated by the Special Forces Flight of 47 Squadron, RAF and the crew and loadmaster knew better than to try and second-guess the needs of their passengers, even though there were only the two of them. Those blokes knew how to look after themselves. If they needed coffee and sandwiches later, after their kip, then there were plenty of rations on board, already pre-packaged and the coffee would always be made hot. Besides which the crew had a job on their hands.

To fly the 6,800 kilometres to Nairobi was a relative doddle. The aircraft had long-range fuel tanks and the payload was minimal so it had the flying range. The Flight Lieutenant pilot had been fully briefed on the ratified flight plan that had come down from Headquarters Director Special Forces to the HQ of 47 Squadron yesterday mid-morning. One could only imagine the amount of staff effort required over the weekend in the various headquarters to get the plans agreed and the permissions approved. Yet another Sunday ruined by operational imperatives! But that wasn't the crew's concern: they *were* the operational imperative, or certainly a sizeable part of it.

The Hercules would transit French and Italian airspace, cross the Mediterranean, giving Colonel Gadaffi's Libya a body swerve, and then, courtesy of President Mubarak's Government, fly almost due south following, albeit at a height of 29,000 feet, the Nile's passage through Egypt. Then the Hercules would cross Sudanese airspace, flying south again until they transited into Kenya through the narrow border area between Uganda and Ethiopia. There had been a coup in Sudan in June, and Colonel Omar Hassan al-Bashir had overthrown Prime Minister Sadiq al-Mahdi. The years of famine and civil war had taken their toll. The country was in bits and pieces. Her Majesty's Government hadn't been able to get any diplomatic sense out of Khartoum but on the other hand didn't believe Sudan's air defences would detect a stealth aircraft at 29,000 feet. Sudan's air defences were non-existent. So that leg of the flight plan was authorised by Whitehall. Officially, the flight was to bring some essential equipment to the British Army's Training mission in Kenya, which went under the code name of Exercise Grand Prix, so the crew would be able to refuel the aircraft at Moi Air Base, where there was a small, permanent RAF presence, before setting off on the leg of the mission that was not a doddle.

From Nairobi the C-130K would fly the 2,500 kilometres in stealth mode as the crew utilised the full suite of sensor systems that were part of the aircraft's Enhanced Vision System. The flight plan was southwards again over Tanzania and then to fly down the border regions - the no man's land areas - between Tanzania and Zambia, Zambia and Mozambique, and Zimbabwe and Mozambique until their drop zone just north of Nyanga. That's when the fun would start, when the Hercules might just need to use some of its Defensive Aids Sub-System. It would be a last resort. The drop off needed to be executed covertly in early morning darkness, and the Hercules needed to be on its way back to Nairobi without alerting any kind of military or diplomatic response.

There was sufficient lack of coherence and capability in the border regions concerned for HMG to have sanctioned the plan. Although there was a British Army presence in Zimbabwe and the Hercules could land at Harare, the British commander there had not been briefed on this mission. This was a need-to-know black operation. He didn't need to know. Anyway, the plan would work. The Hercules would arrive over the designated drop zone with pinpoint accuracy, a drop zone selected for its isolation from any centre of population, and the two men would parachute to the ground. On a second pass, the vehicle would be jettisoned from the aircraft on its own parachute assembly and the Hercules C-130K would disappear, a black blob climbing quietly up into the blackness of the sky. It had never been there.

Of course the plan would succeed. The Special Forces Flight of 47 Squadron RAF did this work all the time all over the world, and the two men in the back of the aircraft were seasoned members of 22 SAS. The vehicle was a civilianised version of the SAS Land Rover 110. It had been repainted in normal livery and distressed to make it look battered and used. The vehicle had special storage panniers built in to the back where there were sufficient weapons, ammunition and pyrotechnics to fight a small war, which they might need to, so they'd been briefed. It had its canopies, front and rear, which could be stripped off and stowed when needed, and it had a special passenger seat in the back that was equally removable. They had suitable civilian clothing, spare fuel, rations and water. They had all the gear required to communicate back to Hereford and to survive and navigate in hostile African terrain. The stop off in Nairobi would only be a refuelling break, a chance to stretch legs, eat and get any up-to-date orders from London. Special Forces had a liaison man there who would come to the RAF's hangar. Cloak and dagger stuff, but it needed to be. They also had the kit for the man they were tasked to meet and support. They were prepared and they would have over a day to get themselves sorted out once they got out of this uncomfortable flying refrigerator.

Staff Sergeant Taff Evans reached down and grabbed his coffee mug 'All right, Lefty?' he asked Sergeant Lefty Shoesmith. 'When was the last time you jumped outta one o' these things?'

'Yes, mate, I am, and it was months ago. But it's like riding a bike. You never forget. You'll be all right. Now, shut up will you and let me get some kip.'

'Fuckin' 'ell, Lefty, we've got 'ours in this flying can an' I was lookin' forward to some social chit chat.'

'No you weren't, you lying bastard. Read that trash book of yours if you can't sleep.' But then Shoesmith leaned over his hammock and looked at Evans. 'Hope Colonel Paul's all right. What do you reckon, Taff?'

''Course 'e is, mate, made of steel Paul is, and tough as old boots. Christ, you should 'ave seen what 'e 'ad to do in that Irish and Berlin job.' Evans took a swig of coffee and grabbed a biscuit, shoving it all into his mouth at once. He chewed for a few seconds. Shoesmith watched and said nothing. 'I wasn't at the Berlin end but we got the full debrief from General Grace. 'E reckons Paul should 'ave got another gong, but he couldn't, being as it was a deniable op.'

'Just like this one, eh?' said Shoesmith.

'Just like this one. Anyways that's all 'istory now,' said Evans.

Shoesmith changed the subject and said, 'So this bloke we have to meet is ex-Selous Scouts then, Taff?'

''E is, Lefty. That's what Major Ted back in Blighty told us. Mind you, mate, they 'ave a long 'istory with us. C Squadron of the Regiment was all Rhodies until about seventy-eight when they formed their own lot. Then when the current mob of politicos got into government in the early eighties they disbanded 'em. Stupid fuckers, if you ask me.'

'And the Selous Scouts did all the clandestine work in the bush against the terrorists?'

'Yes, mate.' Evans put his mug down on the deck, rolled into the centre of his hammock and burrowed downwards into his sleeping bag. 'Now, enough of this talkin' lark, I'm for a bit of kip in this 'ere maggot bag. So put the lights out, Lefty, will ya. And for fuck's sake turn the heating up. I'm freezing my bollocks off.'

Shoesmith laughed and lay back in his hammock.

* * *

THEY WERE ON THE road again and Paul Stanton couldn't wait to get to Harare and then onto Nyanga. It was Wednesday morning, the eighteenth of October, and he had to be in Nyanga tomorrow sometime in order to make the agreed RV with Taff Evans and Lefty Shoesmith. He was stiff from too many hours in the Land Cruiser and gritty-tired, lacking fresh air and exercise. It was hot and the countryside was persistently similar. And despite the essential information he'd been given yesterday during his meeting with Director Stephen Langlands in the NIS, which was significant food for thought, Paul had, for the time being, had enough of the company of Majors Wentzel Schuman and Richard de Castenet.

Paul didn't warm to Schuman and he was pretty sure the feeling was mutual. There was something furtive about the slab-faced Afrikaner's manner. He was of German-Afrikaner origin, Paul was certain of it. Schuman and de Castenet obviously knew each other from military liaison business, Paul assumed, but in contrast to Schuman who wouldn't stop talking and asking questions, his fellow British officer had said very little so far on this tiresome journey. No, Paul ruminated, I neither like nor trust this man with the close-cropped hair and the weathered, sun-hardened face, who chain-smokes cigarettes.

The three of them had set off from Pretoria before lunch yesterday and driven hard for almost nine hours: Schuman and de Castenet sharing the driving of the comfortable Toyota Land Cruiser. Close to eight hundred kilometres, de Castenet had said, to get to Masvingo, the old Fort Victoria. Crossing the Border at Bietbridge had been routine, after which they had powered up the A4 stopping only for fuel, food and the call of nature, until hitting Masvingo just before eight o'clock and booking into a rather shabby hotel.

Schuman's harsh tones broke into Paul's sombre reflections, 'Are you good this morning, Colonel?' which was a normal morning pleasantry after a night before when the three of them had shared a simple meal in the hotel's ill lit and shambolic dining room.

'I am,' he replied. The venison steak had been excellent, Kudu, Schuman had said knowledgeably, but the rest of the meal and the stay were best forgotten. Paul had not had breakfast with the other two. He'd walked down the main street in Masvingo and found freshly baked bread and a coffee. It was all he needed. 'I am, however, looking forward to getting to Harare. When do you think we'll arrive?' Paul sat in the back of the Toyota, as he had done all day yesterday. The two men in the front exchanged looks. Schuman chuckled and glanced back at Paul.

de Castenet answered, 'Four hours, tops, Colonel.' Then de Castenet asked: 'What are your plans when we arrive, sir?'

Paul evaded the question. What he had to do was of no concern to either of these two men. 'I'm guessing we'll stay the night in Harare and then head out to Nyanga first thing tomorrow?' he asked instead. 'What is it,' he followed up, 'only about four hours onto Nyanga?' Christ, he'd be glad when this arduous road trip was over and he could get into his mission without being shepherded by these two goons.

'Correct,' said de Castenet, 'on both counts. But at least we should have a comfortable stay in Harare. We're booked into the Miekles Hotel. The last bastion of the colonial luxury splendour that old Rhodesia was famous for.' Which would actually be nice, Paul thought, especially after the torture of yesterday.

They hit the road intersection at Mvuna. Left to Gweru, right, or straight on, actually, to Harare, said the signpost.

Schuman spoke, 'It's straight up through the Midlands region now. We're heading into Mashonaland.' As if that was meant to be significant to Paul. Schuman expanded on what he'd said. 'This is Mugabe's power base.' Ah, thought Paul, trawling back through the information he'd had briefed to him about the power balance and struggle in Zimbabwe since the Lancaster House Agreement and the election of Robert Mugabe to the office of President in 1980, with Mrs Thatcher's backing, of course. Since when, and certainly within the past year, things had started to go tits-up for the Whites, which was why he was here. Indirectly.

Schuman continued, 'You saw the sign to Gweru back there. Gwelo as it was. From there it's southwest to Bulawayo, the ancient city founded by Lobengula, and a place where you Brits have always fought the Matabele to annex territory and establish rights. Rhodes and company.' Paul listened. For once the man was interesting and his tone had become informative rather than sneering and condescending. de Castenet fidgeted and looked out of the window. What's bothering him, wondered Paul. 'Yes, man,' Schuman continued, 'the area's always been the stronghold of Nkomo and his ZAPU followers, especially since that kaffir madman Mugabe and his ZANU mob seized all the power.'

'The Gukurahundi,' said de Castenet enigmatically. Paul looked at the man, who had stopped gazing at the landscape flowing by and was concentrating on Schuman.

'That's right, bru, the early rain which washes away the chaff before the spring rains, as they say in Shona. Or in this case the fucking treacherous Zimbabwe Fifth Brigade that washed away tens of thousands of Matabele in a Mugabe-inspired rage of ethnic cleansing.'

'The Fifth Brigade,' repeated de Castenet, 'trained by North Korea as part of an arms-for-power exchange deal between Mugabe and Kim Il Sung. Declared operational in September nineteen eighty-two and launched on a mission of mass murder between eighty-two and eighty-seven. Twenty thousand killed, they say. Fuck! And forced to dig their own mass graves sometimes, or often burned alive in their lodgings and halls.'

'Yes, boet, fucking murdering slaughtering bastards, and even us in SA got our hands dirty in that business, hey.' Paul's interest was pricked, but he knew from bitter experience that Schuman would continue. 'Basically Nkomo's army got disaffected when they saw ZANU getting all the power. They started rioting in a small way in their tribal trust lands. Down in Pretoria we decided to send Special Forces into Zim to sabotage the air base in Gweru in eighty-two. That was just one of the things we sanctioned.'

'Why?' Paul felt compelled to show some interest. Besides, the man was informative.

'Because, bru, we wanted to destabilise Mugabe but put the blame on ZAPU. We had hundreds of ex-Rhodesian soldiers and police come south to join our forces. Hundreds, man. They were bitter at what was going on and wanted to oust Mugabe.'

'But then Mugabe and Nkomo came to a reconciliation in eighty-seven,' said de Castenet. 'The Unity Accord.'

'Fucking joke, man,' expostulated Schuman.

de Castenet said, 'It created the ZANU-PF, the Zimbabwe African National Union-Patriotic Front, which supposedly assuaged Nkomo's needs, but of course it didn't. It was two years ago and Mugabe and his henchmen still dominate power and what goes on in society. The white seats in parliament were abolished, Mugabe became President and the post of prime minister was abolished. His old ZANU cronies have all the important posts and the Nkomo factions in the Zim Army are neutered.'

Schuman concluded: 'Christ man, but that kaffir is going to ruin the place, hey.'

No one in the vehicle said anything for a while afterwards. Perhaps, if each had been privy to the others' thoughts, they might have smiled wryly at the irony in Schuman's last comment. The cause and effect of the situation was stunningly paradoxical for the three men in the Land Cruiser. Yes, Mugabe was ruining Zimbabwe and that was precisely why the Whites were moving their wealth offshore;

which was precisely why Paul Stanton was there and precisely why Schuman and de Castenet were, too.

The Toyota Land Cruiser sped on up the A4 to Harare. Mind reading wasn't one of Paul Stanton's considerable skills, but he certainly had the upper hand in this situation.

* * *

NIKKI WALKER-HAIG was strikingly beautiful, unusually, not classically, but mysteriously captivatingly beautiful.

She was also independently minded and dismissive of inefficiency, and this was one of the reasons she had disobeyed her boss, Danny Dalloway, and left the Headquarters of Gurkha Connections Limited in Kathmandu three weeks ago and come to Harare. In Kathmandu the business was running very smoothly, in her judgement. There was little to tax her or disrupt the Nepal end of the lucrative contract GCL had been awarded by MozLon, with the tacit approval of the Brigade of Gurkhas and the direct approval of the Nepali Panchayat. But the reports coming back to Nepal from Mozambique and Zimbabwe had been sketchy, unfulfilling and occasionally quite worrying. So she had come to the business end of the contract to see for herself and to help. She had come to Mutare, to the Mutare Country Club to be accurate, where GCL had secured a concession with the management to use some spare offices and retain a suite of rooms for the Company's personnel. Dalloway had placed two of his Gurkhas there: ex-clerks from the Kathmandu Rifles, who were able to speak good English and had proved themselves fairly competent in handling the administrative tasks that had arisen.

The two Gurkhas were good company for Nikki but she had discovered much they had not been able to do or achieve. For a start they were appalling drivers, so she had hired a Land Rover and gone into Mutare to establish the relationships and contacts with the requisite government, commercial and border officials to ensure everything was as it should be for GCL. The Company's personnel had to be able to transit freely between the two countries and the business needed to move supplies. So far, she had been successful. The officials seemed to want to go out of their way to accommodate her, even though she promised nothing in return except the execution of the MozLon contract, and now everything was working smoothly...except the longer distance communications.

Nikki hadn't been able to crack the problems that had roots in the infrastructure, available technology and the geo-physics of radio waves and the equipment that both propagated, received and converted them into voice communications. So she hadn't actually spoken to Dalloway yet. She had, however, spoken to Omparsad Pun, the wonderful Gurkha commander Dalloway had entrusted with the overall management of the MozLon farm at Manica, only thirty-five kilometres from where she was now. Omparsad had assured her things were going well, as they were at Nhamatanda, so she knew Om would have reported back down the line to Danny Dalloway that she was in country. The fact that she hadn't spoken to Danny personally, fussed her greatly. It was unprofessional. Dalloway would be both worried and slightly pissed off: that was the man he was and he had a right to be. He was her boss.

She took her mug of coffee, leaving the two Gurkha clerks to their morning routine, and went out onto the veranda of the offices and stood and let the warmth of the sun refresh her mood. It was Wednesday, the 18th of October, and it promised to be another hot day under the endless clear blue sky of Africa. She looked across the Mutare valley, the surprisingly green and rural valley, to the southeast, where the rolling peaks of the Vumba Mountains stood proud. She wondered, as she had many times since arriving, what lay on the other side, into Mozambique, in the areas where Dalloway and Omparsad and Gopal and the other lovely Gurkhas were now working.

She had become very fond of the Gurkhas and they had warmed to her and called her Memsaheb. She had become very fond of the mad Danny Dalloway and she had been with him and helped nurse him after the horrendous attack by the Hungarians in Kathmandu that had left him savagely scarred and sightless in his left eye. And she thought of her love, Paul Stanton, who had come to

Kathmandu and, with Omparsad and Gopal and other Gurkhas, killed the Hungarians and effectively rescued Dalloway's enterprise. She realised later that it was at their first meeting, in Dalloway's hospital room, as Paul was leaving Nepal, that she had actually fallen in love with him. And this summer she had gone over to London to secure the MozLon contract and she and Paul had become lovers and truly shared their deeper feelings.

Nikki drank some of her coffee and let her eyes rest on the horizon of hills. She had only spoken to Paul once since she left Kathmandu and had not told him she was in Zimbabwe. Why? Because she knew he would have worried about her and tried to talk her back to what he saw as safer ground. So he would be worried about her, *very* worried. She had to get the communications sorted out and she had to speak to her man and tell him everything was fine. She finished her coffee and made a decision: she would go into town in the Land Rover and try to find Victor Fitzsimons. He would help her.

She remembered when they had met; it had been a Friday, the 29th of September, at the Wise Owl Motel just over two weeks ago. Nikki had treated herself to lunch after a week of running around getting things done. Fitzsimons hadn't exactly tried to pick her up, he'd simply offered her a drink at the bar, and she'd told him straight out who she was and why she was there. He had said, 'I'm Victor Fitzsimons, the MozLon Regional Director for Sofala and Manica Provinces, so I guess we have a shared interest!' And he'd laughed and continued, 'I'm in Mutare almost every week, and if there is ever anything I can do to help you, or if you need some advice about MozLon, then please get in contact with me when I'm here.'

Nikki had liked the man. He was in his late forties, she guessed, and had a warm smile set in the rounded features of his suntanned face. His hair was swept back, a touch too long, she thought, for the climate and a man of his age, but it didn't detract from his genuine nature. 'Thank you,' she had said, 'I will.'

'I've already met your management at Nhamatanda and Manica,' Fitzsimons then said. 'I'm impressed by the way they have structured the security arrangements, and of course the discipline and work ethic of the Gurkhas is exemplary.'

'So you've already had dealings with the mad, one-eyed Danny Dalloway?'

Fitzsimons had laughed again, 'I have, and I think he's exactly right for the job in hand. The farm management and staff seem to worship him. They gain great confidence from him and the militia force he's training up.' This had been news to Nikki for she had no real idea how Danny and the others would actually execute the essentially military tasks on the ground. She was genuinely interested. She felt she had to know as much as possible about how GCL was going to do things.

'That's very good to hear, Victor,' she'd said. 'I'll be sure to relay the information back to the Kathmandu end of our business where the Brigade of Gurkhas and the Nepal Panchayat will be keen to know that things are progressing well.'

'Please do. Things *are* going well. And you might also like to know that my MozLon Regional Headquarters in Beira and the Company's main offices in Maputo are fully appraised of how well your Gurkha Connections is doing.' Fitzsimons had then said, 'And it's not just at Nhamatanda, either. During my visits to the Manica project I've been equally impressed. There's a marvellous Gurkha there called Om, or something like that.'

'Omparsad Pun,' Nikki had replied.

'Yes, that's the man. He also has a strong team.'

Fitzsimons made to leave and said, 'Please remember my offer of help. I'm actually off down to one of the tea estates southeast of here at a place called Melsetter in the Chimanimani, run by an old friend of mine. It's lovely. Then I'm heading back to Manica and Nhamatanda en route to my offices in Beira.'

'Thank you, I will. Have a successful trip.'

'I'm sure I will, thank you. You'll always be able to leave a message for me or find out when I'm next in town from the manager at the Wise Owl Motel.'

Now, having recalled this conversation, Nikki decided that for business purposes she needed to go to Manica. She needed to speak to Danny Dalloway. She needed a more hands-on feel for how things were. And her best bet for getting there was Victor Fitzsimons.

It was Wednesday, and if Victor Fitzsimons was going to be in Mutare at the end of the week then the manager at the Wise Owl Motel would know. So, Nikki, she said to herself, focus on the rest of the working week and then try and find Victor Fitzsimons at the Wise Owl Motel. And at the same time, she decided in a flash of brilliance, she would persuade the manager to let her call Paul in London, whether in his flat or his office in the Ministry of Defence. Yes, that's what she'd do. As for getting to Manica, well, Victor Fitzsimons could, in all probability, take her there. How good would that be?

She felt instantly better having decided these things.

But she had no idea that Victor Fitzsimons would not be coming to Mutare this weekend, or ever again. She had no idea that Fitzsimons was dead: brutally murdered later on that fateful day when she had first met him.

CHAPTER ELEVEN

HARARE WAS NOT quite the beautiful structured and friendly city that Salisbury once had been. Ten years of diminishing self-investment and voracious asset stripping under Mugabe's restrictive regime had made it look careworn, bordering on shabby. Whilst Mugabe and Nkomo continued their internecine struggle, their respective foreign backers, China and Russia, stood by poised to invest; and whilst the Zimbabwean Whites, the creators of the wealth and beauty of the country and this city, were increasingly starved of any say in Government, Harare could only become more bedraggled.

They came in from the southwest, through what Schuman told Paul were the once-prosperous and lovingly tended suburbs of Malvern, Highfield and Parktown. These were prime residential areas, Schuman informed him, but now the Blacks were coming out of the bush and taking over everything, including a lot of the housing, and they were ruining it. Paul could see for himself the truth in the Afrikaner's words. Everywhere he looked closely, at the school, hospital and other municipal buildings they passed, the outward signs of lack of care and the onset of decay were apparent.

The city was not flat. It sat fifteen hundred metres above sea level, rising to this height in gentle folds of ground that swelled and increased in rolling waves from the southwest to the northeast. The heart of the city sat in an enclave surrounded by higher ground on all sides except the southwest. And through it all a network of river tributaries threaded their courses. The roads were wide and not that busy for a weekday early afternoon. However, Paul reflected, although the country's material structures might be failing, the wealth-crazy politicians could not tame the power of Mother Nature. The trees, especially the Jacaranda, were magnificent and the city abounded with parks, golf courses, grasslands and greenery. It was springtime and Harare was coming into flower. That at least was something to gladden the heart and raise hopes.

Then they came into the city centre and to the Miekles Hotel, located on the corner of Third Street and Speke Avenue, with the impressive Anglican Cathedral standing proud behind it in what, Schuman told Paul, used to be called Cecil Rhodes Square. 'No way that name could stay, hey?' The Afrikaner laughed hollowly. 'They'll change all these street names, man, I tell you, and then who'll know where the fuck they are when they come to town.'

Paul loved the hotel. It occupied the pivotal position at the corner junction of the two streets, close to the Harare Railway Station, the National Gallery and the shopping and business districts. It was where Harare's heart was beating. Its two-storey, balconied exterior was classic colonial southern African architecture. There were obviously plans to extend the hotel - upwards, judging by the building site at the rear aspect of the building - but it still held the magic that Paul had somehow imagined was right for this place and this time. The lobby was tastefully decorated and structured so that private meetings and alliances could take place in amongst its public spaces and the secluded bar area. It had elegant charm. The place shouted out history and Paul could only imagine how much this hotel had witnessed over the years in the acts of business and politics that had shaped the region. Fantastic! He loved it.

They checked in.

de Castenet said, 'What do you feel like doing, Colonel?' And before Paul could answer, the man said, 'I have to get in touch with the Embassy in Pretoria to let the Brigadier know we've arrived safe and sound. Then I have to make the arrangements for the journey on to Nyanga tomorrow. It might be useful if I gave you the heads up on

118

how the place operates and who you're likely to meet there.' Paul let the man finish; he could almost see his mind working. 'I'll be honest, Colonel, the brief given to me by the Defence Attaché was pretty loose and so I'm not exactly sure what it is you wish to see and do at Nyanga.' And there's no chance on this earth that I'll ever tell you, Paul said to himself.

Schuman chipped in and said, 'Likewise, boet, I have to call my Director and fill him in. He'll have some jobs for me here, guaranteed.'

Paul knew exactly what he wanted to do; and it was pretty clear from the coded language of his two companions that they didn't want him around for the next few hours. Perfect. He said, 'Take the night off, Richard. I would like to see the town and I'll do it on my own. There'll be a street map at the Concierge's and I'm a big boy who can look after himself. Let's say we meet for breakfast at zero eight hundred tomorrow? You can tell me about Nyanga en route. Have fun. I'm going to find my room.' Paul left them standing and escaped towards the elevators. He had his travel bag with him and he wanted a cleansing shower, a change of clothes, some food, a drink or two, and a meeting with the Head of Zimbabwe's Central Intelligence Organisation, Mr Ken Rose. And he wanted these things in that order.

He'd got across the lobby, out of sight of de Castenet and Schuman but no further than the Concierge's desk, when a man, a tall white man wearing simple casual clothes, walked towards him, engaged him in eye contact and looked down at a note he carried in his hand. As the two men ambled past each other the note was held out and pressed into Paul's hand, and the man said quietly, 'From Ken Rose.' It was expertly done, neither man broke stride, and if anyone were watching them then the action would have gone unnoticed.

Inside the elevator he read the note from Ken Rose. It said: *Meet me in the bar beside the Railway Station at nineteen hundred hours.* Paul checked his watch. He had time to do everything he wanted and to familiarise himself with his surroundings; and he'd get to meet the man he needed to. How good was that. He wondered idly what devilment his two travelling companions would get up to in the meantime.

Back in the Reception area, de Castenet and Schuman were planning the rest of their day. They had their own meeting to set up, for they had the issue of more than two million pounds worth of diamonds to talk about.

* * *

THE BAR WAS cool and Paul was very grateful for it. The late afternoon-early evening humidity had almost negated the effects of his shower during the short walk from the Meikles to the grand old station buildings, and the thinness of his cotton shirt and trousers had no mitigating effect whatsoever. Apparently the rains were due to come in towards the end of the month, and hence the stoking up of the humidity level, but right now it was hot, man, so he'd been told.

So the interior of the bar was a shelter: with its space and high ceilings, where the fans drove the coolish air into the bar's corners. It was crowded, which was good, and although Paul had no description to help him identify his contact, he was on time and he was absolutely certain John Sawyer or Stephen Langlands would have passed his description on to Ken Rose; and so might Fred Etherington, since he and Rose were obviously friends of long standing. Besides, apart from his unique physical distinguishing features, the whiteness of his skin made him standout in this crowded gathering of Harare's post-work business and social groups. Mid-autumn London to mid-spring Zimbabwe in less than a week? Absolutely no chance of a suntan.

He stood for a few seconds and absorbed the atmosphere and layout. The bar reminded him remotely of the Long Bar in the Raffles Hotel Singapore, but clearly did not have such a global cult status. It was, however, stylish and redolent of old colonial charm and obviously very popular. Paul saw a man raise himself up from his chair at a far corner table. He was of medium height, wearing a rumpled beige linen safari suit. As Paul moved towards the table he could see the man was neatly proportioned, with thinning short dark hair and a deeply tanned, slightly weathered face. He wondered if Ken Rose had spent all his adult life in Zimbabwe, if his parents had come out to Southern

Rhodesia and he'd been born here, or if he'd been working somewhere else in the dark worlds of secret intelligence and come on contract to Ian Smith's Unilaterally Declared Independent Rhodesia. Whatever his background, Paul mused, Robert Mugabe had seen fit to keep this man as his Chief of Secret Intelligence despite the move in other areas to oust the Whites.

Ken Rose's eyes were pools of darkness that looked as if they'd been charged with electricity from within. They lit up his face. His handshake was firm. 'You're Lieutenant Colonel Paul Stanton,' he said and gestured to Paul to sit across from him, which Paul didn't really like because he always sat where he could see everything going on. So he sat next to Rose instead, which caused the man to smile wryly.

'How do you do, Ken,' Paul responded, 'and please, no ranks.'

Rose inclined his head in amused agreement and beckoned to one of the bar staff to come over to the table. 'What will you drink, Paul?' Rose spoke with the slight twang of the southern African but it was discernibly of English-speaking origin. His accent had none of the hardness of the native Afrikaner, like Schuman.

The black waiter arrived and greeted them both with a huge smile. Rose gestured to Paul who said to the waiter, 'Gin and tonic, please, in a tall glass with ice and a slice of lime.' Rose ordered another Castle Lager. 'Can we please have some nuts or crisps,' asked Paul, 'I'm starving.' The waiter went on his way and Paul sat back in the comfortable chair and surveyed the scene. No one was interested in them, which was excellent. He turned to look at Rose, who was regarding him with an amused expression, but neither of them spoke until the waiter came back with their drinks and nibbles.

'Cheers, and many thanks for the drink,' said Paul and the two men raised their glasses and chinked them together. Paul took a long drink of his G and T and munched a few crisps. He felt sharp and good.

'Cheers,' responded Rose, as he took a drink from his schooner of chilled lager beer. 'I recognised you from your description, Paul.' Paul raised his eyebrows. 'And your reputation precedes you.'

'In what way, Ken?'

'Well, let me see how I can put this. Fred Etherington told me that you were serious and seemed a touch passive and docile, but that you obviously weren't, given what your General in Whitehall had told him.' Paul munched on some roasted peanuts. 'The Head of Station in Pretoria, John Sawyer, however, relayed to me how impressed he was with you, as did, Director Langlands in the NIS in Pretoria. They both said they didn't envy you your task. And neither do I,' he concluded.

'Well I'm not sure I even know what my task is, yet. And despite Fred Etherington's reservations about me, he needs to be glad that he works for someone or some corporation that HMG regards as having a serious enough problem, in the disappearance of their Mr Fitzsimons, to have me sent from London to the other side of the world in order to try and solve it for them. And by the way,' Paul said, 'please don't ever assume I'm passive and docile,' and he smiled benignly at Ken Rose, who was watching him with interest. Paul drank again and then said, 'So if you also don't envy me my task, perhaps you'd be kind enough to tell me why, and tell me some things I don't already know,' Paul finished by saying.

'Touché,' responded, Rose. Then he became earnest and leant back but inclined his head towards Paul. 'I know you've been comprehensively briefed on the geo-politics of what's going on so I won't repeat it all; but the backdrop *is* vital. For example, Reggie Hanlon is coming out in December to participate, in his way, in the latest round of talks in the Mozambique Peace Process, and before that, at the end of the month, he's in Pretoria. Anything at all that might upset the balance of politics could be disastrous for the region and in business terms for Hanlon.'

'I fully get that,' said Paul. 'So what's the dirty business?'

'The dirty business is, in my estimate, quite simple and devilishly complicated. I believe criminal elements here, and in Beira and Pretoria, have conspired to steal a very large quantity of hard wealth from the Zimbabwean Whites. I believe,' Rose went on, 'these people will try to do it again and I don't believe Fitzsimons was complicit in this criminal activity.'

'So, as John Sawyer intimated as a possibility, Fitzsimons was acting altruistically to help the Whites but was bushwhacked by these criminal elements.' Rose nodded his head. 'In fact you'd go further than that, I'm guessing, and say that Fitzsimons was murdered by these people.'

'Yes. Fitzsimons was well known in Zimbabwe as he was in Mozambique. His responsibilities for MozLon ensured his presence here frequently, and he always, always briefed me on what he had observed in his regular business travels between Beira, his provinces in Mozambique and here. It was part of the *quid pro quo* we had agreed for him being allowed to travel freely across the Zimbabwe-Mozambique border. He had my carte blanche to travel. But,' Rose paused, 'I haven't seen Fitzsimons for over two weeks. He checked in with me by telephone on his last visit but I never saw him after that. No one has. He's disappeared. Murdered, as you say, in all probability.'

A master collector of intelligence, Paul thought, playing every situation to his benefit. He said, 'And this ties in with the physical evidence your Police Anti Terrorist Patrol brought back from across the border?'

'Yes, to a degree. The scraps of clothing most probably were his, but Fitzsimons' remains were not recovered, and certain things don't fit.' Paul said nothing. Rose continued, 'Where the skulls and other forensics were found was much, much further south than Fitzsimons ever, to my knowledge, travelled. He was a man of routine. As I said, he had my carte blanche and he quite often visited old friends on a tea estate in the Melsetter area. He would spend the night there sometimes or he'd return to Mutare and stay at the Wise Owl Motel.' Rose paused and seemed to think hard before fixing Paul with his electric eyes and saying, 'It is just conceivable the man might have stayed on the estate and then crossed the border, heading northwards to get back onto the pipeline road at Manica.'

Paul was recalling the detail on the maps he'd studied endlessly during his briefings in London and subsequently, and he could picture the reasons why Rose was speaking with caution. But there was something else. No, Paul thought, this man knows pretty much exactly what happened to Fitzsimons and it's because he's hiding something. He said, 'But you don't think so.' Rose blinked. 'You don't think so, because the geography there would make it hard for Fitzsimons to get back onto the pipeline road at Manica. I seem to recall there's a socking great dam and forest area around there, the Chicamba Real.' Rose took a drink and watched Paul intently. I'm right, Paul decided, and said, 'And you know Fitzsimons never stayed in Mutare on his last visit because you've checked the register at the motel there, and you know he didn't stay the night on a tea estate because you've also checked.'

'You're right, he didn't. He disappeared.'

'So he erred and strayed from his travel patterns for some reason and was probably butchered and disposed of by the men whose skulls your patrol brought back,' suggested Paul. 'And these men in turn were killed by someone else who was stupid enough to leave his Reconnaissance Battalion Zippo lighter at the scene.'

'Yes,' said Rose, 'Sawyer was right about you. You've given this situation a lot of thought.'

'I had ten hours on the plane to try and piece it all together; and since then two insightful briefings from your British and South African opposite numbers in Pretoria, and over half a day in a Land Cruiser when, amongst listening to a lot of drivel, I've had even more time to think and study the maps. So what was he carrying that made him worth killing?'

Rose screwed up his face in false amusement, and avoided Paul's question. 'But the geography is a little puzzling.'

'No it's not. He was killed in the north, close to Mutare, maybe even on his way to or from staying at the tea estate you mentioned, and his body was moved south and across the border to make its disposal, and the disposal of the other two, easier to achieve and conceal.'

'Which, if so,' said Rose, 'and given the hard fact of the Zippo and the skulls that were recovered, makes a strong case for a South

African and Mozambican presence as well as a local involvement in this.'

'I think you're being coy, Ken. Stephen Langlands is certain of it, as are you, according to John Sawyer. Ex-South African Defence Force soldiers turned mercenaries and finding work just across the border from home, with equally disaffected Zimbabwean white ex-soldiers? It's an alarmingly common phenomenon and not recent. Look at the Congo. And trust me, I know lots of ex-British Army soldiers who advertise themselves as mercenaries and are finding work all over this continent and others.' Just like Danny Dalloway and his Gurkhas, thought Paul, except that Dalloway was doing it legitimately and technically speaking was not a mercenary. 'As for Mozambique, there must be many ex-Renamo rebels underwhelmed by the country's support for the Frelimo power surge and who would be guns-for-hire?'

'You're right. But I tell you what. Let's go and eat. I'm hungry and I'm sure you must be. This country still produces the best beef in the world and I know the place where we can have some. What say you?'

'I say yes, but only on the condition that you cut to the chase, answer my question and confide in me. I'm en route to Nyanga tomorrow morning, ostensibly to visit the Battle School. I'm with a British officer I know well and whom I neither like nor trust, and I'm damned sure he doesn't trust the reasons why he's acting as my escort officer. I'm also with an NIS officer whom I feel similarly about and who reciprocates those feelings. My instinct tells me that both these men have more than a passing interest in the real reasons why I am here, even though I've said nothing to them. I feel it; and I'm usually right. So when I get to Nyanga and I've got some space to move and act, I intend to start getting to the bottom of this situation and solving MozLon's little problem. I have some help of my own in Nyanga but I'm damned sure I'm going to need yours, too.'

Rose had watched Paul intently as he spoke and his head had nodded gently at the references to de Castenet and Schuman. 'Who is your help?'

'I'll tell you later; and only after you tell me why Fitzsimons was murdered.'

'OK. Let's go.' Rose called for the bill, settled it, and the two of them left the Railway Station Bar.

CHAPTER TWELVE

THE FILLET STEAK had been delicious and the red wine good. The restaurant was small and Paul and Rose ate in a booth at the rear of the room. It was extremely private. The two men had talked throughout their dinner. Rose had told Paul much and confirmed a lot of the conjecture that he had formed for himself. They had got to the chase.

'Fitzsimons was carrying diamonds. A very large quantity of diamonds worth a lot of money and belonging to a number of influential people in this country.'

'OK,' said Paul, 'thank you. That makes sense.'

Rose went on, 'You know Mugabe's going to put his closest allies into all the top positions, including mine,' said Rose, 'and it's going to happen faster than any of us and the outside world think.' Then he said something that surprised Paul. 'The reason why I know exactly what the Whites here are doing with their hard wealth is because I'm in on it with them. I stand to lose a lifetime's work on the whim of my increasingly megalomaniacal master and I'm not going to risk it. He'll freeze everything when he ejects us. He'd find it hard in the eyes of the world to have us killed, but he'll take our wealth, that is for sure. We call it the Wealth Protection Collective, the WPC for short. I'm not the organiser, can't be, but I know exactly what goes on and how it works.'

'Tell me about it,' said Paul.

'There is a senior representative in all the key parts of the country. Our man in Mutare is a tea estate manager in Melsetter. His name is Dick Hanney and he's the old friend of Fitzsimons' I was talking about. Given his geographical location he acts as the collecting and holding point for the goods we decide to export and which come in from the other areas in the country. You understand that we have a large number of senior government officials, farmers, mining men and other commercial businessmen, all of whom, for some time now, have been turning a proportion of their personal wealth into hard assets, principally Krugerrands and diamonds. So Dick Hanney is, was, the direct liaison with Victor Fitzsimons. I run the contact with Beira, where the assets are handed over to the Portuguese Embassy's Home Affairs Secretary, who takes them back to Lisbon in the Diplomatic Bag and deposits them, for a small handling fee, into safe deposit boxes in the National Bank of Portugal. With my contacts and access to intelligence, I also keep a watchful eye on the security situation with the Heads of Intelligence in the Frelimo Ministry in Maputo and the Portuguese Embassy in Beira.'

'So you *did* know that Fitzsimons wasn't crooked?'

'I did; but I couldn't tell Fred Etherington without running the risk of the concomitant political ramifications that we've discussed and you've been briefed on. The only recourse for me was for an outside agent to find the truth. That's you. I did tell Etherington that he needed to exert MozLon's pressure on your Government to get involved. That's you again; so it worked.'

'A high-risk game.'

'Very, but this is a high-risk situation for us all. Fitzsimons acted for the WPC for just under a year. His business interests allowed him to travel regularly, normally once a week, between Beira and Mutare and back again. Recently he sometimes staged his journey between the MozLon protected farms at Manica and Nhamatanda. He enjoyed privileged status and he used the pipeline road that runs alongside the railway line from Beira up to Mutare, and which is reasonably well patrolled by Frelimo units.'

'How did it work with this man of yours, Hanney?'

'The monthly shipment was agreed in advance by the WPC regional heads, who planned a fair rota system to ensure those who had assets, could get them offshore in a reasonable timeframe. The regional heads had the responsibility for bringing the assets to Hanney. I was told in advance and ensured the Beira end was informed and that the general security situation was stable. It was a fair system and it relied on mutual self-interest and therefore mutual trust.'

'And the link with Fitzsimons?'

'Fitzsimons always contacted Dick Hanney by telephone when he arrived in Mutare, at the Wise Owl. Hanney and he would meet up in Melsetter, which is about a hundred kilometres southeast of Mutare. Hanney would hand over the consignment and Fitzsimons would normally head towards Mutare and start his journey back, staying on the way at Manica. Occasionally he might spend the night with Hanney and travel back to Mutare the next day. On this occasion he didn't. There are many places very close to the Border where he could have been ambushed.'

'So it would seem that someone here found out about the detailed mechanics of your system, and betrayed it both to Pretoria and Beira, or at the very least decided to act independently. Could it have been Fitzsimons himself?'

'Not in my view. He always acted totally honourably and never took any money from us.'

'I think you're right. It couldn't have been Fitzsimons or he'd more than likely still be alive and you'd have heard about it from someone in your contacts network.'

'I would.' Rose reflected for a few seconds and then said, 'I know it's a selfish thing to say, given that Fitzsimons lost his life, but I, we all, have a personal interest in the success of your venture, Paul.'

'Hmm,' uttered Paul. 'You do, but I'll make it work. Somehow.' And, he thought, I'll find those who killed Fitzsimons and deal with them, too. He had registered everything that Rose said and his mind was working across the range of his upcoming practical options and the detail regarding the personalities that Rose had disclosed. 'In our short meeting, Langlands told me whom he suspected, and he confided to you that he suspected Schuman?'

'Yes. He's been watching the man for a while. Schuman has the contacts in Pretoria with the disaffected ex-Defence Force personnel, people who'd come across into Zimbabwe and people who'd have contacts here, and he has the professional responsibilities to visit here whenever he needs to. It is likely he's also established contacts in Beira, with renegade Renamo bosses.'

'So, if Schuman is the Pretoria end of this criminal ring and the Beira end could be any one of a number of disaffected Renamo warlords or their middlemen, who is the Zimbabwe person? Who is close enough to your plans and your secret organisation in this country to be acting against you?'

'That, Paul, I genuinely do not yet know. But I will find out.'

'I'm sure you will,' and so will I, thought Paul. He said, 'But there's a huge practical consideration we haven't discussed. Your Wealth Protection Collective has an established conduit for moving the diamonds and gold offshore to Lisbon. Fine. But how would a gang of loosely connected criminals take the extremely large consignment of diamonds from Fitzsimons and transport and then dispose of it so that those concerned can all share in the spoils?'

'Again, I genuinely do not know.' I have an idea, thought Paul, and it involves someone with the diplomatic clearances and the street savvy to travel to places and know people who could launder such hard assets.

He needed to think all this through. Certain pieces were beginning to fall into place and become possibly connected, if not obviously so. 'I told you I'm off to Nyanga tomorrow morning, with Schuman and someone called de Castenet, Schuman's opposite number in the British Defence Attaché's staff in Pretoria.'

'Yes, I know the man.'

'Do you trust him?'

'Honestly? No.'

Paul nodded his head gently. 'Neither do I, as I said.' Paul paused. 'I need to be able to contact you covertly, and I have a portable satphone to do this. I also need your assurances that everything I do and where I go, that is not connected to my official visit to the Battle School, will remain undisclosed.'

'Here's my private direct line number,' and Rose handed Paul his personal card. 'I have the number of your satphone from John Sawyer and I'll call you later, possibly first thing tomorrow, to establish comms. On the other matter, you'll have my help and it will remain undisclosed. You've got the travel permits and you've got my endorsements whilst in Zimbabwe. I've never officially met you.'

'Good. Thank you, but call me at zero seven hundred tomorrow, before I set off. We can then arrange a schedule of calls once I'm in Nyanga and for afterwards, wherever I end up.'

'Agreed.' Rose looked questioningly at Paul. 'So, Paul, who is your help in Nyanga?'

'Oh that's obvious,' said Paul. 'The SAS, of course; but you don't know that,' and he laughed.

'And I suppose if you'd told me earlier then you'd have had to kill me!' laughed Rose in return.

'That, too! Of course!'

The men made to leave and Paul offered some money for his evening's drinks and meal but Rose naturally refused. Paul thanked him. Rose said, 'Let me give you something, Paul,' and he reached into his jacket pocket and pulled out a battered Zippo lighter, with a clearly visible insignia or badge on it. 'I'm thinking you might need it.'

'Ah,' said Paul as he looked closely at the Zippo and recognised the Reconnaissance Battalion badge on it, 'the smoking gun, as they say in all good murder mysteries.'

'Indeed,' replied Rose. 'I'm sure you'll find someone who knows its owner.'

The two men shook hands and left separately.

* * *

PAUL STANTON RETURNED to the Meikles Hotel. His mind was still fastened into the threads of the conversation he'd had with Ken Rose, but as ever, he was alert and watchful and deliberately hugged the edges of the Lobby area as he made his way to the stairs entrance that led up to his room.

Which was just as well.

As he was about to go through to the staircase he spotted Richard de Castenet and Wentzel Schuman on the far side of the Lobby, in the dimly-lit bar area, sitting around a corner table that was tucked in amongst the tall potted palms. They sat in high-sided armchairs and the table was crowded with drinks glasses and ashtrays. Cigarette smoke spiralled up from the centre of their intimate little conclave. There was a third chair and it was occupied. It was clear some sort of fairly lengthy social meeting had been taking place, and the fact that it had taken place here in their hotel made Paul think it was innocuous.

Then Paul glimpsed who was sitting in the third chair and he knew in a flash why the three men had met in the Meikles bar: *because Paul Stanton wasn't going to be there for some while*. But it was still a huge risk; and it had misfired for them, because Paul had returned earlier than they'd expected and he saw and recognised who was sitting in the third chair. It was the tall white man who had handed Paul the note from Ken Rose.

Paul climbed the stairs to his room. Somehow he wasn't surprised by what he'd accidentally discovered. Ken Rose had said he had no clue as to who in Harare was betraying the secrets of the Wealth Protection Collective. Now Paul did; and although he didn't know who the man was, he had to be a close confidant or assistant to the Zimbabwe's Head of the CIO to be entrusted to passing on notes arranging his master's covert meetings.

Paul entered his room and locked the door behind him. He poured himself a whisky from the mini-bar and thought through his next steps. He switched on the air conditioning to maximum and opened the window. Leaning out he saw that the windows of the adjacent rooms were fastened shut. Good. He gazed up at the stars, bright as far distant halo-ed spotlights in the clear night sky. Good.

This whole dirty business had little pattern to it. He needed to force some shape into what was going on, because for a start, his cover was blown. de Castenet and Schuman knew exactly what he was here for. So the dynamics of the situation had to shift. He had little time now. He found Rose's card in his pocket and placed it on the side table. Then he went to his wardrobe, pulled out his grip and removed the satphone and his small notebook from where he'd buried them under spare clothing and bits of field gear. He'd made sure earlier the phone was fully charged. He took it over to the open window and pointed the antenna into the crystal-lit darkness.

It wasn't very late and waiting until tomorrow to speak to Rose was not an option. Nor could he trust the landline in his room. So Paul keyed in Rose's number, sipped his whisky and listened to the echoes and bongs of the atmospherics as the phone made its tortuous connections via lower space to Ken Rose's residence only a matter of a few kilometres away. The phone rang eerily, then the noise was broken, 'Ken Rose,' the spooky voice said.

Some minutes later Paul flicked through his notebook and found the two other crucial numbers he needed. John Sawyer had to be briefed. He was a senior spy so getting a call at whatever hour wouldn't fuss him. In London it was an hour earlier. Charles Grace would be having his dinner, but he had to be told what was going on. He would need to start shaking things up in Whitehall tomorrow.

* * *

THE CALLS HAD been successful but Rose had been momentarily silenced by the information. Paul sensed his mind working, and when Rose spoke and said that the knowledge made an awful lot of things fall into place and that they needed to be extremely cautious and take time to ensure they both understood the full compexity of the situation, Paul was reassured. But changes had been forced on him by the new circumstances and he had some notion of where he had to go now. 'Please arrange for me to meet your man in Mutare, Dick Hanney,' he'd said to Rose. Paul had calculated the time and space and continued, 'It can be Saturday morning, Ken. I'll be in the Wise Owl Motel. I'll probably get there late-ish on Friday.' Rose had agreed.

John Sawyer was business-itself. He would compose a short message back to London and pass a factual update on to the Defence Attaché, Brigadier Colin Bullock, the next morning. For the time being, they both agreed, the DA didn't need to know the details of the criminal activity. No doubt London would brief him in when it was right to do so. After all, it would be the DA who would have the responsibility in Pretoria of dealing with the fallout from Major de Castenet's actions.

Charles Grace's responses made Paul chuckle and feel hugely reassured. The man complained about having his dinner disturbed: For God's sake, Paul, I'm actually with a lady tonight, he'd said, and we're dining at home, which is why you've blasted well got hold of me! Well, Paul could say nothing but apologise. Nevertheless, it was unusual, he thought. He knew the General had once been married and that his wife had tragically died some years ago; but nothing Paul had witnessed or discussed with this man during the three years and more he'd known him had ever hinted at a romantic side. Yes, the man was genuinely caring and humane, Northern Ireland and Berlin had shown that to Paul in no uncertain terms, but having a romance himself? Well, you just never knew. Well done, Charles Grace had said, I'll get a full brief from MI6 tomorrow, and I'd better talk to the PM and then that rather odious but necessary character, Fred Etherington. I'll come out, Paul. Expect me. You need help on the ground. I hope your men arrive safely, Grace had finished with, and the call had been terminated. Paul hadn't even had time to say I hope you enjoy your evening, General!

Paul allowed himself another whisky and a few minutes of personal reflection. He felt nicely fatigued. He had the opportunity of a good night's sleep, and he'd take it, before the uncertainty of tomorrow. It was inconceivable de Castenet and Schuman would consider their secret or their secret knowledge to be known to him.

Then his thinking got the better of him. The normality of Grace's situation back in London, a romantic dinner with his lady friend at home, made Paul's heart squeeze as he thought of Nikki Walker-Haig, *his* romance. Where in God's name was she? He'd spoken to Kathmandu, when? Last Saturday, almost five days ago. And they'd told him she was here in Zimbabwe, probably in Mutare where GCL had a permanent base, but they weren't actually sure. Christ! It wasn't good enough. The last thing Paul needed in amongst the violent criminal business in this lost world of southern Africa was for Nikki to be involved, even if only by virtue of her being here.

Paul drank more whisky and forced calmness into his mind. He had reinforcements coming: Charles Grace would arrive somewhere, most probably Pretoria, sometime soon, and be of huge help smoothing out the politics and ensuring whatever needed to be done would somehow have Her Majesty's Government's blessing. And better still, tomorrow Taff Evans and Lefty Shoesmith would be at Nyanga.

Paul wasn't planning on staying at Nyanga long: just long enough to collect Taff and Lefty and satisfy the protocol needs of his official visit. Also he had somehow to manipulate the movements of his two minders, and thinking about it, he believed he could start this once he got to Nyanga. But then he had to get to Mutare. He had a meeting with Dick Hanney on Saturday and the town was clearly a vital centre for all that had been and was still going on. He had to see the place for himself and be there for however long he needed to be. How else was he going to see the patterns in this complex situation? How else was he going to sort out all the bad bastards? How else was he going to find Nikki and make her safe?

Paul looked at his watch. He decided to turn in. He felt better having thought it all through. He would be in Mutare on Friday.

PART IV
BAD PEOPLE, FRIENDS AND LOVERS

CHAPTER THIRTEEN

GENERAL CHARLES GRACE thought the Prime Minister looked tired despite her careful make-up. Thursday. Coming to the end of yet another testing week for the Conservative Government. It was improbable Mrs Thatcher would mention anything of the sort to someone like Charles Grace, but all his inside intelligence had told him that the PM's position was tenuous. Tenuous because of the wretched Community Charge and the machinations of her own party, with outcomes waiting to be pounced upon by the opposition Labour Party, whose main man, Neil Kinnock, was, in General Charles Grace's inconsequential opinion, the most uncharismatic political leader ever imaginable. How was it possible that Mrs Thatcher's leadership could be challenged by her own party? It had to be the madness of politics.

The PM may have been tired, but dampened in spirit? Never! Mrs Thatcher said, 'General Grace, Charles, how *very* good to see you again. It seems, though, we meet only when there are a few little wrinkles in our undertakings which require some clever and clandestine rectification from our wonderful Military.' The Prime Minister offered Grace a seat and motioned, with a practised and not impolite gesture, to her Chief of Staff to pour the coffee that was set out on a table adjacent to the assemblage of chairs. 'This time we are overseas, aren't we?' Grace held his counsel and accepted the coffee with thanks. He waited until the Prime Minister had sampled hers, and then drank gratefully. It had been a frantic thirteen hours since Paul

Stanton had interrupted his dinner last night. How he'd managed to secure this meeting at such short notice was due entirely to the PM's Chief of Staff. A good man, Grace registered, and not for the first time. He must buy the man dinner. 'Sir Reggie Hanlon's letter, I understand, Charles?'

'Yes, Prime Minister, that letter.'

'And you have already despatched a trusted man to Africa to test the urgency and establish the truth of the potential political kick back which Reggie hints at?'

'I have Prime Minister.' Margaret Thatcher's grasp of the situation and her ability to devil out the essentials in any series of briefings had always, and still did, hugely impress Charles Grace. 'It is Lieutenant Colonel Stanton. You might well remember him, Prime Minister.'

'I remember him extremely well, Charles. I have many regrets in my life and one of the smaller ones must be that your man Stanton was never properly recognised for his actions in Berlin three years ago. We ought to be able to do something about that now, oughtn't we?' the PM turned to look at her Chief of Staff.

Grace noted that the PM had deliberately avoided mentioning Stanton's activities in the Republic of Ireland, but he deflected the question anyway. He said, 'Perhaps we should await the outcome of this current situation?'

'Yes. You are probably correct. And what *will* be the outcome?' Mrs Thatcher asked with her customary point of emphasis.

Grace knew enough of the workings of Number 10 not to engender false truths, but neither did he want to play down the highly placed faith he had in Paul Stanton to deliver the desired results. He said cautiously yet firmly, 'This is Stanton's fourth day in country. I've had one long encrypted message from him sent from our SIS station in Pretoria and I spoke to him on a satellite link last night.' Mrs Thatcher nodded, her attention was evident, but get to the point - quickly - Grace chided himself. 'He has confirmed that Sir Reggie's misgivings are well founded. The MozLon man is dead, but is most likely not a criminal. At worst the man acted altruistically to assist the increasingly beleaguered white sector in Zimbabwe. He did so because he could. He travelled regularly between Zimbabwe and his territorial responsibilities for MozLon in Mozambique.' Too much detail, Grace; keep it succinct.

'Hmm,' Mrs Thatcher interrupted. 'I wish to God I'd never supported that man Mugabe now. So why and how was he killed and what does it mean for *us*, Charles?'

'Colonel Stanton is sure there is a criminal ring operating across the three borders of South Africa, Zimbabwe and Mozambique, with control centres in Pretoria, Mutare and Beira. I must emphasise, Prime Minister,' Grace added smartly, 'that there is no evidence to suggest any of the three governments sanction this activity.'

'So Reggie's man is dead, you said?'

'Yes, Maam, killed by a mercenary operative of this gang.'

'Motive, Charles?'

'Money, and a lot of it, Prime Minister, hard money, gold and diamonds.'

'Good Lord.' Mrs Thatcher drank some coffee and looked at the ornate wall clock. 'I have five minutes, Charles. What else must I know and what do we need to do?'

'Colonel Stanton has a developing plan to identify and confirm the exact nature of the criminal activity and how to deal with it.' Mrs Thatcher raised her eyebrows but said nothing. 'We have despatched covert assistance to him, small scale, but adequate. The two parties will meet later today.' The Prime Minister glanced at her Chief of Staff, who nodded gently. The PM turned back to Grace and looked at him to continue. 'Stanton has created an exclusive but highly confidential circle of people who between them will execute the information gathering and sharing, and the hard necessities of the plan.' Grace watched the Prime Minister's face wince momentarily and then reset itself at these last words. 'These people include our Head of SIS in Pretoria, the Head of Intelligence in both Pretoria and Harare and us, Maam. The secret involvement of these people is vital if Stanton is to succeed. In addition, I shall personally brief Sir Reggie's Head of Security.'

'Well, Charles, that all sounds fine.' Mrs Thatcher paused and then said, 'So there is no reason we can know of why we should distance ourselves any further from Sir Reggie's peace initiatives in the region, his continuing dialogue with the Renamo and Frelimo leaders, and the other heads of state, which I understand is set to start again early in December?'

'No, Prime Minister,' replied Grace, with his fingers mentally firmly crossed.

'Excellent. I should hate to have to deny our relationship with MozLon because of corruption in his southern African ventures. It would reflect very poorly on Her Majesty's Government and my judgement in particular. The timing right now would be most difficult.'

Charles Grace glanced at the wall clock. His time was up, which was good, because although there was one more thing he had to tell the PM, he was glad there was no time to discuss it. He said, 'I know I've run out of time, Prime Minister, but there is one final small detail you should know of.'

Mrs Thatcher had risen from her chair and Grace did the same. 'Yes?'

'Colonel Stanton is positive that a British Army officer is one of the members of the criminal gang I've told you about.'

'A serving British Army officer? Good Lord!'

'Yes, Maam, he is part of the Defence Staff in Pretoria. It is the same officer who was implicated in the Berlin situation.'

'Well, how extraordinary! How the fates collide in these things!' Mrs Thatcher smiled. 'You'd better get out there as well, Charles. It seems like Colonel Stanton will need some top cover, literally, to ensure the misdoings of this wretched man cease. As we did in Berlin, please keep us in the picture through the Chief of Staff. There must be no scandal, of course.'

The Prime Minister chuckled as she walked out of the room and General Charles Grace was left admiring, not for the first time, the percipience and pragmatism of his country's Prime Minister.

* * *

THE JOURNEY FROM Harare had been a mild form of torture. The time had to elapse and Paul had to get here, it was a means to an end, but by God was he desperate to arrive. Which had obliquely reminded him of an essay question he'd had to answer in one of his school exams, English, obviously: *It is better to travel safely than not to arrive. Discuss.* Back then his examiners judged he'd discussed it adequately. Today though...he'd arrived but had he travelled safely? He believed so, but the immediate future would tell.

Schuman had done most of the driving and the dour Afrikaner had been strangely sparse with his comments during the journey. He'd smoked endlessly but it was another clear-blue-sky hot day and all the windows were open as they'd travelled through the delightful countryside of rolling, farming uplands with the horizon of the eastern mountains drawing ever closer. Paul had observed the body language between de Castenet and Schuman and it had reeked of masked complicity. The verbal language was also revealing. de Castenet had talked a lot and frequently shot a glance across the front of the car to Schuman, as if reassuring himself that he hadn't inadvertently said something amiss, but by and large the Afrikaner had held his tongue. He'd just driven and smoked.

Once they hit the outskirts of Nyanga town, things changed, and de Castenet took the wheel and the talk focused on the place ahead.

'I don't know if you know the senior British officer at Nyanga,' de Castenet said, 'he's a lieutenant colonel called Robert Sharpe. He heads up BMATT in this part of the country, the British Military Advisory and Training Team, but he's not in charge here. That's a Zimbabwe officer's responsibility.' Paul said nothing, so de Castenet ended, 'But I expect you knew that already. And obviously you're expected by him.'

'I did, and I am.' Paul replied, as graciously as he could muster, hoping that Brigadier Colin Bullock back in Pretoria had cleared the way for this visit without alarming the overall head of BMATT in

Harare. 'But I don't know him.' He wished de Castenet would shut up so he could look for what he needed to see.

de Castenet misread the signs and continued with enthusiasm, 'I come here quite often so I know the set up pretty well.' I bet you do, thought Paul, and I bet Schuman does, too. 'The role of the Battle School here has recently expanded. All the Zim Army units use Nyanga before deploying on operations along the border with Mozambique. And for the past three years Nyanga has also provided limited training for the Mozambique National Army, the Frelimo units, in both conventional and low intensity tactics.'

Schuman chipped in, almost unexpectedly, 'Yes, man, and us in South Africa, we now have to get involved as well. For years these toothless bastards saw us as the number one enemy, but now they ask us to help in their logistics and their equipment needs. What a fucking joke, hey.' The Afrikaner drew heavily on his smoke and spat out of his window. His face tautened. He really hated the Blacks. 'I have to come down here all the time. It's part of my job,' he ended.

'HMG's also involved in this, now,' de Castenet added, in an attempt to deflect Paul's thoughts away from what he must have felt was a leading comment. 'BMATT's helped the Zim National Army establish a Logistics School in Harare. More and more we are acting as strategic advisors whilst carrying out the day-to-day training and assistance tasks. In fact, there's talk back in Pretoria in the DA's offices, that we'll have to expand the scope of BMATT to take in the training of the Mozambique National Army.'

Paul let it all wash around him. He absorbed what was being said to him because of the needs of professional information gathering, but in truth he wasn't the slightest bit interested in what the two men were telling him. Whilst the information in part explained how de Castenet and Schuman had met, professionally, and how they'd come to this part of the world, it didn't, and wouldn't tell him how they'd stumbled upon their criminal, murderous business. But he'd find that out in due course.

The two men were coyly smug. They acted exactly, in Paul's view, as they would if they believed they'd found out his secret and

142

were absolutely confident he believed himself to be undetected. It made them slightly complacent and slightly condescending in their manner. They were even more the reluctant tour hosts than they had been yesterday. But - and this was a small set of signals Paul detected in both the men, especially in de Castenet - he also felt there was a trace of uncertainty in their demeanour. As if the knowledge they'd gained from Ken Rose's man in Harare had been of inestimable value, but that it had also brought unknown and hidden dangers. Good, the more uncertainty that exists in the minds of these bastards, the better. Then Paul stiffened, because suddenly de Castenet turned off the road along a dirt track and Paul saw the sign.

'We're on the approach road. Welcome to the Zimbabwe National Army's Battle School, Nyanga,' de Castenet confirmed. Within a few minutes the dirt track turned into a more solid, better maintained gravel road, and the Toyota Land Cruiser moved slowly through clusters of beautiful trees. 'This leads to the Headquarters building,' de Castenet said.

The road was flanked with Msasa trees, zebrawood, Paul had learned during the course of his journey, which were everywhere in Zimbabwe and beautiful. Their bent, angular trunks supported crowns of dense leaves intermingled with seedpods. Almost all the leaves were now deep green in colour, although some still showed shades of their earlier vivid reds and purples. Planted at regulation intervals they gave shade and provided cover from the glare and heat of the sun. They were Msasa, the sheltering tree.

They started to drive alongside what was obviously the parade square, and across the hundred metres of open space Paul spotted the men he was looking for. He smiled. They were sitting in white plastic chairs on the large veranda of what was clearly one of the permanent staff messes or NAAFI, to use the British Army's familiar term. A corrugated iron awning covered the veranda and there were groups of chairs, all occupied by what must be the instructors and staff, scattered around tables. It looked a touch rough and ready, but that was in keeping with the requirements and general demeanour of the Battle School. They were drinking a beer, he could see from the bottles. All the men were drinking a beer. Well it was a sweltering late afternoon and the work of the place seemed to be coming to a close for the day.

As Paul watched he saw Taff Evans and Lefty Shoesmith stiffen momentarily in their seats and stare across the parade ground at the dust-covered Land Cruiser. Paul was sitting in the back, on their side and his window was down, as it had been most of the journey, so he casually leaned his head out and watched as Evans and Shoesmith registered his sign and then sat back and started talking to each other. Great. They'd made it. Paul knew they'd have the Rover secured somewhere, locked away, and they'd have his gear and weapons and be ready to move at very short notice.

Paul saw the two SAS men because he was looking for them. Schuman and de Castenet weren't and surely didn't notice them as strangers. Paul was positive about this. How could they? They didn't know every single member of staff at the Battle School. Besides, although they were now suspicious of Paul and what he might do, Paul firmly believed they viewed his visit to Nyanga as a legitimate part of his visit and unconnected to their activities. This was Paul's reading of the current situation and he'd spent the last four and a half hours in the close confines of the vehicle with de Castenet and Schuman and felt pretty sure about things. He was persuaded that the two protagonists were unaware that he knew they knew about his false mission.

He was here, in Nyanga, and so were Taff Evans and Lefty Shoesmith. All Paul had to do now was pay his respects to the senior staff here, show some interest, and get down to Mutare, tomorrow, Friday.

But first, he had to change the dynamics of the situation and he knew how he was going to do it. He had to flush the birds out of the covert, so to speak. Schuman and de Castenet were the birds and he had to get them to break cover. What would it take? A few drinks, a measure of shock and the selective disclosure of certain pieces of information.

Paul would begin the process as soon as he could.

* * *

COLONEL JACKSON RADEBE was charming to Paul, and was flattered that his Battle School should host such a distinguished visitor from the British Army. However, as he said with huge apologies, sorry, sorry, sorry, but there had been little notice for the visit, and it is not possible to prepare some live training for the Colonel Stanton to observe. Worse even more, he himself had to drive to Harare very shortly for the Conference of National Army Commanders. It is tomorrow. How embarrassing for him! And the Lieutenant Colonel Sharpe, his British 2IC, was gone out on a shooting exercise in the bush for three days.

Perfect! Paul was instantly reassured that the gods were finally beginning to shape the circumstances so he could act without formal clutter impeding his movements. He said, 'Colonel, that is perfectly all right, and I know you have had very little warning of my coming here.'

'Yes, yes, Colonel Paul,' Radebe interjected, seizing upon Paul's comment as his excuse, 'we have only got the information this morning and now it is afternoon and you have already arrived. Even our training programme has finished for the day!'

The two of them were sitting in comfortable chairs in Radebe's spacious office. Jackson Radebe had offered tea but Paul had politely refused and the Zimbabwean Colonel had ushered his Adjutant out of the door and told him to close it behind him. Paul was conscious of the presence of de Castenet waiting in the Adjutant's office the other side of the flimsy door, and knew the man would be listening as intently as he could without it being obvious. In fact it was obvious that both Radebe's Adjutant and de Castenet would be listening, as it was one way that staff officers stayed ahead of their seniors! Schuman, not surprisingly, had vanished. He'd hopped out of the Toyota before they'd got to the Headquarters, muttering that he had people to see. It was most unlikely that a rabid Afrikaner would have anything in common with one of Mugabe's trusted senior Army officers. Far better that he kept himself out of sight and mind.

Paul turned his attention back to his host. He needed to put the Commandant of the Battle School out of his misery, so he said, 'Please,

Colonel Radebe,' Paul deferred to his rank, 'you must not concern yourself. My visit was very short notice. I really only wished to talk to some of the British personnel and see your magnificent facility, which I have done on my drive around your fine Battle School. It is indeed highly impressive. Also, Colonel, I have to be leaving tomorrow.' Paul paused. He deliberately hadn't said where he was going. Radebe looked relieved. Paul suddenly thought that what he had said might sound rude. 'I have heard extremely high praise from Colonel Sharpe about how effective your training and leadership is here at Nyanga, and these reports have been passed back to the British authorities in UK.' All of which was a barefaced lie. 'You should take great personal credit for it, Commandant.' Radebe sat back and visibly preened himself at Paul's words. He finished the man off, 'If I was you, I would go to your conference knowing that your Battle School is one of the gems of the great Zimbabwe National Army.' Paul could scarcely believe his own unctuousness. He needed to excuse himself, get out in the fresh air and get on!

Fortunately Colonel Jackson Radebe interpreted Paul's intent correctly and grasped the moment to end the meeting. The two men rose from their chairs and shook hands in departure. The Commandant said, 'You will of course stay as my honoured guest tonight, Colonel Paul. In my absence I will ensure you are well looked after. I have a guest cottage. My Adjutant can arrange things. You can eat your fine meal in the Mess,' Radebe added, almost as an apologetic afterthought, as he opened the door to his outer office, his Adjutant's office, and ushered Paul out. Paul was relaxed and smiling. He noted instantly that de Castenet and Radebe's Adjutant were standing stiffly, close to each other. They had been listening at the door. Good. de Castenet's face was strained. Radebe fired off a barrage of what Paul assumed was Shona or Ndebele at his Adjutant, who was instantly electrified, casting a wide-eyed look at Paul and starting to move towards his desk telephone before his Commandant had even finished speaking. Ah well, Paul thought, at least I'll get a good room tonight and be spared the company of de Castenet. And it will allow me to do what I need to, and arrange things with Evans and Shoesmith.

The two British officers walked down the steps of the Headquarters Building to the parking area where the Land Cruiser was. de Castenet affected an air of composure and said, 'I know where the Commandant's guest cottage is, Colonel, I'll show you. And perhaps you'd like me to accompany you to dinner as well? I'm afraid it's not exactly what we'd expect as a proper officers' mess. In fact it's actually an all-ranks instructors' mess, but at least the gin and the beer is normal and the beef will be fine. Well, usually it is.' de Castenet and Paul continued to walk towards the Toyota and de Castenet stooped to the driver's door to open the vehicle. 'What are your plans for tomorrow?' he said, changing the subject, but knowing full well what Paul intended.

Paul's thoughts were mischievous. Now was the time. He stopped, just as the man opened the vehicle's doors. 'You can show me where I'll be staying, but that's all I'll need from you from now on, thanks.'

'That's all? From now on?' de Castenet's discombobulation was almost laughable to Paul. The man continued, 'I mean, what about tonight and tomorrow? What are you going to do tomorrow and where are you going? What about transport? The DA will never forgive me if I just abandon you in Nyanga. Besides, I can't, Colonel.'

Paul had got into the passenger seat of the vehicle and gestured to de Castenet to get in and drive. 'Drive, Richard. I take it you'll meet up with Schuman somewhere later.' Richard de Castenet swivelled his head to look at Paul and there was concern, a touch of fear, in his eyes; he couldn't have failed to notice the distinct change of tone in Paul's voice. 'All you need to do is show me where the Commandant's guest cottage is. I'm perfectly capable of fending for myself after that. I'm sure I can find the messing facilities. Besides,' Paul looked at de Castenet, 'I shall be meeting friends later.'

'Friends? I mean, how is that possible? What friends?'

'Well actually, it's none of your business, but since you asked so nicely, they're from the SAS, and they're waiting for me, and they have transport.' Paul let the bomb drop and blithely looked out of the window. de Castenet's driving wobbled. The man's mind must be in turmoil. Paul turned back to him and said, 'And I'm going on to Mutare tomorrow morning with my two colleagues because we have some work to do. And you, Richard, need not worry about me at all. You can pick up Schuman and carry on with whatever you both feel you need to do having come up into Zimbabwe. As for me,' and Paul looked searchingly into de Castenet's eyes as the man turned his head, 'I'm on a mission which has the blessing of the DA and indeed Her Majesty's Government.' Paul let the bomb fizz a little more before saying, 'Ah, the sign to the guest cottage. We've arrived. Thank you.' Paul got out, hefted his travel bag out of the Toyota's back and left de Castenet to his own devices.

He'd thrown a couple of heavy sticks into the covert and clearly startled the first of the birds, de Castenet. The question was, what would he do now, and where was the other bird and what would the bitter Wentzel Schuman do? How would they show themselves? He'd find out soon enough, he believed. But was he worried? No. He had Taff Evans and Lefty Shoesmith and the three of them could deal with pretty much anything.

Mutare was where he was going tomorrow because he had to find Nikki and he had to meet Dick Hanney on Saturday morning. Also, he was positive de Castenet and Schuman would establish some pretext to follow him, which would be good. It would be good because it was what Paul Stanton wanted and because it would be their undoing.

They were bad men and they needed to be dealt with. Somehow.

* * *

THE SUN WAS dipping and the air cooling to that lovely African evening sundown time when the day's work is done, the soul's stresses can temporarily be laid to rest and the body's needs are waiting to be uplifted by a cold beer or two.

They'd given him a couple of hours, and then the knock came. Paul had already showered, checked and sorted out his gear and was

148

ready for them. He opened the door to the cottage. 'Hello, Taff, Lefty,' he said. He'd guessed they would easily track him down but had not believed they'd give him the time to refresh himself. They must be getting soft. No, they were right to leave him until the day's activities had come to a natural halt and their movements would be less conspicuous to those who might be watching. They were dressed in khaki cotton shirts, lightweight bush trousers and thick-soled desert boots. They held crunched up bush hats in one hand and their black-rimmed sunglasses were pushed up onto their close-cropped, stubbly hair. They looked the part. The Bobbsey Twins. Now in Africa. It was hysterical!

'Watcha, boss,' said Evans, 'see ya made it on time.'

'As you did, too, Taff. Well done, and thank you. Was it the usual RAF mob from Brize that dropped you in? Bloody good, aren't they?' Paul shook hands with his men. 'How are you, Lefty?' Lefty Shoesmith was always going to be the vocally reticent one in the company of the boisterous, cockney-sounding yet Welsh-named, Taff Evans.

'Good, thanks, Paul. It's been an OK trip.'

'So far,' chipped in Evans. 'Are you alone, Paul?' Evans asked, looking beyond Paul and into the hallway.

'I am. Come on inside. I have reassured Colonel Radebe's very solicitous Adjutant that he need spend no more of his precious free time looking after me.' Paul led his men inside and through the small anteroom of the Commandant's guest cottage and onto the veranda area that looked out towards the Eastern Highlands. The place was totally private. Paul had already ascertained that the cottage stood alone. He didn't offer them a drink - he didn't have any. 'Tell me the score, boys,' said Paul, 'then hopefully we can grab a drink and something to eat and I'll brief you in on the plan. I presume the place where I spotted you earlier was some sort of Mess?'

'It is, boss, and we can get some scoff and drinks there,' replied Evans.

'The score?' Shoesmith chimed in. 'As you said, Paul, the Boys in Blue dropped us out into the pitch black yesterday morning, bang on target. The Rover and all the gear landed fine. We've checked it over. Major Ted Bakerswell's contact from the old C Squadron and Selous Scouts days met us, as we were briefed, and took us to his farm where we spent the rest of yesterday and today.'

'So all is well and 'ere we are, now,' finished Evans. Paul laughed. 'What's so funny, boss? It was fuckin' freezin' in that bloody old Herc, an' this place is a far cry from London. Alien, if you ask me.'

'I'm laughing because it's exceptionally good to see you both. I've been seriously deprived of sensible and honest company for days now.'

'There's nothing honest about Taff Evans, Paul, you should know that,' said Shoesmith, and Paul laughed again. Shoesmith continued, 'The local contact's name is Brian Lauwrens, calls himself Vino, and he's solid from what Taff and me can tell. He and his wife looked after us well and he never asked us any questions. Told us a bit about how the country's going down the pan for the Whites since Mugabe took it on himself to be another Hitler. Seems like the farms that have been worked here for generations are likely to be up for grabs as Mugabe re-settles his ex-freedom fighters, and the Blacks pour in from the bush and want their own land.'

Evans said, ''Spose this is part of the reason we're 'ere, is it, Paul?' Paul looked at Evans and Shoesmith thoughtfully. It never surprised him how astute and perceptive his men were: any of them, from all the regiments and units he'd served in. British soldiers could be coarse, loud, drunk and frankly unpleasant for moments in time; but in their souls they were alert to the intelligences of their surroundings and situations, gentlemanly towards ladies and those in distress, fiercely loyal and the best fighters in the world.

'It is, in a way, boys,' he replied. He deliberately changed the subject, momentarily, 'The wagon and the weapons and other gear are secure, are they?'

'Totally, boss,' replied Evans. They're in one of Vino's barns. 'E drove us 'ere today in 'is motor. Bakkie, they call them things in this neck o' the woods. But it seems 'e knows a few of the blokes instructing at this place and 'e's gonna stay around 'til we let 'im know what the ongoing plan is.'

Shoesmith said, 'He'll be at the Mess, Paul.'

'Well, we'd better go and meet him, and then I'll let you all know what I'm thinking. But one thing,' Paul paused the two men with an earnest look, 'our targets are a British officer and a South African officer.'

'I think we've already spotted them, Paul,' responded Shoesmith. 'They came into the Mess building about an hour ago and they looked none too happy if you ask me.'

'Excellent,' said Paul. 'Let's go and meet Vino Lauwrens and then we'll make their day even worse!'

CHAPTER FOURTEEN

THE THREE MEN walked in through the Mess entrance, passing down the hallway and into the main anteroom. It was a rough-and-ready kind of set up, appropriate, some might say for a battle training school. It had seen finer days in terms of the care given to its fabric and property, but that had been in recent by-gone times. Its care now was in the hands of Mugabe's military men. It looked, at best, functional. The faded prints in the faded frames on the ill-painted walls looked down on scuffed wooden floorboards on which rested groups of tired, loose-covered armchairs and settees randomly set around occasional tables. Ceiling fans rotated slowly and noisily, barely disturbing the air. Not surprisingly no one was sitting inside. Its atmosphere was akin to an undertaker's waiting room.

The three men moved outside. Everyone was outside. The whole of the building's edifice that fronted onto the parade square lined by the lovely Msasa trees was open to the outside evening world, the veranda doors all pulled back. And there everyone was. The deck area with its extensive awning of corrugated iron was lit by low-glow lamps, which provided just the required level of ambient light. The men - they were exclusively men - were standing, sitting, crowded around the tables and chairs on which beer bottles, glasses, plates and cutlery gathered in chaotic profusion whilst the cigarette smoke billowed up all over the place like mini chimney stacks. The mosquitoes had no chance at all; besides which, the air was just starting to cool, so not good flying conditions for mozzies. The mood could not have been more in contrast to that of the fading inside world just twenty paces away.

Paul took it all in as the three of them emerged onto the veranda and then stood to take stock for a few moments. To his right, coming out of a doorway that obviously led into the bar and kitchen areas, he noticed the mess staff coming and going, arms laden with trays of chilled beer, clinking together, or plates of steak and chips. He was suddenly ravenously hungry.

Then he saw de Castenet and Schuman sitting with two other men, both white and wearing bush fatigues, at a table towards the back of the deck area and to his left. They were big bastards. Schuman spotted him and made a small gesture of indication to his companions who then leant back in their chairs and stared at him. Later, thought Paul, I'll be on to you all later.

Evans spoke quietly to him, 'There's Vino Lauwrens, boss. 'E's sat on his own so let's join 'im.' Paul was about to answer in the affirmative but saw de Castenet rise to his feet, and make a move, but then hesitate. Paul changed his mind. The moment was right, now, to start it.

'Come with me, boys. You've seen them before but now there are four of them. Bad bastards I need you to meet. But say nothing, OK? I'm serious.'

'Roger that, boss,' the two SAS men said in unison. They knew the score. And they didn't yet know what Paul's plan was. So, no loose talk. They threaded their way through the social chaos to meet the bad bastards. Paul felt the little surge of adrenaline and it made his senses glow with anticipation. He realised he had been inactive for too long. It was time to stand in front of the enemy. His face was grimly friendly as he approached de Castenet's table.

'Ah, Richard,' he offered, 'I see you and Major Schuman seem to be well set and relaxed.' He looked deliberately at Schuman and then the other two men. 'And you have friends here. Well of course you would, wouldn't you.' de Castenet was immobile, caught in the act, almost, about to sit down but transfixed by Paul's sudden presence directly in his and his accomplices' space. Paul said, 'Please sit down. Don't get up on my account.' de Castenet crumpled back down into his chair and started wafting his hands around. Paul felt the presence of Evans and Shoesmith flanking him, quietly still and silent, as requested. 'Oh,' he said, 'let me introduce Staff Sergeant Evans and Sergeant Shoesmith of 22 SAS. I think I told you I was expecting to meet friends and here they are. Mind you,' Paul went on for effect and to play the imp, 'I'm sure *you* do, but I hope Major Schuman and your two friends realise that I've perhaps been a touch indiscreet identifying the regimental parentage of my two colleagues. And if you were to talk about it outside this circle of trust, then we'd have to kill you, of course!' And Paul gave an intentionally brittle laugh, but his eyes were icy cold. No one else laughed. The tableau was rigid. Static. Frozen. Schuman's cigarette gave off a spiral of toxic smoke. Time to move on, Paul said to himself. 'Only joking, of course. Anyway, nice to see you, and thanks for all your help in getting here,' Paul inclined his head to Schuman. 'I'm starving, and my colleagues have told me the steak is good, so we're going to eat. Have a safe onward journey, wherever you're bound.' Paul turned and left the table area and Evans and Shoesmith moved with him. Stanton and the Bobbsey Twins in Africa.

'Think it 'ad the desired effect, boss?' Evans asked.

'Don't know, Taff. What do you think, Lefty?'

'Think the two local boys might have missed the irony, to tell the truth, Paul. They looked stupid.'

Stupid maybe, Paul thought, but perhaps not. He'd quickly surveyed the other three men when he'd been deliberately directing his mild taunts at de Castenet. Schuman remained dark, saturnine and closed, his teak-hard exterior neither flinching nor reacting in any way, his dark eyes flickering as *he* made his assessment of the new adversaries. The other two men looked equally hard and unflinching, ex-Rhodesian Army for certain and probably elite Rhodesian Light Infantry, the RLI, or Selous Scouts. No, he thought, they will not be a pushover. But no matter, his path was set, he had friends and the good guys were with him, and he was getting ready for the consequences as the bad guys came more into focus. The glow of impending battle was still on him. He felt good - and hungry.

'Come on, boys. I need to meet Vino and I need to eat. Take me to the man.'

'Roger that, boss,' the Bobbsey Twins said in unison.

* * *

PAUL INSTANTLY LIKED and trusted Vino Lauwrens. He was one of Ted Bakerswell's old comrades-in-arms and that spoke volumes for his provenance; but as well Paul warmed to the no-nonsense and open manner in which he embraced them all as newcomers to his world, irrespective of what the cost might be to him and his family. He was a member of the Special Forces fraternity, after all, the band of pilgrims.

All of them had ordered steak and chips and Castle lager and were replenishing themselves gratefully. Lauwrens did the talking and he spoke with the slightly softer southern African twang that Rhodesians, Zimbabweans, had, as he brought Paul up-to-date with what had happened since he'd met Evans and Shoesmith at the drop zone rendezvous and taken them to his farm. 'Perhaps cheekily, but I'm working on the assumption you'll need my ongoing help, Colonel,' he added.

Paul paused him with a gesture of his glass. 'No ranks, Vino, I'm Paul, and always will be,' which caused Evans and Shoesmith to smile at each other and tuck into their food with renewed fervour. 'And yes,' Paul continued, 'if you're positive you can help, then I'll accept your offer gratefully.'

'I can, Paul. My farm's not going anywhere and my family and the one or two loyal workers I still have can take care of it in the short term. Frankly, I'm itching to get into something, bru, and you might need some local knowledge.'

'Of that I'm sure,' Paul acknowledged, 'especially as I've just deliberately ditched the help I came with,' and he threw a look across to where de Castenet and Schuman were sitting. No one commented.

Lauwrens was a man in his mid forties, Paul guessed, which would mean that he'd been in his prime, Paul's age now, at the height of the war in Rhodesia. The British Government hadn't involved the SAS in the bush war that had raged against Ian Smith's White Rhodesian regime throughout the seventies, but it had involved them in the Ceasefire and Monitoring operation in seventy-nine that had marked the beginning of the end of the war and presaged the Lancaster House Agreement which had eventually given Zimbabwe the freedom to elect Mugabe as its nascent dictator.

It would have been during that operation, Paul guessed, when Ted Bakerswell, as a young troop commander, would have come across Brian Vino Lauwrens. 22 SAS meets Selous Scouts. But there was no doubt in Paul's mind, having been with him now for close to an hour, and having appraised the toughened external physique, the quickness of his thoughts and the fire in his eyes, that Vino Lauwrens, in spite of his mid-forty years, was still a fighting man. Yes, he needed him.

Paul had been thinking through the next phases of what he had to do during the meal, whilst the four of them had settled into the necessary activity of eating and drinking and talking quietly and inconsequentially. He had not failed to notice Schuman's tatty canvas satchel that the man had brought with him from Pretoria and which had never left his sight throughout their journey. Now Schuman had it on the floor by his chair, the shoulder strap wound carefully around the chair leg. Paul had a very strong feeling that it contained a weapon. But what else?

He was increasingly sure, as Langlands and Rose were, that these men had masterminded the heist and thus sanctioned Fitzsimons' murder. So did Schuman's satchel contain the stolen diamonds? It made sense in a way for the two criminals to bring the diamonds back to their point of origin. They could try and sell or trade them here, or over the Border in Mozambique, rather than attempt to get them out of South Africa. They must have well placed contacts here and in Beira. And despite de Castenet's freedom of movement, Paul didn't believe a British army officer could easily transport the

156

stones back to London or elsewhere in Europe and fence over two million pounds worth of illicit diamonds.

Whilst his men drank and ate Paul had occasionally thrown a glance across the room where de Castenet, Schuman and the two other men were still sitting. They had seemingly entrenched themselves. The beer bottles had mounted up and the plumes of cigarette smoke raged continuously. They're not going to leave until we do, Paul felt sure of it. Everything that had happened since he'd arrived at Nyanga confirmed his thoughts. So, he needed to marshal these thoughts, factor them into his plan and brief his men.

Lauwrens spoke again and it focused Paul's mind, 'Your Rover and all the gear is safe and secure on my farm, so how do you want to play it, boet?'

'Can you take your wheels, your bakkie? Be independent for some time?'

'I can, Paul, my wife has her own. She knows I'm on a mission.'

'Good. What's the driving time from here to Mutare?' Paul asked.

'No time at all, hour and half most likely. Two hours maximum.'

'I have to get to Mutare tomorrow,' said Paul. 'I'm also duty bound to keep up appearances here until I depart, which will be in the morning. So, Vino, I'd like you to take Taff and Lefty back to your farm tonight and then we'll divide our forces tomorrow morning.'

Evans asked, "Ow so, boss?"

'Like this, Taff: We're four and they're four. I need to split them. I need that shiftless bastard de Castenet and the Afrikaner, Schuman to follow me. They know what's going on. They're at the heart of everything and I don't know enough yet to let them out of my sight.' Paul paused and took a drink. 'And they now have two more in tow and I have no idea what their intention is or what they're capable of. No good, of that I'm sure.'

'I do know these two fellows,' interrupted Lauwrens and Paul looked at him enquiringly, 'and they are bad. They're guns-for-hire, mercs, ex-RLI hard nuts but they never made the Scouts. They take work wherever, in SA or Moz and their names are Grenville and Tanyard.'

'G and T, eh,' said Paul, 'pretty much as I'd thought.' He went on, 'So that fits OK.' He looked at Evans and Lauwrens. 'Taff, you're the senior and I need you and Vino to keep eyes on G and T. Tail them wherever they go, even if it leads to where I am. They may try to kill you, put you out of action, they may not. I have no idea. But stay alive, of course, even if you have to put them out of action or kill them yourselves. Do you have a difficulty with that, Vino?'

Lauwrens chuckled. 'Do I have a difficulty? For fuck's sake, Paul, there's nothing more I'd like. Those two bastards are past their sell-by-date, my friend, and if I can assist them to crossover to Hades then I'd jump at the chance.' As an afterthought he said, 'There's no shortage of places to lose a couple of bodies in the bush, and I know plenty of them.'

Paul said, 'Take what weapons and gear you might need, Taff, but leave sufficient for Lefty and myself.' Evans nodded. Shoesmith looked at Paul expectantly. 'We're going to Mutare tomorrow and I fully expect Majors Richard de Castenet and Wentzel Schuman to follow me. I'm pretty sure they think their destiny lies in my hands even though I don't think they're sure that I know it does.'

'Cor fuckin' 'ell, Paul, what does all that mean?' Evans asked.

'What it means is this,' and Paul began to tell the story and at the same time outline his developing plan. 'This is my take, you understand? These two majors are bad, bad bastards who kill people for their criminal ends. The British officer has gone rogue. His and Schuman's business starts here in Zimbabwe but it extends through into Mozambique and South Africa. Not only do they have people killed but their actions threaten the livelihoods of many people and could potentially impact on the highly sensitive politics of the region.' Paul had a fleeting memory of Nikki Walker-Haig and Danny Dalloway's contract. 'Anything more than that I can't say at the moment. They initially thought I was on a fact-finding mission here but they had an inside tip-off when we were in Harare that I might not be.'

'So that's why they have to keep you in sight, boss,' stated Shoesmith.

'Exactly. And that's why they're not sure if I know what they're up to.'

'Gotcha,' said Evans.

'As I said, I have to be in Mutare for a meeting at The Wise Owl Motel on Saturday morning,' and I have to find Nikki there, if I can, Paul didn't add. 'So if you all come into the Battle School in the morning in both vehicles, we'll sort and stow the gear properly, and then Lefty and I will head down to Mutare.'

'Towing the two majors behind us,' added Shoesmith.

'Come to the Commandant's guest cottage at zero nine hundred hours. I'll have a leisurely breakfast in the Mess before then and show my face. The cottage is private and we can sort everything out there before setting off. OK? Vino, Taff, try and lead G and T on a bit of wild goose chase if you can, but get into the Wise Owl on Saturday, in daylight, whatever happens.'

'Roger that, boss,' said Evans.

Lauwrens nodded his head in agreement. Paul guessed by the look in his eyes that he was weighing up the implications and consequences of what he was now involved in; but by the smile playing around his mouth he seemed to be happy with it all. 'I know exactly where we can take them,' he said. 'Show you a bit of the countryside as well, Taff.'

'Oh fuckin' lovely that is,' retorted Evans, 'a bleedin' educational country ramble. That's all I need right now.' They all chuckled at Evans's fake dissatisfaction.

'Keep in touch with Lefty on the satphone if you can,' Paul said. Evans nodded. 'Oh, before I forget and find myself in a bind, did you bring the money with you, Taff?'

'Thought you'd never ask, boss! Thought I'd 'ave a fuckin' great pile of wonga all to me'self. 'Course I did. Just as was requested,' and Evans unbuttoned one of the leg pockets of his bush combats and extracted two neatly banded stacks of banknotes. One was all US Dollars. The other was a mix of South African Rand, Zimbabwean

Dollars and Mozambican Meticals. Paul had brought some travel cash with him but that was almost gone. He'd known it was more than likely he'd need big bucks and it was always better to have too much than too little, and to have more US Dollars than local stuff. Who knows, he might have buy a helicopter in order to get out of the country, although he wasn't planning on it yet.

'Are you boys OK for cash?' Paul asked Evans and Shoesmith. Both nodded.

Shoesmith said, 'The Director back in Duke of York's made sure we had what we might need, so we're well off.'

'Good,' said Paul. He made a quick judgement. US Dollars might be a bit too obvious for Lauwrens but the man must have some money for immediate needs. Paul rifled through the stack of local currency notes and extracted two hundred dollars in twenty and ten dollar denominations. He went on his observations of buying power and the cost of things during the trip up from South Africa. A Dollar had roughly the buying power of a British Pound, so two hundred should do it for now. 'Here, Vino,' he said, 'you must have some of Her Majesty's filthy lucre, even though I'm guessing you're probably a staunch anti-British Government man!' Paul couldn't resist the gentle tease as he passed the notes across to Lauwrens.

'Hey man, that's too much, honest,' Paul resisted the man's attempt to hand it back with a gently insistent push of the man's arm and a genuine smile. 'Thanks. That will buy rations and gas. And no, we're not universally against the Queen, we're mostly from British stock. We were just against being told what to do from London. Anyway, that's all gone, disappeared into history. Now we have the problem of Mugabe. But hey,' Lauwrens looked philosophically at Paul and the others, 'politics is not worth playing here any more, we'll lose. So we have to be prepared for it and make a plan.' Which is what the Wealth Protection Cooperative is doing, thought Paul, but probably on a larger scale than the likes of Vino Lauwrens aspired to. Or was this true? Was Lauwrens part of the scheme, a wealth-contributing member, anticipating the collapse of the country, as he'd just alluded? Did he even know Victor Fitzsimons? Not the time to open that

160

particular can of worms, Paul decided, he'd find out during the coming days.

'Let's call it a night,' Paul stated. He looked across at de Castenet's table to confirm what he'd seen out of the corner of his eye some minutes ago, that the four men had gone. 'From what you've told us, Vino, G and T will know who you are and where you stay, but the three of you take all necessary steps to make sure you're not tailed out of here. And check the surveillance and security back at your farm. Can I trust you blokes to do it?' Paul added teasingly.

'Fuck off, boss, 'course you can. Lefty and me'll do stags when we get back to Vino's place, just to make sure all the gear an' stuff stays secure. One of us'll be in the barn with the wagon at all times.'

'I'll see you all in the morning, then. Zero nine hundred. Ready for action.' Paul stood and stretched his back. It had turned chilly. He would be glad to get hold of his gear tomorrow. He'd made sure Evans and Shoesmith brought all the protective clothing he might need for hot days and cold nights, along with his weapons. 'Taff,' he said, 'since you've got loads of dosh, can you settle the bill with the Mess staff? Thanks for that.'

'Got me again, boss. Good one!' They all laughed.

Paul Stanton made his way back to the Commandant's guest cottage. He saw no bad people. Tomorrow it would be different. But he hoped, too, to see more friends and one woman in particular.

* * *

SINCE STANTON HAD summarily dispensed with him outside the Battle School Headquarters, de Castenet had churned over the possibilities of what it, and all that had followed, might mean. Of course he'd eavesdropped Stanton's talk with Radebe and so knew the man was going to Mutare tomorrow, but what for and why? And then the bastard had dismissed him like he was some fucking corporal! Christ, it made his blood boil! What the fuck had happened in the space of twelve hours to invoke such a change in the man, to make de Castenet suddenly surplus to Stanton's requirements? Well, obviously the fact that Stanton's SAS mates were suddenly, inexplicably coming here. How was that even possible?

Almost in a desperate attempt to grab at a shred of reality, de Castenet had made his duty call back to the British Embassy in Pretoria, to check in with the Defence staff, and the Brigadier himself had come on the line. de Castenet had quickly brought him up to date but did not mention Stanton's unilateral onward plan. Then the DA detonated the next little bombshell in de Castenet's fast-dissembling world when he said, 'I understand Colonel Stanton is going on to Mutare tomorrow, on his own, and he has the means to do so. Well that's fine, Richard, and I'm sure you and Major Schuman have provided every assistance possible. So my advice would be to complete whatever liaison tasks the two of you still have in Zimbabwe and then make your way back to Pretoria when the time is right. The weekend is almost upon us, so have some quality time, too. I haven't spoken to Schuman's boss, Director Langlands, but I feel sure he would be of the same opinion.' *Have some quality time!* Was his DA taking the piss? *Be of the same opinion*? No, not good. It was clear to de Castenet that both the DA and Director Langlands knew exactly what was going on.

As he'd put the 'phone down Richard de Castenet recalled his nightmare in Berlin in 1986. He'd been blackmailed over the security breach in Northern Ireland by one of his corporals, the pestilential Shaggy Drinkwater, and the whole affair had ruined his career. *Stanton had been there in Berlin at the same time*. Although de Castenet hadn't known it then, Stanton had been Drinkwater's nemesis, and therefore, in a way, his own. Now, dangerously embroiled in a new career of crime and killing, *here was Stanton again, for fuck's sake*, up close and personal, right in amongst his affairs, exuding a sense of calm and control as if he knew exactly what de Castenet was involved in! All it needed, de Castenet thought perversely, would be for that bastard, General Charles Grace, to make an appearance. He'd been the man at the top who'd sealed his fate in Berlin. He'd been the brigade commander of them both in Northern Ireland. No, that would be too much.

He'd discussed it with Schuman. The Afrikaner said, 'So, bru, we know Stanton met with Ken Rose in Harare but we don't know why, except that it was a private meet, because Rose's Personal Advisor told us so.' Schuman drew heavily on his cigarette and let the smoke trickle from his nostrils and mouth as he said smugly, 'Christ, but that man is gold dust, bru! He's only been working for Rose for three months, but already he's given us the detail about the diamond shipment. He rifles Rose's mail, eavesdrops some of his personal calls, even tails the man sometimes when he leaves the office. How fucking brilliant is that, hey?'

de Castenet asked in reply, 'I know, and we met the man. But at Meikles, this man told us nothing substantial about Stanton, did he?' They'd been over this before. 'So, just because Stanton didn't tell us he was having a meeting with Rose in Harare does that make it suspicious?' Yes, it most probably does, de Castenet said to himself, because Rose's PA had been told to pass Stanton the meeting note clandestinely and on no occasion had Stanton mentioned it to either him or Schuman during the next day's onward journey to Nyanga. It was pointless to grasp at straws. 'Yes it does,' he answered his own question, and Schuman looked at him almost sympathetically. Keep it together de Castenet. He went on, 'Let's assume the worst and that Ken Rose has had some sniff of what's been going on with the movement of wealth out of Zim and somehow Stanton's bogus mission here is connected to it.' The very statement of this possibility made de Castenet pause for thought. Christ! If true...

Schuman said, 'But Rose's man, my man, told us nothing about this, boet. He said there was no evidence from Rose's notes or calls or meetings that Rose was suspicious in any way.' Which was what the man had said to them in Harare, de Castenet reflected, but Ken Rose was the Head of Zimbabwe's CIO, so of course he had personal secrets! Schuman continued, 'Maybe Stanton was being briefed on the politics, man, maybe, just maybe,' Schuman let his words hang there.

'Maybe. So why is he going on to Mutare tomorrow, without us, and why does he tell me that he has some colleagues from the SAS meeting him here?'

And Major Wentzel Schuman had no answer to that, other than to say, 'Well we have to get to Mutare, too, bru, to meet our contact there, so hey, we'll keep tabs on Stanton and his men whatever.' He added, 'And I've arranged for two mercs, ex-Rhodesian Light Infantry, to meet me here a little later. We'll have more forces, man, which is good for us.' Schuman smiled grimly, tapped the worn canvas satchel that always hung across his chest or tucked by his side, and said, 'And we still have the stones, man, we still have the money. Our contact in Mutare may surprise us and have a way of making us rich.'

So de Castenet and Schumann and the two men called Grenville and Tanyard had been sitting at their table in the Mess drinking beer when Paul Stanton, accompanied by two veterans from 22 SAS had brazenly stood before them at their table and said hello. No, de Castenet had thought, this man is determined to be my nemesis; this was fucking bad juju. He'd had no answer to the swaggering confidence Paul Stanton had exuded in front of him and those he was with, and he'd felt weak and dispirited as a result.

That had been two hours ago. Now Richard de Castenet was dead-dog tired, still uncertain and frankly out of patience with the day. Waiting any longer and watching the bastard Paul Stanton with his two SAS hard men cronies and the Zimbabwean local he had been told was an ex-Selous Scout, was not conducive to his darkening mood. His head was still spinning. The constant nagging talk of Schuman and the two ex-RLI hoodlums who had suddenly joined their party hadn't helped. Nor had the onslaught of Castle lager and the continuous toxic smoke from their cigarettes. He made the decision to call it a night, but Schuman cut in before he could say it.

'We're going to have to kill these fuckers, bru. Trust me. You've said it all. That half-Colonel Stanton knows something.' Schuman was almost drunk.

We might, thought de Castenet, but it would be harder than Schuman imagined. He was no longer totally sure about Schuman's judgement. 'Yes, Wentzel, perhaps, but tomorrow we do as we agreed. I have the feeling Stanton will divide his forces to divide us, which is what I'd do.' He got to his feet, conscious of a flicker of head movement from Stanton where he sat across the room. 'We go to Mutare in the wake of Stanton. We have two bakkies. We stick to him like ticks to a bush dog. You guys,' he gestured at Grenville and Tanyard, 'will come with us if they all move together, but if any of them break away and we have two targets, then you follow that party, unless it's Stanton. Yes?' The men nodded. 'We reveille early, very early, I want none of these bastards slipping away unseen. Meet me here when the Mess opens. I'll make sure about Stanton.'

'OK, boet,' responded Schuman.

The two big Zimbabwean ex-soldiers simply nodded their heads. Their eyes were semi-glazed and bloodshot from all the drink and smoke. What a fucking pair, thought de Castenet. 'One final thing,' he said, 'Stanton is mine. If we have to kill these bastards then so be it. But no one, no one, kills Stanton without my say-so. Got it?' They all did. 'I'll see you at zero seven hundred. Good night,' he said and left.

Fifteen minutes later, standing hidden in the trees adjacent to the Commandant's guest cottage, Richard de Castenet watched Paul Stanton go inside and switch on lights. He was alone. Five minutes later de Castenet quietly slipped out of cover and made his way to his bed in the Mess. He could have no idea that once inside his cottage, Paul Stanton had powered up his satellite 'phone and made three brief calls: to General Charles Grace, to Brigadier Colin Bullock and to Ken Rose. de Castenet could not have known that as a result of these calls, and Stanton's earlier decisions, his personal outcomes were being ruthlessly shaped. For one thing, Charles Grace was putting his affairs in place so he could fly down to South Africa for the coming weekend and base himself initially in the Embassy in Pretoria. No, de Castenet was not the master of his own destiny; his earlier premonition of déjà vu was coming to pass.

But, ignorant of all this, Richard de Castenet felt he was all set for Mutare, and what might ensue. He would follow Stanton there tomorrow. He'd set out his conditions for the man and so Stanton's fate would be his decision. It never crossed his mind that perhaps he shouldn't have made such conditions. It never crossed his mind to question whether such insistence might prove to be his downfall. Only time would tell, and then the fates would decide.

The fates might also have told him that such a reckoning would not be long in coming.

CHAPTER FIFTEEN

THE MOZLON FARM at Manica was slightly smaller than the other of Danny Dalloway's contract responsibilities, which was why he'd based himself at the farm at Nhamatanda and put Omparsad, with his team of Gurkhas, in charge at Manica.

However, having been at Manica now for thirty-six hours, familiarised himself with Omparsad's layout and system, which was, deliberately, a replica of the one he'd put in place at Nhamatanda, and talked through with his Gurkhas and the farm's local management personnel what was going on in the surrounding countryside, Dalloway was beginning to feel he'd got it wrong. He probably ought to be here. There was rebel trouble brewing and leadership and communications would be vital. The Gurkhas and the managers were fairly sure of an impending threat and they were the ones with their fingers on the pulse of the place.

Dalloway had come to Manica for three reasons, he believed: to discuss with Omparsad the possible rebel Renamo threat to the farm, which he now believed was very real indeed; to confirm the whereabouts of Nikki Walker-Haig; and to try and ascertain what had happened to Victor Fitzsimons. Omparsad had been unable to allay his uncertainties about the latter two reasons: the Walker-Haig Memsaheb he had heard from but had not seen, though she must be in Mutare; and he hadn't seen Fitzsimons Saheb recently. And in the wake of their discussions about the rebels, Dalloway came to the conclusion that

Nikki and Fitzsimons would have to remain as lower priorities for the moment. Then he had one of his recurring pangs of guilt when the thought of Paul Stanton suddenly flashed into his mind. Of course Nikki Walker-Haig and Victor Fitzsimons *were* high priorities...but, he reasoned, the rebels *were* on the move and they appeared to have violence in their hearts. What was he to do? Simple. Get out there, find the bastards and kill them.

What he didn't or couldn't know was that everything was linked and that Paul Stanton was the common denominator. But this was all a little way into the future and Danny Dalloway had no notion of it. What he did have was the real and present danger of hostile Renamo rebel activity.

It was now Friday late afternoon and at Dalloway's request Omparsad Pun had gathered all the farm's key players in the canteen room. The working day was drawing to a close anyway. Outside it was still very hot. Inside the room the ceiling fans beat the warm air into a semblance of coolness, but only just. Spirals of cigarette smoke rose up from the clusters of tables and chairs around which these key men sat: the Farm Manager, Philippe Cruz, with his sub-managers and heads of services; the locally recruited militia commanders with their subordinates; and Dalloway's Gurkhas of whom there were twelve in all, with Omparsad as their commander and Kindraman the second-in-command. The canteen bar had been opened and everyone had a cold drink of some type.

As he had done at Nhamatanda for his briefing there, Dalloway had pinned a large-scale map of the Farm and a map of the surrounding countryside on a wallboard behind him. Everyone could see it. He was looking at it intently, thinking his thoughts and subconsciously willing it to talk to him, when Omparsad's words brought his mind sharply back into focus.

'It is the Chicamba Real dam area, saheb, in the forests somewhere that surround it,' said Omparsad Pun speaking in English. 'I am sure of it, and so are the boys,' Omparsad gestured to the other Gurkhas and Mozambicans gathered and sitting there. 'And from what you have told us, saheb,' Omparsad added, 'your contact with the rebels looked like they were heading that way. There is the possibility the *dushman* rebels have a base there.'

Dalloway had shown Omparsad the map and the writings he'd found on the Renamo rebels. They'd discussed it all with Kindraman and they had tried to plot some semblance of coordination between the hand-drawn map and the ordnance survey maps they used.

Dalloway let Omparsad's words hang there for a few moments for all of them to digest as he lit another cigarette and drew in the smoke heavily. He looked around the room and his eye patch seemed to glower at his Gurkhas and Mozambicans. They all ignored its look. They had heard, or knew for themselves, that Major Danny Dalloway was a warrior-man who cared for his men, irrespective of how his scarred and eye-patched face may have presented itself to them or the rest of the world.

Omparsad was undoubtedly correct in what he'd said, but Dalloway felt he needed public corroboration from the Mozambicans. He singled out one of the Mozambican militia commanders, a man Omparsad had referred to earlier, and said, 'Andy, what do you and the other militia commanders think?' Andy Da Silva was a half-Portuguese, half-Afrikaner who had bush warfare experience but had now decided upon a life of more stability and more cash reward.

Da Silva rose to his feet uninvited and went to stand by Dalloway at the wallboard. 'Do you mind if I use these maps, Major?'

'Of course not, please go ahead. Use the pointer.' Dalloway was intrigued. This man had something about him. He glanced at Omparsad who smiled faintly and enigmatically.

Da Silva spoke clearly and persuasively and his English was excellent. 'Our farm here is crucial to the rebels,' he sketched the outline and layout of MozLon Manica as it was on the large-scale drawing pinned next to the map of the countryside. 'We have easy access to the routes into Mutare, south alongside the Zim border, and to the north, and we are a presence in this part of the oil pipeline.' The man was good, thought Dalloway. 'We are building a two hundred hectare farm here and it is almost complete,' Da Silva continued. He was tall-ish, balding with his hair cropped to his scalp, burned brown and weathered by sun and life and he wore the uniform bush fatigues of the farm's militia. He looked fit and capable. 'We have power, water, buildings, security and we will have an airstrip.' Everyone was listening intently. This man had charisma.

'Go on, Andy,' said Dalloway.

'We have brought some of the local townships into our perimeter and we have offered them hope and more importantly, a living. We have planted our crops and we wait to harvest and export. We are a living example of the future of Mozambique.' And this is anathema to the Renamo rebels, Dalloway said to himself. 'These Renamo scum hate us for all this,' and Da Silva gestured to the room, the people and the outside world. He became more focused and looked at Dalloway closely. 'Major,' he said, 'for some weeks now we have picked up some little signs of Renamo movement.' Da Silva looked at Omparsad.

'We have, saheb,' said Omparsad, nodding slowly at Dalloway.

'We patrol outside the perimeter of the farm,' Da Silva continued, 'we talk to the local people and they tell us things in return for some food and some seeds, which Omparsad authorises us to give them.' Good old Om, thought Dalloway, as always, attuned to the needs of poor folk. Win the hearts and minds of the people and the rest will follow. 'These *are* ex-Renamo, and we all believe they are without sanction from the official Renamo Party. We believe also that these rebels operate from a base, a camp that is somewhere to the south and east of here.' Da Silva pointed to the farm's location on the map and traced the distance down to the westernmost finger of the Chicamba Dam area; the tip of the lakes closest to Manica and to the sanctuary of the Vumba Forest and Zimbabwe. Da Silva finished speaking. He'd said his piece. The strategy of the Farm's business was not his to decide, it was Dalloway's.

'Andy, thank you,' Dalloway responded. 'Please sit down.' Dalloway scanned his one-eyed gaze intentionally in panorama fashion across all the people in the room. He'd brought with him his trusted vehicle crew, Ernesto and Pinto, trusted as well as tried and tested in the recent firefight they'd had with the Renamo rebels, but that was all.

170

They sat a little off to one side and looked at him earnestly, as did the others. The expectation and uncertainty of what he would say next was obvious in the eyes of everyone. Dalloway smiled in an attempt to lighten the atmosphere. He knew what they had to do and part of him relished the prospect and the other part held a trace of fear. He said, 'You are most likely to be correct, and in addition to what you say, we will receive no help from the Frelimo military, since their presence is not here. So we have to deal with the situation ourselves. As a first step I believe we must mount a reconnaissance patrol to locate the rebels and determine their strength. Do you agree?' There was a ripple of sighs and exhalation of breath around the room. He looked at the Gurkhas, who all nodded their heads. Omparsad and Kindraman were smiling. Da Silva and the other five Mozambican militia platoon commanders also nodded. The Farm's civilian management team, all direct employees of MozLon, looked less certain.

'How will this happen, Danny, and when?' asked Philippe Cruz.

'Soon, Philippe, we must find these rebels soon. But,' Dalloway said, 'you and your team must keep the Farm's business going. This is *most* important. The recce patrol will be small, nine men only in total, so the security and the production business of the farm will continue as it if nothing had happened.'

'I would like to go, Major,' said Da Silva.

Dalloway smiled. Good, he thought. 'Are you a tracker, Andy?'

'I am, Major. From the bush wars.'

'Then you shall go.' Dalloway had thought about the composition of the patrol. It needed to be small and it needed to move quickly. Its purpose was reconnaissance. Fighting would come later, most probably. 'Here's how we shall do it,' and Dalloway sketched out his plan for them all. They needed to know and to feel part of the overall scheme. 'Two bakkies, mine and Kindraman's, mine with four and Kindraman's with five people.' Dalloway knew Omparsad would be disappointed but he needed to stay at the Farm. 'It is maybe twenty, twenty-five kilometres cross-country to the approximate area of Chicamba where we need to start looking. Each vehicle will have a radio operator.' Dalloway looked at Ernesto. The Mozambican looked

171

worried. 'Ernesto, you will stay with the vehicles, with Kindraman's driver. Om,' Dalloway turned to his senior Gurkha, 'please select three of the Gurkha boys to come with us, two with Kindraman as his radio operator and vehicle security, one with me. Andy, you will come with me. Om, please select one section commander also to travel with Kindraman. *Tik Chha?*'

'Je, saheb.'

'We will do the detailed map planning after this meeting, and Andy you need to be involved. But wherever we decide on for the vehicle harbour area, Ernesto will remain there as radio operator and Kindraman's driver and one of the Gurkhas will provide security. We need radio contact at all times. The patrol itself will be me, Andy, Kindraman, one of the section commanders and two Gurkhas, one as radio operator. Is that clear? And so, Philippe, the farm management and security will be largely normal.'

'Thank you, Danny, I appreciate what you are planning. It will be a great comfort to us all. When do you propose to leave?'

'Tomorrow, in the morning. We shall take two days' rations and water, rifles and one machinegun per vehicle with fighting scales of ammunition, walkie-talkies and spare batteries. We take protection but we do not fight, not yet, unless we absolutely have to. I want to find them and I don't want them to know we have. No fires, no lights. Dress will be bush combats, chest webbing and a daypack. Unless something goes wrong, I plan to be back here on Sunday before dark, at the latest.'

'That will be a relief,' said Philippe Cruz.

Dalloway said to everyone, 'We are all here to serve MozLon. That is our priority and you all are the most important people to do so. However,' and he fixed them anew with his skew-eyed glare, 'if there is the slightest possibility that these Renamo *bastardos* are where we believe them to be and that they will try to disrupt and harm us here, at Manica, then we have to find them and make a plan to stop them.' What Danny Dalloway really wanted to say was: *that if these fucking Renamo scum have any thoughts whatsoever about wrecking this contract with MozLon, then he and his Gurkhas were going to find them and kill the whole fucking lot of them!* Although, he admitted to himself, he wasn't sure he had the capability to do so. But, hey, nothing ventured nothing gained. So instead he said what he said, and everyone nodded agreement.

Danny Dalloway was old, experienced and scarred enough to know he'd thrown down a particular gauntlet and that retrieving it safely might well be at some cost. But it was a cost he had to pay. His Contract depended on it.

So for the moment his concerns for Nikki Walker-Haig and Victor Fitzsimons were lost in his thoughts of the probable impending battle with enemy forces. The bad people.

* * *

NIKKI WALKER-HAIG WAS disappointed. Despite it being Friday, Victor Fitzsimons wasn't at the Wise Owl Motel nor had he been there for over two weeks, said the Manager. Damn and blast she said to herself. OK, she then decided, I'll call Paul in his office. The Manager had reluctantly given her the telephone and advised her on the difficulty of getting an outside line to anywhere, let alone London. Thank you, but I'll try all the same, she'd replied, and had promised not to be long on the call if she did get through. Which she did, only to be disappointed again. Lieutenant Colonel Stanton was not in London, was all she was told and all she was going to be told, according to the faceless staff officer in MOD Whitehall who'd reluctantly taken her call after she'd insisted on speaking with someone in authority, *for God's sake, as I'm in Africa and desperate, please!*

Now it was well after work on a Friday and Nikki was not looking forward to eating a solitary dinner and going to her room to face another period of self-questioning and worry. For a start, what was she going to do tomorrow? Travel to Manica on her own? She could, and in that decision she decided to try and contact Omparsad at Manica first thing in the morning. Or she could be a good girl and go back to managing the GCL offices in the Mutare Country Club. She chided herself: come on Walker-Haig, stop your self-pity and get yourself to the bar before having something to eat. So she went to the bar, sat at a stool and ordered a long gin and tonic. As the alcohol hit her system she sighed with the immediate release of tension.

And then the man spoke and her world changed forever and all her problems were suddenly solved.

'Hello,' the strong, English voice behind her said, 'do you come here often? I can't imagine that a strikingly beautiful woman like you would be on her own? Where, may I ask, is your man-friend, because I'm afraid I shall have to call him out and deal with him, in order to win your hand, fair lady.'

Nikki Walker-Haig's heart leapt into her mouth and her breathing seized momentarily. She turned around on her bar stool and her eyes glazed with tears of relief, joy and love. This tall, broad-shouldered man stood there. He had very short-cut fair-ish hair and the bluest, blue, strikingly icy-blue eyes she had ever seen. Eyes that looked deep into her soul and pierced her heart with the power and love they held. His face was newly tanned with a few days of African sun and grizzled with the day's stubble. She saw his lovely, big bent nose and the warm smile playing around his mouth and her heart soared. She had kissed those loving lips. The man was dressed in journey-worn tan cotton trousers, desert boots and a blue linen shirt with a pullover draped over his shoulders. As always his dress looked fashionably shagged out, but his physical presence was alert, and those eyes told anyone and everyone who met or saw him that this was not an ordinary man. This was a loving man but also a dangerous one.

This was Paul Stanton and he was *her* man. 'Oh, Paul, Paul, oh, Paul, why are you here and I'm so, so pleased to see you...' Her words slipped away as she tried to stand up to hug and hold this man who out of nowhere had re-balanced her world and filled it with the love she realised in a flash she had missed desperately.

Paul Stanton was with her again, *her* man.

CHAPTER SIXTEEN

SHE HADN'T FORGOTTEN how beautifully he made love to her and how completely in tune with him it made her feel; but it had been a long time since they were last together and her passion had been intense and very emotional. She had cried gently and freely as their bodies joined and all her fear, uncertainty and loneliness was washed away in a flood of pure love; and she had cried out in release and happiness at the physical intensity of their lovemaking. Paul Stanton was her man and her body and soul loved him totally and in every way. She knew her emotions would give her the strength to walk with him on their life's journey. Nikki Walker-Haig knew this man was her true love. The thoughts made her shudder in delight and her body generated small tremors which seemed to make Paul Stanton turn on his side, look at her smilingly and rise up out of their bed.

She had, however, if she was truthful, forgotten just a little bit how strong yet battered his body was. All through the night he had held her in his arms and told her through the loving touch of his hands how he felt for her, and she had let herself be taken into his protection and reciprocated his feelings with her own embraces. They had stayed close, locked together, stuck together in their intimacy and the physical heat of love, passion and, if she was honest, the heat of the night. It had been wonderful. Now it was early morning, the light of day was already flooding into their room, and Paul Stanton stood at the bedside and stretched.

'Do they hurt at all, Paul?' she asked him. Nikki was referring to his war-wounds. Although he'd told her what had happened to him, he'd always forestalled her deeper enquiries by saying that he was fully fit and mended. Now, though, he was her man and she needed to know his truths.

There was a matrix of untidy scar-ridges, three in all, low down on his abdomen below his rib cage. Argentinean grenade fragments from 1982. In response to her question Paul fingered them absently with his right hand. Then his left moved to the two stars of scarred flesh just underneath his heart and right pectoral. Berlin 1986. The bullet entry wound where the German gangster had shot him, and where the friendly German surgeon had cut through his chest into the space between his inner and outer lung linings in order to empty his lung of blood. He would have died otherwise.

'No, not really,' Paul answered, 'not unless I really think about it.' He had told her that the German's 9mm bullet had torn its way upwards from below his heart, ripped his lung and lodged in the muscle of his right shoulder. He fingered the series of neat crossed incisions, about four inches long, on his shoulder, where the same German surgeon had operated to locate the bullet, repair the tissue and nerve damage and tidy him up. 'But sometimes,' and he looked at her with those piercingly blue, love-soaked eyes, 'if I'm honest, I almost feel a stab of pain in my heart.' Nikki said nothing. She raised herself on one elbow and looked at him. 'I know it sounds pathetic, and I think it's psychosomatic. I think it's because the bastard almost killed me and it's as if my heart tells me every now and then that I was very, very lucky to live. The jab of thought-induced pain is a reminder of my mortality.' Paul turned from her and started to move towards the en suite shower room. 'Christ,' he said, 'what have you done to me, woman. If the boys ever hear me talking like this they'll really think I've gone soft!'

Nikki leapt out of bed and grabbed him from behind, wrapping her arms around his broad chest and deliberately pressing her breasts against his back. He stopped and stirred. She was conscious of the hardness of her nipples; they were never soft and relaxed when she

176

was with her man. She pressed herself provocatively into his buttocks and started to move her hand naughtily round his hip and felt his body tense. 'You're not soft, Stanton,' she said, 'anything but, it seems to me!' and she laughed out loud.

Paul turned to face her. 'Unhand me, woman, and stop that monkey business. The new day is upon us and there is a whole heap of things to do. There's no time for you to have your wicked way with me again.' He broke free of her and walked into the shower room and put on the tap. He started to brush his teeth and his words were confused by the sounds of water splashing and the gurgle of toothpaste. 'Do you not remember what we discussed last night with Lefty?'

'I do, Paul. OK, I've left you alone. I'll make some coffee. You concentrate on shaving off that skin-grating stubble and getting that disgusting body of yours sparkling clean. But be sure to leave me some hot water, please.'

Yes, the new day was upon them and they needed to be ready to face it.

* * *

NIKKI REMEMBERED CLEARLY what had been discussed the night before.

Although it had been an unexpected and loving reunion for her and Paul, the occasion was salted through with the harsh realities of their situations.

To begin with, Paul hadn't been on his own. He'd had a tough, battle-hardened SAS Sergeant with him, whom he'd introduced as Lefty Shoesmith. Where did they get their nicknames? She'd asked the question and got the obvious answer: Lefty was left-footed. Not Religion, mind, just left footed.

They'd all eaten together and Nikki had discovered she could put aside her desire to be with her man for a while longer because Paul Stanton would never let one of his trusted men, his brothers, feel excluded, even in a situation like this. Nikki loved him even more for it. It showed his soul to be true and fair and reinforced her understanding, as she had learned with Dalloway and his Gurkhas, that the bonds of soldierly comradeship were at least as strong as true love. It made Paul Stanton special in her eyes.

Then, of course, the talk turned to why Paul was there and why she was there, and the whole avalanche of uncertainties surrounding Paul's mission and Dalloway's contract started to slide and it could have overwhelmed her if it hadn't been for Paul's optimism and the deep, deep seated joy she felt at being with him so unexpectedly. Inevitably much was left unsaid; and through the meal, despite Paul's attention and diligence, she saw the tension in the two men and knew there was an imminent, dangerous situation that they had to deal with and into which she had unexpectedly intruded.

Apart from the period they had been true lovers, she and Paul had never spent much time together, with her working in Nepal and him in London. He'd told her a little of his past and Danny Dalloway and the Gurkhas had told her a little more. She did not know who Major Richard de Castenet was, but Paul had told her why he was important now and a brief history of their involvement. She did not know General Charles Grace, or understand how he could influence Paul's life, but she did know that Paul's role was pivotal to a highly sensitive black ops mission sanctioned by the Prime Minister herself.

Nikki had no real awareness of the world of the SAS and she did not know how deeply into the unspoken, unwritten, deniable world of black, Special Forces operations, Paul's life was taking him. She'd seen his scars, of course, and he'd told her about them, superficially. Now, here with them, was one of Paul's SAS brothers, Lefty Shoesmith, who thankfully added a dose of reality to the surreal world they talked about. And most likely, very soon, she'd been told, she would meet one of the other brother-in-arms, called Taff Evans.

Finally, Nikki Walker-Haig would have been a liar if she had said she fully understood the *realpolitik* of southern Africa and how its reverberations impacted on their lives right now. She did understand a little of the Mozambique situation because it was germane to MozLon and Dalloway's contract, but she was truly ignorant of how the encroachment of Mugabe's thugs into the lives of Zimbabwean Whites had brought Paul here, now, and how the endgame of the Frelimo-Renamo civil war, MozLon's activities and illicit diamond smuggling could seriously bugger up Mrs Thatcher's diplomatic position and Danny's contract. Her contract.

During their dinner, Paul's explanations had been clear and succinct and Nikki had been aware that whilst telling her, he was also telling Lefty Shoesmith what was going on. It was, in its way, brutal stuff, despite the care in the words Paul used to try and soften what was happening. Being told of the killing of the lovely Victor Fitzsimons made her cry.

Paul said to her, 'Lefty and I know that de Castenet and Schuman trailed us from Nyanga, but we lost them on the outskirts of town. They must have contacts here and I'm guessing they have to meet them to talk about changes to their operation, so they'll be holed up somewhere close by, and watching us. The other half of their party went on the tail of Taff Evans and Vino Lauwrens when we left Nyanga yesterday.' By being addressed so directly Nikki felt a sense of almost unwelcome immersion in a world of danger and violence but forced herself to be calm and objective about it all. This was *her* man, after all, and he wouldn't endanger her. Paul looked at Shoesmith and said, 'We'll see them tomorrow, Lefty?'

'We will, Paul. Taff will have got it right. He and Vino knew what had to be done, boss.' Which meant, Nikki inwardly translated, that Taff Evans and the local, ex-SAS man, Vino Lauwrens, would *somehow, somewhere*, have ridded themselves of this Richard de Castenet's accomplices. Killed them and disposed of the bodies without trace or possibility of follow up. TIA. *This is Africa.*

Then Paul said, 'We're into the kill phase now because de Castenet and Schuman know I'm on to them.'

'What do you mean?' she asked him. His words had a chilling resonance to them.

'I mean that the enemy has an advantage and will use it soon and look for an opportunity to kill us.' Paul smiled and poured her some more dark red wine. Nikki took a drink gratefully. Shoesmith sat, relaxed, his presence calm and reassuring. He sipped his beer

179

from time to time. His eyes followed Paul's words, but otherwise he seemed unmoved by their import.

'Why?' She asked stupidly. 'Why right now, why not sometime later?' Despite Paul's matter-of-factness and Shoesmith's cool, she was foundering in her incipient fear.

'Because they don't have to wait to kill me, or Lefty and Taff,' Paul replied cryptically.

'And Vino, as well, boss,' said Shoesmith.

'Yes. And Vino. In fact the longer they leave it the greater the risk for them, I believe.' Paul sipped his wine. 'They're going to assume I might know what they've been up to because I had the meeting with Ken Rose in Harare, but they've probably assumed I don't know the detail of it all. They know I'm not here on a fact-finding mission and my actions towards de Castenet in Nyanga and the presence of Taff and Lefty, and now Vino, is an obvious declaration of suspicion on my part.'

Shoesmith said, 'So, boss, you've panicked them, forced their hand, and they're going to assume that by bumping us all off down here, in some form of accident, maybe, they'll get away with it?'

'Pretty close, Lefty.' Nikki couldn't believe the two men were speaking so casually about life and death. Paul said, 'But actually, trying to eliminate all of us would be mission impossible for them. It's me they have to kill. And they need to do it soon before I find out any more about their operation whilst I'm here.'

'In Mutare?' Nikki asked.

Paul smiled warmly and lovingly at Nikki and answered, 'Yes. Mutare *is* part of their operation, I'm sure of it even though I don't know how and neither do Ken Rose or John Sawyer back in Pretoria. It's the gateway into Mozambique. It's the hub from where the Zimbabwean Whites' Wealth Protection Cooperative moves the assets across the Border and ultimately to Beira and offshore to Portugal. It's the place where Victor Fitzsimons transited in order to be the WPC courier. No,' Paul took a deep breath, 'there is someone, or some people and some place or places in and around Mutare which are vital to de Castenet's and Schuman's criminal activity. And there are other people working for them. There have to be.'

'So we find them, boss? No probs.'

'We do, Lefty, we do exactly that. And we start tomorrow, after the meeting with Dick Hanney. And, Nik,' Paul said to her, 'even though the bad men want to kill us, me in particular, they won't find it so easy. Will they, Lefty?'

'No, Paul, they won't. And don't you worry, Miss Nikki, Taff and me'll take good care of your man. After all, I owe him one and Taff's trained to look after his officers. Ain't that right, boss?'

'Yes, Lefty, if you say so,' and Paul chuckled.

But despite the reassurances, it had not made Nikki feel any better.

* * *

PAUL SHOUTED FROM the bathroom, 'Hey, Nik, where's that coffee you promised?'

'Here,' Nikki responded.

Even though it had been many weeks since they'd shared each other's company let alone a room and a bed, she was exactly as he remembered her: uninhibitedly naked, and utterly comfortable in her own skin. Well why shouldn't be; she was beautiful. 'Thank you,' Paul said as Nikki handed him a mug of steaming black coffee. 'A dab of sugar for energy for the upcoming struggle?' He put the mug down on a side table and scrubbed his back dry with the big towel.

'Of course!'

He studied her. Her thick mane of hair had grown longer since London and lightened in the bleaching sun of Nepal and now Africa. Her mint chocolate eyes set above her finely chiselled little nose and warm, loving mouth were serious. The sun flooding into the room caught the flecks of green and brown so that they flashed like sparks off a flint when she turned her head and moved. 'Come with me,' he said and picked up his coffee and put his arm around her waist. He loved the feel of the firmness and smoothness of her body. They

181

moved to stand looking out of the big window of their self-contained room. The Wise Owl was very comfortable. It had all the conveniences they needed, including coffee and a stunning view eastwards across to the Vumba Mountains. 'Somewhere over there is where we have to take you, Nik. Somewhere over those mountains and through the denseness of the forests and the rivers and the bush scrub and tracks is Danny Dalloway's contract farm at Manica.' She turned to look at him. He said, 'So I guess we'll just have to go by road! I hope your papers are in order, miss.'

She punched him pathetically and laughed with him. 'Stupid boy, Stanton.'

'I know. And I stupidly love you, you lascivious, sexy woman.'

'Stop it, Paul. You're clean, I'm not, we have proper business to attend to, and I love you.'

'I can see!' Her small, perfect breasts jiggled and her nipples were rock hard. She was truly lovely. She tossed her mane of hair and stalked off to the bathroom. She waggled her bottom at him cheekily and, as always, it reminded him of the lines of the rugby song: something about...like a jelly on springs!

Paul got dressed quickly and sorted out his gear for the day ahead. He reckoned he needed the weekend to finish his business in Mutare. Despite his jocularity with Nikki he knew it was going to be a vital couple of days, riven with the possibility of extreme danger.

For some time now he'd felt certain that he had to go into Mozambique, to travel the journey that Victor Fitzsimons had travelled, and he had to find out absolutely everything he could that might impact on HMG, MozLon and the British Army. The Prime Minister, Sir Reggie Hanlon and General Charles Grace all demanded it. That was at the strategic level. Lower down at the Operational level, Stephen Langlands, John Sawyer and Brigadier Bullock back in Pretoria needed reassurances. If he was going to remove de Castenet and Schuman then he had to do it in a way that left all of these people blameless. This was the Tactical level, his level and the arena in which Paul Stanton operated: undeniable and most impenetrably black.

But first there was Mutare. He and Nikki had talked about this during the night and made some sort of simple plan, the best kind, in his experience: Nikki would go back to the GCL offices in the Mutare Country Club and stay there, stay out of sight during the day, tending to business as usual and trying to establish contact with the MozLon farm at Manica. Hopefully she would discover what was going on with Danny Dalloway. So far neither de Castenet nor Schuman had seen her and Paul wanted it to stay that way. Having brought Nikki into his mission he had a responsibility to protect her, physically and emotionally. He had to keep her apart from the things he had to do. He didn't want her involved or to bear witness to the dark side of his life.

Paul walked to the bathroom door. He had stowed all his gear in his travel bag and was ready to go, but he wouldn't rush Nikki. He had some calls to make, anyway: to Taff Evans and Charles Grace, whom he fully expected to be in Pretoria by now. 'Nik, I'm going to find Lefty and stow my gear in the Rover. I also have to call Taff and Charles on the satphone. Take your time, but please don't leave the room 'til I come and get you or Lefty does. Lock the door. We'll have some breakfast before we go our separate ways.'

'Roger that, boss!' she said naughtily.

* * *

LEFTY SHOESMITH WAS waiting for Paul in the car park. 'I've spoken to Taff on the satphone, boss, he called in. He and Vino are on their way. Should be here for early afternoon. Taff said Vino's advice was for them to hole up in a place he knows out on the Old Beira Road. He's given me the coordinates. Apparently it's secure. An old abandoned petrol station overgrown with bush and off the beaten track. Said he'd call me when they got there.'

'Good. And their mission?'

'Successful, boss,' Lefty said, 'but Taff didn't give me any details other than he knows where our targets have their base and contacts here in Mutare.'

'Excellent!' said Paul. A great outcome, he thought. Taff Evans and Vino Lauwrens had clearly persuaded the two ex-RLI mercenaries to give over information. 'Any collateral?' he asked Shoesmith.

'No, boss, none, Taff said it was clean and that Vino was happy.'

Good. No forensics or other scraps of evidence. Two unmarked mounds of rocks and stones no doubt, in the rugged bush wilderness of Zimbabwe, concealing just two more victims of the troubled times of the country. Join the rest of the thousands of unmourned. Paul had no moral qualms about what Evans and Lauwrens had done. Anyone who was a threat would pay the price. It was a simple formula; and if you didn't like it then don't get involved. Simple. Now Paul could focus on his own problem.

'Lefty, give me ten minutes. I need to call General Grace. I'm pretty sure he'll be in Pretoria by now. So please round up Nikki, if you would, and take her into breakfast. I'll be with you pronto.'

'Roger that, Paul,' Shoesmith replied. 'The wagon's all set to go. Just need to load your grip. She looks pretty normal really, doesn't she?'

'She does,' Paul said.

The Special Forces 110 Series Land Rover, with its canopies up, looked like any of the other utility 4x4 vehicles that populated the extensive car park of the Wise Owl Motel. Bakkies, the locals called them; essential modes of on and off road transport in this part of the world. But looks could be deceptive, as Paul knew, because he'd been shown exactly how cleverly the Rover concealed its true identity. The beast might look a touch stressed and clearly well travelled, but it was a special mechanical build and would survive pretty much any pounding or battering from the local terrain. It had other special capabilities, too, in the vital areas of firepower, communications, navigation and survival. These secrets were concealed in cleverly in-built storage panniers underneath the seating. Paul's favourite 9mm Browning pistol was there, amongst a considerable range of firepower, which they might need.

Lefty went off and Paul powered up his satphone and dialled in the number of the British Embassy's SIS Station in Pretoria. The Duty

Operator responded. He wasn't aware that General Grace was in the building and John Sawyer certainly wasn't. It was Saturday morning. Paul told him to ensure the message was passed to General Grace as quickly as possible, and John Sawyer could also be told. The Duty Operator confirmed he would pass the message pronto. What was the message? Paul gave it to him: *I'm in Mutare. My team and I are good but there are going to be some incidents over the weekend that you all need to be briefed on and appropriate measures put in place at your end. Stephen Langlands will need to be info.* Paul fully expected Grace to call him back once he'd been given the update.

As yet, Paul did not require direct help; but Grace, Sawyer and Bullock needed to know where he was and the state of play. They would have pre-emptive measures to put in place, he was sure of it, and Sawyer's opposite number in the South African NIS, Stephen Langlands, would need to be updated. After all, there were going to be two unusual incidents fairly soon involving a British Army officer and a Major in the NIS in Pretoria, fatal incidents that would appear to be a combination of a difference of opinions and an accident. Paul had thought about this deeply and knew what he wanted to do. Whether he'd be able to carry it off as cleanly as he would like, still remained to be seen. He was now sure, though, that it would all happen over the weekend. And once finished, he'd have to get everyone across the border into Mozambique. There was no way back for him.

Paul then called Ken Rose in Harare. He knew Rose would have been in contact with Dick Hanney but Paul needed everything to be solid. The meeting was today, but Paul did not know the exact time or place.

'Thank you for the update, Paul,' said Ken Rose. He sounded fatalistic to Paul, but then his voice perked up. 'I've confirmed that my Assistant was the man providing detailed info to Schuman, but I don't think he's been doing it for very long, maybe six weeks at most, because he's only been working for me for three months. I'm fucking depressed by it, but I suppose I shouldn't be. In these times us Whites are taking whatever measures we can to secure a future. I mean, man, what am I doing but exactly that! Anyway, I'm watching him, I haven't

185

given him the hint that I know, but he's been pretty quiet since last week. I guess you've all been on the road, hey?'

'We have,' replied Paul.

'And I guess your Brit officer and that rancorous bastard Schuman have all the Intel they need to do what they are planning in Mutare.'

'I'm assuming so, Ken,' responded Paul. 'That's what I intend to find out today. But in order to do so I need confirmation that the meeting with Dick Hanney is set up?'

'Correct. He'll be at The Wise Owl at eleven hundred hours.'

Paul checked the time. It was eight-thirty. 'Thank you, Ken.' Paul had thought carefully about what he wanted to say next but having told Grace, Sawyer and Langlands, indirectly, Ken Rose had to know. Besides, he was an in-country ally who might prove vital. 'There's going to be a series of fatal incidents over the weekend involving the two individuals you've just referred to. Whatever the incidents are, and I'm pretty sure they're going to be unusual, they should be seen as internal feuding and an act of God. However, given the nationality of the men there may well be some sort of internal collateral effect. You'll be the best judge of this. Also, I think I'm going to have to leave behind some small items of evidence. If I were you, Ken, I would have someone you can really trust, here, who can react as first responder. I'll call you immediately the incidents have taken place. Are you comfortable with all this?'

There was a pause on the satellite line. The atmospherics were suddenly loud. 'I'm assuming that our mutual friends in Pretoria know and that you've cleared your lines with London, so yes, I am. I'll have someone on site who works directly for me and who can initially bypass the local Police. No, on second thoughts, use Dick Hanney. That would work, wouldn't it?'

It would work, thought Paul. Brilliantly. 'That would work really well. Thank you.' Having Dick Hanney close at hand to deal with the collateral would be perfect. It made the plan cleaner to execute than he'd hoped for.

Rose asked, 'Do you need any other help?' What a good man. No histrionics just the offer of help. Well, there was one thing.

'This sounds off the wall, Ken, but I think I'm going to need a handful of low value diamonds and perhaps half a dozen Krugerrands. They'll be crucial to the internal feuding incident I mentioned a minute ago.' Rose was a smart man, he'd work out what Paul was talking about, but it was still a lot of money.

'I'll make sure Dick Hanney has what you need when you two meet. We have time to organise it and I'll call him directly.' Fantastic! There was one other thing Paul needed to tell Rose.

'To complete my mission for Her Majesty's Government, I have to get to Beira. I suspect, and I'm sure you do, that there is a Beira-Pretoria link up in this whole criminal activity, and in some way, Ken, it might well come back to you in Harare. So I plan to go into Mozambique, to Manica initially, and not through the Border crossing here.'

'Why Manica?'

'Because there is a woman involved, and paradoxically, she is a woman most precious to me. I don't really have the time now to explain how or why, but she is, and she needs to be escorted to the MozLon Farm at Manica. I'm her escort.'

'OK,' Rose finished, 'I'm briefed, thank you, and I'm going to be prepared. Please keep me posted when you can and don't wait to ask for help if I can give it.'

'I will. Oh, and by the way,' Paul said tantalisingly, 'If I'm right, I believe there's a good chance I'll be able to return the missing diamonds to you, but you might want to keep this to yourself until I'm more certain.'

There was a pause. 'That would be very welcome, Paul, and more than offsets the extra expenditure you've requested.' Rose's chuckle was brittle at the end of the satphone link. He said, 'Good luck with your girl.'

The line went dead.

Paul Stanton walked back into the Wise Owl Motel to get his breakfast and to join Lefty Shoesmith and Nikki Walker-Haig. His girl. The girl he had yet to tell General Charles Grace about.

Then Paul's satphone rang and it *was* Charles Grace. 'Tell me more, Paul,' he said without any kind of introduction.

So Paul did; but he didn't mention the possibility of recovering the missing diamonds and he didn't mention the girl.

PART V
DEAD BODIES

CHAPTER SEVENTEEN

IT WAS NOW ten o'clock and Charles Grace was conscious of the time and the day. It looked almost certain that for Colin Bullock and John Sawyer the planned family activities for Saturday were going to be put on hold, if not cancelled. Given their lives, Grace fully expected both sets of families to be well used to the so-called *exigencies of the Service* wrecking their plans, but it wouldn't make it any easier for them to accept yet another buggered up weekend. For him, it didn't matter. What mattered was getting this coordination of ongoing actions absolutely right. For two reasons: because Paul Stanton's reputation, and possibly his life, were on the line, and because the Prime Minister wanted it.

He was staying with Colin Bullock in his residence, so it was inevitable that as soon as he'd received Paul's message from the SIS Station's Duty Operator he would bring the DA into his confidence. Besides, Colin Bullock was an old friend and there was going to be an unholy mess to clear up after Paul Stanton had finished his business, and Bullock would have to do it.

Before they'd left Bullock's house, John Sawyer had telephoned and said he was on his way. He was out of town with the family. So having apologised to Colin Bullock's wife, who had been predictably gracious, he and Bullock had left for the Embassy. Now, ninety minutes after Stanton's call into the Duty Operator, Sawyer had arrived and the three men were gathered in Brigadier Colin Bullock's office. Two were seated, Bullock and Sawyer, but Charles Grace was patrolling around the carpet space, marshalling his thoughts and wondering how exactly to put things. The office was spacious and quiet and the bright sun flooded in through large windows.

As if he'd suddenly remembered something, which in truth he had, Grace stopped his pacing, turned to the others and said, 'Please excuse my manners. I haven't apologised for bringing you in at such short notice and on a Saturday. I'm sorry, I really am.' Bullock and Sawyer smiled wryly and continued to say nothing. 'It's obviously about Colonel Stanton and it's obviously crucial. Stanton's doing what I asked him to, what Her Majesty's Government needs, but there is going to be collateral damage, gentlemen, there is, and I fully expected it. So,' he paused, 'the question is: do we endorse Stanton's proposed actions, and if so, what must we do to support him?' They were rhetorical questions and both Bullock and Sawyer sipped from their paper mugs of take-away coffee Sawyer had brought with him. 'As you can appreciate,' Grace continued, 'I simply had to bring us all together and ensure we are totally coordinated. Stanton and I have spoken, so I know where he is, what is happening and what he's planning to do,' which, if he was honest, was potentially political and civil dynamite.

Sawyer cocked an eyebrow and said, 'Give us the outline, Charles, if you would. I most certainly will have to get hold of Stephan Langlands, the sooner the better, and God knows where he'll be on a Saturday.'

Grace had instantly liked John Sawyer. He didn't know the MI6 man, but his reputation and the fact he was here, in a political and intelligence hot seat such as Pretoria, spoke volumes for the regard the Secret Intelligence Service must hold him in. Colin Bullock rated him very highly. Good enough. He said to the two men, 'There are going to be two deaths in Zimbabwe, sometime over this weekend and both will be linked to the criminal activity we all know about.' Grace let the words hang there for a few seconds, as if deliberately challenging the tranquillity and sunlight of Bullock's office. He really needed the two men to buy into his proposal. He said, 'They will be accidental deaths,

191

and if I know anything about Colonel Stanton's methods and skills, they will be highly convincing.'

Sawyer responded, 'Majors de Castenet and Schuman, I presume?' His tone was neutral. He was a seasoned professional and knew enough about operational imperatives in the best interest of HMG, and the charges they might and often did impose on those associated with them. He was a good man to have on your side, Grace thought. 'What else? I have to give Stephen Langlands everything we know or presume, since one of his men is an intended victim. And has Paul kept Ken Rose in Harare up-to-speed?' he added.

Charles Grace sat down and picked up his coffee. He sipped from it, out of politeness, but in fact he hated the taste. He couldn't stop himself wrinkling his nose so he set it down on the table around which their chairs were grouped. 'As for your last question, yes he has. Stanton has been in close contact with Ken Rose throughout, and from what he's told me we need not try to contribute to the delicate balance of things which exists in Zimbabwe.' He looked at the distasteful coffee cup and continued, 'This is what I believe will happen,' and he proceeded to tell Bullock and Sawyer what Paul Stanton had discussed with him. At the end he asked, 'So what are your immediate thoughts, gentlemen?'

Colin Bullock said, 'Very comprehensive, Charles. I can live with it all. Knowing what de Castenet and Schuman have been up to, I'm comfortable. The fact is they're complicit in the murder of a senior MozLon executive and two other men. So, callous it may seem to some, but the British officer has a history, you've told us that clearly, and although it's convenient to hide behind the cover of a series of actions our Government has tacitly sanctioned, the man has to be stopped. And Paul Stanton is the means to do that. There will be practical issues to deal with,' he went on, 'but I'm well used to handling those. The man has no immediate family or next of kin. His mother was all he had by way of family and she died last year.'

Good man, Colin, Grace said to himself. 'Practical issues?' he asked. Even though he knew the answers, Sawyer might not.

'Repatriation of the man's body, the Public Relations furore when the circumstances surrounding his accidental death are revealed or leaked or come out in some way, the Defence Department and Army Board's wrath, the fallout with the Head of BMATT in Harare, all that type of minor stuff. It will certainly spice things up for us.' Bullock raised his eyebrows philosophically as he looked at the two of them.

'Yes,' Grace said, 'it most certainly will.' But, he consoled himself, it might just save Mrs Thatcher's political career as far as foreign relations are concerned, and it might just allow Sir Reggie Hanlon to remain influential in the Mozambique peace process, which of course was inextricably linked to Mrs Thatcher's political standing.

'I'm comfortable, too,' said Sawyer. 'And although this might sound trite, if Colonel Stanton's actions allow the status quo amongst the White community in Zimbabwe to be re-established, then I'm all for it. But that is a personal viewpoint and should not be repeated, please.' Grace nodded. He believed he understood what Sawyer was voicing. Mugabe's dictatorship was a serious threat to many who had committed their lives, and those of their families, to their country, and now stood to lose almost everything. Sawyer continued, 'So, Charles, I'll brief Stephen Langlands, OK?'

'Yes, please do, John. Tell him everything he needs to know but keep those aspects that are germane only to Her Majesty's Government just to ourselves.' Sawyer nodded his assent.

'Does Paul have help in Zimbabwe?' Bullock asked.

'He does, Colin.' Grace told them about the deployment of Evans and Shoesmith and summarised what Stanton had told him about Nyanga. Then he said to Sawyer, 'I might need to establish a personal link to Ken Rose. Can you facilitate that for me, before we leave here today?'

'I can. You have a satphone?' Grace nodded. 'I thought so. We'll exchange the key contact numbers.'

Grace was thinking rapidly. 'I'm confident with what we know and have discussed that Stanton will ensure any possible loose ends in Zimbabwe will be tied up, and Ken Rose will obviously help him, but they're going to have to get out of Zimbabwe very quickly.' In fact,

Grace had told Stanton to get the work done quickly and then get the hell out of the country, which he was sure Paul and the two SAS men would, but Rose was vital to this happening. And so was he. He said, 'I'm going to base myself in Beira, with the First Secretary at the High Commission. I need to be able to report back to London securely and I'll stay in contact with you both, obviously. Colin, if your duty staff could help me with my travel plans I'll travel on Monday first thing.' By which time, if Paul's planning was successful, all hell would have broken loose, Bullock, Sawyer, Langlands and Rose would be firefighting, and Stanton and company would be over the border into Mozambique.

'Of course, Charles,' Bullock replied.

'Thank you, gentlemen, that's all I have. So shall we get on with the rest of the weekend? And let's make sure we stay in radio contact, as they say. It's going to be a challenging and somewhat unpredictable forty-eight hours.'

Charles Grace needed to be in Beira. He needed to be able to help with Paul Stanton's extraction plan.

What he didn't know about was the girl. Nor did he know about the Renamo rebels and the threat to the MozLon farm at Manica.

* * *

PAUL STANTON MET Dick Hanney on his own. Lefty Shoesmith had followed Nikki back to the Country Club and the Gurkha Connections Limited offices there. He would return to the Wise Owl only when Paul called him.

Hanney was a big man, rugged and fit looking. He would be, Paul reckoned, since he ran two very large tea estates. Paul heard him speak to the Wise Owl Manager at the reception desk and intercepted him there. 'I'm the person you're looking for, Dick. Can we go outside for a minute.' The Manager had told Paul earlier that the place would fill up in an hour as local shoppers and town residents would come to the Wise Owl for a Saturday drink and lunch. Paul was also concerned that de Castenet would come scouting for him today and the Motel was an obvious place to look. Why the man hadn't come earlier, yesterday, Paul could only put down to the fact that he and Schuman had more pressing places to be in Mutare.

Hanney took Paul's lead and followed him outside. Paul turned to him as they paused just outside the entranceway and said, 'Can we go for a drive in your bakkie, somewhere private where we can talk.' They drove out of town and then southeast towards the mountains. They were well into the bush, on a dirt track, where the broken savannah countryside was utterly deserted, before either of them spoke.

Hanney broke the silence, 'I really liked Victor Fitzsimons. It was a shock, man, to hear from Ken Rose that some bunch of renegade Renamo bastards had done for him. And,' he paused to look at Paul, 'with a white man involved.'

'One who took your diamonds,' Paul offered.

'That's right, bru! Took our fucking diamonds! A shitload of diamonds, I tell you!' And I believe they're not too far away from us, right now, Paul thought.

'Can you pull off the track here, Dick, it looks totally deserted.'

Hanney did so and the world stilled. Paul got out and stood, scanning the ground to the horizon. It was a jumble of rocky koppies and open savannah scrub, interspersed with clusters of flat-topped acacias. The air seemed to have stopped breathing and was very hot. The sky was blue-clear, the humidity was building and there was absolutely no movement that he could see or hear. Dick Hanney came and stood next to him, opening a flatpack of thirty Peter Stuyvesant cigarettes, offering one to Paul, who refused. Hanney lit up and looked out at the far ridge of mountains.

He was Paul's height and bigger in build. He wore tan coloured bush shorts, shirt and boots and a safari vest with multiple pockets that carried his essentials. His legs and arms were sun-browned and covered in a fine pelt of golden hairs. His face was deeply weather-lined and a squashed nose and friendly mouth sat underneath sparkly blue eyes and bushy eyebrows. His hat was sweat stained around the hatband. He took it off and wafted it vaguely in the direction of the

195

mountains. His fair-brown hair was thick, short-cropped and greying in parts. He must have been in his forties. This was a man's man, no doubt about it. 'The Vumba, man,' he said, 'and beyond them you're into Mozambique. No way anyone, least of all Mugabe's fucking military clowns, could stop any rebels coming in across the Border in this area, or any of them crossing back into Mozambique again, for that matter. That's how they will have done it, bru, I'm sure.'

That's how Fitzsimons' killers would have infiltrated and exfiltrated from Mozambique to Zimbabwe and back again in order to ambush him, take the diamonds and then make their way south to kill him. Where did they kill him, Paul mused? It didn't matter. Paul had the killer's Zippo safely tucked away in his grip. There would be a moment not too far away when he'd declare it. But the fact was, Ken Rose's Police Anti-Terrorist Unit patrol had not found any white man remains, only African. But the find had been much further south. It didn't matter. What mattered was sorting out who was behind it all, namely de Castenet, Schuman and their accomplices.

Hanney turned and pointed almost due south, 'In that direction are my tea estates. I used to meet Fitzsimons in Melsetter on the Friday of his visit and sometimes he'd come and spend the night on the estate where I stay and we'd talk shit and drink whisky, but more often he'd take the consignment from me, we'd confirm the next shipment details, and he'd head back on the Cashel road to the Wise Owl. He didn't get a shipment every week, but Friday the twenty-ninth of September was when we last met. That's when I gave him the package of diamonds. The WPC had calculated the value at over two million pounds sterling. It was a monster shipment. As I said, it took a while to bring together and had inputs from several of our major businessmen, farmers and civil servants. Family wealth, pension provision, start-again-from-nothing life money, man, the diamonds represented all those things. What a fucking shame and a shambles. Christ!' Hanney expostulated. 'Which reminds me,' he said, 'Ken Rose instructed me to give you this.' Hanney reached into an inside pocket in his safari vest and pulled out a small leather pouch tightened by a leather drawstring. 'There's a handful of industrial grade chipped diamonds in there, not fantastically valuable, but they look good, and half a dozen Krugerrands. They're worth quite a bit, but hey, Rose says it's the price we have to pay.'

Paul took the pouch and felt the weight. What he had been given would be perfect for his plan. 'Thank you.' Paul got back to his thoughts, 'Fitzsimons didn't stay with you that Friday, the twenty-ninth?'

'No, bru, he didn't. How I wish he had.' Hanney smoked ruefully and said, 'Hey, but I liked him. He was brave in his way. That fucking pipeline road from Beira can be rough, man, dangerous rough, and he'd come up regular as clockwork every week. It got less dangerous in the past two months because he was overseeing some big farms, he told me, and had some Gurkhas under contract providing the security and training the locals into a kind of militia force. The nearest farm is just the other side of the mountains in Manica. He told me his MozLon farms are large-scale agricultural production. Sure, feed the people use the land and feed the pockets of MozLon, but hey, we can all understand that, and at least it's helping the peace process. And it was helping us, indirectly, big time. He was helping us. You guys out there in the rest of the world have no real idea how fast Mugabe and his goons are wrecking this country. They'll take our farms our businesses and our savings and possessions and we'll be out on our ear, man, I tell you it's true. So under the leadership of Ken Rose we all made a plan to ship it out and now that plan is fucked.' Hanney drew on his cigarette, threw the butt on the ground and trampled it into the gravel dirt. 'As I said, we didn't ship hard assets out every week, that wasn't feasible. But when we did, Fitzsimons never failed on a consignment, until the last,' he said pensively. 'In just under a year we moved ten shipments through into Beira and then offshore. Ken Rose fixed the Beira end.' Paul didn't interrupt. He'd get his chance to ask the questions he needed to in a minute. It was important to let Dick Hanney talk. 'And it's all legal, overseas, in Lisbon.' Hanney then said, 'But somehow we got compromised on this last one, and I have some ideas how.'

'How?'

'Obviously Ken Rose and I have spoken. He told me to give you every assistance.' Paul nodded, encouraging Hanney to get to the point. 'I didn't put it together until Rose told me the details, but I've seen your Brit officer and his South African friend before, twice.' Paul's interest pricked. This was very significant. 'In Mutare,' Hanney continued, 'at the Spar supermarket.'

'How so?' Paul asked, wrestling with the revelation. *Spar supermarket?*

'Well, man, it's bizarre, but I think I'm right.' Hanney dug out another cigarette and lit up. He started moving in small circles by the side of his bakkie as he spoke. Paul scanned the countryside. Nothing moving. He was melting with the mounting heat and humidity of midday. When were he and Lefty meeting Taff and Vino? In about two hours. 'There's a coffee shop by the Spar,' Hanney was using his cigarette for emphasis, not even looking at Paul. 'My wife and I go to Spar every Wednesday for provisions for the estates. We go before the weekend rush. But I can't stand to shop, man, so I help her with the heavy shopping and then go into the coffee shop for a smoke break. I saw them that Wednesday, and I now realise I'd seen the three of them once before as well.'

'Who, Dick? Three of them?'

'Our local Police Chief in Mutare, Oz Macfarlane, your Brit officer and the Afrikaner Schuman, from how Ken Rose described them.'

Paul's thoughts were racing. Having the local police chief involved might explain how Rose's Assistant could get detailed information about the WPC consignments and about Fitzsimons, to Schuman and de Castenet. Also, if the man were complicit, then it would be very good for the pieces of Paul's plan that still needed to be put in place. He said, 'You're positive?'

'I am, Paul. And here's what makes it all fit together for me,' said Hanney. 'I thought nothing of it at the time, until now. It was a meeting that took place two days before Victor met me down at Melsetter and took the shipment of diamonds. So it was a confirmation meeting?' Hanney looked at Paul. He said nothing, but

Paul pursed his lips in thought. It fitted. 'And this is the clincher for me. Thinking back, I remember seeing the same three people at the Spar coffee shop three weeks before.'

Clincher! 'And without putting words into your mouth, Dick, I'm guessing that this police officer, Oz Macfarlane, would have access to Ken Rose's outer officer staff on official business,' Hanney nodded his head as Paul went on, 'and also have the contacts with his opposite numbers in Pretoria and Beira?' Hanney was less certain but Paul was sure: cross-Border liaison was essential and would exist in some form. It would definitely include some form of contact with Schuman's Border liaison function in Pretoria. He finished by saying, 'And this man would know ex-military guys who, for a fee, might be persuaded to assist in bad business?'

'Yes,' said Hanney. 'Like all of us, the guy was in the Army in the Bush War.'

Clincher! Paul looked at his watch. It was after midday. He had to get back to Mutare. 'Dick, can we get going? I have to be back in Mutare and I'll tell you what I'm planning as we go. I'm assuming Ken Rose told you that I needed help?'

'He did, bru. I'll do what needs to be done.'

Excellent. 'It'll be a big ask and illegal in the strict terms of the law. But in my view these bastards have crossed a line and the law no longer applies to them. Comfortable with that?'

'Totally. Tell me what you need.'

'This Police Chief of yours, is he a good friend?'

'No, bru, we all hate the man. If we can stitch up the fat fucker then all to the good.'

'Excellent.' Paul was fairly sure now that his plan would work. In addition to his SAS comrades and Vino Lauwrens, Paul had Dick Hanney to help him and indirectly he would use the actions of the seemingly reviled Mutare Police Chief, Oz Macfarlane.

Then his satphone rang unexpectedly and Lefty Shoesmith said, 'Boss, our targets are at the Mutare Country Club. They're with a third party. Everything's OK and I'm still covert, but you might need to get here.'

'How's Nikki?'

'Secure. In her offices.'

'Keep it that way, Lefty.'

Paul killed the connection and said, 'Can I ask a couple of other favours?'

'Go for it, bru.'

'I'd like you to be at the Wise Owl this evening, not necessarily to stay, but to be there to keep an eye on a woman. Her name is Nikki Walker-Haig and she's staying there. The Manager knows who she is. She was also a friend of Victor Fitzsimons as it happens. I don't believe there will be trouble at the place, but I would like you there just in case. It will also make it easier for me to contact you.'

'No problem, bru.'

'Great. So put your foot on it, please, Dick. To the Country Club, and not, unfortunately, to have a beer.'

The Mutare Country Club, the offices of GCL, Nikki's workplace and her present location.

More importantly: where the enemy was.

CHAPTER EIGHTEEN

IN DIFFERENT CIRCUMSTANCES, the natural beauty of the location and the obvious luxury and comfort of the Club might have impressed Paul, but right now his mind was focused on the enemy and on getting Nikki out of harm's way. Lefty Shoesmith had told him where to come to. The GCL offices were part of the accommodation chalets, a little way from the main clubhouse. Dick Hanney dropped him off and left. They would meet again at the Wise Owl Motel, after the next stage of the plan was in motion.

Nikki was relieved to see him. He could feel it in her swift embrace. 'Nik, as we discussed last night, I need you to stay hunkered down here today.' Nikki nodded. The three of them were in her office. She had given the two Gurkha clerks, who usually worked next door, the weekend off. Paul checked his watch, it was gone one o'clock and he was due to meet Evans and Lauwrens at two o'clock, at a place well out of town. It didn't seem possible, so he might have to change the plan, but the timings might work if Evans and Lauwrens were on schedule. 'Where are de Castenet and Schuman, Lefty?'

'In the Clubhouse bar, boss, they're with a third party, having a few drinks and snacks. Looks like they're comfortably set.'

'What does the other man look like?' Paul had a feeling.

'Short, fat, red-haired.'

Oz Macfarlane, the local Police Chief. Now he could change the plan. 'He's the Mutare Chief of Police, and a man vital to our success.'

'Police Chief?' asked Nikki incredulously. 'I don't understand.'

'Oz Macfarlane's his name. I'll explain everything in a moment, Nik, but Lefty and I need to talk for a minute and we have to contact Taff and Vino urgently. He was thinking ahead, they'd need some rations. 'Nik, I don't suppose you have any food handy, do you?' He'd noticed the fridge in the corner of the office and there were storage cupboards against one of the walls.

'I have some snacky things, Paul, biscuits, crisps and a few packets of sandwiches and some chocolate in the fridge. There are also some cans of Coke. Will that do?'

'It will be perfect. Thank you. Could you please put it all together in a box or carrier bag or something that we can load into the back of the wagon? We won't have time to stop and eat until much later.'

'I'll get on with it.' A no-nonsense girl.

Paul motioned to Shoesmith to step outside. The two men stood for a few seconds looking at the panorama, Paul said, 'Lefty, break out the weapons. Handguns only. Make sure mine's ready to go with a silencer, but keep them hidden. I don't want Nikki more scared than she is already. Have the GPS and comms ready as well.'

'Roger, boss.'

'Give Taff a call now, on the satphone. We're late and if they've made good time they should be close. Whatever, they need to put the foot down. Tell them to come directly here, but to lie up in cover on the approach road into the place and be ready to spring a roadblock on de Castenet's Toyota when he and Schuman come into sight. The approach road into the Club is at least a mile and a half long and there are a number of places where Taff and Vino can stay in cover. Tell Taff I want the block well out of sight of the Clubhouse. He'll find the right spot. Tell him we'll be right behind the Toyota.'

'How do you know de Castenet's going to leave anytime soon?'

'You said the three of them looked set?'

'Yes.'

'So we have a bit of time. He's going to leave when I want because I'm going to make him.'

'Good one, Paul, what's the rest of the plan?'

'Assuming Taff and Vino can be in position in fifteen minutes or so, then I'm going to flush out de Castenet and Schuman. I'll make it so Macfarlane will leave separately. With Taff in position we'll take them down and have a quiet chat with them at that place Vino mentioned, the abandoned petrol station on the Old Beira Road.'

'That's good. What about Nikki?'

'She'll stay here and then head to the Wise Owl until the jobs are all done. She mustn't see any of this shit stuff we have to do. Besides she's safe here.' Shoesmith nodded his head slowly. 'There have to be accidents, Lefty, and then we all have to bale the gaff and cross into Mozambique. After that, I'm not entirely sure, but General Grace will be lurking somewhere close by to lend a hand with the extraction. When we get to it.'

'No problems, Paul, you know me, I'm all for a spot of action. OK, I'll get on the blower to Taff and tell him to move his body and be in position. Assume he needs to be in open comms once he's there and set, so we can tell him when the target's approaching?'

'We do. I'll go and confirm everything with Nikki.'

* * *

IT TOOK TWENTY minutes before Paul received confirmation from Taff Evans that he and Vino Lauwrens were concealed in the bush on the long approach road into the Country Club and ready to spring an ambush when they got the word.

'I'll let you know, Taff,' Paul said into the satphone, 'but you'll get a couple of minutes notice.' Paul had thought about this and he said, 'I want them out of action, Taff. No kinetics, no noise, get them neutralised and into your wagon and then we'll all get the hell out of the place down to the Old Beira Road. You've given Lefty the coordinates for the GPS, the abandoned petrol station, just in case we get separated?'

'I 'ave, boss. No bovver about the other stuff. Vino and me'll 'ave those two bastards silenced, trussed and stowed out'a sight in a jiffy. Lefty an' you can 'elp if you like. Guess you'll drive their motor, Paul?'

'I will. Oh, and Taff?'

'Yes, boss?'

'I need the targets to be neutralised but unmarked.'

'Roger that, see you soon then, boss, 'ave fun.'

Paul handed the satphone back to Shoesmith and turned and put his hands on Nikki's shoulders. He said, 'I'll be back for you, Nik, later tonight.' He hated the thought of leaving her, but she couldn't and mustn't witness what was going to happen during the next few hours. 'Please stay here in the office until just before dark,' he said, 'and then drive back to the Wise Owl Motel. There will be a man there called Dick Hanney. The Manager knows him well as did Victor Fitzsimons. He's a real friend and he'll keep you company until I get back there. You'll be out of harm's way and safe and it will make me feel so much better to know this. OK?'

'OK, Paul, just as long as you come back for me.' He couldn't miss the tone of fear and desperation nor miss the worry shadowed in her eyes. He realised for the thousandth time since he had committed his heart to this wonderful woman, that he truly loved her. Where would this true love lead them? Paul Stanton had a jolt of unexpected realisation, a crystallisation of all the emotions he had experienced: he wanted to spend the rest of his life with Nikki Walker-Haig. They were lovers and they were in love but they knew so little about each other, and how could he step off or slow down the treadmill of his life in order to fulfil this realisation? Christ! And here he was again, about to step into the unknown of violence and killing in unfriendly countries thousands of miles from home. His life. Paul made a silent promise at that moment, as he looked into the lustrous green-brown eyes of his girl, that he would change his life.

'I will come back for you. I will never leave you. That's my promise.' And he kissed her gently and turned to Lefty Shoesmith. 'Be ready to move when I get back. I'm off to find the enemy.'

* * *

THE THREE MEN were standing at the bar. It seemed to Paul a very long time since he'd last confronted de Castenet and Schuman in the Mess at Nyanga Battle School, but it was only thirty-six hours ago. How the world had shifted in a day and a half.

Paul must have transmitted a silent warning signal because as he approached them the three men turned around towards him. All of them looked dishevelled and were unshaven; they looked rough. Macfarlane was instantly recognisable from Dick Hanney and Lefty Shoesmith's descriptions, short, stocky, overweight and bristling with close-cropped red-hair and unshaven beard. The sweat leaked from the armpits of his bush shirt. He looked a thoroughly unpleasant man, but he was needed to play a part in the later stages of the plan and so he had to be separated from the other two men.

Their faces were a picture of mixed feelings. Macfarlane's was uncertainty. He had piggy-small beady eyes that blinked enquiringly at Paul, who was a stranger, but someone he had no doubt been told about. Yes, Paul thought, thoroughly unpleasant. Schuman's was surprise. His dark-tanned, square-blocked face, covered in a bristling sheen of salt-and-pepper beard, became instantly immobile. Paul saw the ubiquitous canvas satchel was slung across his chest and Schuman's immediate action was quickly to tuck it behind him, out of sight. Paul smiled. The diamonds had to be inside it. de Castenet's face wore an expression of disbelief. He looked around him, his mouth slackly open, as if wondering why the two accomplices, G & T, had not put in an appearance at the bar instead of Paul Stanton, his nemesis.

Paul decided to dive straight into deep water. He said to Macfarlane, 'Hello, who are you?' Macfarlane was rooted to the spot and Paul did not offer his hand. He didn't like the man. 'Richard and Wentzel here brought me down from Pretoria. I'm on a fact-finding mission on behalf of my Government and Pretoria and it's going really well.'

Macfarlane then moved and said, 'I must be going. Nice speaking with you, but I'm off.' He swallowed the last of his lager and left.

'Was it something I said?' Paul offered. Schuman lit a cigarette with quick furtive movements. Paul would not be sad when this piece of shit met his demise. He looked at de Castenet who was obviously incapable of speech. 'I'm afraid the two men you were with in Nyanga won't be meeting you.'

'What,' de Castenet squealed. 'What can you possibly mean?'

'Exactly what I said, Richard, they're gone for good. So unless you have other reinforcements you two are on your own.' Schuman was looking intently at Paul who returned his study and winked at him. The man blinked and shook his head in disbelief. This was going well. Surprise: it nearly always worked. Now he had to get them moving out of this place, so he said, 'If I was you two, I'd get out of here and back to somewhere safe where you can regroup.'

And with that, Paul turned from the bar and walked out of the room. If he was any judge of character then he and Lefty and the road ambush party needed to be on their marks.

It was time for action.

* * *

TWENTY MINUTES LATER the Toyota Land Cruiser screeched to a halt. It had to, because the road out of the Mutare Country Club was blocked by Vino Lauwrens' bakkie. There was no one else around. Most people at this time on a Saturday were at lunch or having a few drinks.

Paul had been following in the Land Rover, a distance behind, and now accelerated and closed in behind the Toyota. There was no way out. He sat and watched the action to his front but glanced frequently into the rear view mirror. All clear. He could see back along the road for at least half a mile but the boys had to move fast. They knew this and would. This was bread-and-butter work for them.

Already Taff Evans was out of the bakkie and yanking open the Toyota's passenger door. Simultaneously Lefty Shoesmith leapt out of the Land Rover and wrenched open the driver's door. The two SAS men had their pistols tucked securely into their waistbands as they manhandled Schuman and de Castenet out of their vehicle and towards the open rear doors of the bakkie. There was no need for weapons, just shock action, a roll of duck tape and the means to neutralise them without leaving any physical marks. Weapons, well that would come later.

Vino Lauwrens was now out of the bakkie and he had the duck tape and two sets of harness straps, and as de Castenet and Schuman were bundled into his vehicle he whipped off a large strip of tape and stuck it across the mouth of each of the men. They struggled, the shock was wearing off, so Evans and Shoesmith, as if on a pre-arranged signal, smacked each man hard across their ears, wrenched their hands behind their backs and allowed Lauwrens to secure the harness straps around their upper arms, not too tight, but tight enough so that they could not free themselves. No markings.

Paul smiled grimly. Between the three of them they had de Castenet and Schuman secured and stunned and in the back seats of the bakkie inside one minute. Vino gunned the bakkie and pulled it into the side of the road. Evans hopped into the passenger seat and turned his attention to the two captives in the back. They were still. Shoesmith climbed into the Toyota, its engine still running, and pulled it into the roadside behind the bakkie. The road behind was still clear, so Paul manoeuvred the Land Rover off the road and behind the Toyota.

He got out, went over to the bakkie and peered in the back. 'Don't struggle,' he said to the two muted and dazed figures. 'It will be painful for you if you do. As I said in the Club, your two accomplices will not be joining you. They are dead bodies.' He let the import of these few words sink in. Both de Castenet and Schuman's eyes were stark staringly wide in fear. 'If you two don't want to end up the same way then I suggest you come quietly with us and we'll have a talk and discuss the future.' Paul turned to Taff Evans, 'Give me your clasp knife, Taff.' Paul took the razor sharp blade, leaned in towards Schuman and deftly cut the strap of Schuman's canvas satchel. He wrenched it fiercely from underneath the man's body. It was so quick Schuman hardly registered what had happened. It was heavy, four or five kilograms, at least, so not just diamonds but a pistol most likely. But the important thing was, he had them, he had the diamonds. Paul registered the look of utter defeat in the eyes of the Afrikaner and noticed that de Castenet was struggling to sit up. He said, 'Taff, get them into the floorwells and cover them up. Smack them hard if they're trouble, but I need serious talks with them both very soon. When we get there I want the two of them in the same room.'

'No probs, boss, your wish is my command.'

'Vino, you lead. Lefty, you second in the Toyota, and I'll bring up the rear. Keep spaced out, drive as normal, if we get separated it's not a problem. We all know where we're going. OK, we're good to go, so let's move.'

And they did, a neat three-vehicle convoy, leaving the Mutare Country Club and heading for a derelict petrol station on the Old Beira Road.

CHAPTER NINETEEN

THE OLD BEIRA Road. Which still, Paul assumed, led to some sort of crossing point on the border between Zimbabwe and Mozambique, yet seemed to be little more than a dirt track that contoured the high ground to the south of the railway line, winding its way through the forest and scrub bush which grew thick on both its sides. What mattered for Paul was its isolation and infrequency of use.

The now-derelict service station area must have seen good business in the past since it had been built on hard standing and the layout of the ruined rooms showed it had been reasonably large. Now it was totally overgrown with flowering, thick vegetation, vine and creeper which must have housed hundreds of songbirds, for the birdcalls and the noise of birds in flight through the trees, were almost constant. Fragrance from the flowers provided a sweet counterpoint to the mould and rot of the place.

On the drive in Paul had seen no indications of human life or inhabitants. There were no old tyre marks on the track. Vino Lauwrens had chosen well. The place itself and the immediate surroundings were ideal for what he needed to do. It's proximity to the Border crossing point also fitted Paul's plan, although he and his team would not be using it.

Paul had played this scene out a number of times in his head and now it was for real. Standing outside the ruined buildings, just inside the hanging vines, listening and waiting for a few minutes, Paul admitted to himself that he was slightly worried. He was positive now that de Castenet and Schuman were the men who had ordered Fitzsimons' murder and stolen the shipment of diamonds. Rose's relatively new and corrupt Assistant had provided the information to the Mutare Police Chief, Macfarlane, who had confirmed it to Schuman and de Castenet during a meeting here, in Mutare. The sequence of events had then unfolded...resulting in Fitzsimons' murder. There was a Beira angle, which Paul wasn't sure about yet, but he would be soon, and he would deal with it in due course.

So...he had to confirm the truth of things and then he had to kill both these men. He *had* to. He'd killed men before, a number of them, and not necessarily in combat. He had no compunctions about his job and had firm belief in his moral compass and how it guided him through his dark and dangerous life. It *was* a dangerous life. Many of his enemies had tried to kill him, and on two previous occasions almost succeeded. No, although his conscience was clear and he could look anyone in the eye and tell them so, it was the fact that this time he had to kill de Castenet, a fellow ex-comrade-in-arms and brother soldier in the same army that worried him. But he *had* to; so get on with it Stanton, he chided himself as he went inside to join the others.

He surveyed the scene. The room was largely intact in its shape of ruined walls and doorways and the remnants of a roof structure, and it was flooded with sunlight from the brilliance of the passing afternoon, which brought with it the noise and flights of the birdlife. 'Give them something to eat and drink, Lefty,' Paul said.

'Roger, boss.'

Shoesmith was next to Evans. There was an old service counter at one end and the men had unpacked all the provisions Nikki had provided. Vino Lauwrens was standing behind it, tending the bar. Evans was eyeing the captives. The three men moved to carry out Paul's request, cracking open some cans of Coke and unwrapping packages of sandwiches and biscuits. Schuman and de Castenet needed some final refreshments, and they needed to do some talking.

'Something for you, boss?' Evans asked. Paul shook his head. 'Don't mind if we do, do ya, Paul?' Paul shook his head again.

Paul had mentally planned his approach now he'd got to this moment of denouement. They had separated Schuman and de Castenet on either side of the room, a distance of fifteen feet. They'd unpacked some of the longer harnesses from the Land Rover and bound one foot of each of the captives to a wall joint or bracket. Schuman and de Castenet were on a tether of no more than two feet and the straps would not mark or bruise their ankles. They were stripped of everything and now they were about to be stripped of their lives.

Paul didn't necessarily want to prolong the agony but there were things he had to know first. There was an old stool by the doorway and Paul brought it into the centre of the space and sat down on it. He placed Schuman's satchel in his lap and opened it, and immediately he sensed everyone's attention fixed on what he was doing.

He took out a large oilskin package that looked as if it had been opened at one end and hastily re-sealed. Paul could feel the roughness of the stones and the density of their packing through the coarse material, and he guessed the weight as about two kilograms. He looked at Schuman and de Castenet in turn. They had both frozen, their eyes fixed on his hands and what was in them. Paul placed the package on the floor by his feet and dipped inside the satchel again, bringing out a small cowhide waist pouch, old and sweat stained. He opened it and carefully poured the contents onto the oilskin package. The facets of the stones caught momentarily in the speckled shafts of sunlight filtering through the broken roof structure. They were like a brief brilliant white radiance lighting one spot in this broken place. Paul guessed the additional stones weighed less than half a kilogram, but it was, nevertheless, a shedload of diamonds. This was it, the hard earned and future wealth of many, many families in Zimbabwe, which would have been denied them if these two creatures had had their way. His heart went cold. He could do this now.

Evans couldn't contain himself, 'Cor, fuckin' 'ell, boss, was these two geezers thinkin' they could 'ave it away with all this loot? All this wonga what belongs to other people? Fuckin' lunatics.' Having got that off his chest, Evans took a huge bite out of his sandwich.

Paul smiled tiredly at his men over by the counter and put his hand back inside the satchel finding what he'd always suspected was there, a pistol. He pulled out a Makarov, seemingly in good condition. He checked the safety, released the magazine, cleared the chamber, catching the ejected round, squeezed off the action, checked the chamber and barrel for cleanliness, pressed the loose round into the magazine, reloaded the weapon, cocked it and applied the safety catch. He put the satchel on the floor and rested the Makarov on his lap.

'This will work,' he said, enigmatically, looking first at Schuman and then de Castenet. 'I would suggest you both sit on the floor, it will be less tiring for you.'

'What are you fucking talking about you lousy Brit bastard,' snarled Schuman. It was pathetic. At least de Castenet had the good sense to keep silent for the time being and he sat down.

'Be quiet, Schuman, and sit on the floor,' Paul said, with ice in his voice. 'I'll speak to you in a minute. Taff, if this piece of worthless shit opens his mouth again before I've said so, then smack him really hard.'

'Love to, boss.'

Paul angled his stool towards de Castenet. 'Richard, you and I have known each other for some years, we've soldiered in some difficult places and being here like this with you saddens me more than you can imagine.' de Castenet hardly responded, but a low sigh escaped him and his head dropped a fraction. His eyes broke contact with Paul's. 'You made an error of judgement in Northern Ireland and it cost the lives of my men, but I never really held *that* against you. Christ, but we've all lived by our instincts in that shithole of a killing ground and sometimes got away with it and sometimes not.' de Castenet's head had come up and he was looking at Paul. There was a flash of light in his eyes. The room was totally silent, apart from the birds. Paul was glad of them, in a way, since it lessened the drama, even though it wouldn't lessen the outcome of it. He continued, 'What I hold against you, Richard, is the fact that through moral cowardice

212

and weakness of will you allowed an evil man like Drinkwater to blackmail you in Berlin, indirectly drag down the reputation of my Regiment and the entire British Army, and put good people's lives at risk,' including my own, he reflected.

'It was never meant to be like that,' offered de Castenet weakly.

Paul ignored him. His mind was set and his anger and hurt were like hard knots of pain in his gut. 'I killed that evil worm, Drinkwater. Did you know that? Well, no matter.' Paul took a breath and went on, 'What I hold against you is that three years later, you've learned nothing from the past, you've come out here, and by some means attached yourself to this worthless, stinking example of the worst of Afrikaner prejudice, this loathsome, amoral creature, Major Wentzel Schuman, and the two of you have acted murderously to steal the livelihood of good people whose situation is far worse than yours.'

'Paul...'

'You're a criminal, a murderous, thieving criminal, and you're going to tell me how it worked.' And with that Paul pulled out the Zippo lighter given to him by Ken Rose, flicked it open, lit it, and then closed it up and lay it on the package of diamonds by his feet. He glanced at Schuman. The hatred blazed out of his eyes but it bounced off Paul. 'The man who killed Mr Victor Fitzsimons and stole the diamonds, *those* diamonds,' Paul pointed to the package by his feet, 'was Schuman's contact wasn't he? But did you meet him? I'm guessing you did, in Pretoria probably. He was an ex-South African Defence Force man. A mercenary from the so-called Recces, an elite unit, and that's his lighter.'

'Who was Victor Fitzsimons?' de Castenet asked pathetically.

'As I thought,' replied Paul. de Castenet never knew who the intended target was. Schuman must have kept it from him. But he knew the killer. 'Who was the killer?'

'His name was Coetzee.'

Paul continued, 'You had no idea of how the activity you got involved in would be executed, correct?' de Castenet looked beseechingly at Paul and nodded. 'So Schuman here organised the contacts but you were to be the means of getting the diamonds turned into personal wealth, because you could travel across-borders with diplomatic immunity and back to the UK and Europe, if necessary? Am I right?' de Castenet nodded again. The man was broken. Paul needed to finish this. He spoke to Shoesmith, 'Lefty, give him something to drink.' He turned to Schuman and said, 'Tell me how it worked?'

'Fuck off, you Pommie bastard.' Paul pondered his next move. Schuman stood up and spoke suddenly, 'I heard what happened in Berlin from my family.' Schuman moved towards Paul but was then halted by his tether. Paul's men started to come forward and he signalled them to stay put. 'You brought down Otto Krenselauer, a hero of the Baader-Meinhof.' So what? 'The man was good for the economy at the time. He gave business to my family across the Wall,' Schuman was spitting out his words and his hatred was palpable, 'and you helped ruin that.'

'Tell me the mechanics, Schuman. Tell me how the man you work with, the man in Ken Rose's outer office in the CIO in Harare, gave you information about the shipment of diamonds by courier out of Zimbabwe to Beira.' Paul paused, and continued, 'I saw you with this man at the Meikles Hotel. Ken Rose knows everything. The man has been suspended, and when all this has settled I have no doubt he will be punished suitably. Although, spending time in a Harare gaol will not, I guess, suit him.' Schuman had stopped ranting and squatted down on his heels. He was drinking from his can, watching Paul like a feral cat.

'You'll get nothing from me, you lousy Brit fucker.'

'Well I'll tell you, then. You're Border Liaison in the NIS in Pretoria. You collaborate with Richard, who can move freely on behalf of the British Government and so accompany you on visits into Zimbabwe and Mozambique. You have the contacts amongst ex-SA Defence Force mercenaries, men who will contract to kill for what you pay them. Men like the one who owned this Zippo. You also have contacts in Beira who can arrange for ex-Renamo terrorists to assist in whatever killing is required in Zimbabwe or just across the Border. Am I close to the truth? Oh, and you have the Chief of Police here in Mutare to assist you locally and who is the contact to Ken Rose's

Assistant. This Chief of Police almost certainly provides in-country help such as the two ex-soldiers you were with in Nyanga. And I think I mentioned it in the Club, but both these men are dead, killed by my colleagues over there and buried in the middle of nowhere north of Nyanga under piles of stones. How does all that sound to you, Major Schuman?'

'That's right,' broke in Taff Evans, and Paul realised he hadn't even had the chance to debrief Evans and Lauwrens on their task up country, 'we led them a merry chase north of Nyanga, into some wilderness place. They had nothing useful to say, boss, before they croaked it.'

de Castenet broke in, his voice was quavering with naked fear, 'The contact in Harare is as you said, Ken Rose's Assistant. He provided the info about how the Whites were stockpiling their hard wealth. He was the one who told us about the diamonds this man Fitzsimons was moving. We met Macfarlane here and he arranged the support that you mentioned. That package you have was the only shipment we went for. The only one,' Paul kept his counsel, willing de Castenet to say more, 'and it backfired, Christ it backfired. No one's got anything. The shipment of diamonds is too large to handle.' He looked pleadingly at Paul, 'You've got the diamonds back now, haven't you. You can get them to their rightful owners. That would help.' Pathetic. The man's mind was shot. He was starting to ramble. 'I know the contact in Beira.'

Schuman spat loudly, 'Shut the fuck up, de Castenet!' he shouted out. 'Tell these bastards nothing more, man!'

'They know it all, Wentzel, they fucking know it all!' It was happening, Paul could see the physical evidence in de Castenet's body movements and expressions. His hands were waving around, gesturing to Schuman, pointing at Paul, his resistance had broken down and very soon it would be the moment for Paul to bring the situation to a close.

He took a short breath, 'Lefty, Vino,' Paul signalled to the two men to come to him. He stood up, kept the Makarov in his hand, turned his back on the captives and walked slowly outside. The three of them stood for a few moments and gratefully breathed in the fresher air. Paul spoke softly to Shoesmith and Lauwrens, 'Take the Toyota and drive down the track towards the Border. Find me a place short of the crossing where we can stage a vehicle accident.'

'I know a place,' said Lauwrens, 'it's about two klicks from here. The railway line through to Beira runs north of the track and it loops a bit, but at this point it runs close to the track and there's a hell of a fall off the track down into the thick bush next to the railway. It would be the place, bru.'

'Sounds perfect,' said Paul. 'Please go and recce it, just to make sure it works.' He looked at his watch. It was almost four o'clock. The sun would be down in two hours. They all needed to be well out of the area by then. 'Be back in forty-five minutes if possible. You've got your satphone, Lefty, in case of probs?'

'Yes, Paul.'

'Go then. Oh, and just make sure there is nothing in the Toyota that belongs to any of us. My prints are all over it but maybe that's to be expected.' Paul quickly reviewed the follow-up sequence in his mind. Yes, his prints should be there. Even if the police did bother to check, everyone knew he'd come down from Pretoria in the vehicle. Where he was now, might cause the authorities concern, but he'd leave that little aspect to Ken Rose to sort out. He continued, 'I've spent hours in the vehicle, but wipe yours down. Make some tyre marks on the track close to the push off point you select. You know what I'm saying?'

'Got it, boss.'

'It'll work, boet,' said Lauwrens encouragingly, 'it's a good plan.'

CHAPTER TWENTY

PAUL WALKED SLOWLY back inside the derelict building and sat down again on his stool. He heard the Land Cruiser drive off. Both de Castenet and Schuman were sitting on the broken concrete floor. Taff Evans was waiting, by the counter, now eating biscuits, but poised and ready.

Paul said, 'The contact in Beira, Richard?'

de Castenet's head jerked up and he looked across at Schuman, but the Afrikaner was strangely silent. 'He is called Ramon Lima and I've never met him. Schuman has.' Schuman hissed fiercely at de Castenet.

'Location? Address?'

'I don't know, but he stays near the Port area and he acts for renegade Renamo factions.'

'What else?'

'I've never even talked to him, Schuman has,' and de Castenet pointed accusingly across at his accomplice. Schuman spat again and mumbled some words under his breath. 'That's all I know, you have to believe me.'

Paul did. 'This thug, Lima, provided two ex-Renamo fighters for your Zippo man. The three of them killed Fitzsimons and obliterated his existence from the face of the earth. Good job, eh?' Paul was getting tired of the interrogation and deeply tired of the sordid saga of tragic, corrupt events it represented. 'Tell me about Zippo man.'

'His name was Coetzee, Mannie Coetzee, and he was repugnant. He was Schuman's man, but I had to meet him in Pretoria after he got back with the diamonds, and Schuman had him killed. How do you know about the Renamo?'

Christ, thought Paul, so Fitzsimons' murderer was dead, killed by yet another ex-SA Defence Force mercenary no doubt. Well Stephen Langlands could deal with all this internal mess in the fullness of time. 'How do I know,' Paul replied, 'because their skeletal remains and remnants of Fitzsimons' clothing were recovered by a clandestine patrol of Ken Rose's, and the patrol found this Zippo at the same location.'

'What the fuck are you playing at, man,' said Schuman, 'you think all this talk about how much stuff *you* know is impressive or important right now? What you going to do next, hey, boy?'

Paul ignored him. 'There are two final things you murderers should know. First, your pet policeman, Oz Macfarlane, is permanently compromised with Ken Rose, and so even if you thought he might come to your aid, he won't. Paradoxically he's going to help me, even though he doesn't know it. Finally, the full extent of your activities is known by your respective superiors, and in your case, Richard, by the British Prime Minister, and all of them have given me the authority to try, judge and punish you. There is no way out for you.' Paul stood up and stretched. He looked over at Evans who had stiffened and moved a couple of paces forward, reaching behind him to retrieve his pistol from his waist belt. Paul moved his head from side to side. This was his business. His loyal SAS men would do anything for him, he knew, but not this. He had to do it. His heart was heavy and his feelings numbed by all he had talked about and the sheer desperateness of it all.

Paul looked at Schuman. 'You asked what I'm going to do next?' Paul turned away from the man, flicked off the Makarov's safety and shot Richard de Castenet in the chest. The noise was deafening and the explosion caused the birdlife to screech and trill. The reek of cordite hung in the foetid, humid air. De Castenet was thrown back against the ruined wall, his head crunching sickeningly on the decaying wall plaster. Paul registered Evans moving and said, 'It's OK, Taff, I have to do this, just watch Schuman.'

'Wilco, Paul. Your man probably ain't dead, you know that?'

Paul did. He had to make this look like a shoot out between Schuman and de Castenet, a falling out of thieves. A precision killing would not fit the scenario. He stood in front of de Castenet, five paces away. The man was bleeding out, going into shock, his lungs filling with blood. His heart would seize very shortly and he would go into cardiac arrest. Paul was glad the man's head was down and his eyes closed. A part of him had hated what he'd done. He shot de Castenet a second time in the heart, and the birds screeched and fluttered once more, and the derelict world gained another dead body.

'Take his tether off, Taff, check for a pulse, but leave him exactly as he is.' Paul picked up both the empty cases, clicked the safety catch back on the Makarov and walked over to Schuman.

'I was wrong about you, Stanton,' he said. 'de Castenet warned me you were dangerous and I did not take him seriously. We should have bastard well killed you when we had the chance, hey.'

'If you could have,' said Paul, 'but I'm not that easy to kill.' Paul turned to Evans, 'Dead, Taff?'

'Stone cold, boss.'

'You see, Major Schuman, you killed your accomplice instead.'

'How so?' Schuman asked stupidly.

Paul dropped the two brass cartridge cases on the floor. He said, 'You shot him twice, in the chest, with your trusty Makarov, and all for a few worthless diamonds and some pieces of gold.' Schuman looked stupidly at Paul. 'It's a pity for you, but you're going to die in a car crash and won't get to enjoy the fruits of your criminal actions, but that's life, or in your case, death.'

Before the man could say anything, Paul leant over Wentzel Schuman, and with the palm of his right hand open and extended, smashed the heel of his hand into the man's forehead. It was a violent blow. There was pent up emotional anger there, of course; but the physical power of the blow originated in his upper chest muscles and was transmitted into Schuman's brain by Paul moving his right shoulder into the strike. It jarred his arm but he'd locked his wrist rigid. Schuman's head shot backwards and then with a sickening snap, lurched forwards. Paul guessed it would be Schuman's brain stem tearing. If it was, then it was catastrophic and the man's breathing and the beating of his heart would shut down almost instantly. Just for good measure, Paul hit him again.

He checked the man's pulse. Schuman was dead, too, the second dead body in the derelict petrol station on The Old Beira Road.

As if on cue, Paul heard the engine noise of the Toyota and within seconds Shoesmith and Lauwrens were there, taking in the scene.

'See you had a shoot out, boss. We heard the gunshots down the track, but there's no one about. Everything go as planned?'

'A thieves' tiff, Lefty, with disastrous consequences.' Paul wanted to get out of the place. He'd had enough violence for the day, his feelings were low and he felt heartless. Killing men in cold blood was part of his trade, his mission right now, and these men had crossed into the black world where judgements were swift and violent, but he never derived satisfaction from doing it. He needed to see his girl and get some sanity back into his life. But there was still a lot to do. 'This is what we need to do,' but his words were cut off by an unexpected peal of thunder in the nearby hills. Instantly the world went quiet as if the birds had gone, taken shelter, and Paul could smell the faint tang of ozone. The temperature cooled noticeably.

'It's the rains, bru,' said Lauwrens, 'a little early maybe, but the first of the season. It'll be a heavy burst, if I know anything.'

Déjà vu, thought Paul, Berlin 1986 all over again, the mad, killing shoot out in the derelict cinema down in the Wall Zone during the apocalyptic lightning and rainstorm. It could be useful here. He shuddered at the memories.

'You all right, boss?' Evans asked. Taff Evans knew what had happened to Paul and how the memories and pain still touched him from time to time.

'Never better, Taff,' and strangely Paul did feel better. A load had been lifted from him, and the way ahead was clearer and brighter. He said, 'OK, priorities. You've all worked it out. Make sure they've both got their personal IDs and any other effects they would be expected to have. de Castenet's body stays here, shot by Schuman. Wipe down the brass and leave the cases on the floor. Here's Schuman's Makarov,' and Paul handed the weapon to Evans, 'it's not made safe. Wipe it down, get Schuman's prints on it and put it in the Toyota. I'm not sure about forensics capability in Mutare but no chances. We were never here.'

'I'll clear up all the food stuff and forensics in here, boss,' said Shoesmith.

'Thanks, Lefty, you do that.' Paul dug into his trousers' pocket and pulled out Dick Hanney's leather pouch. He would leave the creation of the accident scene to Evans, Shoesmith and Lauwrens, as it was their skill set. 'Taff, I need the three of you to sort this place out and get Schuman's body into the Toyota with all the incriminating evidence and off the track into the ravine. Fix the accident convincingly. You all OK with that?' The three men paused in what they were doing and nodded their assent. 'You'll need this,' and Paul tossed the leather pouch over to Evans. 'Don't open it, but it's what Schuman and de Castenet were fighting over. It cost de Castenet his life. Put it in the glove compartment of the Toyota along with the shooter.' Paul turned to Vino Lauwrens. 'It's a lot to ask, Vino, but I think we need to use the rain that's coming. You know the place where the accident is going to occur. I suggest the three of you, with Schuman's body, drive the Toyota there. One set of tyre tracks, with skid marks off the track and over the edge of the ravine. Schuman was driving of course, the rains came suddenly, and he skidded off and smashed his head on the steering wheel on crash impact. Makes sense so far?'

'I'm with you, boet,'

'You leave your bakkie here and the three of you tab back from the crash site using the verges of the track, leaving no footprints, and then drive back to the Wise Owl. That's where I'm going in the Land Rover and that's where I'll meet you later. Comfortable with that?'

'A bit of physical's what we need, Paul,' said Shoesmith. The others smiled, each, no doubt, weighing up in their minds what had to be done to ensure Paul's plan worked.

Evans asked, 'What about the diamonds, boss?'

Paul had actually made the decision earlier. 'I'm going to finish Fitzsimons' work and courier them to Beira and make sure they get safely offshore as Ken Rose and those who have put their livelihood into it, would have wanted. You and Lefty are coming with me. We're going to take Nikki with us over the Border, tomorrow, at first light and drop her off at the MozLon farm at Manica.'

'Does Nikki know this, boss, does Ken Rose know?' said Evans.

'No, but when I get to the Wise Owl I shall dutifully inform them.'

'That's a good plan, Paul,' said Lauwrens unexpectedly. 'We all need those diamonds to get to Portugal.' Paul hadn't expected this. So Lauwrens *was* a contributor to the Wealth Protection Cooperative. He was pleased. 'My family's savings are in there, so thanks, bru.' High praise.

Paul smiled at Lauwrens; it made the day a little lighter to know some real good had come from it. 'Rest assured, Vino, I'll call Ken Rose as soon as I get back to the Motel. I have a strong feeling he'll be happy with the decision. He already knows we're going into Mozambique. Which reminds me, boys,' Paul looked at Evans and Shoesmith, 'make sure you've got all your travel documents and IDs. We're crossing illegally but we'll have to be legit at some stage.' Paul picked up Schuman's satchel, carefully rebagged the loose diamonds, and put them and the large oilskin package back inside it. He tied the cut shoulder strap together in a reef knot and slung it over his shoulder. He picked up the Zippo, 'I'm keeping this.' He was ready to go.

'You've got the Rover's keys, boss?' asked Shoesmith.

Paul took them out of his pocket and jingled them. 'I have. See you at the Wise Owl. I'll buy you all a beer.' He looked at Vino

Lauwrens, 'And I need to say a proper thanks to you, Vino, and to let you get back to your family. You've been fantastic.'

'It's been a real pleasure, bru, and I wouldn't have missed it. See you at the Wise Owl inside two hours.'

* * *

PAUL STANTON LEFT the derelict petrol station on the Old Beira Road. The place had served its purpose but now he needed to get back to sanity and to Nikki. Making his calls to Charles Grace and Ken Rose were a priority, because he was taking Nikki and his SAS colleagues into Mozambique and there was a lot of detail and support to be tied up. He needed to see Dick Hanney, who would, tomorrow morning, inform the Mutare Police Chief of an incident he'd heard about; and because Ken Rose would have spelt out Oz Macfarlane's options to him in very clear terms, the accident would be investigated very discreetly, its paperwork buried in bureaucracy, and the bodies of Majors de Castenet and Schuman recovered for the respective National authorities in Pretoria to arrange appropriate repatriation.

Once he'd spoken to him, he believed Charles Grace would brief Colin Bullock and John Sawyer and Sawyer would pass on the information to Stephen Langlands. Grace would somehow keep Mrs Thatcher's Chief of Staff up to speed and possibly, also, Fred Etherington in MozLon headquarters in London. So everyone who needed to know would know, and those who would have to act would know why. There was a price to be paid for this ticking bomb to be defused and it would start on Monday the 23rd of October. The words of Warren Zevon's song came into Paul's mind: *send lawyers, guns and money, the shit has hit the fan!*

Paul still had tomorrow, Sunday, to get his precious people out of Zimbabwe and he knew how he would do it. His first stop would be Manica. Nikki had the location of the MozLon farm and they would make contact with Danny Dalloway as they moved. But Paul had no idea what was brewing there. He had no idea of the series of events that would lead to more dead bodies. Many more.

The first few drops of big rain hit the windscreen of the Land Rover and the sky darkened. Lightning jags streaked across the sky and earthed themselves as dramatic peals of thunder reverberated around the hills. The canopies were up on the Rover, so he would stay dry and warm but he still needed to get a move on. He shuddered again in the aftermath of adrenaline release and drove on, a dark man in a darkening world.

Tomorrow was Sunday. This time last week he hadn't even left London.

PART VI
THE LONG ROAD TO BEIRA

CHAPTER TWENTY-ONE

SUNDAY MID AFTERNOON, and although they were extremely tired they'd made it safely to MozLon Manica. The rains that chased them out of Zimbabwe had not followed them across the mountains into the lower plains of Manica. They had made good time.

'You look shagged out, mate,' said Dalloway to Paul as he greeted the arrival of the SAS 110 Land Rover and its occupants at the Farm's main building.

Dalloway was dressed in olive green bush combats, with matching eye patch, and his clothing and boots were filthy. He looked as Paul felt, knackered, as if he'd just come back off a two-day combat patrol. 'And you, Danny the bush pirate, look handsome as ever!' Paul clambered out of the driver's side.

'Fuck off, Paul, but it's great to see you, even though I only knew you were arriving about an hour ago.'

'How so? We got through to your ops room on the satphone just before midday.' The two men shook hands and Paul noticed the dirt ingrained in Dalloway's hand and in the crease lines of his unshaven face. Yes, he's been out in the bush, and not just to visit his project. Dalloway's one eye looked kindly at him and his mouth broke the rest of his face in a warm smile. It was clear he was glad to see Paul.

'Only just got back from a mission, matey, but I'll tell you about it later.' Dalloway walked over to greet the others as they clambered out of the Land Rover. Omparsad, Kindraman and Andy Da Silva stepped out of the building and Paul moved towards them. All three were dressed like Dalloway, except that Omparsad's working clothes were cleaner by far.

The mutual greetings and introductions became a jolly muddle. 'Stanton, Saheb,' said Omparsad and Kindraman in unison as they presented Paul with the Namaste greeting, *'Tapain kasto hunu hunchha?'* Before Paul could reciprocate with his enquiry of good health and well being, the two Gurkhas spotted Nikki and immediately gave her the Namaste, Omparsad speaking in English, 'Nikki Memsaheb, we have been worried about you, but I see you are very safe with Stanton Saheb.'

'I am very well, Om, Kindraman...' Paul responded in Nepali.

'Oh, Omparsad, Kindraman, it's so very good to see you both, and you Danny, how have you all been? I'm fine, we've had a long journey...' Nikki exclaimed as she moved to give all the men a hug.

Dalloway said, bringing order to the chaos, 'OK everyone, let's calm down and get the introductions sorted out properly so we can go inside. I for one need another beer and I suspect our guests need some refreshments. Andy!' he shouted towards Da Silva, who had remained by the entrance to the building. 'This is Andy Da Silva,' Dalloway said to them, 'one of the local militia commanders here and a top man who is vital to our enterprise.' Paul appraised Da Silva and liked what he saw: lean, fit, a mixture of bloods judging by his colouring, and looked like a soldier. 'Andy, please arrange for some refreshments for us all, we'll go into the Mess where its cool and comfortable. We'll be with you in a minute. So,' Dalloway said, looking at Taff Evans and Lefty Shoesmith, who were standing by the Rover, a smile playing on both their faces, 'I am Danny Dalloway, Miss Walker-Haig's *boss*,' and he deliberately emphasised the word, laughed and looked at Paul, 'and these two good men are Omparsad Pun, who commands the operation here at Manica, and his second-in-command, Kindraman Gurung. In due course I shall introduce you to the other wonderful people who make this Farm the thriving and successful commercial venture and community that it is.'

227

Paul was impressed. Danny Dalloway was a different man to the one he had last seen lying in his hospital bed in Kathmandu, his left eye destroyed and face horribly slashed by the Hungarian criminals who had tried to take away his business, the business that was this contract. Evil criminals that Paul, with the Gurkhas, had dealt with. The eye patch suited him and his demeanour, whilst still extrovert, but engaging, seemed now underlaid with compassion and humanity that Paul had never seen before.

Paul said, 'Danny, may I introduce two dear friends, long-time members of the Hereford Gun Club, Staff Sergeant Taff Evans and Sergeant Lefty Shoesmith. Otherwise known as the Bobbsey Twins of Africa!'

'Delighted to meet ya, boss,' said Evans and walked over to shake Dalloway's hand and those of the two Gurkhas.

'Me too, boss,' added Shoesmith, following suit.

'Lovely to meet you both,' replied Dalloway, 'any friend and comrade-in-arms of Paul Stanton is automatically a friend of mine.' He looked at the Land Rover. 'Nice vehicle, gentlemen. A Hereford special no doubt, and of a type that you certainly can't get hold off in these deprived parts. I expect, in due course, you'll tell me how it got into Mozambique?'

During the journey, Paul had briefed Nikki and his men on what he was going to tell Dalloway and his team. There were a number of things they needed to keep to themselves. They should follow Paul's lead, if in doubt.

Paul said, switching the subject, 'On the journey here, Danny, I told Taff and Lefty all about you. And although Nikki slept a lot, she will have heard things about you that will forever give her leverage over you.'

'No chance, Double-Scotch,' Dalloway responded directly to Nikki, who was standing next to the Gurkhas, 'remember that I pay you.'

'Hah, hah, Danny,' Nikki responded, advancing on him, 'so far I don't think I've received a single pay check!'

228

'In good time, all in good time, madam, its still early days in the success story of the business. Come on, let's go inside and tend to your immediate needs. We'll sort out gear and accommodation shortly. Drinks are in order first, and,' he said to Paul, with an earnest look on his face, 'I have something interestingly serious to tell you about.'

Interestingly serious, what on earth could that be, Paul wondered? He and Nikki followed Dalloway inside the building. Evans and Shoesmith were chatting like old comrades to the Gurkhas.

'We done jungle training with your mob down in Brunei,' Evans was saying, 'your boys ran rings round us, I tell you. We thought we was good in them conditions 'til we met the Gurkhas.'

'Your boys were good in the Falklands, too,' said Shoesmith, 'put the fear of God into the Argies, especially during the nights.'

* * *

PAUL HAD ASKED Dalloway to keep the group of people as it was, to keep it as tight and close as needed, and Dalloway had understood why. He informed Paul that the Farm's senior management, Philippe Cruz and his directors, wouldn't be in for the evening until darkfall as they were out and about on the project. Thirty minutes later the preliminaries were out of the way. Hosts and visitors had eaten, had drinks and now it was time to talk, assess and then make the next plan.

Paul told them of their journey: crossing into Zim just south of the actual Border Crossing Post in the early light, using bush and animal tracks, skirting the Vumba Mountains, gradually losing the rains that had come in the night before. Without the Magellan GPS, pre-loaded with the Farm's coordinates, they wouldn't have made it.

Nikki explained how she dialled into the Manica operations room using the satphone to warn of their arrival. She'd spoken to Omparsad who'd told her that Dalloway Saheb was at Manica, but out at the moment and due back shortly. She had brought them up to date with the state of business in Kathmandu and Mutare, which was good, but she'd been worried about the real-time lack of communications.

Dalloway and the Gurkhas now knew why Nikki was here but not why Paul and the SAS men were.

'So, Paul,' Dalloway asked, 'pleasantries are out of the way and we're rested, fed and watered. And although it wasn't necessarily in the plan right now, thanks for giving Nikki a lift here.' Nikki's face grimaced. 'But what have you and the boys actually been up to in Zim, and what exactly are you going to do here?'

'The answer to both questions, Danny, is indirectly, helping you out,' Paul responded evenly. The two Gurkhas spoke very good English but he'd keep it uncomplicated, sanitised, as well, to what Dalloway and his home team had to know. 'Your MozLon regional director, Victor Fitzsimons, went missing sometime between the twenty-ninth of September and the first of October, somewhere between Melsetter and Mutare, just inside the Zim Border.'

'Yes, I know where you mean,' said Dalloway. His scarred face and eyepatch looked foreboding in the shadows of the dimming light. It was almost five, an hour until dark, when the generators would kick in and the lights could be switched on. Dalloway smoked and sipped from his glass of whisky. 'Which explains, of course why we haven't seen him recently. He used to come by Nhamatanda, the other farm, or here, every week. Go on, please.'

'Well, as we told you, we came through Mutare and Nikki was there, so we brought her with us. She insisted on coming.'

Dalloway coughed and poured himself more whisky from the array of bottles on the table. He said, 'And I suppose a man of your indomitable character simply caves in to the whim of a woman, and I suppose your chance meeting thousands of kilometres from where either of you could normally have been expected to be, had absolutely nothing to do with the fact that the two of you happen to be madly in love?'

Paul smiled, 'You sound like my dear dead Dad, Danny! You're right, but only partly!' The Gurkhas were chirping and laughing.

''E's got you there, boss,' said Evans, 'bang to rights, 'e 'as!' Like the Gurkhas, he and Shoesmith were really enjoying themselves. The beer bottles were mounting up. None of them had been able to relax for some days now. It was what they all needed. Da Silva was joining in, absorbing what was being said but keeping his counsel. Paul liked him.

'Anyway,' Paul said, 'here's the heart of the matter, if you'll excuse the pun.'

'Hah, hah, Stanton, go on.'

Paul hoped this part sounded more convincing, 'A key man for Sir Reggie Hanlon goes AWOL over three weeks ago and no one, here or in London, has any knowledge of what happened to him,' not true, of course, and Paul exchanged a confidential facial sign with Nikki, 'so Hanlon writes a personal letter to the Prime Minister requesting help.'

'What! Requesting help, for fuck's sake! Oh, excuse me, Nikki. How can Sir Reggie do that? Cheeky bastard.'

'For all sorts of reasons apparently, which include the business benefits MozLon, and therefore Gurkha Connections Limited, is bringing to UK, the fact that Hanlon is personally involved in the Mozambique peace process, which Mrs Thatcher supports, and he wants reassurance that everything is above board here, before the next round of talks in Maputo early in December. Oh, and because he's a Knight of the Realm, a personal friend of Maggie Thatcher and because one of his senior men has disappeared, I suppose.' It sounded half-lame to Paul. One day he'd tell Dalloway the full story.

'OK, I'll buy it, so far. So how does one of the British Army's top black ops men, a lieutenant colonel no less, and by the way congrats on the promotion,' Paul inclined his head and sipped his whisky, he needed to be careful, 'how does this man, you, happen to be in Zimbabwe with a mini-cohort of SAS colleagues and a Special Forces 110 Series Land Rover?'

'We were flown by the RAF into the military air base side of Harare Airport, with the consent of the Commander of BMATT, the British Military Advisory Training Team,' Paul explained for Nikki and Da Silva, 'offloaded ourselves and struck out for Mutare. We went via Nyanga, just to pay our compliments to the Commandant there, but the trail ended up in the Border area, which was where MozLon HQ in London last had word of him.' Even though the first part was a total lie, now the story was beginning to sound a touch more plausible, Paul thought.

'How so? What happened?'

'MozLon in London, the Head of Security, your old drinking pal from Hong Kong days, Fred Etherington, had info from the Head of Zimbabwe's CIO, a man called Ken Rose, of terrorist activity close to Mutare, but over the border in Mozambique. He gave us this info and a contact in Mutare. Hence it was our start point and also our end point, as it happened, and it was where we found Nikki, at the Wise Owl Motel, who was looking for Fitzsimons, as she said.'

'Yes, she did, and I believe her. But how come you're here, with Taff and Lefty?'

'Blimey, Danny, what is this, the Spanish Inquisition?' Paul tried to make light of it, but in truth he needed to steer Dalloway onto other things. 'You know my reputation, you know how dispensable I am after the goings on in Berlin, I'm also sort of between jobs at the moment, and I asked for two trusted men to come with me.'

'Paul did, Danny,' said Evans, 'me an' Lefty was on the Counter-Terrorism Role and was getting our briefing in London at Duke o' York's when Paul collared us for this mission. Our gaffer, OC A Squadron, Major Ted Bakerswell, was singularly unamused. You might 'ave known 'im when you was still in the Service?'

Paul interjected, 'Anyway, we picked up the trail of Fitzsimons with the help of our contact in Mutare, covertly crossed the border and scouted around and found the location where he'd been bushwhacked and killed.'

'Where?'

'Not that far from here, in fact, but further south down towards the forests. We found evidence of his clothing and ID, which we took back to Mutare and handed over. We also found evidence that his killers were renegade military of some sort, so likely to be ex-Renamo. They left ammo behind and there were empty cases, seven point six two short, AKs probably, and boot prints. The info has all been passed back to Rose and to London and our task now is to get out of here, via Beira, with an exit plan that's being prepared but which I don't know about yet.' Paul sat back and looked at Dalloway, and took a drink from his whisky. He cast a glance at Nikki who was sitting curled up on a small wicker sofa, nestling her glass in her hands. She looked tired, absolutely lovely in the dimming evening light, but deep tired. He could guess at the emotional strain she had been under these past days.

Paul was waiting for the difficult question: *What about the body?* But it didn't come. Instead, Dalloway said unexpectedly, 'That makes sense, Paul, doesn't it, Om?' Paul sensed a change in his mood and thoughts, a distraction almost.

'Je, saheb,' responded Omparsad. Paul saw Kindraman and Da Silva nod their heads in agreement. Evans and Shoesmith became alert. It made sense? It was a total fabrication!

'It makes sense, doesn't it, Andy?' Dalloway said to Da Silva.

'It does make sense, Major, it sure does. The same rebels, most like.'

'The same rebels?' Paul asked. 'Now it's your turn, Danny, what's up? Is this the something interestingly serious you mentioned earlier?'

'I think so,' Dalloway replied. He looked at his watch. 'We've got twenty minutes before the others will join us for a sundowner and an update on the day's progress and situation. You have to meet Philippe Cruz, and the directors. They run the place for MozLon and they'll want to show their hospitality and be brought up-to-date with events.' Dalloway stood up and started pacing slowly, stopping, drawing on his cigarette and looking at Paul. He seemed to have come to a decision. 'OK, I'll give you the short version of what's happening and where I, Andy, Kindraman and one or two others have been these past two days. We have a real threat from rebel Renamo guerrillas, the same group from which I suspect Fitzsimons' killers came. The geography fits, the timescale fits...'

Danny Dalloway told them everything, concisely and clearly, and one thing Paul was reasonably sure of was that Fitzsimons' killers were not part of the breakaway group of Renamo threatening the

MozLon enterprises; but it didn't matter, it didn't in any way lessen Dalloway's clear and present danger.

Dalloway finished by saying, 'Let's not talk about it any more, other than what I have to tell Philippe and the others. Let us enjoy our evening and relax a little. Paul, if you agree, we'll hold a council of war tomorrow morning, at zero eight hundred hours in the Ops room and we'll make a plan?'

'That's fine, Danny.'

'Come on then, it'll be dark very soon, and we need to show you all to your accommodations before supper.'

* * *

MUCH LATER, DANNY Dalloway and Paul were completely alone, in a corner of the Mess, sharing more whisky and a few last minutes of tired, friendly talk. There were no secrets between the two men.

Dalloway studied the amber nectar in his glass and drew on his cigarette. Paul thought he looked pleasantly smashed, but his mind was still clear. 'So what was Fitzsimons really up to, Paul?'

'Being a courier for White interests in Zim. Taking their hard assets to Beira for shipment overseas. He was totally honest and was murdered for it.'

'I thought as much. You hear things, Paul, in the corridors of Beira and Maputo, just little whispers, nothing you can build a picture with. I'm glad he was honest. I really liked him and he helped us tons. It's largely due to his support and advice that we're making such a success of the contract, and boy do we need to. I'm broke back in Nepal. Still, my first major stage payment comes through at the end of the month and according to Nikki, we've been told we'll get it, in full.'

'So you should. MozLon in London think the world of you, so you'll be fine, and there's nothing I've discovered in Pretoria or Harare to worry you.'

'That's good to know, matey, very good to know. Which makes it imperative that we snuff out these Renamo fuckers that we've found down in the Chicamba Real, before they bugger everything up, for me and the farms. You're OK with helping us, Paul? You're sure?'

'I'm sure, sure, Danny. Taff and Lefty have brought enough firepower to take on the Soviet Forces. There's no way we'd be able to ship it back to UK so we may as well use it, and I've the authority to do so if needs must. But we'll stack the odds in our favour, Danny, minimise the risks.'

'Of course, mate, you're the boss in this, you're the fighting man, but the enemy have played into our hands in my view.' Paul's look asked the question. 'We got pretty close to their base on our recce patrol. We mapped the layout and the routine and we counted their number. Twenty-five, we reckoned. It's not a substantial camp, all open-sided, timber framed communal buildings with bush thatch and crappy furniture, you know the sort, eating hall, utility store, briefing room, classroom, probably some type of comms room and ammo store or armoury, but we only saw light weapons, no heavy stuff. All these buildings were grouped centrally, and on either side it looked like sleeping bashas, probably twenty or so, which would make sense. They were a rabble, mate, in my humble opinion.'

'What about the ground?'

'That's where they've bollocksed themselves, Paul. The camp is on the northern shoreline of the Chicamba Real, on one of the spurs of water right to the very west of the total Dam area.' Paul let Dalloway go on. He was visualising what his friend was describing but until he studied the map it didn't make much sense. 'When the Portuguese created the Dam in sixty-eight, they did what happens everywhere, they flooded a huge networked valley area, because they wanted to create the hydro-electric power for the more industrialised areas of Manica Province which lie to the east of here, down the pipeline road towards Beira. Now, some of the water areas are deep, really deep, but as the water levels settled, the Dam area expanded into gentler valley areas, particularly here in the west, where the ground rises towards the mountains, the Vumba.'

Paul suddenly had the picture, or he thought he did, 'So you're saying that these Renamo have made a camp on the shores of the Dam in an area where they can get at the water, almost like a beach area?'

'Precisely, Paul, precisely! They have no way out to the south, because they are backed up against the water. And, my dear old friend, we saw no boats! These fuckers do not swim instinctively!' Dalloway sighed deeply and took a large drink. He looked at Paul with a tired, half-smile on his scarred face. His one eye was bloodshot with fatigue and whisky. 'Change the subject, Paul. We'll do all this detailed attack planning in the morning, early.' He paused and then said, 'So you didn't find Fitzsimons' killers, but you and the powers-that-be are sure they were Renamo?'

'Yes,' Paul half-lied.

'Good. What was Fitzsimons carrying?'

Damn! 'On this trip, nothing,' Paul lied. 'Fact is, as I learned from Ken Rose, although Fitzsimons came through from Beira quite regularly, as you know, he was only asked to carry hard assets very occasionally. This was an occasion when he was simply going about his normal business.'

'Fucking Renamo bastardos.'

Paul said, slightly tempting fate, 'We didn't find Fitzsimons' body, though.'

'No, mate, I guessed you hadn't. Fact is these Renamo savages will have chopped the poor man up and fed him to the beasts of the bush. The big cats will have fed to satiety, as dear old T S Elliot might have said, and the hyena will have dragged the remains miles across the bush. What an end for a good man. God, I liked him.' Dalloway sat up, stretched his shoulders, leant back again, slouching into his chair and said, 'You're a good man, too, Paul, and Nikki's a lucky woman.'

'Don't know about that, Danny, but I can't bring her into this business. She knows the outline but not the gory detail, and I've still got to get to Beira and sort out something there.'

'I'll keep her with me for a few days, at least until after we've killed the enemy, then I'll take her back to Mutare, myself.'

'That would be a huge weight off my mind. Her Land Rover's still parked at the Wise Owl, but I left a note for the Manager before leaving this morning, along with a sufficient sum of money to pay for our bills.'

'Sure you don't need my help in Beira, Paul, I know the place a little?'

'That's a kind offer, but I have help there, official Government help, and I've got to get Taff and Lefty and all our gear out of country.'

'They're good men, Paul, and they think the world of you.'

'As do your Gurkhas of you, Danny, and the very good people here on the Farm, and so they should.'

Dalloway was now slipping into slumber and there was one other thing Paul wanted to seed into his tired mind. 'Talking of Nikki,' he said, and Dalloway's head shot up, 'We are a couple, and although we haven't discussed the future in detail, I'm pretty sure we're going to marry our lives together.'

'Phew, Stanton, that's a big step for you.' Dalloway's head started to loll.

'Yes it is, and it will change my life. All I would ask, Danny, is that you think hard about how you can get her back to London very soon.'

'I will, mate, I really will. It would be only fair after the favour you did me in Kathmandu and now here...' Dalloway's head drooped forward and then rocked back. A soft grunt escaped from his mouth. He was asleep.

Paul Stanton put a cushion behind his friend's head and left him to his rest. He walked out of the Mess towards the small thatched cottage that was his and Nikki's accommodation for the night, towards a woman with whom he hoped he'd share a bed forever.

For the time being he put from his mind the fact that from tomorrow there would be a small action to be fought. There would be risks, there always were in combat and Paul knew it better than most. So did Danny Dalloway. Never underestimate your enemy. So they would stack the odds in their favour. They knew the enemy's location and layout, they had surprise on their side, a boldness of approach, massive firepower and the SAS and Gurkhas. What enemy force on earth could withstand that combination?

Tomorrow they'd find out if there was one.

CHAPTER TWENTY-TWO

HIS VOICE WOKE her. He was talking on his satphone, quietly, but loud enough for him to have brought her to wakefulness. Nikki opened her eyes and looked at him. Paul was sitting in a chair, naked, his long legs propped up on the ledge of the open window, his back half-towards her where she lay in bed underneath the mosquito net. Thankfully it had been cool in the night and the net had not felt claustrophobic. She'd been vaguely aware of Paul climbing in beside her last night, much later on, but the accumulation of emotional and physical stress had finally caught up with her and she had fallen into a deep sleep. She looked at her watch. It was not quite six o'clock, but she'd had eight hours sleep.

Her movement must have alerted Paul because he got up, looked out of the window, turned and moved towards the bed. She loved his body and the way he walked. He was a warrior and bore the scars to prove it, but he was tall and compactly put together, every part properly proportioned. He thought the same of her, he'd told her with love in his eyes, so it must be true: the two of them fitted, they were a team. Where would it lead them, she worried? Not for the first time.

Paul smiled at her, lifted up the mosquito net and tucked it over the metal frame so that the cooler air of the room could waft in. He was listening. Who was he speaking to?

'Ken Rose,' he mouthed silently to her as he sat down on the edge of the bed and idly stroked her bare arm. Nikki loved the softness of his touch. How could this man of war be so soft and caring? He cared for everyone. He carried their burdens and never seemed to tire or lose his sense of direction. God alone knew what black deeds he had locked away, yet they did not appear to taint his soul or harden his heart. She lay back and watched him and her love for him made her sigh. Paul looked at her, smiling his lovely smile whilst also listening intently. He lent forwards and gave her a gentle, simple kiss. He stood up and wandered back towards the window. Nikki's mind turned quixotically to her concerns, the worries she would tell him about later. She knew she had to be strong and brave, but she would tell Paul about her fears. She needed him to reassure her and then it would be all right.

'So, Ken,' Paul said, 'Dick Hanney's told you everything and the follow up actions in Mutare are in progress and you're content all is in order?' Nikki watched him listen to the reply. His face was calm.

'And with Macfarlane?' The answer must have been yes. Paul said, 'Good, and thank you. I will deliver the package to your man in the Portuguese Embassy, you have my word, and in return I really need any information you can gather on Ramon Lima.' Nikki's mind fastened on these snippets. They'd had a small council of war at the Wise Owl Motel last night and Paul had said he'd recovered the diamonds and he and Dick Hanney had talked about the horrid Police Chief, Macfarlane. Then Hanney had left. She'd been too afraid to ask any of the men what had actually happened. They were all safe and that was all that had mattered. But who was Ramon Lima?

'I'll speak to you in a couple of days, Ken. I'm staying at Manica probably until Wednesday, all things being equal, and then I'll move on to Beira.' She wouldn't be going with Paul, Nikki knew this; how would she bear the sudden separation?

'Don't be sad, Nik,' Paul said and lay down on top of the bed beside her. He propped himself up on his elbow and fixed her with his startlingly blue eyes. He smiled, 'You know the plan, my love, I have to finish the job and that means going on to Beira.' He rolled onto his back and held her hand. 'There is the little matter of the Renamo to be dealt with first but that will happen later today and tomorrow. We'll all be back here by the afternoon.'

'Are you sure, Paul?' She couldn't stand it if anything happened to him. This was her worry.

'Yes, and I never count my chickens on these things. I'm sure. You ask Taff or Lefty or any of the Gurkhas. We'll firm up the plan in a couple of hours and we'll all make it work.' Paul faced her again. 'I love you, Nicola Walker-Haig, and I couldn't bear it if anything should happen to you,' her heart lurched and she felt the tears squeezing into her eyes, 'and that includes me not being there to be with you,' he finished.

'Oh, Paul, I love you so much!'

'I know, I know, which is why Danny and I made another type of plan last night.' Nikki held her breath as Paul went on, 'After we've moved on to Beira, he's agreed to take you back to Mutare personally, for which I am indebted to him, and he's agreed to let you return to London if you so wish.'

'Why would I want to do that?'

'To marry me?' And her heart crashed and she burst into tears.

'That is the most beautiful thing anyone has ever said to me, Paul.'

'If I had my duty hankie I'd offer it to you, baby, but I don't and I'm assuming that's a yes, then?'

'Yes, yes, yes!'

'When I've finished the job in Beira and Charles Grace has helped me get the boys and the gear back to UK, then I'm going to have a serious think about my military future, which, when we can, I'd like to discuss with you. How does that sound?'

'It sounds absolutely great, Paul! I'm so happy, so, so happy!'

'Well then happiness, I'm happy, too. And as for Ramon Lima, he's the last piece in this dirty puzzle, Nik, and I have to find him, which I will.' Paul leapt up and moved towards the bathroom. 'Come on lazy lover, we have a busy day. We need an early breakfast. There's lots to do.'

Nikki realised that she was the happiest and luckiest woman on earth.

Because of Paul Stanton. Her man.

* * *

CHARLES GRACE ENJOYED some moments of solitude sitting in Colin Bullock's office. The Defence Attaché was about his business, briefing his staff and firefighting with the rampaging British general in Harare, the Head of BMATT, not that ultimately it was any of the man's business, but he was a notoriously noisy senior officer. However, there was the not-so-simple issue of getting Major de Castenet's body released from the Zimbabwe police and having it repatriated to Pretoria for onward shipment to UK, and having the general's help in this was essential. Thankfully, the Head of the Zimbabwe Central Intelligence Organisation, Ken Rose, was also helping, and apparently the local police chief in Mutare was being very cooperative, which wasn't a surprise given what Paul Stanton had told him on Saturday night. Well done, Stanton, yet again.

Grace had an hour before he needed to leave the British Embassy and be driven to Johannesburg Airport for the flight to Maputo and then on to Beira. He had his small amount of luggage, his satphone and all his travel documents with him, so he was good to go. Grace was basing himself in the High Commission, and the First Secretary had persuaded him to stay with him and his wife in their spacious apartment there, for however long he needed to, which Grace was glad about.

There was still work to do in Beira. According to Stanton, and Grace believed him, a man called Ramon Lima contracted renegade Renamo to do mercenary work, and this man was the final link in the criminal network and so had to be questioned and possibly silenced to ensure total success of the mission. Grace had asked John Sawyer yesterday if he could use his intelligence sources to help locate Lima's whereabouts and with whom he associated. Sawyer said he would try, but it would have to wait until Monday; and as frustrating as it was for him, Grace knew he had to be patient and get to Beira, where he could speak to Sawyer in a secure environment, pull all the information together and start the groundwork in earnest.

Grace thought about Stanton and his men. He had to arrange their exit plan. It was Berlin all over again. He checked his watch. It was time for him to call London. After the frenetic goings on of yesterday he had to be sure the Prime Minister had all the information she required. He walked over to Bullock's desk, sat down in the chair, picked up the telephone and dialled the private number in Downing Street of the Prime Minister's Chief of Staff. The line warbled and sang for a few seconds and was then answered. The connection stayed strong.

'Chief of Staff.'

Grace responded, 'Good morning, Chief of Staff, it is Charles Grace, calling from Pretoria, do you have time to talk to me for a few minutes?'

'I do, General Grace, the PM is having her breakfast and reading up on what has been happening here at home. I take it you must have news. Have events turned out the way we hoped for? And if so, how may I help you?'

'They have, thank you.' Grace swiftly ordered his thoughts. He had at best two minutes before either the PM's Chief of Staff would be called away, or the blasted telephone line would fail in some way. He said, 'There is a hullabaloo, based in Zimbabwe, which broke out late on Saturday. It is being handled very well, in my view, by our staff here, but it is likely to echo all the way back to the UK, but how loudly I do not know. The British officer we talked about has met with an unfortunate accident and is dead. His body was found on Saturday evening in a remote location close to the Mozambique Border. It appears to the Zimbabwe Police that he was involved with a member of the South African National Intelligence Service in criminal activities, and that this person killed him. We do not know the full detail of their activity yet, but I believe it involved the smuggling of diamonds and gold, probably across the borders from Zimbabwe into Mozambique and South Africa.' Charles Grace deliberately paused. The man on the line had a mind that could process prodigious quantities of data at lightning speed, and pare it all down to the essentials equally swiftly.

The Chief of Staff said, 'I shall brief the PM and we shall prepare a statement with the Ministry of Defence to satisfy the media. We will also need to decide our position regarding the South African Government.'

Grace responded, 'I believe the latter will be made easier by the fact that the South African man involved died in a traffic accident, later the same night, during a violent rain storm and whilst attempting to cross into Mozambique using a remote track through the mountains. Evidence of their criminal activity and a weapon, presumably the killing weapon, were found in his vehicle.'

'That does make it easier. Thank you. I take it that we have offered all support to the requisite national authorities?'

'We have.'

'I also take it that in the fullness of time the wretched man's body will be repatriated?'

'It will. The Defence Attaché in Pretoria will lead on this and is highly competent. He knows the full story.'

'Very good, General Grace. Should Mrs Thatcher be concerned about anything else?'

'I don't believe so. There is nothing that in any way implicates Colonel Stanton in what has happened, and he and his men are no longer in South Africa. I am also confident that Sir Reggie Hanlon's business and political initiatives in the region are all above board and remain on track.'

'Excellent. Anything else?'

'One final thing, Chief of Staff, if I may.' Grace didn't stop to let the man say anything, 'You recall the contingencies we put in place for Colonel Stanton and his team in Berlin, their exit requirements? Well I shall need your assistance, please, to ensure something similar this time, from Beira.'

'Quick details, please, General?'

'There will be three of them and an SAS vehicle. I would suggest an RAF transport aircraft on standby in Nairobi at Moi Airbase, from Wednesday, and with special clearance from Portugal to fly into the military air base facilities at Beira at very short notice.'

'I shall speak with the necessary people today. Thank you once again, General Grace.' And the line went dead.

Charles Grace sighed deeply and allowed himself a moment of satisfied reflection. He looked again at his watch. He still had time to make his other telephone call, to Fred Etherington in MozLon's London HQ. The man had been very patient and not pestered him since he'd been in Pretoria, but he did owe Etherington a positive situation report. Then it really would be time to start the journey to Beira, where he had more work to do, to find Ramon Lima, and meet Stanton and his men. Stanton had said he hoped to be in Beira by Wednesday at the latest. Grace hoped it would be so.

But when Stanton had told Grace that, neither of them had known about Chicamba Real.

* * *

IT WAS A properly orchestrated operational briefing in the Manica farm canteen. Everyone was seated close up to the low stage on which the briefing would take place. They could see the large-scale map of the Chicamba Real area pinned up on the wall, and they could see the sandbox model of the Renamo rebel camp that Andy Da Silva and the Gurkhas had made. The model was up on the stage and it was excellent. It showed everything: topography, vegetation, routes and enemy dispositions. The scale was clear to see. Paul remembered how brilliant his Gurkhas had been at making tactical models out of the bits and pieces they carried or found, no matter where it was. This was another example of their skill.

The model brought to life everything Dalloway had described to him last night. And so with his help, Paul had devised the Troops to Tasks, the manpower that would carry out the action in the various required roles. All those involved were sitting in their battle groupings, slightly apart from the senior management of the Farm who were there of course, because they would keep the enterprise running and had to know what was going on. They also had to be prepared to receive the men back at the Farm after the action, Paul had said, because there could be casualties. Nikki was in the front row, next to him. Paul and Dalloway had agreed they would share the briefing. The stage was quite literally set and it was time to start.

Dalloway stood up and moved onto the platform. Everyone hushed their chattering. He said, 'We are going to attack the Renamo rebel camp and kill every single one of them.' His opening statement of the mission couldn't have been more riveting or clear. 'We will move from here this afternoon and be in position before last light. We will move in vehicles, with weapons and equipment, and in tactical groupings organised for the tasks that need to be carried out. The detail of this will be given to you in a few moments. At the same time, we will continue to run this Farm as normal.' Those listening were spellbound. Paul smiled to himself. Dalloway was good. He felt his heart quicken. Now that they were committed to battle, there would be no turning back, and as he always had, Paul experienced a growing sense of excitement underlaid with a healthy frisson of fear. This was his world! He reached for and squeezed Nikki's hand. She glanced at him and returned his look of keen anticipation with a worried frown.

Dalloway walked across the stage and said, 'The reason we are doing this is because these rebels are rogue. They do not represent Mozambique. They are not owned by either of the two main parties discussing the independent future of this country, *your* country and *your* future,' he emphasised. 'We are doing this because these rebels want to harm us and cause the farms to fail. We all work for MozLon,' he continued, 'and these rebels certainly do not share the interests of our Company, in fact, quite the opposite. And so, we must kill them, and then forget them and work towards the future. They will not be missed and they will not be mourned. And we shall remove all traces of them from the face of this earth.'

This last statement caused Paul a moment of thought, because he and Dalloway hadn't exactly worked out how they would achieve the forensic clean up they had agreed was necessary. But, the two of them had reasoned, the Gurkhas had great skill and imagination in such matters, and besides, once on the ground with the battle over, options and ideas would become apparent. Paul's thought was interrupted. Dalloway moved to stand in front of him, and his friend turned his blazing single eye on him and said, 'And this fighting man, Colonel Stanton, will now tell us all how we shall achieve this outcome.'

'Nice one, boss,' chirped Taff Evans from behind Paul, 'no pressure then?'

'Why aren't you sitting with your task group, Evans,' Paul muttered from the side of his mouth as he started to get up.

'I am, Paul, I'm with you. Some poor bastard's got to protect you, else what would Nikki say?' Nikki turned round and nodded her head to Evans.

'Lord help me,' Paul responded, 'disobedient subordinates.'

'Over to you, Paul,' Dalloway said as Paul finally got up onto the stage and turned to look at everyone.

He scanned the pool of faces and saw the mixed looks of worry and uncertainty amongst Da Silva's militia platoon of thirty men, the impassive, serious expressions of the wonderful Gurkhas, all twelve of them, with Omparsad and Kindraman at their front, and the quizzical concerns of Philippe Cruz and the other senior management of the Farm. Then he looked at Shoesmith and Evans, both of whom were making faces, and he chuckled out loud, which seemed to ease everyone's tensions, including his own.

Paul said, 'Danny's right.' He set his face and spoke in a firm and forthright voice that he knew would carry to everyone listening, 'We have to remove these rebels and we shall. We will ensure, through our own forces and the planning we have made, that there is no possibility of the rebels succeeding against us.'

Paul needed to identify those taking part, to bind them personally into this action, in which it was possible some would be injured and even killed. He also needed to reassure those who would be staying behind. So he said to each group, 'We have the fantastic support of the Farm itself and those who lead it and make it work, we have your brave and skilled militia, we have the wonderful Gurkhas,

247

and we have two very experienced warriors from the SAS.' Evans and Shoesmith were now watching Paul intently, they'd got serious. 'We know where the enemy is and how he is deployed and the enemy knows nothing about what we plan. So we have the forces to kill him and we have surprise. Do we have the firepower and the resources? Yes, and far more than he has. We have all the tactical ingredients required to succeed. We shall attack the enemy at dawn tomorrow morning when he is at his weakest and do it quickly and surgically. We plan to be back here by early afternoon tomorrow, so please look out for us.' There was a ripple of amusement at this remark. Paul walked over to stand by the map and the model and picked up the length of bamboo to be used as a pointer. He said, 'This is how we shall do it. Please listen carefully and if you have any questions then save them until I have finished. Don't worry, we will all be absolutely clear about how this plan will be carried out.'

And Paul Stanton took them through the plan of battle and how it would be executed. Like all good plans, it was simple. It was also capable of adjustment, if and when the enemy didn't do exactly what you had thought it would do, which more often than not, in Paul's experience, was the case.

No plan survives contact with the enemy.

CHAPTER TWENTY-THREE

IT WAS THE time when the earth had no colour except the greying of coming dawn. There was sufficient light for Paul to check the layout of the Renamo camp through his binoculars. They'd marked and confirmed it all yesterday before the sun had gone down, and Paul had made some slight adjustments to the plan. They'd monitored any movements through the night from their static positions, but the short burst walkie-talkie transmissions had been few. Now he could see nothing had changed, and there was no one up and about. It seemed the enemy suspected nothing.

Paul felt the moment and knew it was almost time to start. Everything and everyone was in place. All the fighting forces had Kevlar body vests, weapons, bullets and water. There would be time to eat after the action. Each group had a medical satchel and each man carried a field dressing. They had used most of the Manica Farm vehicle fleet to get here, and the vehicles were secure at the rendezvous location five hundred metres away, guarded by Dalloway's driver and radio operator and two of Da Silva's militia, both of whom could drive. Paul had checked the walkie-talkie communications with the vehicle group. It was possible they might be needed in a hurry.

Paul had an errant thought: Tuesday morning, in London, walking up to Sloane Square from his flat in Pimlico, getting into Duke of York's and Headquarters Director Special Forces, grabbing a coffee, chatting to the rest of the staff, checking his in-tray... What in God's name was he doing here? He was killing renegade Renamo guerrillas in Mozambique, of course, what else would he be doing on a Tuesday morning in late October? Christ! In which case, Stanton, get on with it.

'Lefty,' Paul said quietly to Shoesmith, who was behind him and to his left, 'get ready.'

'Roger, boss.' He heard Shoesmith move off back towards the Land Rover, their mobile weapons platform. The Gurkhas had silently manhandled the vehicle into position last evening. Now it was ready to fire and ready to move, just ten metres away.

'Om,' Paul turned to Omparsad who was five paces to his right, 'get ready to move, as soon as Lefty opens fire, but on my command.'

'Hunchha, saheb.'

Paul squeezed the pressel on his walkie-talkie and spoke quietly, 'Danny, Andy, get ready.'

The answers came immediately into his earpiece, 'Roger, Paul,' said Dalloway first, followed by the same affirmative from Da Silva.

They had established an all-informed walkie-talkie communications network before they left the Farm, that way everyone would know what was going on. It required a modicum of radio discipline: answer when you're called; report when you have to; otherwise maintain silence. Simple. The distances between the killing groups in Paul's plan were relatively short and the system's range was more than adequate. Radio communications would have been a nightmare.

As Dalloway had told him, and as the model back at the Farm had shown them all, the enemy had played into Paul's hands. The Renamo camp housed a force of twenty-five men, maybe one or two more, that looked like a rabble, living in a rambling bush camp of sleeping and working accommodations made of wood and brush. Washing lines of faded bush clothing were strung between building frames, and small piles of boxes and equipment lay close to the buildings. The camp was in a large clearing right on the northern shore of the Chicamba Real. They were backed up against the vast expanse of water that was the Dam, and that was a big mistake. Furthermore, their base was surrounded by sporadic plantations of trees, low koppies of rocks and scrub, and undulating bush savannah, criss-crossed by tracks into and out of their encampment. The tracks were well worn from Renamo use and from the elephant and buffalo that came to drink from the watering access places close by, but Paul's plan had them all covered. The enemy were trapped.

No, Paul thought, as he scanned the area once again, the enemy was a force of isolated, probably un-owned Renamo rebels, that looked poorly done by, but they were trained bush veterans, and of all things they still had weapons and bullets, their pride and ambitions, and they would fight.

Enough speculation. The sun was climbing up from the horizon. Grey was turning to dull colours. It was time to start killing the bastards.

'Fire!' he hissed to Lefty Shoesmith, and immediately the Minimi 5.56mm machinegun, mounted on the forward roll bar of the Land Rover, burst into rapid fire. Lefty had belted ten thousand rounds of mixed tracer and armour-piercing rounds, loaded the gun with the first five hundred, and laid the spare belts on the floor of the wagon, ready for use. The red, lantern-lit tracer bullets arced down onto the Renamo camp and started to smash it to pieces and kill the enemy. From a range of four hundred metres and an elevation of fifty feet, which was the height of the koppie that Paul had chosen for the Rover's fire position, the bullets were lethal. Half-dressed bodies burst from the groups of bashas closest to them, and stood transfixed as the bullets crashed all around them. Bodies fell and jerked and men ran in all directions. Paul's plan was to use Lefty's gunfire and Om's Gurkhas to drive the enemy north-eastwards along the shore of the Dam, into the traps waiting there, and to kill as many of them as possible.

Now the sun was up and becoming bright. The world had been brutally awakened. The gunfire was relentless and the smell of cordite and burned powder filled the air. Paul's ears bounced with the harsh, staccato sound and empty bullet cases pinged and rattled in the back of the Rover. It was cacophonous and the thousands of birds in the trees around the Chicamba Real burst from their roosts, cawed and

251

screamed in disturbed protest and flocked in swarms above the scene of increasing chaos and carnage.

Down towards the enemy, on the edge of the fringe of trees two hundred metres to the north, a blanket of gunfire burst out. It was Danny Dalloway's group, with Taff Evans, Kindraman and a section of militia, sited to block any exit that way but also to get in amongst the enemy's communal buildings and kill them hand-to-hand if necessary. Beyond the camp itself, at the eastern end of the scrubby open ground, was a low ridge over which tracks criss-crossed. It was the final cut-off position that dominated the other group of bashas, and that was where Paul had located Andy Da Silva and two sections of militia. They had machineguns, and they dominated a killing zone into which any enemy survivors would move to escape. From a range of three hundred metres they were also pouring fire into the rapidly disintegrating encampment.

'Lefty!' Paul shouted. 'Switch left!' The gunfire immediately traversed slowly to the left, annihilating the enemy and clearing the attack approach for Omparsad's band of six Gurkha killing machines. 'Om!' Paul shouted to his right, 'Move now!'

'Ayo Gurkhali!' was Omparsad's immediate screamed response as he and the Gurkhas burst over the crest of the low hill and raced down towards the enemy camp. 'Jai Gurkha!' his men roared, some firing from the hip with their AK-47s, blazing bursts of aimed fire, and the others with their kukris out, held high, the wickedly sharp blades glinting in the coming sunlight. Four hundred metres downhill? Even with Kevlar body armour, chest webbing and ammunition, the Gurkhas would close with and start killing the enemy inside forty seconds. It was no contest.

With his orders to fire and move, Paul had unleashed the full coordinated killing plan. The enemy was caught in three-way crossfire and trapped against the depths of the Chicamba Real. It was slaughter, but it wasn't finished. Not by a long shot.

* * *

252

DANNY DALLOWAY, WITH Taff Evans, Kindraman, four of the remaining Gurkhas and a section of Da Silva's militia, were in a series of blocking positions in the trees, covering the tracks into and out of the north and north-western areas of the enemy camp, which they could see clearly, two hundred metres to their front. They had infiltrated into their assault positions before dark and stayed undetected all through the night. Dalloway was tired, his eye ached and the fucking mosquitoes had been merciless. Thank the Lord for his water bottle of Gurkha rum.

Paul's voice broke into his earpiece and after listening he responded, 'Roger, Paul.' He turned on his side, 'Taff, Kindraman,' he whispered, 'be ready. Any moment now. Pass it on to the militia boys.' And within a minute the world to his front exploded in rapid gunfire. 'Fire!' Danny yelled. Thank the fuck, he thought. Now let's kill the bastards. He squeezed off a fifteen round burst from his AK-47. All around him the rifle fire broke loose. Next to him Taff Evans was firing short, aimed bursts from his HK MP5. Dalloway was glad he had the reassuring presence and experience of the SAS man with him.

The world to his front was disintegrating in a mass of broken scrub and exploding dirt and stones as the weight of fire tore apart the meagre foliage and arrowed in towards the camp. The noise was deafening and was added to by the screeching flocks of birds. Dalloway shook his head, adjusted his eye patch and scrambled up on to his knees, releasing the tension and ache in his joints. He couldn't really see what the hell was happening. He needed to get closer.

'What you thinkin', boss?' Evans said, close to his ear. 'A coupla minutes more for Lefty to move the bastards beyond our killin' area and then we get in amongst 'em? Do a few of 'em in an' 'elp shift the remnants up towards Andy's killing zone?'

'You've got it, Taff,' and Dalloway, with some difficulty, unfastened his alcoholic water bottle and offered it to Evans. God he hated all this chest webbing and body armour bollocks, you couldn't get to the important things in life.

'Don't mind if I do, Danny. Top stuff,' and Evans took a pull and handed it back to Danny. Evans peered to his front and said, 'Paul's plan's working, Danny. The bastards are moving and Lefty's fire's almost past us.'

'It is. Let's go. If we don't, Om's team will have all the spoils.' He stood up and roared above the noise, 'Stop! Stop firing!' Dalloway quickly moved to his men. Leaning over Kindraman, he said, 'Kindri, we go in on my command. Get the boys ready. Weapons and kukris. Kill any dushman you find. Omparsad's men will be coming in from the west, from our right hand side, so be careful.'

'Hunchha, saheb.'

Dalloway scrabbled through the scrub and found the section commander of Da Silva's militia platoon, a young Mozambican with wide staring eyes and cordite marks all around his face. The man looked happy! 'Rodriguez, you know your tasks?' The man nodded energetically and poked a finger into his ear, shaking his head a little. Don't blame you, Dalloway thought, it's enough to deafen us all. 'I'm going into the camp with the Gurkhas. We'll clear it to the edge of the water, to our front, ahead,' he signalled the direction with his hand. 'Then we'll move to our left, that way. Omparsad's Gurkhas will come from the right.' Christ, Dalloway thought, this is too complicated. 'Do you understand, Rodriguez?'

'I do, Major, sir. Don't worry, I understand it clear.'

Thank God for educated local men. He said, smiling in return, 'Good man. Just remember, if any, *any*, of the enemy come this way to escape, then you and your men kill them. Kill them. No prisoners.'

'I understand, sir,' and the young Rodriguez smiled again, bright white teeth in the midst of a camouflage-blackened, cordite smeared face.

'When it's all over, Colonel Stanton will give the signal, and then I or one of the Gurkhas will come for you. Stay here until that time. You have done really well, Rodriguez, but stay strong, now.'

Dalloway gathered Taff Evans and his Gurkhas and broke cover, racing, bobbing and weaving, towards the dust and debris of the broken enemy camp.

Then the first bursts of enemy fire rang out, zipping all around them, and the fight was on. 'Ayo Gurkhali!' roared Dalloway, 'Kill them all!'

* * *

'COME ON, LEFTY, let's get in amongst them.' Paul was on his feet, racing the short yards to the Land Rover, 'Can't sit here all morning, let's get tore into the bastards!' They'd rehearsed this drill. He leapt into the driver's seat and turned the ignition key, gunning the engine, engaging the gears and roaring off the top of the koppie amidst a violent scattering of stones and grit. 'Mark your fire, Lefty,' he roared above the deafening chatter of the Minimi's relentless fire. How many rounds had Lefty used? It didn't matter. They had plenty and Lefty was a highly skilled gunner. 'Watch Om's Gurkhas, my friend, and Danny and Taff coming out of the trees. They'll stick to the attack lines we agreed but who knows what they'll do when they close with the bastard enemy.'

'Got them, boss. No bother. Look to your left,' he shouted, 'Danny's Gurkhas are getting ready to break cover from the tree line, they're going in as planned.' Paul looked, saw, and then concentrated on driving the bucking Rover down off the hill. The steering wheel tore from his grip and he quickly grabbed it again, hardened his grip and fought the beast of a vehicle. He was making directly for the western edge of the Renamo camp, to a place where he and Lefty would dismount. Shoesmith said, 'Om's Gurkhas are almost there, boss, look right. We're coming up on their flank nicely. Good one, Paul, keep that line. Christ, there's gonna be blood on the ground when those boys hit the bad men with their guns and kukris.' Paul could have sworn he heard Shoesmith laugh, but the noise was fiercesome. Shoesmith's fire was controlled in short bursts now, aimed with precision. The man was a genius. He was killing the enemy, the ones too slow to have taken cover and go to ground, and literally shepherding the survivors into Da Silva's killing zone.

But he wasn't killing all of them, because suddenly there were at least three separately targeted bursts of automatic fire, machineguns, probably RPKs, Paul thought, big bullets, 7.62mm, and the fire was spraying towards Dalloway's group as it was breaking cover, and churning the ground to Paul's right where Om's Gurkhas were leaping down the slope like bobbing, hurtling hill creatures, but grimly focused on closing the remaining few metres between them and the enemy.

Lefty yelled, 'Incoming, boss! From your half-right! Get this fucker down into the camp, Paul!' And the third burst of fire was aimed at the Rover. Paul heard the ping and clang of some rounds hitting the vehicle's sides, just one or two, nothing serious. His blood was up. He had fifty metres to go before they would dismount and join Om's killing group. But he had to stick to the methods of the plan. *All* the enemy had to be killed and accounted for. They knew there would be resistance. It just made the fulfilment of the plan more difficult. What's new?

Paul hit the brakes and the Land Rover swerved, jerked and shuddered to a halt. The dust and stones clanked and swirled. 'We're here, Lefty. Get that gun dismounted. Chuck me the bag of grenades.'

'Roger all that, boss,' and Shoesmith shovelled a canvas bag of fragmentation grenades into the front seat area, which Paul grabbed, along with his MP5, as he killed the engine and leapt out into the mayhem of the battle action he had created.

The first thing that struck Paul was that there was no cover. 'Lefty! Make a fire position and cover Om and me! Put down suppressive fire. Watch for Danny and Taff coming in from the left!'

'Got it, boss.'

'You might need to head for the shoreline to find where they are, I don't know. But you have to identify their fire positions and then murder the bastards. They could still do us damage.'

'Leave it with me, Paul.' Lefty Shoesmith, laden with firepower, ducked low behind the Rover and sprinted backwards to the rear of Om's Gurkhas towards the shoreline, to find a suitable fire position.

Paul did the same, head down, bobbing and weaving, but he ran hard to his right, for cover from fire he'd spotted amongst the remnants of what looked like some kind of community building, and which he quickly found was a wood framework with a thatched roof, but was now pulverised by Lefty's machinegun fire. It would do, for a few seconds. He needed to orientate himself with Om's Gurkhas, take stock and then get in amongst the various habitats and structures that made up the Renamo camp. It would be house-to-house clearing, close quarter engagements, perfect for grenades and kukris. But he needed Lefty to neutralise the enemy's fire positions. He was pretty sure they were to his half-right, to the northeast, holed up in some last ditch positions of resistance. Well they'd get to those in due course.

He subconsciously checked his personal state. He felt good; organised, comfortable and in balance. He hadn't worn a fully loaded set of chest webbing and body armour for some while, but, as ever, all the gear seemed to meld into his body; he was at one with his fighting gear. He fastened the satchel of grenades around his waist and slung his MP5 across his chest, shoving it around into the small of his back, and unholstered his beloved Browning. Before they'd all left Manica, Omparsad had offered him a field kukri. Paul had felt a moment of honour and thanked Om graciously. There had been a time when he'd worn the prized kukri as part of his combat equipment, a time when Paul had served with the Kathmandu Rifles and first met Omparsad Pun. But those days were gone. Gurkhas knew how to kill with the kukri, he knew how to kill with the Browning, and he had ten magazines' worth of bullets, which was surely enough.

Paul scanned his arcs. Lying scattered amongst the ruins of the bashas and clear to see, he counted eight dead Renamo, blown into tattered fragments by the hurricane winds of Shoesmith's bullets. Probably twenty more to kill, Paul thought. He saw that Omparsad and his Gurkhas were close, crouched and lying down, spaced out, dispersed, alert and watchful, absolutely ready to move into the house clearing phase. Christ, but they were wonderful warriors. Paul had a sudden lurch in his heart. He needed to bring all these men, *all these men*, back to Manica safely, and damn it, he would.

They needed a sign and Paul shouted it to them, his voice carrying over the space of the bullet-blasted wasteland, 'Om, I'll join you!' Paul rolled onto his side, crawled three paces and ran crouched to where Omparsad was. Immediately he drew fire and the crack and thump of the heavy enemy bullets rang out and the ground to his left was churned by the spattering of the bullets. Simultaneously, Paul heard the roar of Lefty Shoesmith's Minimi machinegun. Good! He'd found a suitable fire position. Crack and thump. How to identify the enemy's fire position. It was the thump that gave it away, and Paul had been correct. The enemy were holed up to his right, at the end of the encampment and Lefty had identified them. Omparsad pulled him down into the ground next to him. 'Fire and movement, Om,' Paul said. 'Clear every building. Use grenades. Demolish the place. Kill every dushman. Be aware, *bhai*, Lefty will provide covering fire from your right!'

'Hunchha, saheb, the boys know what to do. We will be a team.' Omparsad roared the words of movement and action to his men and the Gurkhas readied themselves to move. Paul took out two grenades, pulled the pins and lobbed them one after the other fifteen metres to his front, into the nearest clutter of partially destroyed buildings.

'Grenades!' There was a dull exploding crump, then a second, the ground trembled, broken debris blew in an upwards arc to their front, and then there was another, to the right, and the Gurkhas broke from cover screaming their war cries as they went into the unknown to find and kill any remaining enemy.

Paul shook his head slightly, releasing the pressure and tension, and chose his target, just where his first grenade had exploded. 'With me, Om! Where the first grenade landed!' Paul shouted as he rolled and twisted to his left. He heard Om's rapid burst of AK-47 fire, and with the bullets tearing into the target, almost guiding him, Paul got to his feet and charged.

* * *

258

DALLOWAY AND EVANS operated as a pair, one moving a few metres to cover, the other firing and then joining his partner, making sure their ground was clear of enemy before moving and firing again. Kindraman's Gurkhas were operating the same way. All of them dodged the incoming fire, which was sporadic and seemed to lessen as they fought their way into the clutter of Renamo buildings.

Two dead Renamo were strewn across the open ground, caught in either his group's volley fire from the tree line or Shoesmith's savage covering fire from the high ground to their right. And as they'd manoeuvred past these prone bodies Taff Evans fired a short aimed burst into each, just to make absolutely sure they were dead. No sense in taking chances.

It was the Gurkhas who flushed out the next three Renamo and killed them. The actions were swift and lethal: a massive overkill of short-range rifle fire into the building or shelter where the enemy hid, followed instantly by one or two mad-eyed Gurkhas with a slashing kukri blade. The blood flowed but the momentum did not slow. His small force had cleared the central part of the enemy's camp area to within fifty metres of the Chicamba Real's northern shoreline, and now Dalloway told his group to go firm for a moment.

He and Evans crouched low around the entranceway to a utility store, shattered bags of rice and mealie lay everywhere. Something wasn't right, Dalloway could sense it, but he didn't know what. The constant noise of gunfire had subsided to short, sporadic bursts that came from his right, which would be Paul's group, and from his left, Da Silva's cut off group. The visibility was shocking: the air was full of dust, grit and splinters of wood, churned up by the gunfire. The ground, in amongst the wrecked common rooms and utility buildings, was littered with the detritus of a community of soldiers: clothing, military and personal kit, cooking pots, books and magazines. But something was not quite right. There should be more enemy here.

Evans' words burst into his thoughts, 'Looks like Lefty's gotta bead on them enemy, Danny, an' 'e's keeping their 'eads down nice an' low for us.'

'You're right, Taff.'

Dalloway looked at the grinning, blackened visage of Evans and smiled thinly. The man was dressed in his version of bush combats, topped off with a stained, khaki bush hat, jammed on his head and held in place by an old bootlace chinstrap. His sleeves were rolled up and his arms were filthy with the stains of battle. His chest webbing was clearly personalised and bristled with nothing more than full magazines for his MP5. He had a webbing belt on, from which five pouches hung, one full of grenades, one full of emergency medical kit, and three full of water. Taff Evans was a pocket battleship of fighting power. Thank God he was on his side!

'How many enemy have been killed, do you think, Taff?'

'We've found five, boss, 'an there's maybe one or two more yet, but I reckon there was more of 'em in Paul's area. We've 'ad most of what we knew was the common rooms, so not many was sleepin' 'ere. An' whatever force was sleepin' up to the northeast, will 'ave baled the gaff towards Andy's mob.'

'You're right. Come on let's get to the shoreline and take stock. We need to be totally clear of enemy and secure so we can help the others.'

Dalloway gave a rapid set of hand signals to Kindraman and his two teams started to move. Evans rolled to his right and crawled into the next piece of shattered cover. 'Move now, Danny,' Evans whispered urgently.

Dalloway did, but, with his mind on other things, he stood up. Instantly two rapidly fired shots rang out. Dalloway was conscious of their proximity, Christ they were very close! Then simultaneously two pulses of shocking power hit him in the chest and left shoulder and he was falling on his back. Fuck! What a time to get hit. 'Taff...' he heard himself saying as he looked to his right.

But Evans had gone mad, charging across his front, MP5 blazing rapid fire, and screaming and shooting. Then he was back at Dalloway's side, ripping open his medical pouch and ripping off Dalloway's chest webbing.

'Kindraman!' Evans bellowed. 'Get one of your lads over 'ere, now! The boss 'as been 'it. Quick, pronto! Just one o' your lads. Then you an' the others get the rest of this bleedin' area cleared. Kill everything! You understan' me, Kindraman? Kill every livin', breathin' thing an' go firm on the shoreline. The saheb'll live.' That was good news, Dalloway thought. Evans said to him, 'You stupid bastard, boss, what you wanna do a daft thing like that for? Mind gone AWOL, 'as it? Anyways, we killed one more o' the fuckin' enemy, so that's a plus.' The Gurkha arrived. Evans said, 'Get the Major's kit off an' let's find the wounds.' He turned to Dalloway, 'I 'ave everythin' we need in this 'ere medical pack, so no worries, boss, OK?'

'I'm in your hands, Taff.'

'You are, an' lucky for you.'

CHAPTER TWENTY-FOUR

THE ENEMY'S SLEEPING huts were destroyed and now Paul and Omparsad were in amongst the western edge of the main settlement of the camp. Paul crouched low down on one knee amidst the ruins and Omparsad was three paces to his right. The rest of the Gurkhas had taken the ground close up to the shoreline, moving in two further teams. Paul reckoned they had about twenty metres still to clear before they'd meet up with Dalloway and Evans. In addition to the eight confirmed dead, they'd killed three more. Omparsad was keeping the tally, the short bursts of fire and the yelping martial cries of his men as they went in with their kukris, prompted his shout, '*Maryo? Kati*?' Dead? How many? And on each of the three occasions the shouted reply came back, '*Yota dushman, saheb. Pukka maryo.*' One definite kill each time, so eleven of the enemy accounted for by his group alone.

The business wasn't finished. Paul hurled his last two grenades, shouted the warning, and ducked down again. As the blasts rocked and shook the battered fabric of the large structure to his front, he and Om were on their feet, charging and firing. Om fired short bursts into the building from his AK-47 and then slung it around his back and wrenched free his kukri. Paul dodged and jigged into the entranceway, Om was to his right and through into the space beyond. It was a big room, with tables, chairs and maps on the walls. Paul thought he saw military hardware on the tables.

But was it clear? No! Somehow the enemy had survived the grenades, there had been sufficient cover for them. Omparsad spotted the first man, crouched down against what had been a rudimentary low wall, and leapt for him. The Gurkha was lightning quick and his kukri slashed viciously downwards, almost taking the man's head clean off his shoulders.

In that instant of awareness of what this building might be, Paul knew something was wrong. There was at least one other enemy here! He hit the deck and rolled to his right as a burst of fire rocketed over his head, smashing out through the walls and roof. The noise was absolutely deafening. But he'd been right. This was some sort of central base in the camp, a comms rooms, perhaps, and it had been manned all the time. He saw the Renamo, a big man, now on his knees, bringing his AK-47 back into the aim. Paul shot the man twice in his body and as the enemy toppled over Paul was on his feet, rapidly checking to see all was clear, and this time it was. He leant over the Renamo and shot him twice more in the head.

Thirteen of the enemy accounted for. Now he had to bring this attack to its conclusion and get into the next phase of the plan. 'Om, check the boys. Find Danny and Taff and go firm. Locate where Lefty's fire position is.'

'Hunchha, saheb.'

Paul moved out of the building and keeping low he stopped and listened. The battleground was strangely silent, but then it wasn't! Over to his right, no more than fifty metres away, he heard the recognisable sound of Shoesmith's Minimi machinegun, just spitting out short bursts of fire, obviously aimed, but also, it seemed to Paul, intent on neutralising a target. It must be the enemy position that had fired at them during their approach. They'd have to deal with that very soon. Paul looked up to the sky and then checked his watch. The sky was now brilliant blue and the sun was getting hot. It was five forty. They'd been killing the enemy for less than half-an-hour! It always amazed Paul how time slowed in situations of life and death.

He felt a wash of tiredness as he realised how much still had to be done, but he shook it off and listened again. To his front and left there was no fire, which meant that Dalloway and Evans' group had completed their tasks. Om would find them and report back very soon. Which just left Da Silva's men. He pulled out his walkie-talkie. He had no feel for what was happening at the north-eastern end of the enemy's position. He squeezed the microphone's pressel and said, 'Andy, give me a quick sitrep.'

'No casualties. At least five enemy killed, but there is an enemy stronghold one hundred and fifty metres to my left. I don't have eyes on but I can see the muzzles flashes. Two automatic weapons, I reckon, sound like RPKs.'

'Can you get closer to dominate it with fire and can you get to such a position unseen?' Paul interjected, thinking rapidly. This was the enemy's last stand, two men, possibly three, with machineguns, and it looked as if it would have to be taken in a final assault. Shit!

'Can do, sir. It will take me ten minutes to get in position, but I can.'

'Do it, Andy. You and one section. Split your machineguns, take one of the FN MAGs and leave the other with a section in your current position covering the exit tracks. Let me know when you're in position. Try not to draw fire, but if you do, don't worry, there's no surprise left in this game, and the more ammo the enemy uses up the better. But don't take casualties, you hear me?'

'I do, Colonel.'

'And don't expend all *your* ammo until I tell you to give it the maximum. Speak to me when you're in position and set. This will be over quickly.'

'I will.'

Paul took a deep breath and started to move towards Omparsad and the other Gurkhas. He had the plan in his mind: a frontal assault with covering fire from Da Silva on the left and Shoesmith on the right. He needed Dalloway, Taff and their Gurkhas and he needed Shoesmith to relocate his fire position. Then Taff Evans' voice broke into his earpiece.

'Boss!' Evans' voice was strained, even in the tinny earpiece.

'Tell me, Taff. Is your area clear?'

'It is, boss, an' we're firm, but Danny's 'it, shoulder wound, but 'e's OK. Bullet went clean through. I've stopped the beedin', swabbed 'im down wiv antiseptic, an' plugged both the 'oles. Oh, an' 'e took another in 'is Kevlar, but nothin' there save a little bruisin'. 'E'll be fine, Paul, and I've got 'im secure with one o' the Gurkhas. 'E's smokin' and drinkin' that Gurkha rum, which is fuckin' rocket fuel if you ask me.'

'He's fine, then. Well done, Taff.' As heartless as it sounded, Paul had to know, it would make all the difference to the next ten minutes. 'How many dead enemy in your sector, Taff?'

'Six accounted for, boss. 'Ow's the tally goin'?'

'Twenty-four, but we've got a last stand.'

'Where?'

'At the north-eastern end of the camp. Andy can't bring fire to bear but Lefty's got them covered.'

'So what's the plan, boss?'

'Two interlocking covering fire positions from Andy, who's moving into position as we speak, and Lefty, who I'm moving to now. Then a frontal assault with all we've got. You, me and the Gurkhas. You up for that?'

'Fuckin' right, Paul! Wouldn't miss it for the world!'

'Good. H Hour in about fifteen. Leave Danny as he is and get to the edge of the shoreline with all the other Gurkhas ASAP. Bring everything you have, especially grenades.'

'Roger that, boss, see you in three minutes.'

Three enemy left alive. With Omparsad's men and those with Evans, there were twelve of them, ten of them Gurkhas, who were thirsting to kill and who would be mad with rage at the injury to their Saheb. OK, Paul thought, that's good odds for us.

* * *

IT HAD ONLY TAKEN ten minutes and Paul was pleased. They were all set. Da Silva had checked in on the walkie-talkie, he was good to go. One of the Gurkhas had scuttled back to the Land Rover and gathered up all the spare ammunition for Shoesmith's Minimi and a further pouch of grenades. Shoesmith was set in a new fire position, with a clear line of sight onto the enemy stronghold only three hundred metres from him. He would pulverise them.

Omparsad distributed the grenades and bullets, they checked weapons, and then the twelve men quietly infiltrated through the wreckage and carnage of the Renamo camp to its north-easternmost edge and went to ground in their assault formations. Paul had his binoculars out but they could all see the enemy position and it was a poor one, which was good for Paul. The enemy were not dug in but lay in line abreast - and there were three of them - in a shallow scrape in a slightly elevated fold in the ground. As he had correctly assessed, there were two machineguns and he could see they were RPKs. The third man had an AK-47. The Renamo position must have been a night observation post. Tellingly, though, they'd stopped firing, so Paul reckoned they were conserving the remainder of their ammunition, for a last stand. They had to know the wrath of their enemy was about to fall on them.

Paul's men were one hundred and fifty metres from the piece of ground they had to take. It was a suicidal distance, some might say, but it was the final play in the plan and it had to be done. There was little cover, only a few patches of low scrub, but the plan didn't depend on cover. It depended on overwhelming firepower, shock attack, speed, and the killing rage of Gurkhas with kukris. Stack the odds in your favour. Don't think of Nikki. Don't think about anything other than killing the last three enemy.

Paul looked left and right. The Gurkhas were either side of him, in fighting pairs, weapons fully loaded and cocked. The grenadiers were detailed off. Each pair would fire and manoeuvre in a rushing, mad skirmish for eighty metres, and then, not stopping, all the grenades would be thrown, kukris unsheathed and the killing rage would take over. Let it start. Paul nodded to Omparsad and Evans who were either side of him. Every Gurkha looked inwards, Omparsad made the hand signal to be ready. Paul clicked the transmission switch of his walkie-talkie and spoke into the microphone, 'Lefty, Andy, acknowledge this order and then open fire. Give them everything you have. Mark our advance and switch your fire when you have to. Fire, now!'

'Roger, boss,' said Shoesmith.

'Roger, Colonel,' said Da Silva.

And the world went mad.

* * *

THE MADNESS LASTED only ninety seconds. It was enough. By then the enemy was dead. Now they were clearing up. It was the penultimate phase of the plan, before their exit from the scene.

Paul was weary but relieved. Shoesmith had brought the Land Rover into the central part of the clearing and the Gurkhas had put Dalloway into the back of it. Paul walked over to talk to him. He was propped up on a mattress of cushions scavenged from the wrecked Renamo camp, his upper torso bare, his left shoulder swathed in bloody field dressings. Across his heart was a huge blue-black bruise. He looked like shit. He was lucky to be alive. The Kevlar saved him, taking the energy out of the low velocity Makarov bullet.

'How did it go, Paul?'

'Your Gurkhas were magnificent, Danny.'

'Any casualties?'

'No, you're the only one.'

'Fucking typical!' Dalloway was slightly tipsy, which was fine. He'd finished his substantial supply of Gurkha rum, which on top of an empty stomach, blood loss, shock and fatigue, had put him into a pleasant state of euphoria. 'What happened, mate, after I copped it and your blessed Taff Evans doctored me?'

So Paul told him.

It had been no contest. The incoming support fire from Da Silva and Shoesmith had smashed into the Renamo, broken their weapons, fixed them, terrified them, and mortally damaged them. The Gurkhas had charged, firing from the hip, running helter-skelter like mad, whooping, animals, they'd thrown the grenades, which had simply added more carnage and destruction, and then leapt like wild things onto the already neutralised enemy. Paul had been there with them as the kukris had delivered the final despatch of the three Renamo. It made no difference that the enemy had run out of ammunition. Too bad.

'Your men are here, Paul,' Dalloway said.

Paul looked around and saw Omparsad, Kindraman, Da Silva, Evans and Shoesmith making for the vehicle. They were battle-stained and looked shocking, but they had smiles on their faces. Evans and Shoesmith went round to see Dalloway and then leaned against the Rover's side. The others stood in front of Paul, ready to report.

'We are ready, saheb. Come and see,' said Omparsad.

'I will, Om, thank you.' He had a sudden thought. 'Taff, seeing as you're the chief medic, please continue your care of Major Dalloway.'

'No bovver, boss, love to.'

'Lefty, do you reckon your satphone survived?'

'No doubt about it, Paul, had it cushioned and wrapped safely in one of the internal panniers.'

'I thought as much, so in that case, give my number a call, I left the satphone with Nikki, and tell her we'll be back in two hours. Bring the wagon to us when you've done.'

'Roger that, boss,' said the two SAS men in unison.

Paul walked slowly towards the shoreline. The vehicles had been shuttled in from their harbour location and stood line abreast at the western end of the camp ready to move out. Everyone had worked furiously to complete the clear up phase of the plan. It had taken an hour. Some had lit fires and boiled water and made coffee for everyone. There was nothing to eat save some hard biscuits and rusks, which had been handed around. It was enough until they got back to Manica.

'You've all done well,' Paul said.

Da Silva responded, 'All bodies have been stripped and every piece of personal belongings and papers are bagged and loaded in the trucks.'

'Thank you, Andy.' Paul was looking at the transformation scene around him. The place was clear. The Renamo camp no longer existed. Had it ever existed? All the structures had been fully dismantled and the timbers either dragged back into the trees or used to build and fuel the fire platforms that now sat like sentinels on the shoreline looking over the water. The camp and cooking fires had been broken up and ashes scattered and scraped into the dirt and grit.

Omparsad seemed to read his thoughts, 'All weapons and ammunition are also loaded, saheb. Andy's men have done a sweep through the fighting areas and collected all the brass they can see. Lefty fired many, many bullets, saheb!' What a job! 'We have all brushed and swept the area to make it look like animals.' It would do, Paul thought. The rains would come and wash away the signs, the beasts of the bush would come and forage and repossess their habitat. It would do.

'Thank you, it is fantastic work.' They had reached the shoreline where everyone else was gathered loosely, sitting, standing, waiting, smoking and sipping water or coffee. Paul heard the noise of the Rover and Shoesmith parked it up close by and he and Evans climbed out. Dalloway was propped up in the back and could see everything. There was almost a ritual significance to these moments, Paul felt. There was something else, too, a sense of déjà vu! Paul looked at them all, smiled, and turned to Omparsad, 'It is almost like Kathmandu again, Om. Like the Pashupatinath Temple.'

The Gurkha's face split into a huge grin and the other Gurkhas chirped and nudged each other. It was a big joke and the story had obviously been told many times.

'What 'appened in Kathmandu, then, boss. Come on, share the 'umour,' Evans chided.

'We burned bodies, Hungarian bodies, on the cremation *ghats* at the sacred Hindu Temple. Well, strictly speaking, Omparsad and the Gurkhas burned bodies. And in order to do so, Omparsad and the others had to shave their heads. I don't think he's ever forgiven me, have you, Om?'

'*Tik chha*, saheb, I have. My hair is back,' and he stroked his thinning hair lovingly and smiled his huge smile.

'Lovely reminiscences, Paul,' shouted Dalloway from the back of the Rover, 'and if you recall, mate, I was in a similar state as I am now! So can we please get a move on and get the hell back to the Farm. I need a drink!'

Everyone laughed.

Paul raised his voice and spoke to them all. 'There is much I would like to say to thank you, but we must move soon from here, so I will be short. You have saved yourselves today and protected your business and your families. The enemy had to be killed and you have done this without a single casualty. I do not include Major Dalloway because he will be fit again very soon.' Dalloway raised an arm in acknowledgement but did not interrupt. Paul finished, 'I am honoured to have been with you and to count you as comrades. Be very proud of yourselves, because I am.' Paul turned to Kindraman and asked, 'Kindraman, we are ready?'

'Je, saheb.'

'Then do it.'

There were six fire platforms, each separated by ten metres and built right on the edge of the shoreline escarpment, from where there was a two metre drop into the deep waters of the Chicamba Real. Kindraman and the Gurkhas had wrapped the twenty-seven Renamo bodies in all their clothing and rags and piled them on the platforms along with the remnants of the equipment. Now they took a jerry can and sloshed petrol over the six burning *ghats*, and at the signal from Kindraman they lit faggots of dried wood and set the structures alight. Everything was bone dry and the flames caught and roared. Everyone moved back and watched, fascinated by the six funeral pyres, consuming the dead enemy, whose ashes would soon be swept into the waters of the Dam.

Paul was deep tired. It would take an hour to complete, but they had to stay to finish the job. He wasn't worried about this site being found by anyone really, it was just the need to finish the plan and leave the battle scene as forensically clean as possible.

His mind turned to other things. It was Tuesday today. He'd told Charles Grace he would be in Beira by tomorrow, which now would not be possible. And then he realised that he'd forgotten to call the General yesterday; but how could he have? And besides Grace had been travelling to Beira. He would call later today. It would be his last two days with Nikki until...he didn't honestly know. His heart saddened, so he turned and walked over to the Rover, and with Danny Dalloway and his SAS men, watched the fires rage and roar as they burned the dead.

PART VII
CLOSING THE LOOPS

CHAPTER TWENTY-FIVE

NIKKI HAD JOYFULLY told Philippe Cruz the news, and it spread like wildfire throughout the Farm. Nikki and Cruz quickly made a plan; they had two hours, maybe less, to prepare a homecoming fit for their heroes, the men who had risked their lives for the security and future prosperity of all who lived and worked on the Farm. They summoned the help they needed and everyone got to work. It was a happy day, a day of celebration.

The first vehicles were spied from a distance by the young boys, and they telegraphed the word along the chain of boisterous look-outs, so that by the time Paul's Land Rover, bringing up the rear of the convoy, came into the Farm's main building area, everyone was there, cheering and throwing flowers and rushing to greet the men and get them in their arms. It was lovely, and it reminded Paul of *The Magnificent Seven*. Thankfully, though, they had no tears to shed because there were no dead to bury.

'Fucking wonderful, aren't they, Paul,' said Dalloway from behind him.

'Truly, they are.' He pulled into the chaos of vehicles and people outside the main building and carefully parked up the Land Rover. He was emotionally and physically shattered. He spotted Nikki, standing with Philippe Cruz, on the deck, a little back from the rest, and could see the look of happiness on her face and the sparkly

273

teardrops in her smiling eyes. As it always did, nowadays, his heart lurched. He had some serious life adjustments to make, and very soon. His defences had been well and truly smashed down by this beguiling woman whom he loved very deeply. He said to Evans and Shoesmith, 'OK, boys, please help the wounded Major out of the wagon and into the loving care of these wonderful people.'

'Enough of that veiled sarcasm, Stanton, I'm fine to walk, thanks, men, a little unsteady on my pins, but nothing that a couple of cold beers and a bite of proper grub won't steady.'

The SAS men helped Dalloway out of the Rover. Nikki rushed forward to greet him and hug him gently. 'Steady, woman, steady! I'm wounded, the only one, I might say. Shows how close I was to the real action, eh!' And Dalloway winked to Paul and the others.

Paul laughed and said, 'Danny's been a true hero,' then he got serious and said aloud so that all could hear, 'actually, *everyone* of these men has been a true hero! And now, please, you must feed them and give them drink and listen to their stories!' And the foreground of the Manica Farm building erupted in cheers and shouts of joy and the bustling movement of people, and above it all Philippe Cruz's voice shouted out and all paused and listened.

He said, 'Yes, Colonel Paul, you are correct. But please, first, I must welcome you all home properly.' He turned to all the fighting men who were now gathered, many with their womenfolk and families, 'I am so proud of everyone and I thank you with my heart!' And the people cheered again.

Cruz walked up to Dalloway and gave him a gentle embrace and a look of respect and affection. Paul could hear his quiet words, 'Danny, we are proud to have you caring for us and our safety.' Before Dalloway could react, Cruz quickly moved to Omparsad and said, 'We will have the opportunity to thank you and your brave Gurkhas, properly, Ompasad, but please accept my personal thanks. We are in your debt.' The two men bowed their heads to each other. Then the Farm Manager was in front of Paul, but looking past him at the Bobbsey Twins of Africa, Evans and Shoesmith, who stood to his rear flank. 'You are truly fighting men, and I thank you with all my heart.'

Definitely *The Magnificent Seven*, thought Paul, and even Taff Evans was silenced. Paul looked at his two SAS men, and they were genuinely humbled. Good for them! It was his turn. Cruz held his arms and looked up into his face. The man was six inches shorter than Paul but his grip was passionately intense and his dark brown eyes were swimming with emotion and the release of worry. 'Welcome home, Colonel Paul! Welcome back! I do not have words to say what is in my heart.'

'I think I understand, Philippe,' Paul replied, 'and I thank you in return,' and Paul bowed his head to the earnest, emotional man who still gripped his arms. 'I believe you are, but you should be very proud of your men, especially Andy Da Silva who is a fine and brave person, true to everything you seek to achieve at Manica Farm.' Cruz nodded his head thoughtfully and the tears were now visible.

Then he released Paul and said, 'I have been selfish, sir. I think there is a special lady waiting patiently to say hello to you, no?' But before Paul could do anything the man turned to everyone and shouted out, 'We are roasting food, it is on the spit braais at the back of the Mess, and we have many tables laid out with your food and drink! Everyone, everyone, come! And there will be music! So we must eat, drink and dance, celebrate and let the children play!'

'We must,' said Nikki quietly in his left ear, 'but first, *my* wonderful fighting man, may I say hello and tell you that I love you?' And she gave him a crunching hug and kissed him with a warmth and tenderness that he hadn't thought could be.

'Crikey! What a corker!'

'No one outside the *Beano* or *Dandy* speaks like that anymore, Paul, no one except you, obviously! Did I tell you I love you? And what have you to say to that?'

'Phew! I love you! Christ, but it's good to be back! Danny's going to be absolutely fine. It's a flesh wound, nothing vital hit and Taff's a brilliant combat medic. And I love you, Nik, seriously I do.'

'Good. I'm glad. But it's just like you, Paul Stanton, isn't it, always worried about others before yourself, and,' she looked into his eyes and he saw the chocolate mint flecks light up in the sun and glisten with lingering tears, 'so it should be. But, my man, everyone is going to eat and drink, in case you hadn't noticed, even Danny Dalloway, who's going to be treated like a king, so maybe we should join them, yes?'

'We should, my girl. Perhaps the wonderful aroma of roasting meat will disguise the fact that I and the others smell pretty horrible, but then the onset of much strong drink will remove your olfactory sense all together. What think you?'

'I haven't a clue what you're talking about, Stanton! You look like a scarecrow but you smell fine to me. Eating roasted meat, consuming lots of strong drink and dancing? Now you're talking! Take me there, my man!'

Paul Stanton and Nicola Walker-Haig walked hand-in-hand to join the party, each wrapped in the special glow of their feeling for the other.

* * *

THE SAS AND Gurkhas were three sheets to the wind, gloriously drunk, camped in a tight group around a dying fire, impervious to the chilling night, unaware of the expanse of stars that blazed in the night sky above them, unhearing of the calls of night creatures echoing faintly in the distant bush. It was Africa at its richest and most beautiful, and it was all totally ignored by the band of warriors whose beatific smiles were captured in the glinting shadows of the fire's embers as they drank Gurkha rum, smoked cigarettes, laughed and swapped tales of derring-do. They would be there all night.

From their own small group of armchairs on the deck, Nikki said, 'I'm going to fetch some blankets. Our brave men will get very cold otherwise.'

'Good on you, Double-Scotch,' responded Dalloway, 'they'll appreciate it.' He turned to Paul, 'She's some woman, Paul.'

'As I well know, Danny.'

'I sense, my battered brother, a change in your priorities, even from when we talked two days ago.'

'You're right.' Had it been less than two days since he and Dalloway had agreed Nikki should get back to Mutare and then to London as quickly as Dalloway's business could release her? 'And it's going to change my military priorities and probably bollocks things up with Charles Grace.'

'Did I hear the name of Charles Grace mentioned?' Nikki said as she approached from inside the Mess, her arms laden with a stack of soft blankets.

'You did, Miss Eavesdropper.'

'Well, I forget to tell you that I spoke to him, yesterday evening, as it happened.' Paul looked at Nikki and let her finish. It correlated: Grace had said he'd be in Beira sometime on Monday and must have called on the satphone to check on Paul's progress and plans. He and the Bobbsey Twins were supposed to be in Beira tomorrow. 'He called your satphone, Paul, and I told him you were helping out with a local emergency on the MozLon Farm at Manica. He was very charming and interested, although I don't think he knew anything about it.' She left them.

Paul watched her drape a blanket over the shoulders of Evans and Shoesmith, who both glanced up and thanked her kindly. Then she handed the remaining blankets to Omparsad who threw one at each of the Gurkhas who immediately rolled themselves up like maggots in a cocoon, lay on the ground and carried on. The glow of cigarette ends lit their smiling round faces eerily and they drank heartily from the tin mugs that contained the rocket-fuel rum called *raksi*.

'Who's Charles Grace?' Dalloway asked.

Nikki rejoined them. She had three blankets left and pulled one across her lap and gave the two men the others. 'Paul's mentor and controller,' Nikki said.

Paul pulled the blanket over his shoulders to ward off the chill. He said, 'You've heard of him before, Danny, when I came out to Nepal after the Berlin job and we talked.'

'Yeah, you're right, mate, I vaguely remember it now, so how come he's involved in this job then?'

Nikki interrupted, 'He had no idea who I was, and he had no idea that you knew Danny and the goings on of Gurkha Connections Limited here in Mozambique. In fact, lover boy, I could almost hear his mental processes at work as I told him, and it was almost as if several pennies dropped into the slot machine of his mind.'

'I can imagine,' Paul replied. It was time for some truths, so he said, 'Charles Grace had not heard of you from me, Nik, nor had I told him that I knew the inside story of your contract with MozLon, Danny. Why? Because rightly or wrongly at the time when I was being despatched to find out the truth concerning Fitzsimons, I didn't want Grace or anyone else to believe there were reasons why I might be less than objective in the search for answers.'

'That's a fair one, Paul,' said Dalloway.

'It is,' Paul replied. 'Because of my personal involvement with both of you, I wanted to be absolutely sure that the Fitzsimons incident had no adverse impact on your business, Danny. That's the truth of it.' Which it was, partly. The other part was, he reflected, that had it been necessary, he would have done his utmost to ensure Nikki Walker-Haig and GCL were not damaged in any way.

'I knew that was the reason, Paul,' Nikki said, 'but I'm afraid General Grace now knows a little bit more than he did before. He sounded pleased, in a way,' she continued. 'I think he liked the sound of my voice.'

'You're a bit of a tart, Double-Scotch, if you don't mind me saying so. "Spect you charmed the man off his feet on the end of a satphone, and all at the time your man and I were exchanging high velocity bullets with the bloody enemy!' Dalloway reached for his whisky, took a huge gulp, and then lit another cigarette.

'And you're very rude, Dalloway! I hope you set fire to yourself!'

'Well,' Paul said, 'it doesn't matter a hoot, now. Grace has an iron will when it comes to job and duty, but he's a proper man with a soul and a touch of romance which occasionally breaks through his hard exterior. I happen to know he might also have a lady in his life.'

'Talking of romance, mate, pass the bloody whisky bottle will you. Grab a dram on the way past. And Nikki here, needs a toppers.'

'So what does it all mean then, Paul?' Nikki asked.

'It means, Nik, that Taff, Lefty and I have to get to Beira as planned, but a day late, now. I'll call Charles Grace in the morning and update him. It'll give him a little more time and we'll get there on Thursday. Soon after that we have to return to London.' Paul looked at Nikki and saw the look of disappointment on her face. It wouldn't be that bad. They had a personal plan to make and execute, but he had to finish this mission first. He asked, 'What's the running time to Beira, Danny?'

'Two hundred and seventy klicks, patches of rough road, the odd hold up for wandering wildlife and beasts, time taken out for anti-ambush drills, I'd say four hours tops.'

'Danny!' Nikki exclaimed.

'Yeah, Paul, about four hours. Honest. But,' Dalloway said, 'and you'd be doing me a favour if you did, you could take an hour or two extra and stop off at Nhamatanda, say hi to Gopal, bring him up to date with all the stuff that's been going on, and drop off some bits and pieces for me. If you left at zero nine, for example, you'd be in Beira for an early sundowner.'

'Sounds good to me,' Paul responded, 'I'd be delighted to see Gopal. That's a plan, then, and it gives us tomorrow to have a rest and get set.'

'Talking of plans, Paul, and I mean those that extend beyond the next few days,' said Dalloway, 'what are you and this lovely woman here going to do about getting together on a more permanent basis? You know she's central to the success of this enterprise, the great Gurkha Connections Limited, and cannot be spared?' And Dalloway chuckled at his own mischievous humour.

'Of course I can be spared, Danny Dalloway!' Nikki exclaimed hotly. 'And I can be based in London.'

'Fell for it, hook line and sinker, what a girl, eh, Paul!'

'She is. We're going to marry, Danny.'

'Fuck me, apologies, Nikki, I mean, Christ, that's a bit fast, isn't it?' Dalloway sat up, poured himself a healthy slug of whisky, gulped it down, poured another and lit a cigarette, sitting back, all in a seamless string of motions, founded on years of practice.

Paul smiled broadly. 'Yep, we've decided. The exigencies of the British Army and Her Majesty's Government can go on hold for a while. Stanton and Walker-Haig need to take care of some life-changing personal business.'

'And I hope, dearest Danny, that the exigencies of GCL can go on hold for a similar period of time? You know I'll never leave the business and you know I can win us some more deals back in London, but only after Paul and I have married and had a little time to ourselves.'

'Blackmail! We'll talk about it, we will,' Dalloway prevaricated, 'I'm sure there's a way around that fits all the requirements.'

'You sound boring now, Danny, and most unlike yourself. What do you know about requirements? Who actually won you this contract and therefore saved your bacon? Who charmed that smarmy creature Fred Etherington off his feet at those meetings in MozLon HQ back in July? Eh? Well. It was me, in case you've forgotten!'

'Okay, okay, I give in. We'll make a plan that fits us all. I promise.'

'Thank you, darling Danny!'

'Seriously, Paul, have you got a date or time in mind?'

Paul hadn't really. He'd been sitting there feeling slightly overwhelmed by the talk, realising that he and Nikki were at the centre of the biggest change in their lives, certainly his, and yet his deep rooted sense of duty kept interrupting the euphoric thoughts with reminders of what he still had to do. Find Ramon Lima, for a start. Pass on the diamonds to the Portuguese Home Affairs Secretary. Ensure Nikki continued to be safe. Then get Taff and Lefty out of country, and himself. Close the loops. And then there was the situation in London...his continuing career as a newly promoted lieutenant colonel.

He said, 'Christmas, Danny, a white wedding.' Nikki raised her eyebrows, smiled and said nothing. No wasted remonstrances or interjections. Of course they hadn't decided on this time. He really *liked* this woman!

'White wedding, mate?' Dalloway questioned. 'Isn't it a bit late for that?' And he roared with laughter at his own naughty insinuation.

'Danny,' Nikki gently reproached him, with humour in her tone.

'Couldn't resist it, Nikki. You see, unlike your lovely Paul here, I'm a simple grammar school educated bloke, rude and brash. None of that posh public school heritage in me I'm afraid. God I love you both, I really do!' Dalloway levered himself to his feet. 'Come on Paul, let's go and join the boys and get totally smashed. Good night dear Nicola.' Dalloway grabbed the whisky bottles from the table

'Good idea, Danny,' Paul responded. 'See you later, Nik. Don't wait up; but do please remind me tomorrow that I have to call Charles Grace on the satphone. Please?'

'I will. And I won't wait up! Good night to you both, you naughty men. Just please make sure you don't all freeze to death with low blood temperature and a rising cold dew.'

'We have your lovely blankets, Nik.'

'Tell you what, Paul,' Dalloway said, lurching down the steps, 'as we've got some time tomorrow we can go hunting.'

'Cracking plan, Danny.'

'We'll go out with your lovely SAS boys, Om and Kindraman, and Nikki can come too, and we'll hunt some wild pig. You remember how addicted Gurkhas are to *shikar garnu*, especially hunting pig!'

Paul did. He remembered it well from Brunei and Hong Kong days. 'I do!'

'Settled! That's what we'll do! Come on, Stanton, let's roust these boys up a bit. Throw some logs on the fire, stoke up the heat, find some light, and get some serious drinking done. Think we can mix *raksi* and whisky? 'Course we can! No probs! Come on, my warrior *sathi*, we need the boys to get the drums out and give us a beat so we can dance. You remember the classic Nepali dance step, Paul? 'Course you do.' Dalloway shouted to the Gurkhas, 'Eh, bhai! *Nach garnu parchha! Madal haru lyaunus!'* And to Paul, 'That'll get them going. Bet your boys are excellent dancers. Follow me, Stanton, this is my place and I am your leader!'

There was no stopping the man. Tomorrow was another day. Tonight was for celebration and it wasn't over yet.

Commitments had been made and Paul Stanton felt a glow in his heart as a result of them.

CHAPTER TWENTY-SIX

GENERAL CHARLES GRACE was footsore and hot, furthermore he was now convinced he did not have the skills required for covert investigation. So far, and it was three o'clock in the afternoon, he'd had no success in finding the address that John Sawyer in Pretoria had given him, and which the British First Secretary in the High Commission here, had provided directions for. The blasted place didn't seem to exist. So where exactly was Ramon Lima? No, Grace thought for the umpteenth time, this is not my skill set. It's Stanton's.

Frankly, the Port area of Beira was a maze. It was also ugly and filthy and the people had been unhelpful and suspicious. For a start the noise had been horrendous: the constant mechanical cacophony of cranes shifting hundreds of containers, vehicle movement in and out of the quays and oil terminals, and the unique screeching of locomotives within the railway workshop and marshalling yard, had frayed his nerves and worn down his tolerance. The rank odour of port waste, rotting vegetation and fuel oil, mixed together in the late October humid heat, had made him feel nauseous on several occasions. Grace wasn't a man to be affected easily by his environment, nor was he a sensitive type, Christ, he was a bloody Infantryman, but he was admitting defeat in this minor enterprise. It was time to get back to relative civilisation and await Stanton's arrival. The blasted SAS could find Lima!

Having come to a decision, Grace strode out purposefully for the Old Quarter, heading due south away from the soiled waters of the Pungue River, towards the Avenida Poder Popular and the safe haven of the British High Commission. It was where he'd told Stanton to come to. Yes, damn it all, the blasted SAS could find Ramon Lima!

Grace felt better and almost immediately the air, starting to blow in from the Indian Ocean, smelled fresher.

*　*　*

'RECKON THIS IS it, boss,' said Taff Evans.

'Got it, Taff. Thank God for the GPS.' Paul glanced at his watch, five o'clock, later than he'd hoped, but not by too much.

'Hear, hear,' said Lefty Shoesmith from the back of the Land Rover. The vehicle's canopies were down and had been since they'd broken out of the dust roads and entered the outskirts of Beira, over thirty minutes ago.

Paul turned off the Avenida Poder Popular and into the entranceway of what was rather shabbily declared on the signboard, in dual Portuguese and English, as the United Kingdom High Commission. A solid looking double metal gate guarded the entrance and it was closed and almost certainly locked. The walls were at least ten feet tall. 'We've made it, boys. Lefty, hop out please and ring the bloody bell, will you?'

Evans said, 'Looks a bit down on the 'eel, don't it, Paul?' It did. But then so had the rest of Beira that they'd threaded their way through during the last half an hour.

'It's not surprising really, Taff, the city has been in a state of civil war for over ten years.' Paul had found the drive through the old colonial city an experience of mixed emotions. Driving past the almost derelict Grande Hotel, set on the shore overlooking the Indian Ocean, had been sobering. It had become a wrecked shell of a place that looked as if it now provided refuge for countless families. Then they'd driven along the miles of seafront into the old residential area, and Paul could see the appeal of the blocks of classic Portuguese villas, albeit in varying states of repair. They hadn't been into the port area. When he'd spoken to Grace yesterday on the satphone, the General had told him it was the place where the search for Ramon Lima should focus. They'd get to that tomorrow. Now, though, what the hell was holding them up? 'What's going on, Lefty?'

'Can't seem to raise anyone, boss.'

'Climb over the bleedin' wall, Lefty,' said Evans helpfully.

Shoesmith was evaluating the possibility of scaling the wall, possibly made easier by overhanging branches of glorious bougainvillea, when one side of the double gate creaked open and a scared looking black face peeked out, and under instruction from someone in authority standing behind him, hastily unbolted both gates and laboriously drew them back to let the Land Rover drive in.

Charles Grace walked through, immediately engaging all of them in banter. 'You're late, Colonel Stanton, a day and some hours late. Oh, it's you Corporal Evans. I might have known you'd be lurking around close by. And I suppose you must be Mr Shoesmith. Good to meet you, I'm General Grace.' Evans and Shoesmith made some attempt to brace up and look respectful and tried to respond to Grace's deliberately tongue-in-cheek comments, but Paul just sat back and smiled. The engine was ticking over so he revved it gently and Grace said, 'Oh come on in, all of you. Let's get off the street and inside into the cool. Park the old wagon anywhere, Paul, there's plenty of space. I expect you're all dying for a drink. Well I know I am! The First Secretary's looking forward to meeting you, and he has a lovely wife, so be on your best behaviour. You're still late, though.'

Welcome to Beira.

* * *

THERE WAS A guest cottage to the rear of the High Commission, which had been given to Evans and Shoesmith for as long as they were to stay in Beira. The two SAS men had driven the Land Rover around to it, unpacked, cleaned and re-stowed all the gear, showered and changed. Now they were politely guzzling cold Mozambican beer and chewing their way through small dishes of olives, crisps and nuts, but behaving beautifully and engaging the First Secretary's lovely wife in amusing conversation. She was laughing her head off. They were happy, relaxed soldiers and Paul liked to see it. The tempo would change again tomorrow, so make the most of it boys.

Paul also felt good. He had been given a spare room in the main building and it was spacious and cool, with big windows that overlooked the extensive gardens at the rear of the High Commission. At least the water supply seemed to be fairly consistent in Battered Beira, so he, too, was clean, freshly shaved and had found almost his last set of unused clothes buried in the recesses of his travel bag. The diamonds were there, too, in Schuman's satchel, the main package and the cowhide pouch, and no one else other than Evans and Shoesmith knew he had them. He'd decided it would be a step too far to tell Grace, especially after the revelations about Nikki, MozLon and GCL, all of which Grace had yet to talk to him about.

Paul quietly sipped his beer and took in the surroundings. It was a beautiful room, high ceilinged with ornate cornices, and the large sash windows gave on to the same riot of mature, slightly overgrown garden that he could see from his bedroom. The ceiling fans whirred above them and moved the humid air just enough to make it comfortable. The rains were coming, but not quite yet. The rugs were old, frayed at the edges and a touch faded, but the patterns and colours must have been striking once upon a time: exotic birds and animals, jungle and savannah. Portuguese style and local Mozambican lamps, with fringed, patterned shades, were scattered around the big room on hardwood tables with elegant, bowed legs. The sofas, divans and armchairs were similarly styled and solid in their dark wood frames, some with carved backs or arms, but all with well-used cushions or fabric upholstery, still full of life, but tired. The whole building, but especially the living apartment, must have been magnificent in the heyday of Portuguese colonial rule.

Grace was talking to the First Secretary, who said, so that all could hear, 'Well, Charles, we'll leave you to discuss your business, but we shall look forward to having dinner with you all in, say, an hour's time? Would that suit you?'

'It would, indeed, how kind of you,' replied Grace. 'I apologise for evicting you from your own drawing room.'

'Don't be silly, Charles,' said the First Secretary's wife, 'we have plenty of rooms! We shall sit and have another aperitif and await your charming company at dinner. I look forward to seeing you all soon, and to talking to you, Colonel Stanton!' And with that, the couple left the room.

'Have a seat, gentlemen,' Grace said. 'What a gracious couple and how lucky are we to have their kindness at our disposal. But, now to business.' He sat in a big armchair, as did Paul and the SAS men. 'Tell me about those last days in Zimbabwe and then about Manica and this young lady of yours, Paul,' and Evans and Shoesmith looked at Paul, perhaps wondering, mischievously, exactly how much he *would* tell Grace.

So Paul told Grace. And he told him that the diamonds had been recovered and given back, via Dick Hanney, to Ken Rose, who would ensure they were returned to those whose property they were. Her Majesty's Government had not been implicated in any way. Which caused Evans and Shoesmith to look sideways at Paul when he said it, but they knew better than to say anything. Paul was their boss, and he knew best.

* * *

'GOOD,' SAID GRACE decisively. 'Very good. Well done, all of you. It must have been quite testing in parts, especially for you, Paul, with the de Castenet involvement. God,' he paused, 'how perverse are the fates that we should find that poor, inadequate, yet detestable man, buried at the bottom of this latest pile of trouble, and here, in bloody Africa, of all places! Unbelievable.' Paul was relieved. Grace, with his usual perspicacity had foregone making any irrelevant comments that some lesser mortals may have made and focused on the heart of what was important, namely the successful outcome of the mission and its impact on Her Majesty's Government. But he hadn't finished. 'So, as you instructed me, Paul, this Ramon Lima is the final piece in the puzzle. The closing of the loop, as you put it to me?'

'He is, General.'

'Well, I haven't been able to find the wretched individual. Not even locate the address I've been given. So you, Taff and Lefty here will have to do it. You have the skills and the equipment. And by the way, gentlemen,' and here Grace looked at Evans and Shoesmith, 'I need hardly remind you, need I, that everything we talk about here is only between ourselves?' Evans and Shoesmith nodded. They knew the score. Grace hadn't needed to remind them, but no matter. He went on, 'You must do it quickly, tomorrow. Despite the pleasantness of the company, I can't sit around in Beira twiddling my thumbs for too long, and neither can you. You have honest jobs to get back to. Don't you?' Paul smiled broadly. He really liked this good man. 'Something amusing in what I've said, Colonel Stanton?' And now Evans and Shoesmith couldn't resist a silent chuckle and a squirm in their seats, before both, as if on cue, reached for their beers and took a huge swallow.

'We'll find him, General. Tomorrow,' replied Paul, feigning seriousness; well he was being serious, about the task, at least, 'and I will personally close the loop.' And I'll personally close the other loop, the one I haven't told you about, the handover of the diamonds to the Portuguese Home Affairs Secretary. As much as he had a duty to Her Majesty's Government, Sir Reggie Hanlon, et al, he had a bigger duty, in some ways, to the people of the Zimbabwe Wealth Protection Cooperative. They still had to live in that fast-collapsing country where they had families and futures to protect, and he, Paul Stanton, was the guardian of a large chunk of that future. The diamonds.

'I know you will, Paul. I know that.' Grace became serious and changed the angle of the conversation. 'de Castenet's body is being flown back to UK, tomorrow, to Brize Norton. The Defence Attaché received the body yesterday. Good old Colin Bullock. You found him helpful and supportive, Paul?'

'I did, sir. He was great.'

'Yes, a tried and trusted friend, and I knew you could count on him. It seems Ken Rose personally escorted the man's body to the border crossing at Bietbridge, or some such place. It seems also that the Head of BMATT Zimbabwe was only too pleased for the matter to be handled internally, so to speak. As for Colin Bullock, well he's a Green Jacket, so he knows his career is God-blessed. Says it all really, doesn't it?' Paul's face split in a huge grin: even amongst the most serious of talk, the Army's pecking order of regimental pedigree could always find an introduction and be a topic of contentiousness. Charles Grace was also a Green Jacket. Grace continued, completely unabashed, 'Thank God we had friends on the inside, eh?' Indeed, Paul thought. And it reminded him that he needed to speak to Ken Rose on the satphone tonight - and to Nikki. When would Grace get to the question of Nikki, he wondered? 'Our friends in the Royal Air Force are working overtime on our behalf,' Grace's words interrupted his thoughts. 'Yes, they are, because also, as of today, as it happened, they have one of your Special Forces Hercules aircraft standing by at Moi Air Base in Nairobi, in the hangar area leased by the RAF.' Evans and Shoesmith leaned forwards in their chairs.

'Our exit, General?' chirped Evans.

'Of course, Taff, absolutely, so you and Lefty can get back to proper work, as well as recover all the highly expensive and accountable equipment I understand you have with you. No doubt secreted in that rather battered Land Rover you arrived in, which also has to go back, you understand.'

'What notice is the Herc on to arrive here, General, and where is she coming in to?' Paul asked.

'Vital questions, Paul. The aircrew are on two hours notice to fly from Moi and into the military side of Beira airport. I understand the flight in will take somewhere between three and four hours.'

'It does,' interrupted Evans, 'me 'an Lefty 'ave done it once, 'an it takes the thick end o' four 'ours. You're spot on, General.'

'Thank you, Taff, that's good to know. So, Paul, we have to plan on a minimum of six hours from calling the aircraft in, before we can plan on its arrival and the subsequent evacuation of you and the boys here and the vehicle. I understand the Hercules will have enough fuel to make the return trip.'

Paul was thinking. 'And it takes at least thirty minutes to get from this part of Beira up to the Airport,' they'd passed the signs to Beira Airport on their drive in earlier today. 'We can work with that. Tomorrow we'll find Señor Lima and once we have, we can firm up the exit timings. You obviously have the contact satphone numbers for Moi, sir. Perhaps you'd like me to handle things from now on?' Paul really wanted Grace out of the way. He had other clandestine things to finish, but the General shook his head thoughtfully.

'No, thank you, Paul. I take it you don't envisage a hot exit, not like Berlin?' Grace hurried to add to his last comment, 'And I'm not prejudging anything, Paul, please understand, but I really do not want any of you being left high and dry with me not here to add that little bit of top cover, so to speak.'

Yes, a good man. 'I understand, General, and thank you, as always. No, I don't anticipate we shall need to bale out in a tearing hurry. If things go even remotely according to plan we'll start really early tomorrow morning and finish things, no matter how long it takes. It will allow us to call in the Hercules for an exit flight on Saturday, in the morning. They can leave Moi tomorrow night or early Saturday morning, pick us up and we'll be back in the UK for the end of the weekend and work on Monday.'

'Lovely, boss,' said Evans, 'the RAF'll love us for that, they will.'

Paul continued, 'Will the First Secretary and his wife be happy if we stay with them until then?'

'I'm absolutely sure they will, but we'll just ask them to make sure. Let's go and join them for dinner. They really have been very kind and it would be churlish to keep them waiting for too much longer. Oh, and afterwards, Paul, you and I can have a little private tête-à-tête and you can tell me all about Gurkha Connections Limited, Kathmandu, where I understand you helped your old Gurkha colleague Major Dalloway, and of course the mysterious Ms Nicola Walker-Haig. Yes?'

'Think the General's got you there, boss,' said Lefty Shoesmith.

'Done up like a kipper, Paul!' added Taff Evans.

'Be quiet, you reprobates!'

They all laughed and went to join their host and hostess for dinner.

* * *

GRACE SAID, 'I'M not prying, Paul, wouldn't dream of it,' the two men were on their own, enjoying a last whisky, 'but I'm assuming what you've just told me was not planned. Oh, and by the way, we can drop the formalities now we're alone.'

'Thank you, Charles, and yes, it was all rather unexpected, and it started off being a totally private matter.'

Grace sipped his drink and smiled at Paul. He said, 'As I thought, and that's fine, it really is. Nothing has happened that has clouded the mission in any way or compromised your integrity, has it?'

Paul could honestly answer the first part, 'No, nothing. The fact was we had to exit from Zimbabwe via Mozambique and the action we engaged in around Chicamba Real was a spontaneous act. We had the means, time and resources and they needed help. The whole event is deniable. The MozLon workers at the farm were sworn to secrecy and that was the best we could do. I trust them. And I expect Sir Reggie Hanlon and Fred Etherington will, in the final balance, owe HMG a big debt.' As for the second part of the question: Paul wasn't sure if his integrity would be compromised by his intended handling of the diamonds, but he was going to close that particular loop on his own, come what may.

'Indeed. But we shall not be able to call it in, I suspect. It doesn't matter.' Grace took a drink and looked thoughtful. Paul hadn't checked the time but it was getting late. He needed his bed and he needed to agree the plan with Evans and Shoesmith first. It would be a very early start in the morning. The two SAS men had made their excuses after dinner and would sort out the gear in readiness, but they still needed to be briefed.

Paul said, by way of finishing what he wanted to tell Grace, 'I met Nikki by chance in Kathmandu, just before last Christmas, when she was working for Dalloway, before they'd got their act together and bid for the MozLon business.' Now he'd started he wanted to tell Grace all he needed to know. 'I was there on a few days leave, to catch up with Dalloway and my old Gurkhas from the Kathmandu Rifles. You know they had all been really good to me after the Berlin shooting. Helped me recover in more ways than one.'

'I know, Paul. I do understand, and God knows how sorry I am that it should all have happened to you.'

'Then Nikki came over to London in the summer to have the talks with MozLon and we got together. When you briefed me on Mozambique and showed me Hanlon's letter, I had no idea that GCL would be directly involved. I assumed that they had to come into the business somewhere, just because of the MozLon factor and the geography, but that was all. And,' Paul added, 'that was the case when we met Etherington in London and he briefed us on the Fitzsimons situation.'

'You saw no connection, Paul?'

'I didn't, Charles,' which was true. 'I had no idea Nikki was even in country. I'd thought she was in Nepal.'

'Difficult, Paul, how very difficult for you, but I assume that the lovely Ms Walker-Haig is safe? For clearly, my dear Paul, she means a huge amount to you personally. Am I right?'

'She does, Charles, and I hope she will soon be safely back in Zimbabwe, and shortly after that heading to London.'

'Marvellous! Well, the mission has been a success, Paul, and you can be on your way back, too, can't you?'

'We still have Lima to sort out, but as I said earlier, I'm determined we'll finish it tomorrow.' Then I still have the diamonds to deal with, he thought.

'Well, I'll not ask you how you will go about it, that's strictly between the three of you, but you know well the conditions of deniability, Paul?' Paul nodded, of course he did. 'So, in which case,' Grace said, 'I'll book an open ticket back to London and make a provisional plan to fly out on Saturday's morning departure. That should work, shouldn't it? As you said earlier, we can call in the Hercules to lift you all back the same day, to be home for the end of the weekend.'

CHAPTER TWENTY-SEVEN

PAUL HAD THE code, and the three of them were able to slip out of the secure postern gate at the rear of the High Commission unnoticed. Not many people were up and about yet. They bomb-burst silently in separate directions, and then started walking purposefully towards the Port area. It was as if they were exiting a security forces' base in West Belfast or Crossmaglen to start a foot patrol. In some ways the situations, although world's apart, were quite similar: there was danger out here in the backstreets and there was an enemy who was not readily identifiable as such.

Each of the men had a small pocket street map, but they'd studied it closely, agreed the different routes and where they would first rendezvous. This RV was close to the Beira Railway Terminus and it would take them less than an hour to get there, even by circuitous routes, but by then the day would be awake and the city bustling with activity.

It was going to get hot, but it would also be a long day, Paul believed, so the three of them had dressed in tough cotton trousers and desert boots. Their safari shirts and vests had all the pockets required for their gear. They'd get water and basic rations off the streets, as they needed to. Paul had given Evans and Shoesmith sufficient Mozambican Meticals for their needs. Most importantly they all had a silenced 9mm Browning pistol with two spare magazines. For communications they had a walkie-talkie with an earpiece, which

Paul had deliberately borrowed from Dalloway. With a sunhat and sunglasses they looked like tourists, but there was nothing benign about their intent. Ramon Lima was to be found and dealt with.

In no time, it seemed, Paul was on the northern road bridge and crossing the Rio Chiveve, which dribbled its way through small clumps of trees and shrubs before emptying into the Pungue. The Chiveve provided a neat division in this, the south-western part of City, between the old style villa and commercial district and the ugly sprawl of Beira Port. Evans and Shoesmith had gone east from the High Commission and crossed the Chiveve on the larger, southern road bridge.

Paul's earpiece chirped into life, and Evans' tinny voice said, 'Comin' up on the Terminus, boss and there's loads o' people cover. Gonna buy some sustenance. Lefty's 'ere, too. See you in a minute, out.'

Paul acknowledged the progress to himself and was thinking. The Rail Terminus sat at the southern end of the Port and it was where the three of them needed to take stock. Grace had described the maze of the Port area from his abortive reconnaissance yesterday, and just from the map, Paul believed they had their work cut out to find Lima's supposed location. Grace had described exactly the information John Sawyer in Pretoria had given him and what the First Secretary had told him by way of directions. But Grace had had no success whatsoever, which wasn't a surprise to Paul.

Ramon Lima was a criminal, one who worked closely with renegade guerrillas, so he would have buried himself behind doors of overt respectability and deniability; but he was also a businessman and he needed people to be able to find him, to feed his business needs. Which was what Paul intended to do. He had money, the US Dollars Evans and Shoesmith had brought with them, and he had diamonds. He touched the inside pocket of his safari vest and felt the hardness of the cowhide pouch of diamonds that Coetzee had tried to steal away from de Castenet and Schuman. Yes, he had diamonds, and he would use them to find Ramon Lima.

Paul saw Evans and Shoesmith lolling at a street vendor stall, eating bread rolls and drinking from a bottle of water. His stomach rumbled at the thought of freshly baked warm bread rolls. It reminded him of the morning in Kathmandu after Danny Dalloway had been brutally attacked by the Hungarians. The morning when he and Omparsad and the laconic but lethal American, Brad Trevelyan, had made the plan to kill them. Where was Brad Trevelyan now, Paul wondered? The American was ex-CIA and had proved to be a true friend to Dalloway.

''Ere, boss, 'ave some 'ot bread rolls. They're delicious,' said Evans as Paul joined his two men. 'Lefty, get the boss a cuppa, mate.' Shoesmith turned to the stall owner and indicated what he wanted, then handed Paul a glass of hot, sweet tea thickened with condensed milk. Just like Gurkha tea. Lovely!

'Thanks, boys.' Paul sipped the brew and munched on a soft roll. The sun was up, it was getting warm and the local people and some tourists were beginning to grow in numbers and move into the human ebb and flow of another Beira Friday morning. The Rail Terminus was a hub of humanity and the three of them were not out of place. Paul relaxed a notch. He said, 'So, just to confirm the next moves, Taff, Lefty, head up through the Port to the area described on the map as the North Pier. There's a line of warehouses on the wharfs, and if I know anything, there will be offices above them. But, if what Charles Grace told us is accurate, it'll be like working your way through the Harland and Wolff shipyards in Belfast.'

'That'll be home from home, then,' said Shoesmith.

'Fuckin' lovely,' was Evans' rejoinder.

'I'm going to make my way there the long way round, via a few office calls on the Port Ring Road.'

Shoesmith asked, 'Can we kick a few doors down, Paul?'

'No, Lefty, we're doing this quietly. I'll give you a buzz on the comms if I find out anything hard to narrow down the search for this bastard man.'

'Then, when we do find 'im, Paul?' Evans asked.

'As we planned last night, Taff, we get the info I need and we walk out of there.'

'So no Gunfight at the OK Corral, then, boss?'

'No, Lefty, not if I can help it.'

'Pity,' said Evans, 'There's nothin' quite like baling the gaff in a RAF-Herc with the countryside on fire be'ind us!'

* * *

PAUL HAD HIS first break in the offices of the unlikely sounding South African Timber Trading Company, which sat behind a derelict façade on the Port Ring Road, a pot-holed, woebegone thoroughfare between the City and the docking storage and transportation yards. The whole area was how he imagined post-War Eastern Europe had been, and it surprised him in a way that the structural investment Portugal had put into this part of its Empire had decayed away so rapidly. It was actually worse than Belfast.

The door was open and the outer office was furnished with a simple steel desk and chair, an antique telephone, three stand-alone metal filing cabinets, and a kettle on a gas ring. There was no secretary and it didn't look as if the place had seen any business for some time. There was, however, an inner office and Paul could see the silhouette of someone through the glass panel in its door.

Paul knocked and entered the careworn, darkened little cubbyhole. The place stank of cigarettes and body odour. 'I have some business to transact with Señor Ramon Lima. I am told by my associates that the Señor has offices close by?' Paul addressed the man sitting behind the paper-littered desk and the pall of rank cigarette smoke. He was thin, balding, swarthy and oily. His shirt was huge, filthy and incongruously, was a print of large palm trees and a tropical beach. It was open over a sweat-stained singlet vest. The man was a midden. 'You understand English, I am sure?' The manager nodded his weasel-like head slowly and his reptilian eyes watched Paul guardedly. Well at least he hasn't instantly denied knowledge of Lima, which Paul thought was promising. All of his prior enquiries had been nugatory. Press on, Paul, 'I believe this might help you remember, Señor?' Paul extracted a large US Dollar bill and placed it amongst the chaos on the man's desk. 'May I sit down?' Paul didn't wait for an answer but shut the office door behind him and moved the only other chair into a position where he could see the man and the door. He waited and smiled. The man coughed and sat forwards, his hand shot out and trapped the banknote, which he held up to the few rays of sunlight which penetrated his hole.

He was obviously satisfied it was genuine. 'You say you have to meet Señor Ramon Lima?' His accent was thick but his English was good. He seemed to become animated, and having stuffed the banknote into his trouser pocket, lit another stinking cigarette, coughed again, and said, 'The Señor is a hard man to locate and to do business with.'

Bollocks, thought Paul, I'm not giving this creature any more money. 'Señor, I have just offered you one hundred US Dollars, for some information. You have taken my money and put it into your pocket,' and Paul imitated what the man had just done to ensure he understood. 'By doing this, and by what you have just said, you know the answer to my question, and by taking my money I expect you to give me this information. So I will ask you again: where can I find Señor Ramon Lima?'

The Manager of the South African Timber Trading Company seemed to come to the conclusion that this tall, travel-worn man with the bent nose and fierce blue eyes was not to be messed with, for he became instantly compliant. And he had just been given a hundred US Dollars. He said, 'Señor Lima imports some timber through this agency. He rents some docking space at the North Pier. But understand, Señor, I do not know this man personally.'

I'll bet you do, thought Paul. 'Show me where on your map,' Paul instructed. The man got up and traced the route on his wall map from where they were now to the North Pier. Paul had it. 'One final thing, describe this Ramon Lima to me, so I shall recognise him.' Once again the Manager did as requested and his description was surprisingly clear. Paul left the man with these words, 'You have taken

298

my money for some simple information, and I thank you. But you will tell no one of this visit. Do you understand me?' The man nodded his head vigorously and his skin visibly paled in the shaded room.

Paul left the building and headed off briskly in the direction he now had to take. His threat to the Manager was a calculated risk. He fully expected the man to make a telephone call to Lima but in a way Paul wanted him to. It might precipitate events, which could be to Paul's advantage. They had so little time. The risk lay in the aftermath of meeting Lima and what the Manager might say subsequently. Conversely, the Manager would be unlikely to bring danger to himself, and he'd taken money. Paul wasn't quite sure how much collateral damage there would be, but, he mused, they wouldn't be in Beira long enough to find out and so far none of them officially existed.

He put such thoughts out of his mind. Paul checked his watch and saw that, unbelievably, it was already midday. He'd heard nothing from Evans or Shoesmith. He activated his walkie-talkie, 'Taff, Lefty, it's the North Pier. Northern warehouse. What's your location, over?'

'We're there, boss, watchin'. North of the wharf, in the tree line, opposite the gas storage tanks. What's your ETA, over?'

Paul had done the calculation, 'Twenty minutes, maybe longer. The target looks like this,' and Paul gave the outline description of Ramon Lima. He finished by saying, 'Watch for an increase in activity, out.'

In the event it took Paul just over thirty minutes to join up with his men. Before he came in sight of the open stretches of the Pungue River, which would mean he was past the wharves, he broke off the pot-holed ring road and navigated his way to the north and west, where he believed Evans and Shoesmith had to be. Eventually he found himself on the edges of a thick copse of trees that looked as if it ran directly towards the River. He'd passed on his left the vast compound that housed the gas storage tanks.

He must have been spotted, because Shoesmith's voice suddenly broke into his earpiece, 'Keep coming straight on, boss, keep in the cover of the trees. Watch your left side. That's were the enemy is. We're about two hundred from where you are now, over.'

'Thanks, Lefty, be with you in a minute, out.' Evans and Shoesmith had eyes on Lima's lair. That was good.

Five minutes later Paul slithered into position alongside his two men, where they had gently parted the branches and undergrowth to create a field of view onto the last warehouse on the wharf and the hard standing area in front of it. So this was the place in which Ramon Lima had his office. Paul was looking forward to meeting him.

He pulled out his binoculars and screwed them to his eyes. 'There's only two of 'em, boss,' said Evans, 'an' they don't seem to 'ave shooters. The geezer you described as this Lima bloke, 'e came out to talk to 'is boys some twenty minutes ago, then 'e went back inside. There's the doorway on the end, an' the office is upstairs, boss. Since then the boys outside 'ave been a bit more active, but they don't seem too concerned.'

'Which means they're not totally suspicious, which is good for us.' He studied the enemy he could see. They were big men and similar in size and physique to those they had killed at Chicamba Real. Shangaans, Danny Dalloway had said. They wore civilian coloured combat fatigues, multi-pocket jackets with the sleeves cut off, and thick-soled boots. The men carried no side arms, just a sheathed tapanga blade. They looked like gangster-soldiers but they would know how to fight and would do so, for they had been Renamo guerrillas and now were beholden to a paymaster who expected total loyalty. As he watched them, one of the men disappeared through the doorway and the other sat down in a discoloured plastic chair by the doorway. No, they were definitely not expecting an attack.

Paul rolled on his back and checked the time. It was twelve fifty hours. Any others returning to work would do so in just over an hour.

Shoesmith said, 'Move when it's dark, boss, or before?'

'Before, Lefty, in fact, very soon, I don't want to lose the target and I want to get this over with. Anything left to eat, Taff?'

'Water, bread an' some o' that dried beef stuff,' replied Evans.

'That'll do fine. Let me have a drink and a bite whilst I tell you how we're going to play this.' Three minutes later Evans and

Shoesmith just nodded their heads and thought about what Paul had told them. He was going in legitimately, to do business with Lima, and he'd take Evans with him. Shoesmith would stay in cover to see them into the building and then move in and respond as required. 'We'll get Lima to come down to us, Lefty, and to take us upstairs, then you'll know if there's one or two of the guards left outside.' He added, 'No heroics, Lefty, no close quarter stuff, just silenced bullets at close range. Bring the body or bodies inside and stand watch from the doorway. Wait for my call.'

'Wilco, boss,' acknowledged Shoesmith. 'What about the forensics?'

'Leave them for the time being. We'll sort it all out afterwards.' Paul took a final swig of water and cleared his mind of everything extraneous to these next moments. He felt the first telltales of impending action and his senses started to heighten as adrenaline kicked in. 'Lefty, you just be ready for war. Taff, you and I have to look innocent, so we'll stow our weaponry accordingly, but cocked and locked. Take your earpiece out. One spare mag only and put it in your boot.' He looked at both of them, 'This will start off clean but it's going to get messy. I see no other way, but we contain it within Lima's place. There will be blood on the tracks, boys, but not ours. Make ready and let's go.'

* * *

PAUL AND EVANS cut back through the trees and approached the wharf in front of Ramon Lima's warehouse from the rough road that came in from the east. Two things struck Paul: how vast the expanse of the Pungue River was ahead of him, and how quiet the area was at this end of the wharves. Then they were spotted by the Shangaan watchman, who got up from his chair and shouted something into the doorway of the building.

'Do you speak English?' Paul called loudly to the man and held his hands up showing they were empty. Evans did the same. There was a clattering of footsteps from inside the building and the second

Shangaan appeared. Lima's guards stood together and unsheathed their wicked tapanga blades but held them down by their sides. 'I wish only to speak to Señor Lima,' shouted Paul as he and Evans walked slowly towards the two guards and then halted, several paces from them. They had reached the corner of the warehouse and Paul could see more. To his left the wharves ran due south and there were open-hold lighter vessels berthed, bow-to-stern, against them. The lighters were empty. Cranes stood dormant and there was no movement. It was lunchtime, siesta time, the early afternoon working stand down. Perfect timing. Paul was struck by the smell of rotting vegetation coming from the swirling muddy waters. It reminded him instantly of the Brunei jungle. 'I have some business for him,' and Paul carefully extracted the pouch of diamonds from his inside vest pocket, held them up and jiggled them so that the movement of the stones could just be heard. It was a stand off. They didn't speak English.

'I speak English, and I am Ramon Lima. Who are you, Englishman, and why do you not come alone?' What a stupid question, Paul thought. But there was the man, standing on the corner of the warehouse, ready to meet him. His Shangaans stepped back and Paul and Evans walked the few steps towards him.

Ramon Lima was exactly as he had been described. His eyes caught Paul's attention first, since they were jet black and flashed in the sun with a friendly menace, if that was possible. They were eyes not to be trusted and they said: you are welcome; but they meant: My men will kill you if I do not trust you. But actually it was his physicality that marked him out as unmissable. The Portuguese blood was evident in his skin colouring, which was bronze, coffee coloured, and in his grizzled greying hair, stubbled salt-and-pepper beard growth and moustache, which was set below an incongruous looking aquiline nose. Then there was his physical bulk, which was abnormal. Paul glanced at Evans, and the SAS man had a frown of amazement on his face.

Paul needed to gain the initiative, so he tossed the pouch of diamonds to Lima and the man moved like a snake, whipped it out of the air, clenched it in his huge paw, looked at Paul quizzically and then examined it quickly by rolling it in his hand. 'I think you know, Señor, that I have business to discuss with you, and that is my proof.' Lima's face had lost its hostility and he nodded to his Shangaans, who also relaxed and re-sheathed their blades. Paul asked, 'Do you think we might get inside, out of the sun and out of sight of anyone who might be watching us?'

Lima stuffed the pouch of diamonds inside his trouser pocket and said, 'There is no one watching us, Englishman. I control these wharves here and the unloading has been finished for some days. The containers are in my warehouses. Yes,' Lima looked hard at Evans, 'we can go inside my humble offices where you can tell me how you have so many diamonds and what you want of me, but who is this man?' Lima hissed the last few words.

'He is my business colleague. That is all you need to know. I assume these men are your colleagues?'

'Good enough, Englishman, please follow me.' The man was supremely confident. Lima led the way and gave instructions in some local dialect to his men. One of them followed Paul and Evans up the stairs and the other assumed his previous posture in the plastic chair. OK, so Shoesmith had just the one to deal with, but that was bread and butter business for him.

The staircase was narrow and Lima's bulk seemed to fill the space in front of Paul. The man was huge, not tall, six inches shorter than Paul, but he was built like a wall, and Paul could see evidence of massive physical strength in the bared arms and the strain on his voluminous shirt and trousers from what could only be a barrel of a chest and thighs like oak trees. Christ, thought, Paul, normal bullets might not stop this man! It was no wonder Ramon Lima was a local warlord: his physical presence and obvious business acumen marked him out from the hoi polloi.

Then they came into a corridor, with a blank, stained wall on the left and two offices on the right, each with a glass window at chest height and each with a window on the outside wall. The first was almost bare, just a table and some chairs, a meeting room, perhaps. The second was Lima's, and it was full of the clutter of his working domain. The corridor was a narrow defile but just as Lima opened his office door and stepped inside, Paul took the moment.

Without looking at Taff Evans, Paul said, 'Take him, Taff!' There was a sudden frenzy of movement and noise and Paul heard the soft, rapid explosion of bullets as Evans shoulder barged the man behind him and then shot him three times. Judging by the noise, the Shangaan's body must have hurtled backwards against the wall before crashing to the floor. Well done, Taff! Paul's eyes had never left Lima, who was transfixed for a second and then lurched towards his desk. 'Don't do it, Lima!' Paul shouted at him and moved into the open office doorway. The man froze again.

'Need help, boss?' Evans had his Browning levelled at Lima's chest.

'No thanks, Taff, I'll deal with this one. Dead is he?'

'Yes, boss. No vital signs. Want me to get Lefty?'

'In a minute.'

Ramon Lima stood for another few seconds, as if trying to decipher this burst of dialogue, and then decided to make a move. Paul read it in his body language and smashed his foot into Lima's left kneecap. It had all Paul's weight behind it, propelled by a surge of acceleration over a distance of five feet. It was a crippling blow on a target he couldn't miss. Lima went down like a wounded buffalo, and made a similar amount of squealing and snorting.

'Fuckin' monster of a man, boss. Scary, if you ask me. Want me to shove a sock in 'is gob to shut 'im up? Or even better, shoot the bastard?'

'No, Taff, give him space. Give Lefty a call.' Paul heard the noise of the brief exchange on the walkie-talkies, but he was watching Lima who was clasping his broken kneecap and struggling to raise himself up onto his good knee at the same time. Impossible agony. 'Sit in that chair, Lima,' Paul ordered.

Evans stuck his head into the office, 'Lefty's good, boss, all went according to plan.'

'The two of you start the clean up. Get the bodies together up here. Pick up the brass and start wiping things down. We'll get all the gear from the trees on the way out. Don't be seen, Taff. Lock the door and join me soonest.'

'Roger all that, boss, don't forget your diamonds, an' don't take too long.'

'I won't, but this man and I have just a little talking to do.'

CHAPTER TWENTY-EIGHT

'ANSWER SOME SIMPLE questions, Señor Lima, and we will leave you.' Lima had managed to hoist himself into the office chair, his massive bulk squashed into its frame. His face was ashen and he was perspiring visibly.

Paul was standing on the opposite side of the office, against the wall. He'd checked the time and they needed to get out of this place. It was twenty past one. Evans was in the office doorway leaning on the frame, his eyes flicking constantly between Paul and the end of the corridor, where Shoesmith was watching the outside of the wharf area through the window. It was as if Evans was mentally willing Paul to get a move on.

'What questions, Englishman,' Lima gasped.

'You have a contact in Pretoria, a man called Schuman who works in the NIS and you do business with him? He gives you money and in return you give him men, like these ex-Renamo who lie dead in your offices? Am I correct?'

'So what? Why should this be of interest to you, foreigner?'

It was an OK start. Paul continued, 'You remember providing two men to do a job at the end of last month, September?'

'How should I remember this, English filth, I do much business.'

'This job was for Schuman. The target was a white man coming from Zimbabwe, a man carrying a lot of money. In fact the man was carrying many, many diamonds. Schuman sent a killer to meet with your two Renamo, close to the Border.' Lima's face was wincing with pain, but his eyes were focused and he was trying to stop his body from convulsing. He knew what Paul was talking about. 'Did you ever hear what happened? Do you know why you never got your payment, why Schuman betrayed you and why your men never came back to you?' It was a long shot, but Paul needed this grotesque man to talk.

'I'm interested to hear, Englishman, go on, but your questions are pointless and I am in much pain.'

'Schuman's man killed your Renamo. Their bodies were found by a Zimbabwe military patrol.'

'This I do not believe!' Lima interjected hotly, his pain forgotten momentarily.

Paul ignored his protest, 'I have proof of this from the Head of Intelligence in Harare, but it is no matter if you do not believe me. Schuman's man took the diamonds back to Pretoria. He never contacted you. You were never going to be paid and you were never going to be told about the diamonds.' Which was not necessarily true, but the lie would serve the purpose.

'Schuman would never cheat me!' Lima spoke the words fiercely but there was an undertone of doubt now.

'Tell 'im 'ow you know, boss, and let's get the 'ell outta 'ere,' said Evans. Lima's eyes swivelled to look at him and quickly fastened back on to Paul.

'He was going to cheat you. He told me this, just before I killed him. Those diamonds you have in your pocket were part of the shipment which he had with him.'

'He had these diamonds? And many more, you say? You killed him? How so, English, how did you know and do all this?'

'It's not important. It is important only that Schuman cheated you and betrayed you. I wanted to tell you the bad news personally.' There was an old safe in the corner of Lima's office. It had a large keyhole and a single opening handle. 'Where is the key to your safe, Lima?' The man's eyes momentarily flickered towards the desk and then reset themselves to look at Paul. It was a trick that often worked: change the subject completely to see what subliminal responses it provokes. Paul said to Evans, 'Check the desk drawers Taff, and find the key to that safe and the weapon that Lima has there.'

'Roger, boss.'

'Señor Lima, you must tell me if you have any more people you talk to in Pretoria? Any more contacts in official places who give you inside information such as this Major Schuman?'

'And why should I do this?' Lima's voice sounded uncertain. He was watching Evans rifle through his desk drawers and there was a look of panic on his face.

Evans held up an old fashioned steel bangle of keys, on which the largest must be for the safe. 'Think we've got the jackpot, boss. Want me to try it?'

'Where's the shooter, Taff?'

Evans dug around some more and then a big grin broke on his face as he held up a Makarov pistol. 'Another piece of Russian junk.' He unloaded it and checked magazine. 'Full mag, boss.'

Excellent! Paul's forensic plan would work. 'Load and cock the weapon, please Taff, and pass it over.' Evans gave Paul the Russian pistol and Paul checked the safety was on and held it loosely in his right hand. 'Open up the man's treasure chest, Taff, we need to see what he has in there.' Paul turned his attention back to Lima and said, 'I asked you a question, Señor, and I need an answer. I also need you to tell me if there is anyone you deal with in Zimbabwe? Anyone who provides you with the same type of information that Schuman did?' Lima was half-listening. His eyes were watching Evans closely and he was leaning forward in his chair, his pain seemingly forgotten. What was in his safe?

Evans provided the answer as he cranked the heavy door open, stuck his head inside and said, 'Bingo, boss, fuckin' bingo! Look at this bad bastard's stash! There must be millions in 'ere!'

Paul glanced inside the safe as Evans stood back from it, and could see mounds of banded banknotes and small pouches of what must be coins, gold coins, and precious gemstones, in all probability. Evans was correct, there must be a fortune in Lima's safe.

'Get the stuff out, Taff, bring it all on the desk. Let Señor Lima look at his wealth whilst I ask him one last time to answer my questions!' And Paul directed the last comment at Ramon Lima. 'Tell me, Lima, or I burn it all and empty the gold and stones into the river.' Paul took out Coetzee's Zippo lighter from one of his vest pockets and flicked it open. 'This cigarette lighter belonged to the man who killed your Renamo, the man who worked for Schuman who was going to cheat you.' Paul could see the look of bemusement on Lima's face. 'It is true. This was found at the site where your men's bodies were left. Anyway, it doesn't matter, Lima. But you see, Señor, unlike Schuman, I don't want your money, I just want the answers to those two questions,' and Paul struck the flint and watched the flame burn, as he picked up the nearest banknotes, Meticals, and began to hold the flame close to them.

'Schuman?' Lima's voice faltered, and he looked at Paul almost beseechingly, 'There was only Schuman. He was the only one. In Zimbabwe? No, I have no friends in Zimbabwe.'

Paul believed him. He closed the Zippo and said, 'Thank you.' Paul put the unsinged notes back on the desk, flicked off the Makarov's safety, walked over to Lima and shot the huge man twice in the heart. It was point blank range and noisy but the shots were muffled by the man's clothing and instantly fatal. He checked Lima's pulse, nodded gently to himself and then ferreted in the man's pocket, extracted his pouch of diamonds, turned to Evans and said, 'OK, Taff, now let's do the forensics.'

'Roger, boss.' Evans yelled down the corridor, 'All clear, Lefty? If so, give us some 'elp, mate.'

'How many bullets used, Lefty?' Paul asked.

'Two, boss, that's all that was needed.'

'OK. The Brownings are untraceable, yes?'

'Yes, boss.'

In which case we'll leave Taff's and the Makarov.' Paul handed the weapon to Evans, who started to wipe it down with a rag he pulled out of one of his pockets. Paul walked over to the safe and took out the small sacks of money and stones, placing them on the desk. He said, 'It was yet another case of thieves falling out and the staff not being paid enough by the management. 'Lima shot his two Renamo thugs whom he caught taking his money, but not before one of them had shot him twice. We need the five cases from the Browning and the two for the Makarov.'

'An' the bodies, boss?' Asked Evans.'

'The bodies, Taff, good question. One of the Renamo in the corridor and the other, with Lima, in here, yes, that should work.'

Evans clearly couldn't resist it and said, 'We gonna burn 'em again?'

'No, Taff, not this time, too much collateral, and too close to those bloody gas storage tanks! The way it is right now, I reckon we can pass this off as an internal feud.' Paul was seeing it as it would be found, and said, 'The Browning with Lima, the Makarov with the Renamo in the office. Two Browning cases in the corridor, where Lima came across the first man and shot him, which means the other three browning and the Makarov cases in the office. Yes, that's it. Wipe it all down, the safe, door handles, weapons, the whole nine yards. Stuff some bundles of banknotes in the pockets of both the Renamo and leave the rest on the desk and in the safe. Have I missed anything?'

'Nah, yer good, boss, leave it to me an' Lefty. But what 'about these 'ere bags o' goodies, Paul?' Evans asked pointing at the pouches of coins and stones.

'We're taking those, Taff.'

'You sure about this, boss?'

'I am, call me Robin Hood, but I'm distributing the ill-gotten wealth from the evil rich to the poor and needy.'

''Ow so, boss, an' 'ho's the needy then?'

'Well, for a start there are the Whites in Zimbabwe. Then there's Danny Dalloway's Gurkhas and the lovely Mozambican workers in Manica and Nhamatanda. And then there's you two hoodlums. How about that?'

'Ah, boss, that's fuckin' brilliant, that is!' exclaimed Evans, and Shoesmith was smiling and nodding his head. 'But me an' Lefty don't need no gelt, we'd only spend it.'

Shoesmith said, 'Speak for yourself, Taff, you thickhead!'

Paul swept up the small pouches off the desk, stuffed them all into his various pockets and said, 'We'll look at this lot later, when we get back to the High Commission and we'll make a plan accordingly. But remember, boys, Charles Grace does not need to know about any of this. He's a big picture man and I'll explain to him what happened in appropriate terms, OK. I'll see you downstairs.'

Within minutes, Taff Evans and Lefty Shoesmith joined Paul at the bottom of the stairs. Paul had the door open and the hard area alongside the wharves was still empty of people. They stepped out into the fierce sun of the early afternoon and jogged across to the trees. As he ran, Paul swivelled towards the Pungue and hurled Mannie Coetzee's Zippo lighter into its swirling depths. Retaining it served no useful purpose anymore.

* * *

WITHIN FORTY MINUTES the three of them were back at the High Commission, and then the pace of things accelerated.

Charles Grace was happy to be reassured that Paul's mission was complete and made the call to the duty officer at the RAF Hangar in Moi Air Base to request the Hercules for its evacuation of three British Service personnel, ranks and names unspecified, and a Land Rover vehicle half-loaded. Given the notice to fly and the transit time, it was agreed that the people and the vehicle would be at Beira Airport at zero six hundred hours tomorrow, Saturday.

Evans and Shoesmith paid their respects to Grace and went to their cottage to get everything sorted out. There would be no excursion into the red lights of the city for them this night. This was the final, vital stage of the mission, the exit, and nothing could get in the way of its success. They knew the score. Within a week their African odyssey would merely be one of their many operational memories, because work awaited them. So a quiet dinner with their hosts was the order of things for this last night in Africa.

Now Paul and Grace were drinking a cold beer and finalising what remained to be done. They were on their own. The First Secretary was still in his office and his wife was elsewhere in the apartment. Paul was anxious to make his final call. Time was slipping by, though, and it was already after three o'clock. Making the call was getting quite urgent.

'So, Paul,' said Grace, 'I think that just about does it. Is there anything else you can think of?'

'Just the return of the satphones, Charles, mine came from John Sawyer and is therefore the rightful property of Her Majesty's Foreign Office. Is yours the same?'

'No Paul, it is mine, brought all the way from London. There is only yours to worry about, so we'll ask the good First Secretary to parcel it up and send it back to Pretoria in the Diplomatic Bag on Monday. That should work.'

And talking of Diplomatic Bags, Paul thought, I really need to get on and out again. He said, 'If it's all right with you, Charles, I'll go and check the men and then start sorting out my own gear.'

'Yes, Paul, of course you must. Oh,' Grace added, as if suddenly remembering something, 'I didn't tell you that I spoke with the PM's Chief of Staff whilst you were out and about.' Paul said nothing. 'Well the furore we might have expected over de Castenet has not happened, and the PM is much relieved, of course. So that is good, Paul, very good, don't you think?' Paul didn't respond. The General had more to say, he could tell, and frankly, Paul had ceased to think about de Castenet, who had become a lost man who never redeemed himself. Paul had killed the man, but the events were now in the dark place in Paul's soul where he kept such things. He hoped no one other than God ever looked there. Grace went on, 'There's been scarcely a ripple back home and the Ministry of Defence Press Office is handling what there is. Anyway, I thought I'd just let you know that.'

'Thank you, Charles. I believe we have our allies out here to thank, don't you?' Thanks, John Sawyer, Stephen Langlands, Ken Rose, Vino Lauwrens and Dick Hanney, Paul acknowledged silently.

'We do, Paul, very much so,' Grace replied, 'and I also contacted Fred Etherington and provided him with a full update. He was extremely grateful and reminded me that Sir Reggie Hanlon was actually on his way to Pretoria for talks there. So a timely conclusion, eh?'

Paul remembered the letter Hanlon had sent to Mrs Thatcher. It *was* a timely conclusion. He did the calculations: he would be back in UK on the twenty-ninth of October, one calendar month after Victor Fitzsimons had been given the diamonds by Dick Hanney and then brutally killed by Mannie Coetzee. It would be nineteen days after Sir Reggie Hanlon signed his letter to Mrs Thatcher and sixteen days since Paul had arrived in South Africa. *Sixteen days!* Christ, no wonder the world hadn't noticed, there hadn't been time! Just as well.

Paul took his leave. He would see Grace later at dinner - if all he had left to do went to plan.

* * *

'THANKS FOR THE update Paul,' said Ken Rose, 'it's very good news. And as far as your superiors are concerned the diamonds were returned to me by you, which is indeed the way it should be. Except that it isn't, but that is between the two of us.' Paul said nothing. He smiled to himself. Rose went on, 'So all I have to deal with is one of the men who sit in my outer office. Well I can do that without too much further trouble. Now,' Rose paused and the hiss of the satphone link played in Paul's ear, 'the man you must meet with is the Portuguese Embassy's Home Affairs Secretary. Their Embassy is very close to you, on Rua Antonio Enes, you can be there on foot in minutes. Just head south from your place. I'll call the contact now, Paul, presumably you want to meet sooner rather than later?'

'I do, Ken, I'm out of here at first light tomorrow and this is the last play I have to make. Also, I'm housebound from about seven this evening, so it has to happen very soon.'

'Got it. Let me think for a second. Yes, that should do. There's a small eating-place called Inico, it's in the shopping complex on

Antonio Enes, you can't miss it. I'll get our man to meet you there at, say, five. How does that suit you?'

'Perfect, Ken, I can do that.' It was now four o'clock.

'Good. I'll give him your description, but so as you know him, he's tall and slim, has thinning black hair and a moustache. I imagine he'll be wearing a lightweight suit since he'll be coming from the office. You'll spot him easily in the Inico.'

'Thank you, Ken.' Paul paused and then said slowly, 'By the way, during the course of my questioning of Señor Ramon Lima, I happened to come across some other gemstones, emeralds and rubies, two small pouches of each. I have no idea of the authenticity or value of them, but I shall add them to the satchel of diamonds, if that is all right with you?' Paul had thought about this. The gemstones were no use to the people he wanted to give some financial reward to. Fortunately most of Lima's pouches of valuables had been gold coins, Krugerrands, which were considerably more tradeable, and Paul had a plan for getting a fair share of them to Danny Dalloway and his people. They would be bundled up with the satphones and Paul would trust to John Sawyer's integrity to get them to Rose.

Rose laughed and said, 'Christ, Paul, you're some operator, you really are. That would be fantastic, man, and I'll make sure those concerned know there has been some additional deposit to their savings now going to Portugal.'

'There is one final thing, please, Ken, and it will come from John Sawyer, but I'm asking him to get a valuable package to you, and I'm asking you to get this package to Dick Hanney as quickly as you can. Would that be OK? It sounds massively convoluted but I need to get this package to Nikki Walker-Haig at the Wise Owl in Mutare and Dick has met her. Nikki works for Gurkha Connections Limited. That's the long and the short of it, really.'

'We can manage that and it's the least we can do. Which brings me to you, Paul,' and Rose paused. 'I've been thinking and talking to the key members of the WPC about how we might show our appreciation for you single-handedly sorting out this total clusterfuck with Schuman and everyone associated with him, and we concluded that a man like you could probably make use of a few diamonds. Would we be right?'

Of course he could use some diamonds! How good would that be, with what he had planned coming up! Paul said, 'It's not necessary, Ken, it really isn't.'

'Yes it is, Paul, it *really* is. We have a deep-rooted tradition of showing appreciation to true friends and comrades in this country and this is what we intend to do. Dick Hanney told me that in the satchel Schuman carried, there was a smaller cowhide pouch of stones. I believe the man Schuman employed to kill Fitzsimons had intended to steal these. Well, Paul, you are to keep that pouch of stones for yourself, to do with as you wish, and we will not take no for an answer. If you want the truth, we never thought to see the diamonds again, and now we have them, and you have added emeralds and rubies, no less. So, that is an order from the Head of the Zimbabwe Central Intelligence Organisation!'

Paul gave in. There *was* a member of his family who could do with a windfall, his elderly mother. 'Thank you! Tell everyone so, please.'

'I shall. Now I will make the call to the Portuguese Embassy. Good luck, Paul.'

Back in his room, Paul extracted the cowhide pouch of diamonds from Schuman's old satchel and stuffed it into his travel bag where he'd stored Lima's gemstones and Krugerrands. He transferred the four sacks of stones into the satchel, which left six small sacks of coins. He'd counted the Krugerrands, and there were fifty in each sack, and decided that Evans and Shoesmith would have one between them, and the other five would be for the good of the GCL enterprise. As he'd told Rose, they'd go in the Diplomatic Bag to John Sawyer, wrapped inside his satphone equipment.

Paul bound up the satchel with tape and put it inside an old parachute sack that he'd got from Evans and taped that up, too.

Using the coded door to the High Commission's postern gate, Paul set off for his last meeting.

315

***

IT HAD BEEN a celebratory dinner, fresh fish, fruits, and cheese with fine Portuguese wines. The conversation had been bright and light and after coffee and a dram of whisky, Evans and Shoesmith had sensibly excused themselves.

'Thank you very much, Maam, and Sir,' they had both said and the First Secretary and his wife had beamed at them and said how much they had enjoyed having them to stay and that their cook would be on hand to provide them with an early breakfast. A *very* early breakfast! 'Do yer need a wake up call, boss?' Evans had asked Paul.

'No thanks, Taff, see you both for breakfast at zero five hundred. We'll leave for the airport at zero five-thirty.'

And as it was still relatively early, only nine o'clock, the First Secretary's wife had said, well, let's have a rubber of friendly Bridge, shall we? You can be my partner, Colonel Stanton, and Charles can partner my husband. I'm sure you must be excellent at Bridge, she'd said, which Paul wasn't, but he was good enough to hold his own with Mrs First Secretary, who actually, was a charming and very lovely woman, and as it turned out, not a bad Bridge partner.

So, an hour, two successful game bids, two whiskies, and the exchange of polite and warm farewells later, Paul was glad to get to his room to check over all his preparations for the early morning and to make his final call.

Before he'd left Manica Paul had prearranged the call for this evening but he was now fifteen minutes later than he'd hoped. She answered the telephone in the Manica operations room after two uncertain warbling rings, 'Paul?'

The line was strong and his heart lurched unexpectedly as he heard her voice. It levelled all the feelings he'd ever experienced. It was like being brought right down to earth with a crash from whatever heights he had previously been at, as he realised there was nothing more important in his life than this person. 'Hello, Nik, I'm really sorry I'm late, but Charles and I got dragged into a rubber of Bridge with the First Secretary and his wife.'

'Were you sociable and brilliant, as you always are?'

'I was quite good, as it happened,' and Paul laughed. 'Are you well, Nik, and how is Danny?'

'I am, Paul, and Danny's recovery has been surprisingly rapid. It is, as you said, a flesh wound. Although he's a bit of a baby for attention occasionally,' and she laughed. 'The good thing is that Philippe Cruz and Andy Da Silva and the others have been out and about around the farm and the countryside these last two days and there is no talk of any kind. It's as if the Chicamba Real didn't exist. How good is that? Tell me you love me, Paul, totally, because I do you. I miss you as well!'

'I love you, totally.'

And the two lovers chatted for a few minutes during which Paul gave Nikki the Charles Grace version of the Ramon Lima incident.

'I'm leaving with Taff and Lefty tomorrow morning, Nik, really early; Charles is following later, by civilian air. We're going in the back of a Hercules - I suppose being a general must have its privileges.'

'Of course it does, silly man, and you'll be one, one day. Give him a goodbye kiss for me.'

'Of course I won't! When has Danny planned to take you back to Mutare, Nik? He promised me he would and you must hold him to it.'

'I will, and it's planned for the end of next week. And once I've spent some time in Zimbabwe, giving our lovely Gurkhas there some tender loving care and checking all is well, Danny's threatened to let me get back to London. Did you have anything to do with that, Stanton? If so, well done, and I can't wait. You'll be back at work. Will you have leave? We can stay in my flat *and* yours!'

'Whoa, slow down, Nik! Tell Danny that when you get back to Mutare you must contact and meet up with Dick Hanney. He has a package for Danny. It's from Ramon Lima. So Danny must take you to Mutare and wait for the package.'

'Ramon Lima! Don't be daft, Paul, how can that be? The man was a criminal.'

'Tell Danny it's from Ramon Lima and that he is to use the contents to provide suitable reward to his Gurkhas, his Mozambican people and his Company. OK?'

'Being Robin Hood again, Paul?'

'Something like that.'

'You're a good man, Stanton.'

'Now, my Nicola, I have to go. Please promise you will somehow let me know when you are due in London.'

'I will. Be there, Paul.'

'I shall,' Paul said and he really meant it. No matter what was planned for him when he got back to London, he would be there to meet his girl.

Then Paul Stanton and Nikki Walker-Haig said their personal farewells.

The southern African odyssey was over.

REQUIEM FOR THE GOOD GUYS

PAUL STANTON KNEW where to find the Jewish goldsmith and gem dealer, since he'd been there before, earlier in the year. The small, highly secure and private shop front was in premises on Leather Lane off Hatton Garden.

The owner, Isaac Benowitz, greeted Paul as he stepped out of the early November rain, 'Ah, Mr Paul, how good to see you again. What have you brought me this time? More gold bullion?' Gold and jewel merchants never forgot a customer, even if they were infrequent.

'No, Isaac, diamonds.'

As improbable as it sounded, the gold coins Benowitz referred to once belonged to a Great Train Robber, whose wife, just before their tragic deaths ten years ago, had entrusted them to Nikki's sister. The only problem was that Nikki's sister hadn't known this, and the case in which the coins and other valuables were stored had remained hidden in the chaos of her home possessions for over a decade. But then, back in the summer this year, Nikki's sister had been threatened by those who sought the money, and because she was Nikki's sister, Paul had got involved, found the case, denied it to those who would steal it and harm Nikki's sister, and with the exception of the gold coins referred to by Isaac Benowitz, handed the money into the Police. For which he had been rewarded. It was with this reward, and the proceeds from Isaac Benowitz's fencing of stolen bullion, that Nikki and her sister had purchased new properties. Paul hadn't kept a penny. Robin Hood never did. This time, though, he might.

'Diamonds?'

'Yes, Isaac, diamonds. African diamonds, which are completely untraceable anywhere in the world, and I know this because I went there to recover them. Oh, and I was given them by their rightful owners. Can we perhaps discuss this in your private room?'

Benowitz prised himself out of his protected cubicle, walked the few steps to his door, locked it, lowered the burglar shutters and beckoned Paul to follow him into the back room.

The hide pouch lay on Benowitz's desk as he checked each of the stones with his eyeglass. 'You were given these stones, Paul?'

'I was, Isaac, but in fairness to you, I can produce no provenance for them so you must sell them for me as you can. I would like you to keep out for me the largest and best stone, which I will pay you to make into the most beautiful ring.'

Benowitz unscrewed his eyeglass and raised his eyebrows quizzically at Paul. Smiling, he said, 'Romance Paul, it is good to see it in your eyes.'

'Romance, Isaac. Now, what is the value here?'

'The value, Paul, is close to three hundred thousand pounds. I will be able to sell them for that, but I will deduct thirty per cent for handling these diamonds for you. To take out the most beautiful stone and make it into a fabulous ring I will charge you ten thousand pounds. I can pay the balance of the money, two hundred thousand pounds, to you in any way you wish. Our business is strictly confidential. Do we have a deal?'

'We have a deal, Isaac. I'll tell you when I shall need the ring, but it is likely to be soon.'

It would be a beautiful ring for a beautiful woman.

* * *

'WELL, PAUL, IT'S happened,' said General Charles Grace. 'The Berlin Wall is being torn down, as we speak. Dear old President Reagan's call for action to Gorbachov has actually materialised. It's taken just over two years. Amazing!'

'It really is, General.' The familiar style of addressing a general by his christian name had been dropped. Paul was back in the Military.

It was the morning of 10th November 1989, and Lieutenant Colonel Paul Stanton knew all about what was happening. Like millions of others, he had been monitoring the news all through the night.

'But the speed of it, Paul, is stunning!' The big, well-groomed, smartly dressed man turned to him and looked earnestly at Paul. There was softness in his eyes. They stood at the large sash window in the Historical Room on the second floor of the Old Admiralty Building, the room where almost exactly a month ago, Grace had briefed Paul on the mission to Mozambique.

Somehow, even though Paul had been back in London less than ten days, the memory of Africa was becoming ever more distant. 'Yes,' he responded, 'it seems Günter Schabowski's press conference yesterday afternoon, lit the blue touch paper, as they say.' The Politburo spokesman in East Berlin had announced that with immediate effect the border would be open, and when pressed by journalists, had said that this applied also to the crossings between West and East Berlin. Last night the local people started to demolish the Berlin Wall.

'You sound a little flat, Paul.' Grace had turned back to look out across Horse Guards.

If he was honest, Paul did feel flat. The warmth and exciting uncertainty of Africa - South Africa, Zimbabwe, Mozambique - was an all-too-soon distant series of events, and it had only been ten days since he was there. Here he was back in London working once more in Headquarters Director Special Forces as if he'd never been away, and Nikki hadn't arrived yet - he didn't know when she was coming - and he was staring out across a frosty Horse Guards Parade talking about bloody Berlin. So yes, he felt flat; but it wasn't Grace's fault. 'One of the first crossings in Berlin they opened was the Bornholmer Straße. It brought back memories, General. I was just reflecting for a few moments.' Memories of the crossing point close to the Wall Zone where Paul had been shot.

'My dear Paul, of course, I truly understand. Grace walked over to the table that served as a desk and picked up a sheet of notepaper. 'Here, Paul, read this. As you can see it was written two days ago. It might bring a smile to your slightly solemn face.'

Paul took the sheet of stiffish paper, and instantly, southern Africa was in the room with him. He looked at the familiar heading of the letter.

This was where it had all started.

<u>Private Office</u>
Sir Reginald Hanlon, KCMG
Chairman and Chief Executive, MozLon Corporation
46-48 Lombard Street, London EC3

Personal for The Prime Minister
The Right Honourable Mrs Margaret Thatcher, MP
10 Downing Street
London SW1

8th November 1989

Dear Prime Minister

It is with a grateful heart that I write this letter. When I wrote on the 10th October 1989, I realised I was asking a great deal of you to note my concerns, which as you know, impacted not only on my business interests in southern Africa, but on what I believed to be your Government's Foreign Policy stance in the Region. Due to your boldness and kindness I have been able to play a small part in the ongoing Peace Process in Mozambique.

Your new Foreign Secretary, Mr Douglas Hurd, will have been briefed on what has occurred. As a result of my dialogue with the Maputo Government and visit to Pretoria, we have gone some way to persuading Mozambique's President Chissano that there is sufficient basis for strengthening Peace talks with Renamo's leadership. The US State Department also supports this initiative and sees it as the best way forward for peace in Mozambique and wider regional stability. My personal observations, Maam, are that President de Klerk will shortly lift the ban on the ANC in South Africa, which will shine a beacon of tolerance across the Region, and which must help. I therefore remain very optimistic about political stability, which of course benefits MozLon's business interests, since a Renamo fully engaged in a peace process is the best way to help re-grow Mozambique's indigenous wealth.

In this latter regard, Prime Minister, the concerns expressed in my earlier letter, have proved unfounded. The Regional Director I talked of, died as a result of an accident whilst going about his legitimate business on behalf of MozLon. Mr Fitzsimons had no family and no next of kin. He had proved to be inspirational in overseeing the establishment and development of two of our huge agricultural enterprises, the security of which, I have contracted to a Kathmandu-London based business called Gurkha Connections Limited. GCL is bona fide, has the endorsement of your Ministry of Defence and Nepal's Panchayat, and of course utilises ex-Gurkhas of Her Majesty's Army. They are a well-led and very exciting organisation and I commend them to your notice. I would also commend to you, Maam, Mr Victor Fitzsimons, and would ask if there might be some small way in which his legacy might be remembered.

I thank you again, Prime Minister, for everything you have done.

I remain, respectfully,

Reggie Hanlon

Sir Reginald Hanlon, KCMG

Paul smiled broadly. 'A suitable requiem for the good guys, General.'

'Exactly my thoughts, Paul, exactly, and it *has* brought a smile back to your face, so I'm especially glad.' Grace took the letter from Paul, placed it on the table and came and stood again by the window. 'Anyway, mission accomplished, Colonel Stanton, and you should know that Mrs Thatcher has asked for her personal thanks to be passed to you. I spoke to Number Ten this morning.'

'That's very gracious of the Prime Minister, General. How much did she actually know?'

'Everything, Paul, absolutely everything, and she is a devoted fan of yours, so watch out!' What exactly did Grace mean by that? Grace continued, changing the subject, as he did frequently and unexpectedly. 'Poor old St James's Park looks bleak and dreary at this time of year, doesn't it.' It was a rhetorical question. 'Quite a contrast in colour and feeling to a month ago, eh, Paul.' Another statement. Paul knew that Grace had something or things still on his mind that he needed to say. 'Sir Reggie's letter is full of optimism for the future of Mozambique, but I'm afraid that events now in Europe will consume the world's interest and energies. Dear old southern Africa will be placed on the back boiler once again whilst the new world order between East and West is established. It will be an exciting time.'

'It will, General, and it will shift the focus of our military activities dramatically.'

'Crystal ball gaze for me some more, young Stanton,' Grace said. 'In what way?'

Paul didn't really know why he said it but he did: 'Well, we'll gradually dismantle our Cold War posture and all the plans that support it, and in the vacuum created by the phenomena of perestroika and glasnost we shall adopt a new foreign policy that sees us selectively choosing limited war engagements to protect vital, or perceived vital, interests, such as oil, or more philosophically, the freedom of sovereign states. All, of course, within the framework of treaty alliances, United Nations resolutions and world-sanctioned coalitions.' Having said it now, Paul thought he sounded pompous and marginally flippant; but it was what he believed. No Cold War equals a vacuum, which has to be filled, and by future military actions of more limited and affordable scope. All the Cold War plans would be ripped up and new contingencies developed. It made sense to him.

Paul was conscious of the interest sparking in Grace's face as he spoke, the General's look encouraging him to say more. 'Go on, Paul.'

So he did, 'And I don't believe southern Africa, or Africa as a whole, will necessarily go onto the back boiler. If what John Sawyer in Pretoria said is true, then South Africa's recognition of the ANC and the probable release of Nelson Mandela will cause an equally seismic shift in power politics in the Region. Sir Reggie says the same in his letter. And as for Zimbabwe, well I saw at first hand the actual and the potential impact of Mugabe's effect on that country.'

Grace interrupted his flow, which was probably just as well, 'It seems to me, Paul, that you're a dead ringer to become a member of the fabled directing staff at the Army's Staff College in Camberley.' He eyed Paul with a quizzical but interested expression. 'It can be arranged.'

'No thank you, sir, I'm happy where I am.'

'But are you, Paul? Are you really? And what about the lovely Nicola Walker-Haig, whom I've yet to meet? If I understand the little snippets of gossip I pick up correctly, the two of you may marry?'

Not for the first time Paul had been gazumped by Charles Grace's intelligence network, or in this case his ability to pirate information out of the Army's rumour mill. How had he known this? It had to be Dalloway, via the Gurkha network back to London? Or was it the MozLon network from Mozambique back to Etherington in London? Damn the man for the upper hand he always seemed to hold!

'We may, General, we may, and before Christmas if God, the Army and you are all willing.' But at least, thanks to the diamonds Ken Rose gifted to me, we can afford it. Paul said, somewhat wistfully, 'That is, if I even knew when Nikki was returning to London.'

'Well, my rather poor intelligence tells me that the good lady, your wife-to-be, will be arriving within a week. You will, I very much hope, bring her to meet me and *my* good lady, and to share some dinner with us both, and nothing, *nothing*, dear Paul, would give me greater pleasure!' Paul Stanton found himself nonplussed by Grace's information and his genuine manner. He was speechless. *Nikki was going to be in London next week!* 'And given this news, Paul, I urge you to consider my offer.'

'Your offer, sir?' Paul wasn't thinking straight.

'Yes, Colonel Stanton, my offer to you, to become a member of the directing staff at Camberley, starting at the beginning of the New Year. I have it on good authority from the Military Secretary himself, that it is likely, should you want it. At Camberley you can settle for two years as a married man, pontificate with experience and a modicum of wisdom to the impressionable young future commanders of our Army, and gain the insights into future conflicts, which you can later engage in, as a commanding officer of either your beloved SAS or Scottish Infantry. What say you?'

'I say, thank you, General. It sounds wonderful.' And suddenly it did.

'Well, Paul Stanton, I'm pleased. You are a man of whom I have become very fond and nothing must happen to you.' Paul found himself welling up with emotion. Then Grace said, 'And I and my good lady friend shall expect an invitation to the wedding!'

'You will, General, you most certainly will.'

HISTORICAL NOTE

As with the previous Paul Stanton thrillers the historical and political contexts of this novel are accurate. However, like the others, the events I have described that take place within them, are not necessarily so.

October and November 1989 were hugely important months in the political history of the UK, Europe and the southern African region. In London, Mrs Thatcher was beset all around by foes within and outside her party. She would, in early December that year, be challenged in her position as Leader of the Conservative Party. The challenge would fail, but the accumulating pressures were building up against her. Cabinet dissension and resignations were seriously destabilising her position. Nigel Lawson resigned as Chancellor in October and more trusted allies, such as Michael Heseltine and Geoffrey Howe would abandon her in 1990 as she was seen to be more-and-more out of step with her party. The public uproar over the Poll Tax was becoming a personal nemesis and the economy was sliding inexorably towards recession. In November 1990 Margaret Thatcher would be ousted as Prime Minister and replaced by John Major, the man rather disparagingly referred to by General Charles Grace as having a dull mind with little to occupy it other than cricket!

Whether it was a major factor or not in her demise, Mrs Thatcher's anti-views on wider European integration were at odds with the reality of what was happening in 1989. Charles Grace and Paul

Stanton reflect on these massive changes in Europe and the likely impact on the West's Cold War stance in Chapter Two. References to the Wall of course bring the chills of near-death back into Paul's soul. Hungary started to dismantle its border defences with Austria in August 1989, two-and-a-half months before the Wall came down in Berlin, and it was all these events that sat heavily on Paul's mind when he was summoned by Grace to the Old Admiralty Building at the end of Chapter One. We have to remember that Paul had witnessed first hand the early impact of Hungary's moves to freedom. The previous December, with the help of his ex-Gurkha soldiers, he'd faced down a gang of Hungarian criminals in Kathmandu. Charles Grace knew nothing of this when he started his dialogue with Stanton.

It is rather apposite, in a way, that by the end of this novel, the Berlin Wall has started to be pulled down, bringing light into the dark lives of the many thousands imprisoned for generations inside the repressionist regimes of the East. One can almost feel the sense of catharsis and accompanying calm in Paul as he and Grace reflect on what the future might hold, especially as Paul seems to be moving into a rare hiatus in his military life. But of course these reflections are tempered by Sir Reggie Hanlon's thank-you letter to the Prime Minister, bringing Grace and Paul back to what had happened in southern Africa.

When Stanton meets Grace in Chapter Two, he is pre-occupied with the ongoing threat of Provisional IRA terror acts on mainland UK; he's the SAS's point man on this, working from inside the Director Special Forces' HQ in Duke of York's Barracks. Stanton has also been watching the developing events in Europe. So when Grace introduces the subject of Mozambique, Paul is momentarily nonplussed. Why did the Prime Minister sanction Stanton's mission? What was the relevance of the region to the UK's foreign policy, if any?

There is more than a passing correlation between the character and enterprises of Sir Reggie Hanlon and Tiny Rowlands, and between the fictitious MozLon and the real life Lonrho. Through Hanlon's character and the specific business ventures described in Mozambique I have tried to reflect, without taking sides in any way, the significant contribution Tiny Rowlands and Lonrho made to the wider southern African peace initiatives and to Mozambique's peace settlement and future prosperity in particular. Throughout the novel I have tried to be faithful to the *actual* geo-political and social events of the time. This can be evidenced, for example, in the discussions between Grace and Hanlon's Head of Security, Fred Etherington, in Chapter Four, between Paul and the Head of Station, John Sawyer, in Pretoria, in Chapter Seven, and when Paul is talking to Ken Rose, Head of the Zimbabwe Central Intelligence Organisation in Chapters Eleven and Twelve. There was a lot happening in the region!

Tiny Rowlands did actually try to broker peace between Frelimo and Renamo, much as Hanlon is doing, probably at some not inconsiderable cost to himself and his business. However, he must have felt ultimately that these costs would be worth it. I have no idea whether or not they were commercially, but in terms of regional change and stability, the period was as seismic in its outcomes as the events in Europe I described earlier. In February 1990 F W de Klerk would reverse the ban on the African National Congress and release Nelson Mandela! In the spring of 1990 President Chissano of Mozambique would draft a new constitution for anticipated free elections later on. It would take a further two years to reach a peace accord and to disarm Renamo fully, but by 1990 regeneration of agriculture and industry through the efforts of Lonrho and others, and the isolation of renegade Renamo, was underway. Perhaps Mrs Thatcher had a sniff of the positive outcomes that might be realised from sending Stanton to Africa? Besides, as Grace tells Stanton, she owed Reggie Hanlon. Perhaps Stanton's despatch was her honouring the unwritten contract she had with MozLon?

The real Contract, though, was Danny Dalloway's: the one between Dalloway's private military company (PMC) Gurkha Connections Limited (GCL) and MozLon. We remember the eccentric, ex-Kathmandu Rifles, Major Danny Dalloway being savagely injured (losing his left eye) by the Hungarian criminals in Kathmandu, the same Hungarians Stanton and the Gurkhas killed. Now almost a year later Dalloway's contract is underway and successful. Whilst Dalloway is a fictional persona, his character is rather loosely based on my real life, ex-Gurkha friend Major Jon Titley, to whom I owe great thanks for providing me with insights and facts about how it was in Mozambique at the time. His PMC, which used ex-Gurkhas, has been referenced in an edited collection of essays entitled *Mercenaries An African Security Dilemma*, put together for the Centre for Democracy and Development.

Despite this strand of authenticity, everything that Dalloway does in Mozambique is a fiction – but a fiction based on real equipment and tactics and on the emotional themes I have been told about. The MozLon farms at Nhamatanda and Manica are my creations, as is the last stand of the renegade Renamo on the northern shore of the Chicamba Real reservoir. The geography is accurate, though, and so I hope they provide the structures within which Dalloway, his Gurkhas, Stanton and his SAS men, and of course the MozLon employees and the local people of Mozambique, fight off the Renamo attempts to de-rail their future livelihoods. There is nothing like the smell of cordite, masses of empty brass cartridge cases and a few dead bodies to ensure the future gets protected.

On the subject of the SAS, Taff Evans, whom we first met in Northern Ireland, and Lefty Shoesmith, who we now know was with Stanton in the Falklands War, are my creations. Everything they do is fiction. Nor is there any evidence (to my knowledge) that the Special Forces Flight of 47 Squadron, RAF, based at Brize Norton, ever flew a C-130K mission over Africa on two separate occasions during the month of October 1989. It was, however, necessary to get some Special Forces assistance to Stanton (and Dalloway, as it happened) and these boys were (are) superb at this type of work.

Which brings me to Zimbabwe. I paint a fairly bleak picture of Zimbabwe and perhaps this is unfair. My mother and father lived there in the 1970s and I visited Salisbury (Harare) and Umtali (Mutare) as well as travelling within the country a little. At that time, in the early years of the Rhodesian Bush War, the country was still gloriously prosperous. What a fantastic place! All my Zimbabwean friends who now live in South Africa talk of its wonders and its tragic decline and fall, particularly since the late eighties and nineties. I won't comment further other than to say that this decline is what I have attempted to presage by my descriptions of the country in the novel. The ravages of Mugabe's regime will be chronicled in history and, in my opinion, stand as testimony to the blackest stains ever put on the fabric of that country.

There is no evidence that I can find of white Zimbabweans stockpiling their hard wealth and establishing some sort of collecting and courier system to move it all offshore. Conversely, I have heard a lot of unattributable talk from people who were there and could know, that this might have been the case! How the system worked is again a product of my imagination, and it added to the spice mix of personalities and situations to have Ken Rose, Head of the Central Intelligence Organisation, involved at the heart of it all. Sometimes the good guys have to win. Dick Hanney, the man in the Eastern Highlands, is based on my father, who worked for Tanganda Tea and ran the tea estates at New Year's Gift and Rattleshoek in the

Chimanimani, south of Melsetter. This is the lovely part of eastern Zimbabwe where poor old Victor Fitzsimons lost his life one Friday evening after his regular meeting with Dick Hanney. It was a relief to have it recognised at the end of the novel that Fitzsimons was an innocent man acting altruistically.

Major Richard de Castenet certainly wasn't an innocent man! For me there was always unfinished business between Stanton and de Castenet and I'm sure Paul felt the same. Three and a half years had passed since de Castenet's acts had, one way or another, culminated in Stanton's shoot out in Berlin's Wall Zone. Paul might have killed de Castenet's 'accomplice' the evil, twisted Shaggy Drinkwater, but he'd nearly lost his life and meanwhile de Castenet hadn't come remotely close to the consequences of what he'd started. No, there was definitely unfinished business for Stanton. Thankfully de Castenet had, during his time in Pretoria, decided to forego any kind of redemption in the Army and become a criminal. There was just cause, once he knew this for certain, for Paul to kill de Castenet. The setting, in a derelict petrol station close to the Mozambique border, is my creation, but it was a necessary location in order for Paul to gather up Nikki Walker-Haig and with his men, cross the border into Mozambique.

Nikki Walker-Haig...Well we knew from Stanton's encounter with the Great Train Robber that he and Nikki had fallen in love and that their relationship, albeit hampered by their respective physical locations, was serious. Nikki was never going to be in harm's way, although Paul feared she might be because of her in-country work for Gurkha Connections Limited. For me the focus of the story was always for Stanton to deliver the contract placed on him by Grace and the Government to establish the truth of what was going on and sort it out. Having Nikki caught up in firefights in the bush of Africa was never something I wanted nor believed was credible. Stanton had too much dark, dirty work to do – best left to the SAS and Gurkhas.

In the end though, finding himself improbably even wealthier than he was – thanks to Ken Rose – and being encouraged by Charles Grace to take some time out, Paul decides he will settle down and marry Nikki. Who knows how that contract will work out!

I hope the career plans being discussed by the powers-that-be for Lieutenant Colonel Paul Stanton, MC, do allow Paul and his lovely Nikki to enjoy some stability in the early years of their lives together. I can't believe though that Stanton won't be back in the thick of things once again, sometime in the future. He is a genuine British dark hero and there are dark times ahead.

Chris Darnell
Weymouth, England and Knysna, South Africa
March 2016

ABOUT THE AUTHOR

Chris Darnell is a retired British Army Colonel.

He was commissioned in 1971 into the 2nd Gurkha Rifles and later transferred into The King's Own Scottish Borderers. After thirty years of regimental duty all over the world, staff tours in large headquarters in Germany and UK, and too much operational service in Northern Ireland, the Persian Gulf War and the Balkans, he resigned from the Army and worked for global companies in Defence and Technology specialising in the NATO Region.

Now he gives his time to charitable activities, being a Governor of his old school, Haileybury, and writing, amongst other things, Paul Stanton thrillers.

He and his wife live in Weymouth and Knysna, South Africa.

20250738R00194

Printed in Great Britain
by Amazon